D

the Edge of Nowhere

ELIZABETH GEORGE

the Edge of Nowhere

VIKING
An Imprint of Penguin Group (USA) Inc.

VIKING

Published by the Penguin Group

Penguin Group (USA) Inc., 345 Hudson Street, New York, New York 10014, U.S.A.

Penguin Group (Canada), 90 Eglinton Avenue East, Suite 700, Toronto,

Ontario, Canada M4P 2Y3 (a division of Pearson Penguin Canada Inc.)

Penguin Books Ltd, 80 Strand, London WC2R 0RL, England

Penguin Ireland, 25 St Stephen's Green, Dublin 2, Ireland (a division of Penguin Books Ltd)

Penguin Group (Australia), 250 Camberwell Road, Camberwell,

Victoria 3124, Australia (a division of Pearson Australia Group Pty Ltd)

Penguin Books India Pvt Ltd, 11 Community Centre, Panchsheel Park,

New Delhi – 110 017, India

Penguin Group (NZ), 67 Apollo Drive, Rosedale, Auckland 0632,

New Zealand (a division of Pearson New Zealand Ltd.)

Penguin Books (South Africa) (Pty) Ltd, 24 Sturdee Avenue, Rosebank,

Johannesburg 2196, South Africa

Penguin Books Ltd, Registered Offices: 80 Strand, London WC2R 0RL, England

First published in the United States of America by Viking,

an imprint of Penguin Group (USA) Inc., 2012

10   9   8   7   6   5   4   3   2   1

LIBRARY OF CONGRESS CATALOGING-IN-PUBLICATION DATA

George, Elizabeth, date–

The edge of nowhere / by Elizabeth George.

p. cm.

Summary: When her mother abandons her on Whidbey Island, Washington, a fourteen-year-old girl with psychic abilities meets a Ugandan orphan with a secret.

ISBN 978-0-670-01296-1 (hardcover)

[1. Whidbey Island (Wash.)—Fiction. 2. Psychic ability—Fiction. 3. Abandoned children—Fiction. 4. Secrets—Fiction.]   I. Title.

PZ7.G29315Ed 2012   [Fic]—dc23   2011050741

Printed in U.S.A.   Set in Warnock Pro   Book design by Kate Renner

For Bob Mayer and Debbie Cavanaugh,
in acknowledgment of a breathtaking lesson
in both friendship and appreciation.

Be not afeared: the isle is full of noises,
Sounds and sweet airs, that give delight, and hurt not.

—WILLIAM SHAKESPEARE,
THE TEMPEST

How Things Began

On the last day of Hannah Armstrong's existence, things were normal for a while. She made a 94 percent on a math test, and she accepted a movie date for later in the week.

She walked home, as usual. She didn't use her hearing device since she didn't really need it outside of school. This gadget had the appearance of an iPod, but it didn't play music. Instead it played a form of static that removed from Hannah's hearing the disjointed thoughts of other people. Since babyhood, she'd heard these broken thoughts of others, which she'd learned to call whispers. But they came into her head like a badly tuned radio; she could never tell exactly who the whisperer was if more than one person was present; and they made school a nightmare for her. So a mechanism that her mom called an AUD box had been manufactured for Hannah. She'd worn it since she was seven years old.

When she arrived home, she went to the stairs. She headed up to her room, only to see her stepfather come stealthily out of it.

They locked eyes. *Damn . . . what's she doing . . . why didn't . . .* came into Hannah's head from Jeff Corrie as whispers always did, disconnected and seemingly random. She frowned as she heard them, and she wondered what her stepfather had been doing in her room besides trying once again to gather reassurance that she wasn't going to tell her mother how she'd been helping him with his latest scheme.

It wasn't as if she'd wanted to help him, either. But Jeff Corrie had Hannah's mom in some sort of thrall that had more to do with his looks than his character, and caught up in their dizzying relationship, she'd told him what went on inside Hannah's head when she wasn't wearing the AUD box. It hadn't taken him long to figure out a way to use Hannah's talent. He decided to "employ" her as the cake and coffee girl at his investment house, just the person to bring in the refreshments and listen to the whispers of his clients in order to read their weaknesses. He and his pal Connor separated old folks from their money in this way. It was a grand scheme and it was making them millions.

Hannah had never wanted to help him. She knew it was wrong. But she feared this man and she feared the fact that his whispers, his words, and the expressions on his face never matched up. She didn't know what this meant. But she knew it wasn't good. So she said nothing to anyone. She just did what she was told and waited for whatever was going to happen next. She had no idea it would happen that very afternoon.

Jeff Corrie said, "What're you doing home?" His gaze went to her right ear where the earphone to the AUD box usually was.

Hannah dug the box out of her pocket and clipped it on the waistband of her jeans, screwing the earphone into her ear as well. His eyes narrowed till he saw her turn up the volume. Then he seemed to relax.

"It's three thirty," she told him.

"Start your homework," he said.

He went past her and down the stairs. She heard him yelling, "Laurel? Where the hell are you? Hannah's home," as if his wife was supposed to do something about that.

Hannah put her backpack in her room. Everything seemed to be the way she'd left it that morning. Still, she went to the bedside table to check the drawer.

The tiny piece of clear tape was ripped off. Someone had opened the drawer. Someone had read her journal.

It wasn't enough, she thought, that she helped him and his friend. He had to possess her thoughts on the matter, too. Well, good luck to figuring out how I feel, Daddy Jeff, Hannah scoffed. Like I'd write something honest and actually leave it in my bedroom for you?

She left her room and descended the stairs. She heard her mom and Jeff Corrie talking in the kitchen. She joined them there and turned away from the sight of Jeff Corrie nuzzling her mother's neck. He was murmuring, "What about n-o-w?" and Laurel was laughing and playing at pushing him away. But Hannah knew her mom liked what was going on between her and her husband. She loved the guy, and her love was as deaf and as dumb as it was blind.

Hannah said, "Hi, Mom," and opened the refrigerator, reaching for a carton of milk.

Laurel said, "Hey. No hi to Jeff?"

"Already saw him upstairs," Hannah told her. She added, "Gosh. He didn't tell you, Mom?" just to see how she would react. Don't trust him, don't trust him, she wanted to say. But she could only plant seeds. She couldn't paint pictures.

There was a silence between Laurel and Jeff. With the refrigerator door still open, hiding her from them, Hannah turned off the volume of the AUD box.

He's not . . . he can't be . . . had to be from her mother, she thought.

She tried to hear Jeff, but there was nothing.

Then everything changed, and life as Hannah had known it ended.

Little bitch always thinks . . . a break-in . . . surprise . . . Connor . . . if she hears that a gun . . . because dead isn't always dead these days . . .

The carton of milk slipped from Hannah's fingers and sloshed onto the floor. She swung around from the refrigerator and her eyes met Jeff's.

"Clumsy," he said, but inside his head was something different.

His gaze went from Hannah's face to her ear to the AUD box on her waist.

She heard was the last thing Hannah heard before she ran from the room.

PART ONE

The Cliff

ONE

Becca King's mother, Laurel, had traded the Lexus SUV at the first opportunity after they'd descended interstate five on the serpentine stretch of highway known as the Grapevine in California. She'd lost money on the car, but money wasn't the issue. Getting away from San Diego along with getting rid of the Lexus was. She'd traded it for a 1998 Jeep Wrangler, and the moment they'd crossed the California state line into Oregon, she began looking for a place to unload the Jeep as well. A 1992 Toyota RAV4 came next. But that only took them up through Oregon to the border with Washington. As quickly as possible and making sure it was all legal, Laurel then dumped the Toyota for a 1988 Ford Explorer, which was what mother and daughter had driven ever since.

Becca hadn't questioned any of this. She'd known the desperate reason it had to be done, just as she knew the reason there could be no more Hannah Armstrong. For she and her mother were traveling as fast as they could, leaving house, school, and names behind them. Now they sat in the Explorer in Mukilteo, Washington. The car was backed into a parking space in front of an old wooden-floored store called Woody's Market, across the water from Whidbey Island.

It was early evening, and a heavy mist that was not quite fog hung between the mainland and the island. From where they were parked, Whidbey was nothing more than an enormous hulk surmounted by tall conifers and having a band of lights at the bottom where a few houses were strung along the shore. To Becca, with an entire life lived in San Diego, the place looked forbidding and foreign. She couldn't imagine herself there, trying to establish a new life far away from her stepfather's reach. To Laurel, the island looked like a safety net where she could leave her daughter in the care of a childhood friend for the time it would take her to establish a place of refuge in British Columbia. There, she figured that she and Becca would be safe from discovery by Jeff Corrie.

Laurel had felt overwhelming relief when her longtime Bohemian lifestyle had been enough to quash any questions from her friend. Carol Quinn had not even acted surprised that Laurel would ask her to care for her daughter for a length of time she couldn't begin to name. Instead of questioning this, Carol said no problem, bring her on up, she can help me out. Haven't been feeling so great lately, Carol had said, so I could use an assistant in the house.

But will you keep this a secret? Laurel had asked her over and over again.

To my grave, Carol Quinn had promised. No worries, Laurel. Bring her on up.

Now Laurel lowered her window two inches, to keep the windshield from fogging up. The middle of September, and she hadn't had a clue the weather would have changed so much. In southern California, September was the hottest month of the year, a time of forest fires driven by winds off the desert. Here, it already felt like winter. Laurel shivered and grabbed a sweatshirt from the back of the car, where it lay against the wheel of Becca's old ten-speed.

She said, "Cold?" Becca shook her head. She was breathing deeply, and while she usually did this to calm herself, she was doing it now because on the air was the scent of waffle cones meant for ice cream, and it was coming from Woody's Market behind them.

They'd already been inside. Becca had already asked for a cone. Laurel had already made the automatic reply of "In through the lips and onto the hips." She was a woman who, on the run from a criminal, could still count her daughter's intake of calories. But Becca was hungry. They hadn't had anything to eat since lunch. A snack certainly wasn't going to blow up her thighs like balloons.

She said, "Mom . . ."

Laurel turned to her. "Tell me your name."

They'd been through this exercise five times daily since leaving their home, so Becca wasn't happy to go through it another time. She understood the importance of it, but she wasn't an idiot. She'd memorized it all. She sighed and looked in the other direction. "Becca King," she said.

"And what are you to remember as Job Number One?"

"Help Carol Quinn around the house."

"Aunt Carol," Laurel said. "You're to call her Aunt Carol."

"Aunt Carol, Aunt Carol, Aunt Carol," Becca said.

"She knows you have a little money until I can start sending you more," Laurel said. "But the more you can help her . . . It's like earning your keep."

"Yes," Becca said. "I will become someone's slave because you married a maniac, Mom."

Oh God what did he do to you when you're my only—

"Sorry," Becca said, hearing her mom's pain. "Sorry. *Sorry.*"

"Get out of my head," Laurel told her. "And tell me your name. Full name this time."

There was a parking lot to Becca's right, across the main road that ended with the ferry dock. People had been sauntering from cars in that lot to a food stand just to one side of the dock. A sign declaring the place to be Ivar's was shining through the mist, and a line of people making purchases had formed. Becca's stomach growled.

"Tell me your name," Laurel repeated. "This is important." Her voice was calm enough, but beneath the gentle tone was *come on come on there's so little time please do this for me it's the last thing I'll ask*, and Becca could feel those words coming at her, invading her brain, perfectly clear because that was how her mother's thoughts always were, unlike the whispers that came from others. She wanted to tell her mom not to worry. She wanted to tell her that Jeff Corrie might forget about them. But she knew the first statement was useless, and she knew the second was an outright lie.

Becca turned back to her mother and their eyes met and *listen my children and you shall hear of the midnight ride of Paul Revere* came from Laurel.

"Very funny," Becca said to her. "It would've been nice if you'd memorized something else in sixth grade besides that, you know."

"Tell me your name," Laurel said again.

"All right. All right. Rebecca Dolores King." Becca grimaced. "God. Does it *have* to be Dolores? I mean, who has a name like Dolores these days?"

Laurel ignored the question. "Where are you from?"

Becca said patiently because there was no point to anything other than patience at the moment, "San Luis Obispo. Sun Valley, Idaho, before that. I was born in Sun Valley, but I left when I was seven and that's when my family moved to San Luis Obispo."

"Why are you here?"

"I'm staying with my aunt."

"Where are your parents?"

"My mom's on a dig in . . ." Becca frowned. For the first time since they'd fled California, she couldn't remember. She assumed it was the fact that she was so hungry because she was never at her best when there were physical needs that had to be taken care of. She said, "Damn. I can't remember."

Laurel's head clunked back against the headrest of her seat. "You *have* to remember. This is crucial. It's life and death. *Where* are your parents?"

Becca looked at her mother, hoping for a clue but all she picked up was *on the eighteenth of April in seventy-five hardly a man is now alive*, which wasn't going to get her anywhere. She looked back at Ivar's. A woman bent over with osteoporosis was turning from the counter with a carton in her hand and she looked so old . . . and then it came to Becca. Old.

"Olduvai Gorge," she said. "My mom's on a dig in Olduvai Gorge." Nothing could have been further from the truth, but shortly before they'd made their run from Jeff Corrie, Becca had read an old book about the discovery of Lucy, aka *Australopithecus afarensis,* in Olduvai Gorge by an ambitious postgraduate fresh out of the University of Chicago. She'd been the one to suggest that her mother be a paleontologist. It sounded romantic to her.

Laurel nodded, satisfied. "What about your father? Where's your father? Don't you *have* a father?"

Becca rolled her eyes. It was clear that this was going to go on till the ferry arrived because her mother wanted no time to think of anything else. Least of all did she want to think of how she'd endangered her daughter. So Becca said deliberately, "Which father would that be, Mom?" and then she reached in her pocket and pulled out the single earphone of the AUD box. She shoved it into her ear. She turned up the volume and her head filled with static, soothing to her as always, the way satin is soothing against someone's skin.

Laurel reached over and yanked the earphone out of Becca's ear. She said, "I'm sorry this happened. I'm sorry I'm not who you want me to be. But here's the thing: no one ever is."

At this, Becca got out of the car. She had money enough in her jeans to buy herself something to eat, and more money in the pockets of her jacket. She fully intended to use it. There was even more money in her backpack if she wanted to buy everything on the menu, but the backpack was with her bike in the back of the Explorer and if she tried to get at it, she knew her mother would stop her.

Becca crossed the road. To her left, she could see the ferry coming, and she paused for a moment and watched its approach. When Laurel had first told her that she would get to Whidbey Island on a ferry, Becca had thought of the only ferry she'd ever been on, an open-air raft that held four cars and sailed about two hundred yards across the harbor in Newport Beach, California. This thing approaching was nothing like that. It was huge, with a gaping mouth for cars to slide into. It was all lit up like a riverboat and seagulls were flying around it.

The line at Ivar's had diminished by the time Becca got there. She ordered clam chowder and made sure it was the New England kind, made with milk and potatoes and therefore possessing a dizzying number of calories. She asked for an extra bag of oyster crackers to float in the container, and when she had to pay, she did it in coins. She placed them carefully one at a time on the counter, and *oh damn . . . what the . . . stupid chick* told her that the cashier wasn't pleased. Becca saw why when the cashier had to pick up the coins with fingers minus their nails. She'd bitten them down to the quick. They were ugly, and Becca saw the cashier hated them to be on display.

Becca thought about saying sorry but instead she said thanks and took her chowder over to a newspaper stand. She balanced the soup container on top and dipped her spoon into it as she watched the ferry come nearer to the mainland.

The chowder wasn't what she expected. She'd been thinking it would be like the chowder her stepfather two stepfathers ago had made. He was called Pete and he used corn in his, and Becca was a corn girl. Popcorn, corn on the cob, frozen corn. It didn't matter. Laurel claimed corn was what was fed to cows and pigs to make them fat, but since Laurel said that about nearly everything Becca wanted to eat, Becca didn't give much thought to the matter.

Still, this particular chowder wasn't worth fighting over with Laurel. So Becca ate only half of it. Then she jammed her container into a trash can and sprinted back toward the Explorer.

Laurel was on her cell phone. Her face, now without its spray tan, looked gray and weathered. For the first time, Becca thought of her mother as old, but then Laurel smiled and nodded and started talking in that way where no one could squeeze in a word. Carol Quinn was probably getting an earful, Becca thought. Her mom had been calling her twice a day to make sure every detail of the plan was hammered into position irreversibly.

Their eyes met, and when they did, what Becca heard was *no one's ever going to hurt*, but that was cut off the way a radio gets cut off when someone changes stations and what came over the airways next was *one if by land and two if by sea and I on the opposite shore will be*. It was just like static from the AUD box and it worked as well. Laurel said something into the cell phone and ended the call.

Becca got into the Explorer. Her mother said sharply, "Was that New England clam chowder you were eating?"

Becca said, "I didn't eat it all."

Ready to ride and spread the alarm through every Middlesex village and farm took the place of what Laurel wanted to say but it didn't matter and Becca told her so. "Stop it," she said. "I know what you're thinking anyway."

Laurel said, "Let's not fight." She reached over and touched her daughter's hair. "Carol will be waiting for you when the ferry docks," she said quietly. "She has a truck for the bike, so there's nothing to worry about. She knows what you look like and if she isn't there when you arrive, just wait because she'll be on her way. Okay, sweetheart? Hey. Are you hearing me?"

Becca was. She was hearing the words. She was also feeling the emotion behind them. She said, "It's not all your fault, Mom."

"There's more than one kind of fault," her mother replied. "If you don't know that yet, believe me, you will."

Becca reached for her backpack in the back of the Ford. Laurel said, "Where are the glasses? You'll need to put them on now."

"No one's looking at me."

"You need to put them on. You need to get in the habit. Where's the extra hair dye? How many batteries do you have for the AUD box? What's your name? Where's your mother?"

Becca looked at her then. *Listen my children listen my children*, but there was no need for Laurel to recite that poem over and over, even if she couldn't recall the rest of the words at that moment. For Becca read her expression as anyone could have done. Her mother was terrified. She was going on instinct alone just as she always had, but because her last instinct had been the one telling her to marry Jeff Corrie, she no longer trusted what her gut was telling her.

Becca said, "Mom. I'll be okay," and she was surprised when Laurel's eyes filled with tears. Her mother hadn't cried once since they'd left San Diego. She hadn't cried at all since she'd spent herself crying when she'd learned who Jeff Corrie really was and what Jeff Corrie had done. We can't go to the police, her mother had told her through her tears. God in heaven, sweetheart, who will believe you? No one's reported a body yet and if we do . . . we have no evidence Jeff was involved. So she'd laid her plans and they'd made a run for it and here they were on the brink of something from which there was no return.

Becca reached out and took her mother's hand. "Listen to what I know," she said.

"What do you know?"

"Rebecca Dolores King, Mom. San Luis Obispo. My aunt Carol on Whidbey Island. Carol Quinn. Olduvai Gorge."

Laurel looked beyond Becca, over her shoulder. The sound of traffic said that the ferry had arrived and was offloading its vehicles. "Oh God," Laurel whispered.

"Mom," Becca said, "it's okay. Really." She shoved open the door and walked to the back of the Explorer. Her mother got out and joined her there. Together they lifted her bike from the back and arranged its saddlebags on either side. Becca struggled into the heavy backpack, but before she did so, she dug inside for the glasses with their clear and decidedly useless lenses. She put them on.

"Map of the island?" her mother asked her.

"I've got it in the backpack."

"You're sure?"

"I'm sure."

"What about Carol's address? Just in case."

"Got that too."

"Where's the cell phone? Remember, it's limited minutes. Yours is programmed with the number of mine. So emergencies only. *Nothing* else. It's important. You've got to remember."

"I'll remember. And I've got it in the backpack, Mom. And yes to the rest. The AUD box. Extra batteries. More hair color. Everything."

"Where's your ticket?"

"Here. Mom, it's all here. It is."

Oh God oh God oh God.

"I better get going," Becca said, gazing at the stream of cars heading into the town beyond the ferry line.

"Look at me, sweetheart," Laurel said.

Becca didn't want to. She was afraid, and she didn't need to hear more fear. But she knew the importance of giving her mother this reassurance, so she met her gaze as Laurel said to her, "Look right into my eyes. Tell me what you see. Tell me what you know."

And there was no midnight ride of Paul Revere now. There was only a single message to read.

"You'll come back," Becca said.

"I will," Laurel promised. "As soon as I can."

TWO

The walk-ons and the bikes went first. There was a crowd of them, and Becca followed their lead. Those with bikes moved toward the front of the ferry, wheeling them along a three-lane tunnel toward an opening at the far end. The walk-ons went for a stairway. Among them were people fishing in their pockets and their purses, and Becca concluded that there was something to buy up above. She guessed it was food or hot drinks. Either would be welcome to her, because a cool breeze was coming off the water, she was shivering, and she was still hungry.

At the front of the ferry, people parked their bikes. Becca did likewise. She had intended to go back to the stairs to find the food, but the sudden roar of motorcycles stopped her. The noise was intensified because the motorcycles were coming through the ferry's tunnel. There were only four of them, but it sounded like twenty, and what followed them was a line of eighteen wheelers. The cars followed, arranging themselves in four lanes, two to each side of the main tunnel.

None of this would have been a problem, since Becca had the AUD box with her. She plugged in the earphone and turned up the volume and concentrated on the static the AUD box produced. But as she did this, she saw that the first car coming into the side tunnel and parking just behind the spot where she was standing next to her ten-speed was a police car.

If it can be said that blood can run cold, Becca's did at that moment. All she could think of was the logical first move Jeff Corrie would have made when he found his wife and his stepdaughter gone: phone the cops and report them both as missing persons, sending out the general alarm to find them as quickly as possible, so that Becca and what Becca had gleaned from his whispers could be wiped from the face of the earth. Jeff's favorite motto had been about the best defense being an offense, and what better offense could there be? Becca could even picture the flyer he'd come up with and circulated far and wide. It would be fastened to a clipboard within the police car, she imagined, her face and her mother's face upon it.

She turned away from the police car slowly, determined to look straight ahead. Anything else like a sudden turn would have given her away, and the thought of giving herself away not ten minutes after she'd left her mother was so frightening that she felt as if neon arrows were pointing down from the ceiling of the ferry right at her skull so that the cop inside that police car would get out and question her.

But the suspense of not knowing if she'd been noticed was too much for Becca to bear. She knew it meant exposing herself to even more of an assault pounding like hammers inside her head, but she did it anyway because she had to do it: she turned down the AUD box to try to catch some useful information.

It was nearly impossible to distinguish anything. There was *Nancy damn it* and *dinner won't be* and *nail polish all over* and *talked to my boss* and *William for a haircut . . .* then suddenly with all of this came a warmth that should have been impossible to feel in this cool, damp place. With the warmth came scent, equally out of place. Where she should have been smelling diesel fumes from the big rigs or exhaust from the cars and the motor-cycles, instead what she smelled was the sweetness of fruit being cooked. It was so intense that before she realized what she was doing, Becca actually swung around, exposing her face to the police car behind her. But she didn't think of what might hap-pen. Nothing seemed as important as finding the source of the warmth and the scent.

That was how she first saw him, the boy who would ulti-mately change everything for her. He was a teenager like her, and he was sitting in the police car. He was in the front seat, not the back, and he and the policeman were talking. They both looked serious, and the contrast between them could not have been greater.

The boy was black, deeply black, and the pure midnight of his skin made the policeman with him look white beyond white. He was also completely bald, not the bald of illness but the bald of choice. This suited him and, in contrast again, the policeman had lots of hair that mixed gray and brown.

Becca realized as she looked at the boy that he was the first person of any color other than white that she'd seen in the vicin-ity of the ferry. She didn't intend to stare and she *wasn't* actu-ally staring when the boy looked at her. As their eyes met, the warmth Becca was feeling increased along with the scent of cooking fruit, but something else floated on that warmth and it was the unexpected hollowness of the boy's despair. Along with the ache of it floated the whisper of a single word repeated three time: *rejoice, rejoice, rejoice.*

Becca half-smiled at the boy the way one does. But in return the hollowness grew, and when it began to feel as if it might take her over, she dropped her gaze. As she did so, the policeman got out of the car. He shut the door neatly and walked toward the stairs, punching in numbers on a cell phone.

While this was the moment that Becca could have approached the boy, she knew far better than to do so. She decided that now she could go for the food she'd been thinking about when the police car had stopped behind her.

She shrugged out of her backpack. She left it next to her bike and walked in the direction of the stairs. She couldn't risk another look at the boy but she saw as she passed the police car that on the side it said ISLAND COUNTY SHERIFF.

As luck would have it, she found herself climbing upward just behind the policeman, who she assumed was a deputy of some kind, or perhaps the sheriff himself. He seemed to be well-known, because people passing on the stairs called him Dave and asked how Rhonda was and inquired about his daughter's new baby. Becca huddled into herself to stay unnoticed to him, but it didn't matter as things turned out, because his call went through and he started talking about a cliff to someone.

Becca caught snatches of conversation but not any whispers. The conversation that came to her said that next week was going to be too difficult for Dave because of his schedule and maybe the week after might work if it works for you too. Also, was the cliff completely safe because it was pretty exposed, wasn't it, and you-know-who was starting to hang around there with his little brother. This made Becca wonder more about the island. She was used to southern California, which had suffered from every possible kind of natural problem: earthquakes, fires, floods, drought, windstorms, and landslides. But now she saw that disasters were, perhaps, common here as well, and she wondered what sort of disasters they would be if they had to do with the safety of cliffs.

Upstairs, the policeman paused to continue his conversation near the windows, while Becca followed the crowd to a cafeteria where a line had formed to purchase food. Aware of money and how she was going to have to make it last till her mom started sending her more, Becca chose cookies. There was a package of three, sugar cookies that were frosted in orange, and she concluded this was something special when she heard a little girl's voice behind her say, "Look, Gram! They're not pink this time," and Gram say in reply, "Maybe it's for Halloween."

Halloween. Becca felt a tug. It had always been her favorite holiday. Laurel usually said this was because of the free candy she could collect and it was important that they "take a look at your addiction to sugar, sweetheart, because Type Two diabetes is becoming an epidemic these days among kids your age." On the other hand, Becca's grandmother noted that it was all about the fun Becca had in knowing who each child was behind the mask since their whispers almost always gave them away. Becca's grandmother always advised her to stay near the whispers of children anyway. "They don't know how to lie to themselves," she said.

Becca missed her badly. She missed hearing, "Laurel, just let her *be*, okay? She's going to adjust," and although Laurel's answer was always the same, "I want her to be *normal*, Mother," her grandmother's reply of "Pooh. Nothing's more boring than normal," generally made Becca feel special, not odd.

It was in the cause of seeming normal, though, that Laurel had come up with the AUD box. She'd claimed it was entirely for Becca's benefit, so that she could concentrate when she was in school. But the truth was that while the AUD box worked perfectly to help Becca focus, it also served to keep other people's thoughts away. Laurel's in particular, of course.

BECCA DIDN'T TAKE any note of the girl in front of her in the cafeteria's line till they reached the cash register. Then she saw her holding a foil-wrapped hamburger and talking to two boys who were waiting for her by the condiments, a short distance away. One of the boys was long-haired and spotty-faced, wearing a rolled-up ski cap on his head like a beanie; the other was neatly dressed and neatly combed, looking worried and swallowing compulsively. As for the girl, she was very small and very trim, not an ounce of fat on her, virtually all muscle. She had a pixie haircut and a voice whose tone was one of snarky irritation. All three of them together made the suggestion that something was going on. It came to Becca as she watched them that, no matter what, high school kids were probably the same pretty much everywhere.

The long-hair boy muttered, "She doesn't have the guts to try it," as the girl reached the cash register.

"Probably shouldn't, Jenn," the worried boy said.

Becca thought idly, Shouldn't what? as Jenn handed over a ten to pay for her food.

The cashier took the money, and Becca watched the exchange and admired the woman's nicely buffed nails, so different from those on the cashier at Ivar's. They were smooth with a pretty sheen to them and Becca wondered as she handed change back to Jenn—

"Hey," Jenn said to the cashier, "I just gave you a twenty."

Becca spoke without thinking. "No, it was a ten. I saw it."

Jenn swung on her. "What the . . . Are you calling me a liar or something?" And what came with this was *who the hell . . . oh great, Dylan . . . more cool ideas?*

"Oh, sorry! No," Becca said. "I just noticed because I was look-ing at her nails." She added, "They're really nice," to the cashier, who blushed prettily.

Jenn said, "What are you, some kind of perv?" and to the cashier, "It was a twenty, and I want my change."

"It really wasn't," Becca said as, behind the counter, a man came out of an inner room. He asked what the problem was, and the girl Jenn spoke right up.

"I'll tell you what the problem is," she said, as the younger of the two boys with her murmured, "Jenn . . ." in a voice that sounded like a warning. "I gave her a twenty," Jenn declared. "This chick's seeing things."

"Let's take a look, shall we?" the man then asked. He swung a small screen around to face the line of customers. It displayed the cash drawer, and it filmed each time the drawer opened. He pushed a button and there it was. The ten-dollar bill went from Jenn's hands to the cashier's hands. "Move along," the man said in a steely voice. "Next customer please."

Becca stepped to the register and paid for her cookies. But not before Jenn said into her ear, "You little bitch," and then vanished with her two companions.

AN ANNOUNCEMENT TOLD everyone when to head back to their vehicles. Becca followed the crowd. She was careful when she passed the sheriff's car not to look at it or the boy within it, although she caught a glimpse of his shoulder because he was leaning against the window.

Everything was as she'd left it at her bike. The saddlebags still bulged on either side of it, and her backpack leaned against its rear wheel. She worked her way into this again and gazed forward as the ferry dock loomed up ahead. She saw that here the mist was more like fog, a billowing gray veil that hung between her and whatever there was that defined this place. Mostly, what defined it appeared to be trees. There were more trees here than she'd ever seen in an area where people also actually lived.

Becca was used to hillsides sketched with the bony definition of chaparral and a landscape that developers scraped clean to the desiccated dirt before they filled it with thousands of identical houses. Here, though, if there were houses at all, they were somewhere in the trees, because what Becca was looking at was a vast forest: Douglas firs, hemlocks, and cedars that would remain untouched by winter weather, along with alders, birches, maples, and cottonwoods that would lose their leaves and thus bring light to the forest floor. This landscape rose steeply from a beach along which a few houses were strung, brightly lit against the growing gloom.

The ferry workers waited till a ramp was lowered from the dock. Then they took down the barrier chain and waved at the bicyclists and the foot passengers to disembark.

The foot passengers headed to the left, and the bicycle riders headed to the right. Becca went along and found herself on a dock far vaster than she'd expected. Here, she realized, everything was larger than life. Ferries, trees, docks, everything.

As soon as she had walked her bike to the end of the dock, she began to look for Carol Quinn. She didn't know a thing about what her mom's friend looked like, but she assumed that there would be someone waiting with a pickup truck into which she could dump her bike.

But there was no one, just a local bus that pulled away and headed in the direction of a highway, just a few cars in a distant parking lot to which ferry passengers walked and then climbed inside. Becca looked around, but she felt no panic. Her mom had phoned Carol Quinn. Becca had seen her do it. Carol Quinn was on her way.

Becca waited ten minutes. Slowly, she ate one of her cookies as those ten minutes stretched to twenty. Another ferry came and went with no Carol Quinn turning up to get her. After the departure of yet another ferry, Becca rustled through her backpack and found the cell phone that was programmed with Laurel's number.

The call to her mom didn't go through. *Out of range* was the reply she received. She would wait awhile and phone again, Becca decided, but in the meantime she would start on her way to Carol Quinn's house because, obviously, something had come up to detain her and she would no doubt meet her on the way.

Becca pulled out the map of Whidbey Island, along with Carol Quinn's home address. She plotted the most direct route she could find to Blue Lady Lane. Right off the highway, she saw, a street called Bob Galbreath Road would take her there. She wasn't in the best shape in the world for a bike ride, she knew, but this appeared to be only six miles. A piece of cake, she decided. She had a ten-speed. And anyone with a ten-speed could ride six miles.

Wrong, she discovered. When she pedaled to the highway that led away from the ferry, Becca's first thought was, Oh my God, and her second was, I'll never make it. For where the road began, it climbed at once. It curved up and away from the dock, and it disappeared into the fog. Along its right side a few businesses were lined up, hopeful buildings that seemed to cling to the ground with the expectation of otherwise sliding into the water.

Becca actually made it about one hundred and fifty yards before her breath was shrieking through her chest and her heart was slamming so hard that no AUD box was going to be necessary to drown out every other sound around her. Then she turned into a small parking lot. A sign reading CLINTON NAIL AND SPA identified the business, and a red neon sign indicated it was open. There was also a light above its door that cast a pyramid glow down to a welcome mat, and it was this light that Becca approached.

She took out the map again. She tried to find another way to get to Carol Quinn's house. There wasn't one. So she watched the highway for a good ten minutes, hoping to see a pickup truck slowly going by, with someone inside it searching for her.

That didn't happen. She had no choice. She set off again.

The pedaling was so difficult that she was practically standing still. She managed to inch past a low-slung Wells Fargo bank and an ancient restaurant with Pizza! Pizza! Pizza! advertised and that same sheriff's car parked in its lot and, no doubt, the sheriff and that boy inside, scarfing down a king-size pepperoni and cheese. When she crawled past a used-car lot, she thought about how she and her mom could have driven onto it and traded the Ford Explorer for whatever came next. Thinking this made her eyes sting, though, so she looked away from the car lot and what it promised and instead looked ahead with the hope of seeing the road she was looking for somewhere in the shrouded distance.

Instead she saw a Dairy Queen. Her heart sang. She'd make for this, she decided. She'd buy herself a hamburger there. French fries and a strawberry shake. Eating her way through her fear was the only answer. She *certainly* could make it as far as the Dairy Queen, she told herself, especially since there was a meal waiting for her at the end.

As it happened, however, what was also waiting was Bob Galbreath Road. It lay a short distance before the Dairy Queen, giving Becca another option. Since the shadows were lengthening and darkness was approaching, she went for virtue instead of calories. She set off along Bob Galbreath Road.

THREE

Becca discovered quickly enough that Bob Galbreath Road was worse than the highway she'd ridden to get to it. It began with a descent that allowed her to coast, but within fifty yards it started to climb

Soon enough there were trees everywhere. On the right, the edge of the lane ended abruptly. It gave way to a hillside that fell steeply, with thin-trunk alders bursting out of it. This same kind of tree grew in profusion on the other side of the road as well, and in the fog the leaves on the branches above Becca made a tunnel from which drops of water plopped onto the glasses she wore.

Becca shook her head to get the water from the lenses, but she knew better than to remove the glasses altogether. For they were now part of who she was, along with the dismal brown that Laurel had chosen in order to change her hair from strawberry blonde to completely ugly.

The important thing was neither her glasses nor her hair, though. Getting to Carol Quinn was paramount. Yet Blue Lady Lane seemed as far away as the moon, and with every revolution of the pedals it became more difficult for Becca to breathe.

The fifth time she came out of the forest to climb yet another hill, a sob leaped out of her chest. She couldn't tell if she was sobbing for breath or simply sobbing, but what she did know was that she had to rest. She made it to a point where the road wasn't so narrow, and she got off her bike.

She leaned over the handlebars to catch her breath. That was when she heard the siren approaching, followed in short order by flashing lights.

She thought the worst at once. As the vehicle came closer, she could tell it was a police car. She steeled herself and waited for something to happen, but the car screamed by her as if she were invisible to its occupants.

Becca saw them, though. In the brief instant it took for the car to shoot by, she saw the boy from the ferry again. Their eyes met. She felt the hollowness within him. And then it was gone. What had he *done*, she wondered, that his insides were so empty? Where was he being taken?

The silence was profound once the police car's siren faded away. Becca had no idea how much farther she had to go, but she assumed she had little enough hope of reaching Blue Lady Lane before the gloom of the evening became utter darkness. She set off again.

She'd gotten only a quarter mile when she heard a vehicle coming up behind her. She moved as far to the edge as she could, but the engine noise didn't get any louder. She realized that whoever was coming along in her wake had no intention of actually passing her, and she turned to see a pickup truck, a group of dogs moving restlessly in its bed.

Hallelujah, Becca thought. Carol Quinn at *last*.

The truck pulled to the side of the road. Someone got out. Becca could see a baseball cap, work boots, and a heavy jacket. A woman's voice spoke pleasantly. "Looks like you're struggling. Do you need a ride?" Obviously, Becca thought bleakly, this was not Carol Quinn at all.

She listened for whispers. On the side of the road there was a woman. On the side of the road there was Becca. What there wasn't was a single whisper.

Becca wasn't sure what this meant. The lack of whispers from this woman said she was completely different from anyone Becca had ever come into contact with. Although Laurel would have declared that this was the precise reason Becca should avoid her like poison oak, Becca's grandmother would have taken her aside and said, "Special defines itself by absence as well as presence, hon."

So Becca said, "The chain keeps slipping," in reference to her bike. This was a lie, but a small one since the chain had been feeling like a chain with the clear intention of slipping every time she had shifted the bicycle's gears. "I'm going to Blue Lady Lane," she added.

The woman said, "This is your lucky day. I'm going to Clyde," as if Becca would know exactly what that would mean. She strode over and said, "Let's get this in the back," and she picked up the bike, its weight and the loaded saddlebags nothing at all to her. She carried it to the side of the truck and hoisted it into the bed, saying to the animals, "All dogs move," before she said to Becca, "Hop in the front. Oscar'll move over. Just let me get this settled."

Oscar turned out to be a standard poodle, without what Becca thought of as a poodle's froufrou haircut. He was black, and he was secured into the seat with its regular belt. Since Becca wasn't sure if she was intended to unfasten the belt, she waited until the woman opened her door, climbed in, said "What're you waiting for?" and then laughed when she realized the seat belt was the problem. She said, "Sorry. Let me get that. Come on over here, Oscar," and when she had the seat belt off the dog, she pulled the poodle over, and then said to Becca, "Diana Kinsale. I don't know you, and I thought I knew everyone on the south end."

"Becca King," Becca said. She thought the rest: Rebecca Dolores King from San Luis Obispo, California, by way of Sun Valley, Idaho, where I was born. I do not ski. You'd think I would, considering, but I don't.

Diana Kinsale said, "Pretty name." She put the truck into gear.

Becca glanced back through the window at the pickup's bed. There were two labs back there and two mixed breeds. She said to Diana, "Doggie daycare?"

Diana laughed. She took off her baseball cap and Becca could see that her hair was gray. Becca found this quite strange. She couldn't remember if she'd ever actually seen gray hair on a woman before this because where she was from women dyed their hair the moment the first strand of gray came in. But Diana Kinsale was the definition of *au naturel*. She wore no makeup, and her hair wasn't even styled.

"They're all mine," Diana Kinsale said in reference to the dogs. "I didn't *intend* to end up with five of them, but one thing always leads to another and here I am. What about you?"

"I don't have a dog," Becca said. "I like them a lot, but my mom's allergic."

"Ah." *Who is she?*

Becca felt a pressure inside her head. *Who is she?* was, of course, the logical question. Who is your mom, this woman who is allergic to dogs, and does she know you're on your bike all alone in the growing dark with the fog coming in heavier each minute? But these questions weren't asked. They weren't even thought.

Becca stole a look at Diana Kinsale. Diana Kinsale glanced at her and said nothing. She punched a button on the radio, and the Dixie Chicks began singing at a volume that precluded conversation.

It didn't take long to get to Clyde Street. One and a half Dixie Chicks later, and Diana was pulling into the driveway of a gray clapboard house that overlooked water that Becca would come to know as Saratoga Passage. Below the house, a group of cottages sat directly on a spit of beach, and across from this another island rose up in a mass of trees, darkness, and a fistful of flung lights coming from the houses that stood at its south end.

Diana got out of the truck and Oscar followed her. The other dogs began to pace. When Becca joined the woman at the pickup's tailgate, Diana had lowered it and the four dogs leaped out and began bounding around the front yard.

"No pooping," Diana shouted at them as she heaved the bike out and set it on the ground. She rearranged the saddlebags upon it, and extended her hand to Becca. "I hope to see you around, Becca King," she said.

Becca reached out for the shake. When their hands met, a tingling shot up Becca's arm, something between an electric shock and her arm coming awake from sleep. Her eyes met Diana's and in that moment, Becca knew what her grandmother had said was true. Sometimes the absence of something indicates the presence of something else. The only difficulty lay in discerning what that something else was.

Diana said quietly, "Things aren't always your fault."

Becca said, "Huh?" because she needed whispers now in order to understand this woman, and in the absence of whispers she was only too aware of how lost she could become on Whidbey Island.

Diana said, "The chain on your bike? It probably needs some work but it's natural not to notice that kind of thing till it's too late. It's not your fault that the ride was a tough one if your bike's not in good condition."

The dogs returned. They began sniffing the ground around Becca's feet and they'd soon made it up her leg to the vicinity of her jacket pocket where the last two sugar cookies remained.

Diana said, "The dogs like you. That's good," and then she said to the animals, "Chow time, dogs!" and the dogs set up a chorus of barking. "Stop by anytime," Diana said with a wave, and she disappeared toward the back of the house. The dogs followed.

BECCA REMEMBERED TO push her bike. She figured that Diana Kinsale might have known she was lying about the chain slipping, but still she wanted to keep up the pretence. So she pushed it till she came to a streetlight some distance away from Diana's house and there she unfolded her map to see where Blue Lady Lane was from Clyde Street.

A single glance told her why Diana had said this was her lucky day. Blue Lady Lane broke off from a street at the end of Clyde, and the end of Clyde was clearly visible by the stop sign on its corner.

So, it turned out, was the sheriff's car that had passed Becca on Bob Galbreath Road. When she made the right turn that would take her to Blue Lady Lane, she saw the car sitting in front of a house midway along the street, where Blue Lady Lane began.

Becca knew, then. She couldn't have put everything into words, but something had happened and it wasn't good. At first she thought the police were looking for her. But the presence of at least eight people on the upstairs deck outside of the house and the bright lights within the building seemed to suggest something else.

She rolled her bike to a mound of vegetation, and from within its shelter she gazed at the house. A low sign in front of it said Horse Haven and lights shone on house numbers on this. She dug out Carol Quinn's address, but she was sure of what she would find. The numbers matched.

She crept forward. She crossed the street in the shadows from the trees, and she'd reached the side of the sheriff's car before she realized the boy was still in it, although the sheriff was not.

She began to back off, but the boy got out. He rubbed the back of his neck and gazed at the house on its little rise of land. She froze where she was. Then he turned to her.

Their eyes locked on each other's. *People leave . . . someone . . . if death was easy . . . rejoice rejoice . . .* caressed the air between them. Then voices broke into the darkness around them as two men approached, coming down the walk from the house.

"I'm so damn sorry, Mr. Quinn. If there's anything . . ."

The boy glanced their way, then back at Becca. *Go*, he mouthed. *Now. Go.* He got back into the car.

But Becca couldn't go until she heard and knew, and the knowledge came quickly with the other man's words. She could tell he was crying. "Just a little under the weather," he said. "She felt bad but she thought it was the flu and so did I. And now this."

"She's not the first," the undersheriff said. "With women, a heart attack . . . it doesn't feel like they think it would feel. She didn't know that."

"She was so strong, Dave." He started sobbing.

Becca backed away. She returned to the vegetation and sat. She put her head in her hands and listened to the sound of the Island County sheriff's car as it drove off. She had no idea what she would do.

WITHIN AN HOUR, everyone had gone as Becca sat and thought and tried and failed to contact Laurel. *Out of range, out of range* was the message each time, feeding into Becca's deepest fears. At the end, she had only a single hope. She would have to talk to Carol Quinn's husband.

Becca stepped out of the vegetation. She approached the house, and as she did so, Mr. Quinn came outside and stood on the deck. She hesitated, half-hidden behind a rhododendron. She could see him, but he could only see her if he knew where to look, and he wasn't looking. Instead, he stared out at the water across the street from his house in a way that told Becca he wasn't actually looking at anything.

He lit a cigarette and smoked for a few moments in silence, and in equal silence Becca watched him. Then *what now . . . she never thought . . . no plan* came to her, a scattering of thoughts, like bread cast on the water for ducks. But the feelings that came with them made them heavy like boulders and they rolled toward Becca till she stepped into the light.

"Mr. Quinn?"

"Yeah," he said heavily. "Who're you? You lost?"

"I'm Becca King," she said. And then she waited, for the recognition, for the realization, for the remembrance, for anything. She hoped he would say, "Oh yes. The girl Carol was going to take in till her mom comes back," but he said nothing. So Becca knew from this that Carol Quinn had taken Laurel's request for absolute secrecy right to her death. Her lips felt stiff and sore as she murmured, "I just wanted to say . . . I'm sorry for your loss."

But he was already deep within his own thoughts, and none of them related to a girl from San Diego on the run from a man who'd murdered his business partner in a phony break-in into the man's million-dollar condo.

———

BECCA WENT BACK to her bike. She pulled the cell phone out and she tried again. She heard her mother's words. It's programmed, sweetheart. Press one on yours and it'll connect you to mine. But only in an emergency.

Everything related to Carol Quinn had turned into an emergency, Becca thought. She pressed one and tried for Laurel again. She waited in agony for the connection to go through. But the message was the same as before. *Out of range, out of range, out of range.*

Wait, she told herself. Just wait for a while. Cell phones got out of range all the time, and she expected that they got out of range frequently in this part of the world. There were mountains and bodies of water and islands, and surely all of these things indicated it would be very simple for someone to be out of range for a time.

So wait, wait, wait, she told herself. Just wait, wait, wait. Because the last thing she could face at the moment was the possibility that the very same mother who'd planned their escape from Jeff Corrie so perfectly had ended up leaving her to fend for herself on an island she knew nothing about.

FOUR

In that moment, Becca was afraid of a lot of things. Like other girls her age, she'd never been on her own. She'd had her mother and, before her breast cancer death, she'd had her grandmother. Now what she had was a cell phone connecting her to exactly no one unless she wanted to call San Diego and exchange happy greetings with Jeff Corrie. The fact was that Laurel had laid very careful plans, and the big one had just blown up in Becca's face.

She crossed the street in front of the house where Carol Quinn had lived. The man had gone back inside, and she could see him through the brightly lit windows. She couldn't hear his whispers from this distance and because of the glass between them but she could easily imagine them: *Carol . . . Carol . . . what do I do . . .* He was moving aimlessly around the living room.

Becca was on a stretch of open grassy land, high above the water. A log lay here, bare like a piece of driftwood that had been brought up from the beach below to serve as a bench. She sat and tried not to think about anything else but an answer to the question, What next? To keep herself from going to a place of total panic, she dug in her jacket where the sugar cookies were, and she ate the second one slowly, in order to kill time. A soft rain began to fall, and she put up the hood of her jacket. Then she looked out at the lights across the passage and wondered how far Laurel had gone.

She was heading for British Columbia and a mountain town called Nelson. She had *said* her reasoning had to do with *Roxanne*, that old film with Steve Martin and Daryl Hannah. Laurel liked it so much that she had her own DVD of it, and she played it whenever life got to her. It wasn't the romance of the film that seemed to interest Laurel, though. It was the little town of Nelson where it had been filmed. She studied that town every time she watched *Roxanne*. She stopped the film and looked at the scenery. She did it so often that Becca had wondered if Laurel was actually *looking* for someone, like an extra hired from the town. But she never was able to figure this out. For when Laurel watched, she kept her mind going on *listen my children and you shall hear of the midnight ride of Paul Revere*, and when Becca asked her why she was doing that, her mother said, "Discipline, sweetheart," as if she was afraid she'd forget the poem because the film would sweep it from her mind. She'd add sharply, "And why aren't you using the AUD box?"

"The AUD box is for your protection, hon," her grandmother would say. "It's to give other people their privacy, sure. But it's also because you can't go through your life being bombarded with noise."

"*You* have," Becca would answer, for she'd inherited hearing whispers from her grandmother instead of the woman's flaming red hair.

"Sure. But your talent's stronger than mine. It'll take you a while to learn to control it."

"So, I have to wear this dumb thing for the rest of my life?"

"Just till you learn where the knobs are on the volume in your head," her grandmother said. "Your mom's only trying to protect you, hon. It's for the best."

But Becca couldn't see how her mom was protecting her now. So when she'd finished the cookie, which she'd eaten as slowly as she could manage by letting each bite melt on her tongue, she took out the cell phone and called Laurel again.

Out of range was the message another time. Becca gave a little cry, and she shoved the phone back into her pocket. She wanted to be angry with her mother, but she knew there was no point to that. She also wanted to return to Diana Kinsale's door and ask for help. But despite not having the AUD box plugged into her ear, the fact that she'd gotten no reading off Diana Kinsale worried her. She wasn't sure what it meant. Still, she couldn't stay here on the driftwood log, so she roused herself and trudged back to her bike. Under a streetlight nearby Becca fished out her map of Whidbey Island and traced the route into Langley, which was the nearest town. It wasn't terribly far at this point: back to Clyde, a few miles to the end of a road called Sandy Point, and then a right turn would put her in the vicinity of downtown, whatever went for downtown in this place. But she didn't know what she would find there, and she was so tired that she didn't know what she'd do when she got there. So she refolded the map and returned to her bike. She had to do something, and riding was better than nothing.

When she reached Diana Kinsale's driveway, Becca paused. In the darkness just beyond the house, she could make out the silver outline of the dog run where the shapes of Diana's dogs were moving about, settling down for the night. Becca found there was comfort in thinking about those dogs. They'd been friendly to her, sniffing around her feet and her pockets but not jumping on her or anything.

She glanced around. As she did so, the porch light on Diana's house went off and somehow that seemed like an invitation.

She saw that next to Diana's driveway, an enormous heap of shrubbery grew. In the darkness she couldn't tell what it was, just that it was thick and ungoverned and that it had copious thorns, which she discovered when she removed her saddlebags from her bike and slid them and the bike beneath its branches.

The dogs began barking as she approached the dog run. The back door of the house opened and Becca shrank back into the shadows. Diana's voice called out, "Enough, dogs. No bark," and they fell silent although they increased their restless pacing. The door closed once more.

Becca waited. She wanted the dogs to settle down and she wanted to make sure that Diana Kinsale wasn't going to open the door again. She shivered and stuck her hands into the pockets of her jacket, and her right hand found the last of the sugar cookies. This told her there was an easy way to handle what had to come next.

At the run she extended her fingers, sugary now from the

cookie and its icing. The dogs jostled one another for a smell and a lick, and they were delighted when she climbed over the fence, joined them, and broke the sugar cookie into pieces, saving one for herself and giving them the rest.

There was a doghouse at the far end of the run. It was the size of a chicken coop because of the number of dogs that slept there. It was also big enough for just one more creature to fit inside, and that was what Becca did. She crawled through the opening, out of the rain.

The dogs crowded in after her. The smell was terrible, since there's very little that smells worse than wet dog except, perhaps, wet dog plus dog blankets in need of washing. But for Becca it was a beggars and choosers situation, and even if it hadn't been, she thought she probably would have chosen the dogs anyway as her sleeping companions that first night on Whidbey Island. For as they settled around her and she settled in with them, one of the dogs sought out her face and licked her lips. She knew at heart that the dog was after one more crumb of sugar cookie, but she decided to call it a good-night kiss.

SHE WOKE UP early. It was still dark, but through one of the boards that made up the side of the doghouse, she could see a slice of dawn. It was the color of an apricot near its pit, and threads of that color bled out into the sky.

Becca was stiff in every way. Her neck hurt from how she'd positioned herself with the dogs. Her legs were sore, her back ached, and her arms felt as if she'd been carrying weights. Even her wrists hurt.

She smelled just like one of the dogs, and she was very hungry. She lay there with her head on her arm and wished more than anything that she'd stopped at that Dairy Queen.

She moved tentatively. The dogs roused around her, and the air filled with the dog breath of their morning yawns. None of them barked, however. She was part of the pack now, and there was no reason to sound the alarm at her coming or going.

Becca petted each one of them in farewell. She didn't know their names, only Oscar's, and he was apparently inside the house. They nudged her with their noses, and one of them whimpered while another went to an enormous stainless steel bowl that glittered in the ambient light and lapped noisily. Becca was as thirsty as she was hungry, but member of the pack or not, she drew a line at sharing the dogs' water.

At the mass of shrubbery along the driveway, Becca rustled for her saddlebags and then for her bike. In the weak light, she could see that the shrubs were blackberry bushes, completely untrimmed and insanely wild, with the late summer's fruit still upon them. But she had no time to pick some berries and make them her breakfast. Diana Kinsale would be up soon, and Becca knew she couldn't run the risk of being caught there and facing her questions.

She walked her bike to the road. From looking at the map on the previous night, she knew where the town of Langley was. She had to find this place, and once there she had to figure out what to do next. She'd phone Laurel again when she got there.

She reached the end of Clyde, Diana's street, and she made a little jog onto Sandy Point Road. This ran in the same direction as the waters of Saratoga Passage although within moments, Becca discovered that Sandy Point Road was as bad as Bob Galbreath Road had been. The only difference was the lack of curves. It was as straight as a ruler but otherwise it was hills and valleys all the way.

It was terribly cold. Becca's breath came from her like cumulus clouds, and she was soon grateful for the exertion necessary to get up the hills because, at least, this kept her warm.

At last she came to the end of the road, where at a T-junction she saw in front of her the barnlike shapes of the county fairgrounds. She went to the right, in the direction that the map had told her she would find the town. As she did so, the chain on her bike slipped suddenly. The pedals turned with nowhere to go, and her leg hit the serrated pedal edge. Becca winced with the sudden pain.

She got off the bike and took a look at it. She had to do something to keep it functioning. The problem was that she didn't know what was wrong with the thing aside from the obvious. Did the gears need oiling? Did the chain need cleaning? Did something need to be replaced?

She had to push the bike the rest of the way into the town. It wasn't far. The road she was on was level at last, and she followed its curve. Finally, in the growing dawn, Langley spread out before her, tucked into trees, easing its way down a slope speckled with wood-framed cottages, then rising again into another hill. It was more a village than a town, and it sat on a bluff high above the pulsing water. She pushed her bike along this bluff toward what looked like a commercial area.

She quickly discovered that the business part of Langley consisted of only two streets. She chose the first one, simply because it went downhill and she could get back on her bike and coast. She wasn't sure where she was going at this point. She only knew she needed some food and she hoped to find it.

She had a bit of luck quickly. On her right a short distance along the street she came to a parking lot. Not a large parking lot, as nothing in the village seemed large, but a parking lot all the same. At one side of it squatted a white building with STAR STORE in red neon letters above a double door of glass. The lights inside this store were on, and from what Becca could see, it looked like a market.

She rolled her bike up to its door. She thought about removing her saddlebags while she was inside the place, for security's sake, but no one was around to steal them and anyway, she had a feeling they'd be fine where they were. So would her backpack, she figured.

Although the lights were blazing inside the Star Store, when she pulled on the door, Becca found it locked. She muttered and jiggled the door in irritation. Nothing—it seemed—was going right. It was time to call Laurel again.

Becca turned to dig her cell phone from her backpack, but at that point a little miracle happened. The store doors opened behind her and a boy's voice said, "Hey. Not opened yet. Sorry."

Becca swung in the direction of that voice. An older teenager was standing half in and half out of the store, a trash bag in one hand and the other hand holding the door open a few feet. He sported baggy jeans and a long-sleeved black T-shirt with DJANGO REINHARDT ROCKS featured on it. He wore an unbuttoned flannel shirt over this. His hair was long and held back in a ponytail, and a black fedora sat on his head. He looked about eighteen years old.

He said to her, "Two hours till we open. Sorry." He leaned a mop against the wall inside and came out into the cold. He had odd, thick-soled sandals on his feet and even odder red-and-orange socks. He sauntered over to a Dumpster, heaved the trash bag up and over, and wiped his hands on the sides of his jeans.

Becca's eyes fixed on the Dumpster. Her thoughts went quickly from Star Store to groceries to trash bag to what might be in the trash bag, but the boy seemed to know what she was thinking because he fingered one of the ear gauges he sported and said, "No way. There's nada in there worth even a look. If there was anything, I'd take it down to the seawall and give it to the gulls. Believe me, you do *not* want to mess with what's inside this thing." He slapped his hand against the Dumpster the way another boy might have slapped his hand against his car.

He came her way. Becca could tell that he was nice because what came off him felt like a pleasant bath. He paused at her bike and looked it over. He gave her a glance, then squatted down for a closer look. He shook his head as he deftly put the chain back where it belonged. "Ride this thing far?" he asked. "It looks like it's been sitting in the fog for a decade."

This wasn't exactly an incorrect surmise because leaving something outside in the eternally salt-laden air of San Diego wasn't far removed from having left the bike in the fog. Becca said, "Yeah. It's pretty bad. I've got to get it fixed. Or something."

He said, "Definitely 'or something.'" He rose again. He was

closer to her now, and he made that clear when he went on with, "Whew, you smell like a dog. You been sleeping with them?"

"More or less," Becca said. "I was hoping there was a place I could buy something to eat."

"Yeah? Bummer. This hour? Nada." He looked at his watch. He said, "Mike's'll be open earliest. It's up on the corner." He pointed vaguely. "First Street and Anthes? You could get breakfast there. But not till later," he added.

She said, "Oh. Double bummer," and made a move to go, which was when he said spontaneously, "On the other hand, I think I can help you. You got to keep it under your hat, though. Can do?"

She nodded, and he led the way back into the Star Store, scooping up his mop as he entered. He rested this against one of two checkout counters and continued to the far side of the store.

The place was bigger than it looked from the outside, Becca found. It was a full-service market, only in miniature, with short aisles stocked with groceries and an area with fresh vegetables and fruit. The place also had a deli, and it was to the deli that the boy led her.

He pointed to some trays that sat on the counter behind a display of meats and cheeses. "It's still good enough to eat but too old to sell. I give it to CMA"—with a glance at her—"Christian Missionary Alliance. They do soup a couple days a week for anyone who needs it. When there's stuff here to be thrown away, I make sandwiches for them. If you want to make yourself one, have at it."

He washed his hands and set to work. Becca did the same and joined him at the counter. Side by side, they made sandwiches for a few minutes in silence till he brushed up against her and she sensed an aching hole within him. Something had been torn away from this boy, and she said without thinking, "Other stuff'll cover it up eventually and finally you won't even know it's there."

He stopped what he was doing and said, "What the heck?"

She said quickly, "Oh. Mustard. Sometimes I put too much on but if I cover it up with mayo and other stuff I forget it's there. Know what I mean?"

He didn't look like a believer. "Who are you?"

She said, "Becca King." And it came to her that saying the name this third time to a stranger was claiming a new identity. That didn't feel good.

He said, "Becca King. Okay. I'm Seth Darrow."

She said, "Seth Darrow. Okay."

He waited a moment, for a reaction from her. When she didn't give one, he said, "You're not from around here, are you? If you were, you'd know."

"What?"

"My last name. What it means."

Becca felt Seth relax next to her. It seemed she'd passed some sort of test. He said her name again and asked her if it was short for Rebecca and she said it was. He asked why she was called Becca and not Becky like most girls, but to answer this was going to mean constructing a history of lies. She didn't want to do that, knowing she had to stick to the main story, so she said she didn't know and she told him that she'd only got to the island yesterday. She said she was supposed to stay with Carol Quinn, over on Blue Lady Lane and—

"Wow, *triple* bummer." Seth's tone told her he knew that

Carol Quinn was dead and as if to assure her of that, he went on to say, "Small town. Everyone knows what's going on."

"Yeah, triple bummer," Becca agreed. "She was my mom's friend, since they were kids." She let him fill in the rest of the information the way people tended to do when you told them something.

She ate her sandwich. She made quick work of it. Seth left her and went over to a cold cabinet where he took out a plastic bottle of orange juice. He brought it to her and said, "It's on me," when she took some coins out of her jacket pocket.

He handed her another sandwich, this one wrapped in plastic. He said, "For later. Just in case." Then he took a napkin and a pencil from the deli counter and he began to draw upon it.

Becca saw that he was making a map. It was simple enough, just two streets with two others running perpendicular to them. "First and Second," he said, pointing. "Anthes and Park."

Near Second and Anthes, he said, there was a public bathroom where she could do . . . well, whatever she needed to do. It would be open. It was near the bank and behind a yellow cottage, which was the visitors' center. He drew an X-marks-the-spot and then he drew another, this one on the corner of Second and Park.

He said. "You go to this place at one o'clock, okay? Little white house there, but don't go inside or knock on the door. It's an AA meeting and they won't want you listening."

"Okay," Becca said slowly, drawing out the word and waiting for more information. Did he think she was an alcoholic?

"Just wait outside at the picnic table," he went on. "There's a lady? Debbie Grieder? She goes to the meetings. She'll help you out."

"Why?" What sort of place was this? The last thing Becca was used to was people who handed over sandwiches and pointed out other people who would help you out.

"It's just who she is," Seth said. "She's okay. You won't need to ask her to help you, even."

"How will I know who she is?"

"You won't need to," he told her. "She'll know you."

FIVE

Seth walked outside with her. He took another look at the bike.

"It's not really that bad," he said, "but you got to know how to ride a ten-speed. A mountain bike would be better here, but a ten-speed will work if you're in decent shape. You know how to ride one?"

Becca didn't know there was any particular way to ride a ten-speed. All she knew was that you shifted when the pedaling got too tough, and that was what she told him. He said that she had to rely on her legs to tell her when to switch gears and if she didn't do it right, she'd wear the gears out. She said that her legs weren't telling her anything but to get off the bike and push it. He smiled and said, "Look, I can show you. Not now, because I've got to get back to work. But I'm here every morning. You have the map?"

She said, "Nope. You've got it," and he looked at his hand. He said, "Oh. Right," and he pushed the map in her direction. "Remember. Debbie Grieder," he told her. "Wait at the picnic table. Okay?"

Becca nodded, mounted her bike, and took off. She knew he

was watching but it didn't matter, because she also could tell that Seth Darrow was going to be a friend.

———

SHE FOUND THE public bathroom. She was able to clean herself up in the place. She looked more horrible than she'd ever looked in her life, though, and she understood at once why Seth had suggested she check out the public facilities.

It wasn't just that she'd slept with the dogs. That was bad enough, and it contributed to her rank smell. But it was also how Laurel had altered her appearance so that she looked gross, so unlike her normal self that should Jeff Corrie pass her on the street, he'd never notice her.

Aside from the ugly color, her hair was also a chopped-up mess, hanging just beneath her ears. She was wearing more makeup than she'd ever worn in her life, sort of like a marginal goth, and at the moment it was streaking on her face, the eyeliner looking like sooty tears and the mascara creating semicircular smudges.

Becca removed the phony glasses and looked around. There was soap and water, so she washed her face. If she was going to meet this woman called Debbie, she didn't want to give her the wrong impression.

When she left the restroom, she still smelled like a dog but at least she didn't look like one. She went out into the open air, dug out her cell phone, and made her next call to Laurel. She was feeling much better all around. She knew this had a lot to do with having eaten the sandwich provided by Seth Darrow and having found the restroom. These two circumstances were the kind of thing that made a person believe in possibilities.

Becca's contentment did not last long, though. Once again the cell phone told her that Laurel was out of range.

Well, she thought reasonably, her mother would have stopped somewhere for the night. She and Laurel had gone over the route together, the highways she would take to get to Nelson, B.C., so she'd have paused somewhere in the Cascades. Some small town or a motel in the middle of nowhere. She could even be on the other side of the mountains by now but in an area without a cell tower. A few more hours would take care of the problem. Since she was fed and warm and somewhat clean now, Becca knew that she could wait.

In the open air, the morning was cold and damp. With time to kill until she was meant to find this woman called Debbie, Becca decided to warm up by riding her bike and practicing with the gears, as Seth had told her to do. She'd explore as well, she told herself. There didn't appear to be a lot to explore in the village, so that wouldn't take long, but it was something to do.

Langley, she discovered, couldn't have been less like San Diego, with its housing developments all painted beige with red tiled roofs. Here there was nothing but seaside cottages, with clapboard and shingle siding on them and with roofs that were often green with moss. There were trees everywhere, trees gone wild, trees gone completely beserk, and their leaves were just beginning to turn in what would eventually become a panoply of red, orange, yellow, and gold.

Becca found that her initial impression of the village had been correct: It was a town in miniature. She discovered a squat brick city hall–cum–police station, a library with a purple front door, a pizza parlor, several restaurants, an abandoned old tavern called the Dog House, and—this being Washington—four coffeehouses competing with each other.

Becca ended up at the place she'd always felt the safest: the public library. She gazed in the windows and thought she might wait till it opened so she could find a spot to remain until it was close to one o'clock. She'd read a book, she decided, and she'd be perfectly at ease among whatever whispers were in the air since library whispers had always been soothing to her as people's minds drifted into the worlds of what they were reading.

———

IT WAS TWELVE-THIRTY when she left the library and consulted her Seth-drawn map. She saw that the place she was looking for was right up Second Street, and since the library stood at the corner of Second Street, she wasn't going to get lost trying to find the spot. It was, of course, all uphill. By the time she found the small white cottage that Seth had described, she was breathing like a steam engine.

The cottage was the smallest she'd seen so far, and no one had bothered to plant a garden out in front. Instead its yard was beaten down and being used as a parking lot by the people who were inside at the AA meeting. But a weathered picnic table and benches stood to one side of the paint-peeling front door. Becca dismounted her bike and rolled it over to this. She sat to wait.

It wasn't long before the meeting concluded, and the front door opened. A swarm of people came out. They lit cigarettes and talked and laughed, and not a single one of them glanced Becca's way. Becca watched all of them and waited.

She fixed the earphone of the AUD box into her ear. It seemed the polite thing to do, giving people their privacy as her grandmother would have advised her.

The crowd slowly dispersed, not a single one of them approaching Becca. They called out good-byes to each other, making promises to "call you later, okay?" Too soon there was simply no one left in the parking lot. Just Becca accompanied by her ten-speed bike, her backpack, and her saddlebags, along with an ancient SUV that looked abandoned at one side of the parking lot.

She was thinking that Seth Darrow had been wrong. She was thinking about what she would do next. Then the front door opened a final time, and a woman came outside. She lit a cigarette. She was motherly looking, somewhat overweight but not obese, with squishy bosoms of the sort that children get lost in when they're hugged. She had short hair growing out gray from a dye job and the kind of bad skin that comes from decades of smoking. She also had a terrible jagged scar that worked its way across her forehead, and seriously stained teeth. But she was dressed neatly in jeans, tennis shoes, an Oxford shirt, and a bulky sweater, and when her eyes locked with Becca's, the distinct scent of baby powder seemed to fill the air.

Things happened as Seth Darrow had said they would. The woman walked directly over to Becca. She said to her, "I'm Debbie Grieder. And you look like a girl who needs a hug," and before Becca could answer one way or the other and before she could even decide if that was the kind of girl she was, Debbie drew her up from the bench and into her arms. The feeling for Becca was utter comfort.

"What's your name, darlin'?" Debbie said.

"Becca King. A kid downtown told me to find you."

"That so?" Debbie didn't ask which kid, so Becca wondered if going to Debbie Grieder for help was a regular things for the kids of Langley.

Debbie rubbed the horrible scar on her forehead. As if it advised her what to do next, she nodded and told Becca to come with her. She strode over to the SUV. Half of it was Bondo-repaired and half of it was rust. She said, "Get in, darlin'. I'm giving you a ride."

Becca said, "Uh . . . I've got a bike and some stuff," and she pointed out the ten-speed.

"No problem," Debbie said. "Bring it on over here. It'll fit."

She waited while Becca scooped up her belongings and wheeled the bicycle over to the SUV. She stowed the ten-speed inside. Then she told Becca to climb aboard, and she did the same.

The SUV smelled like a car inside of which two million cigarettes had been smoked. Debbie added another one to the overall stench, although she rolled down the window when she did so. This didn't help much, since the ashtray was stuffed with butts and there were even some on the floor of the truck.

Debbie put on music, the way people tend to do when they don't want to be alone with their thoughts and they don't want to talk about anything serious. It was hard rock. But just as abruptly as she'd switched it on, Debbie switched it off and said to Becca, "So where can I take you, darlin'?"

Becca didn't know what to say. She realized that while Seth had told her Debbie would help her, he hadn't said how this help was supposed to come, what it would look like, or whether she was supposed to ask for it herself.

Debbie was studying her with the sort of look mothers direct to their children. She said, "You don't have a place to stay, huh? Couch surfing, are you? You run away from home?"

Becca's fingers went for the AUD box at this, and she turned it off. If there were going to be whispers, she needed to know what they were.

. . . *Come on now, girl* . . .

Becca could feel how important her answer was going to be. She could sense Debbie's need for truth. But she *couldn't* tell Debbie the full truth, so she told a form of it, which was the best she could do.

"I'm meeting my mom here," Becca said. "She dropped me off, but she'll be back later."

"Today?"

"I don't know exactly when . . . I'm just supposed to wait for her."

Having said this, Becca *did* wait, although what she waited for was Debbie's reaction. She added, "I guess I'm looking for a place to stay," she added. "Till she gets here."

"How old are you, darlin'?" Debbie asked her.

Becca thought about lying, but rejected the idea. "I'll be fifteen in February."

"And your mom just dropped you in the middle of Langley?"

"Just to wait," Becca said. "She'll be back."

"Fourteen years old?"

"Almost fifteen," Becca said.

Debbie looked long and hard at her, but her face was altering. It was softening for some reason and she said, "Almost fifteen years old." She put the SUV into gear and added in a contemplative voice, "Well, how about that."

Becca didn't know what Debbie meant, but the way she looked at it, she would probably find out.

SIX

Debbie drove them to the edge of town, to an old motel called the Cliff that Becca had actually passed without noticing on her way into Langley earlier that morning. It wasn't much to look at, just a string of ten rooms with old-fashioned rusty metal porch chairs in front of them and dismal flowerbeds, most of them empty. The front of the motel was planted with Japanese maples, though, and these added lovely color to the place.

At first Becca thought that Debbie had driven her here to help her get a motel room. This worried her because while she had the money to pay for a motel room, she didn't have the money to pay for it very long. But then Debbie said, "This is where I live," and Becca altered her thinking to consider that Debbie was one of those poor people who had to live in motels because they'd lost every possession they had. But *then* Debbie got out of the SUV and led her toward the motel office, the only part of the business that had a second floor. She walked directly through the office and into the living room of an apartment behind it.

The old furniture inside reminded Becca of her great-grandmother's house. It was that unappealing early-American style, done in maple with tufted cushions. These were leaking stuffing at some of their seams. There was a coffee table in front of a sofa, littered with copies of *National Geographic* and *Travel + Leisure* that gaped open and had pages torn from them. Some of these pages were on the floor, and others had been used to make collages. These hung on the walls as decoration along with pictures of children and adults. Members of Debbie's family, Becca reasoned.

As Debbie continued into a kitchen, Becca said, "Are these your kids?"

Debbie said, "Kids and grandkids," over her shoulder, and she added, "I'm starving. Let's have something to eat before I have to pick up the Indians."

In the kitchen, Debbie took hot dogs from a refrigerator and dumped them into a pan of water on the stove. She took buns and opened them into a baking pan and slapped this onto the stovetop as well. She lit another cigarette, took a hit off it, and coughed. Her cough was deep and chesty.

As the water heated, Debbie said to her, "You can stay here and wait for your mom."

Becca said, "Gosh. That's . . . I don't have a lot of money."

Debbie waved her off. "We'll work something out." Cigarette hanging from her mouth, she went back to the refrigerator and began to hand things over to Becca, who put them on the edge of an extremely cluttered table: mustard, ketchup, relish, chopped onion inside a Baggie, shredded cheddar cheese, cold chili in a can. Debbie continued talking. "I'm lucky to have the place," she said, in a voice that told Becca important information was on its way. "I didn't build it, but my dad did. I didn't inherit it, thank God, which would have meant the ex would have had a stake in it. My dad's still alive, up in Oak Harbor in one of those retirement communities. I'm running the place for him. We split the profits."

Becca nodded and wondered what kind of profits there could be. The motel seemed fairly decrepit. With only the ten rooms, no one here was getting rich off the takings from tourists.

"Anyway," Debbie said, flicking ash from her cigarette into the sink, "me and the grandbabies live here. They're in first and third grade—Chloe and Josh—and they're real good kids. You'll like them."

Debbie didn't say where the kids' mom and dad were, and Becca didn't ask. For when Debbie had said the names of the children, what Becca had also heard was *no suffering for sins*, and she figured that the kids' parents were the people who had probably done the sinning.

She directed her attention away from Debbie and onto the kitchen table. It was a mass of magazines, newspapers, and coloring books. It held a Lego set being built into the *Millennium Falcon*, as well as a pile of those connect-the-numbers kids' games that she'd liked so well when she was little.

When the hot dogs were done, Debbie dumped the water from the pan. She used a yardstick to shove everything on the table as far to the wall as she could, and she handed over a dog in its bun along with a couple of paper towels that Becca saw were intended to be their plates and napkins. Debbie loaded her dog with the works: mayo, mustard, ketchup, onions, pickles, relish, cheese, and cold chili. She even threw on some green olives with pimentos. Becca used only mustard, wondering how Debbie was going to fit her hot dog into her mouth.

It didn't turn out to be a problem as Debbie was a master in the eating of hot dogs. She could also chew and talk at the same time, and she was able to do this without showing the chewed-up food in her mouth, which took some skill. She said, "Here's what we're going to do, Becca. We'll barter till your mom gets here. It's a good thing to learn, anyway, if you and she are going to spend any time on Whidbey."

"Okay," Becca said slowly. She wasn't sure what Debbie was talking about, but she found out soon enough.

"You can stay here at the motel in exchange for doing some work for me. I'll pay you a bit, too, to keep things completely fair. The place needs some attention, and I can use your help. I'd also want you to babysit the kids now and then. Mostly Chloe, because Josh's just signed on with a Big Brother from the high school. Think it'll work?"

Becca nodded. "I'm pretty good at stuff. Like painting and things. And I can clean good. And I babysat all the time where I'm from."

"Deal then." Debbie held out her hand for a shake. She said, "We can renegotiate things when your mom gets here," but she added this in a way that told Becca Debbie had concluded for some reason that Laurel probably wasn't going to show up anytime soon.

When they'd finished their lunch, Debbie pushed away from the table, lit a cigarette, and told Becca she would show her her room. "Let's grab your stuff from the car," she said. "It'll give you a chance to settle in before I get the kids. They'll want to meet you."

They went back through the office, where Debbie took a key

from a holder shaped like an enormous fern frond. Nine other keys were hanging there, each of them on a completely different fob. The one Debbie held was numbered 444 as if the motel was a huge Las Vegas resort or something, and its fob was Las Vegas as well: a slot machine the size of a checkbook. As they went back outside, Debbie explained that her father had collected the key fobs during the old days when hotels and motels actually *had* keys and he had traveled for Boeing. He had a whole box of them as souvenirs, and when he built the motel, he decided to use a few. They had nothing to do with the order of the rooms, but what the heck. Since there were only ten, what difference did it make, huh?

Becca saw what she meant when they walked along the line of rooms that were numbered haphazardly to match the stolen fobs. Room 444 was third along the way, and its door was warped and tough to open. Debbie had to use a shoulder on it.

Becca saw that the room was very clean, which encouraged her to think well of the place. It was also very old and very simple, but for a girl who'd spent her first night on Whidbey Island inside a doghouse, it looked celestial. There were twin beds with a table and lamp between them, a dresser with a kneehole in it to tell people it could also be used as a desk, a straight-back chair, a clock, a television without a remote, and some paint-by-numbers art hanging on the walls.

The bathroom was what Becca wanted, though. She was used to bathing daily and washing her hair as often, and what she desired more than anything was a long soak in the tub. The towels, she saw, weren't thick like those she was used to, but they were clean and white.

Behind her, Debbie said, "We need to talk about the rules.

There's only two. No boys for overnighters and no using. Okay?"

Becca could see that her agreement was going to be crucial to Debbie. She nodded and said, "I don't know anyone for an overnighter, and I don't use. You mean, drugs? I don't use drugs." Drugs were the last thing she would ever use, Becca thought. She had enough trouble with the whispers when she was perfectly straight. God only knew what would happen if she were ever stoned or lit up with something.

"Drugs, yeah," Debbie said. "But I mean drinking too. Especially drinking. Above all, drinking. I know how kids are and I know it's tough to say no. But you got to promise me or we can't do business. We can't do business if you lie to me, either. About anything. And I'll know if you lie. I always do."

"I promise," Becca said. "No drinking, no drugs, no overnighters, no lies."

Then she brought up an issue that she knew was going to be a delicate one, especially considering what Debbie had just said to her about lying. She said, "I have to go to school, though. Mom's going to take me when she gets here but I'm sort of worried 'cause it's my first year, and I'm already a couple weeks late. I'm worried I'll fall behind if Mom doesn't show up fast." This was three-quarters the truth and one-quarter a lie, and Becca supposed it was a good way to see if Debbie really could tell when someone lied to her.

Debbie looked at her long and hard. Becca heard *Reese . . . try to find . . . dear sweet baby . . .* in a whisper that got choked off the way whispers did when they hurt. Still, one sharp needle from them flew into the air and landed somewhere near Becca's heart and although Becca didn't know it, it was her flinching from the pain of that needle that helped Debbie make her decision.

She said, "I'll get you into school. No trouble. Do you have anything with you? Transcripts or something?"

"I've got my records from middle school. But that's all. I mean, I don't have any other records, like a birth certificate or shots or anything."

"Good enough," Debbie said. "Nothing about school will be a problem."

There was a sudden firmness to her voice that was different from the firmness with which she'd spoken about lying. It felt hard like a boulder. It felt smooth and unmoving like marble. This made Becca ask, "It won't? Why not?" without thinking about her questions much.

Debbie smiled but it wasn't a smile about anything other than vindication. She said, "Why won't it be a problem, you mean? Because a few years ago, the registrar at the high school killed my daughter."

DEBBIE SAID NOTHING more on that subject, and when she left Becca alone in room 444, Becca was too intent upon having a bath to think very much about it. This bath was a real pleasure to her, and washing her hair in the shower afterward was practically ecstasy. When she was finished, she wiped the steam from the mirror and thought long and hard about Laurel's instructions to her.

"Makeup. Lots of makeup, sweetheart. Particularly eye makeup. The point isn't to make yourself gorgeous, and I'm sorry about that. The point is to make sure Jeff Corrie wouldn't know you if you served him a cup of coffee somewhere."

Becca didn't want to, though. What teenage girl anywhere *wants* to make herself deliberately hideous? But the point wasn't to capture some errant Prince Charming, and Becca *did* know this. She sighed and set about making herself into goth-meets-Dumpster. At least she wouldn't smell bad, she thought.

She was just finishing when she heard laughing and a little boy's shouts of fun and excitement coming from outside her bathroom window. "No fair! You kicked it way too hard!" he cried as another boy—a deeper voice this time—laughed and said, "Bro, if you can't block that one, you are hurrrr-*ting*."

This had to be the grandson, Josh, Becca concluded, play-ing soccer with his Big Brother in the vacant lot next door. She flicked the window curtain back to see if she was correct. When she saw who was out there, though, she drew in a sharp breath. It was like they were fated, she thought. For the Big Brother was the boy from the ferry, the boy from the sheriff's car outside of Carol Quinn's house.

She dropped the curtain hastily. As she did so, a knock sounded on the door to her room.

"Becca?" Debbie Grieder shouted. "You in there, chick? Come here and meet my Chloe."

Becca had no choice. It was, after all, part of the deal. She only hoped she could avoid seeing the dark-skinned boy another time, although she couldn't have exactly said why she was so reluctant to be in his presence again.

Outside her room, Debbie was waiting with a little girl who was clutching her hand. She had enormous eyes the color of cornflowers. She was wearing overalls and bright pink rubber boots that matched the color of her Hello Kitty T-shirt.

"This's Chloe," Debbie said. "An', Chloe, this is our new friend Becca."

Chloe's mouth was an O. Becca couldn't blame her. Only facial tattoos would have made her look worse than the makeup did. Becca said to her, "Hey, there, Chloe. D'you like Barbie or Bratz?"

Chloe grinned and cried, "Barbie!"

"Me too," Becca said. "Only I don't have any Barbies with me. What about you?"

"Oh, I got lots of Barbies."

"Could I visit them?"

Chloe looked at her grandmother. "Grammer . . . she could *look* at them, huh? But they got to stay in my room. C'n we take her to my room to see 'em?"

"Sounds good to me," Debbie said. "But first she's got to meet Josh, okay?"

Becca smiled but gritted her teeth behind her closed lips. No way to avoid it, it seemed. She was going to come face-to-face with the handsome black boy again.

She followed Debbie to the back of the motel, where in the vacant lot a maple tree showed leaves edged in crimson and wild green grass grew in profusion up to a bluff. This was thick with blackberries and with ocean spray bushes, purple fruit on one, creamy flowers on the other. In this area, the two boys were kicking a soccer ball, the taller boy laughing as he danced the ball gracefully toward a makeshift goal. The smaller boy was clinging to his waist and shouting, "Hey, no fair! You stole it from me!"

The dark boy tripped. Both boys stumbled. They fell onto the grass and laughed up at the sky.

"Hey, you guys," Debbie called out. "Come meet Becca King."

The older boy was the first to get up. He did so, still laughing, and he scooped the little boy under his arm like a football. He called out, "Ready to charge for a touchdown!" and his companion squealed till he set him down again.

He turned then. Becca steeled herself for whatever might happen. His eyes met hers, as dark as the nighttime of his skin. And there it was again. Something passed between them as one random thought struck another.

. . . if someone could only . . . rejoice . . .

Then the boy crossed the lawn. He said, "Happenin', Chloe?" and touched the little girl's head softly. Then he said to Becca, "I'm Derric. You just move to Whidbey?" as if he'd never seen her before this moment.

"Did," Becca said, and felt like a fool. One word was all she could manage in reply?

He smiled. He had the whitest teeth Becca had ever seen. His skin was so smooth it looked painted on. Standing before him, Becca wanted to wipe the hideous makeup from her face. She wanted to lose twenty pounds. She wanted to say, "I'm actually strawberry blonde." She also wanted to kick herself for wanting all this. How lame *was* she? she asked herself.

Derric said, "I think maybe I saw you coming over on the ferry?"

"I think I saw you too," Becca replied.

"Well," Debbie said, "that's as good as married on Whidbey Island. Come on then, troops. Let's have a snack."

The word *snack* set Josh's and Chloe's feet in motion. Chloe yelled, "Popcorn!" Josh yelled, "S'mores!" and both of them tore toward the front of the motel. Their grandmother followed.

Derric and Becca brought up the rear. Derric walked at Becca's side. He was very tall. He was like a dancer when he moved.

He said quietly, "I saw you at Carol Quinn's last night. That *was* you, right?"

She ventured a quick glance his way. "Yeah. Why did you tell me to go?"

He was quiet for a moment. She glanced at him. He met her gaze and she saw him swallow. "I completely don't know," he replied.

SEVEN

Becca was ready for school more than an hour before she needed to leave. She'd washed her dog-scented clothes in the bathtub on the previous night, but because of the cold and the damp, they were still hanging wetly over the shower curtain rod when Debbie knocked on her door. Debbie saw them and said, "You don't need to wash your own clothes, darlin'. I c'n throw them in with ours."

Becca said, "Gosh. That wouldn't be right," because she had a feeling Chloe and Josh generated lots of laundry, especially Josh since during their snack the previous day he'd asked her if she wanted to slide down the bluff with him and Derric and look for dead crabs at the edge of the water. Debbie had mouthed "There aren't any" in case Becca was worried about having to pick them up. Becca had said sure to Josh and the little boy had looked delighted. Still, it didn't seem fair to throw her laundry in with theirs, no matter how much she played with the kids.

Debbie said, "Well, if you feel that way," and Becca could tell she'd hurt her feelings somehow although she couldn't quite figure out why. Debbie went on with, "There's a Laundromat. It's way the heck up hill, though, at the top of Second Street, almost out of town."

"That's okay. I need the exercise," Becca said.

"Whatever you want." Debbie stepped back out of room 444 and lit a cigarette. Becca knew she was doing so in order not to feel something, and she wondered if it had to do with Debbie's daughter. She couldn't have said exactly why this might be the case other than having caught a glimpse of a single picture of a teenage girl among the others hanging on Debbie's wall. She looked the same age as Becca herself.

Josh and Chloe were outside in Debbie's SUV. They would be dropped off first, since their school was on the way to Becca's. Both of the schools sat on Maxwelton Road, which was not far from the Cliff Motel, and getting there involved a ride down a twisting road that was sided with forest: huge Douglas firs creating deep pockets of shadows that were crammed with ferns and shiny with the glistening leaves of salal.

As they passed a narrow driveway that disappeared into the undergrowth, Josh informed Becca that a white deer roamed the woods around here. Only the *luckiest* people ever saw it, he proclaimed. It was there in a flash and gone in a flash and *if* you saw it, it meant a Big Change was coming to your life.

Becca looked at Debbie. Debbie said to Josh, "'You just keep thinking, Butch, that's what you're good at,'" and she rolled her eyes, telling Becca he was making things up. Becca liked this about him although what she couldn't tell was whether he was making up the part about change coming to your life or the part about the white deer.

When the kids got dropped, Debbie waited till they'd disappeared into the front doors of the school. Then she waited some more as if worried they'd run off the minute she drove away. But her expression said more than worry was involved and Becca knew there'd be whispers coming off Debbie, which she would have heard had she not had the AUD box chugging away in her ear.

It was time, anyway, to mention the AUD box because from Becca's experience, she knew that earphones and schools didn't mix without an explanation. She was ready with one, and she gave it as Debbie drove out of the parking lot.

She had an auditory processing problem, she told Debbie, using the same lingo she'd heard Laurel use so many times to one school official or another. It had to do with eliminating secondary ambient sounds so that she could focus on one main sound. That was why she wore this device (here she showed it clipped onto her jeans, along with her earphone). She didn't want anyone to think she was listening to music or something like that.

Debbie glanced over at her, giving Becca one of those looks that said she was evaluating the truth quotient in Becca's words. She said, "Auditory processing problem, huh?"

"I can't always tell where I should pay attention," Becca told her. "This thing helps. It's called an AUD box. A-U-D, not o-d-d. It masks the noise I'm not supposed to listen to."

Debbie nodded, her gaze back on the road. "AUD box," she said. "We'll make sure they know about it."

When they pulled into the parking lot of South Whidbey High School, classes were already in session. Debbie jerked the truck to a stop in a stall marked ADMIN ONLY and led Becca toward the school building. This resembled a bent shoe box with a brick extension tacked onto it. It was into the brick extension that Debbie took Becca.

To their left stood a birch desk. Behind it a student was doing service as a receptionist, and Debbie strode over to her and announced, "We need to see Ms. Ward, Hayley."

Hayley said, "Ms. Ward?" with a glance at Becca. She shot her a smile, said, "Hi," and then added, "Let me get her, Mrs. Grieder," and she took off down a hall.

Becca watched her. She turned the AUD box way low and glanced at Debbie because Debbie seemed like an entirely different person inside this school, like someone getting ready for a battle. But instead of taking a weapon out of her jacket pocket, Debbie said firmly, "Give me those transcripts, darlin'."

Becca had the transcripts in her backpack. She rustled for them and brought them out, slightly crumpled and definitely unofficial but the best thing Laurel had managed to come up with considering the time she had, always receiving reassurance from Carol Quinn that she would manage the rest when Becca arrived.

Debbie gave the transcripts a glance, then tossed a look at Becca. Hayley was coming toward them down the hall, a rabbity-looking woman following close behind her.

The woman said, "Hello, Debbie," in a friendly way, although her expression reminded Becca of a dog that's ready to be punished. "Hayley says you need to see me?"

It was power, Becca realized, that was flowing through Debbie. It had altered her completely. She had no soft parts left. Debbie said, "This is my niece, Becca King. She'll be staying with me for a while. My sister wants her to be enrolled in school. C'n we get that handled? She's got a bit of a hearing problem, too. Becca, show Ms. Ward the AUD box."

Debbie handed over the meager transcripts that Becca had given her. Becca heard the flutter of terms flying back and forth between the two women: *records . . . nonsense . . . immunization . . . can't expect . . . when will it . . . sister? . . . there's no stopping . . .* It was a battle of wills without a word being spoken, and always between Debbie and Ms. Ward was the great unspoken of the death that had occurred.

Becca waited for something to happen. The atmosphere was tense; it seemed the very air would explode. Finally Ms. Ward said, "Lovely. Come with me," and she took them along the hall to what looked like another reception room. This one had yet another birch desk with a name plaque on it reading Stephanie Ward, Registrar. Beyond it two small offices were peopled by the A–L counselor and the M–Z one.

Ms. Ward told them to have a seat and she took some paperwork out of her desk. She asked Becca how she'd liked living in San Luis Obispo, although her whisper was actually *God . . . what makeup.* For a moment Becca forgot what her question actually referred to, especially since what Ms. Ward was also thinking was *how the hell am I going to* as clearly as if she were screaming it.

Becca told her she liked San Luis Obispo well enough except that there'd been a lot of sun and she had to be careful about the sun since she was prone to sunburn.

Ms. Ward said, "Well you won't have that problem here, will you? I hope you like rain."

"Keeps a girl's skin young," Debbie said. The *girl* and *young* part seemed rather like poison darts.

Ms. Ward did some typing. There were various forms that needed to be filled in and signed, and Debbie sat there without moving until Ms. Ward had filled in each one. Becca had no idea what they were, but she had an inkling that what Debbie Grieder had said to her about being truthful wasn't going to apply in this situation.

When it was all finished and Becca was as enrolled as Ms. Ward could make her, the registrar said, "Come and meet your counselor, Becca," and took her to the A–L office where the name Tatiana Primavera was printed on a placard on the door, and a woman inside the office was speaking on the phone.

Becca was wondering what sort of name Tatiana Primavera was when Debbie, standing behind her, said quietly, "It's really Sharon Prochaska."

Becca said, "Huh?"

"That's who she is. Sharon Prochaska. She changed her name when she came to the island. It's something people do. Azure St. Cloud used to be Phyllis McDermott. Sage Sorrell was Susan Jones. You get the idea."

Tatiana Primavera hung up the phone. She said, "Hey, Deb," as Ms. Ward started to introduce them. She got up and shooed poor Ms. Ward out of her office, grabbing the file of information from her and saying to Debbie, "Who've we got here, then?" and to Becca, "A hearing problem, huh?" in reference to what Ms. Ward had evidently typed about the AUD box.

Becca explained the AUD box again, and she showed it to Tatiana Primavera. Tatiana told her to hand it over, and she listened through its earphone to make sure it wasn't music. Becca watched her expression as she heard the static. She hoped the strangeness of it would see her through.

"Unusual," was Ms. Primavera's reaction, and she handed the AUD box back to Becca. She made a note, shoved it into the file, and swung her chair around to face her computer. She said, "Let's get you set up, then."

There wasn't much to do. Since Becca was a freshman, she got one elective and the rest were classes she had to take. As her elective, she chose Yearbook. It seemed like a safe bet.

Ms. Primavera banged away and finished up by hitting *print*. She'd get the schedule from the printer, she told them, and in the meantime . . . She opened her lowest desk drawer and brought out a jar of jelly beans. She said, "Welcome to South Whidbey High, Becca. Help yourself," and she disappeared out the door of her office.

Becca took a handful of the candy and shoved the beans into her jacket pocket. She put one in her mouth.

Tatiana Primavera returned. She had the schedule in hand along with a slip of paper with a locker number on it. She said to Debbie, "You c'n leave her with me now. I'll see to it she gets where she needs to go."

Debbie told Becca she'd pick her up after school but not in the parking lot. After today, she'd have to ride her bike because the hours were different to get Josh and Chloe to and from school. Today, however, she'd come for her and she'd wait across the road where the water treatment plant was.

Becca could tell that being in the building was difficult for Debbie now. The power she'd felt was diminished.

Before Debbie left, Tatiana said to her, "See you next week.

I think," and Debbie seemed to know what this meant. She didn't appear to like it, though, because she shrugged and said, "Whatever, girl. I hope you know what you're doing." There was something left unsaid between them, but hints as to what it might be were blocked by the AUD box.

When Debbie was gone, Tatiana said, "Let's get you going." She looked at a wall clock, said, "Eastern Civilization," and headed out of the office.

At the front desk, she stopped to speak with the girl Hayley, motioning Becca over to join them. "New student," she said to Hayley. "Becca King, this is Hayley Cartwright."

Hayley smiled. She was pretty in an old-fashioned way, with straw-colored hair cut in a neat bob. She had ruler-straight bangs, frameless glasses, and large blue eyes. When she stood up to grab something from the top of a cabinet, Becca could see that she was tall.

She handed over a calendar of sorts and told Becca it was the athletic schedule. "Welcome to the home of the Falcons, Becca." She said this in a friendly enough way, but sadness came off her, then faded quickly, like something she knew she had to hide.

Tatiana said, "Nice girl," as she shooed Becca out of the office. "Let's get you to class."

Tatiana hummed as she walked. She wore stiletto heels, which made her taller and made her ample breasts bounce. They also made her the first person Becca had seen on Whidbey Island who wasn't wearing sensible shoes.

They went across a large room that Tatiana said was the "old commons." It had a bank of windows on one side and a wall of bulletin boards on the other, and in between was a scattering of tables. At one side of this room they climbed a stairway, and at the top the classrooms began. Tatiana ushered Becca to one of the doors and flung it open. She tilted her head, meaning Becca was supposed to go in first.

Becca did so, acutely aware of all eyes turning in her direction. At once, she dropped her gaze to the floor so she wouldn't have to meet the stares because she knew exactly how she looked, which was bad, very bad, extra bad from the top of her dyed head to the tip of her tennis-shoed toes. She had an enormous urge to look up and say to the class, "I'm prettier than this. Really."

Becca felt the other students' interest like mice scurrying around her ankles. They were extremely happy to have the diversion. She glanced warily at the teacher to see if he was why.

His name was Mr. Powder. He shot one look at Becca and another at Tatiana. His expression said that he hated them both, but it also said that he hated anything having to do with South Whidbey High School. He was going to be a lousy teacher.

Tatiana handed over Becca's schedule, which Mr. Powder signed. He looked at the class in front of him and said to Becca, "Take that seat over there. Class, this is"—he referred to the schedule before he handed it back—"Becca King. Thank you, Ms. Primavera."

He'd said that last part because Tatiana hadn't left the room yet and he wanted her to, that much was obvious. But she was looking around and she said, "Good. Take the seat next to Derric. Derric, will you show Becca around the campus today so she can find her classes?"

Becca looked up, absolutely horrified. There *had* to be more than one Derric, she thought. The first Derric had looked too old to be a freshman.

But it was the same Derric from the ferry, she saw, the very same Derric from in front of Carol Quinn's house, the Derric who was Josh Grieder's Big Brother and who would probably be hanging around the Cliff Motel.

"Some things are written in the stars, hon," Becca's grandmother would have said about all this.

Becca's response would have been, "*What* things?"—a question she wanted desperately to have answered as she crossed the room to take the vacant seat next to this boy.

EIGHT

For Becca, it was the oddest sensation. For the first time since that terrible moment in the kitchen in San Diego when she'd heard Jeff Corrie's whispers and she'd known what he'd done, she felt safe. Sitting next to this boy to whom she'd barely spoken, she felt *perfectly* safe, and she didn't know why.

She couldn't stop herself from shooting glances at Derric's arm. It was bare, it rested on the side of his desk, and it was roped with muscle. An athlete, she decided.

Her feeling of safety didn't last long. The classroom door crashed open as Becca was opening her notebook. A girl entered and Becca recognized her with an internal *uh-oh*. It was the girl from the ferry, the girl who had tried to cheat the cashier.

At the front of the room, Mr. Powder took one look at her and said, "That's your second tardy, Jenn. One more and it's detention. Got it?"

Jenn didn't answer him because she'd seen Becca, and what came out of her was a galloping horse of astoundingly dirty whispers, audible even over the AUD box. She said to Becca, "You're in my seat."

Mr. Powder said, "So tomorrow try being on time. Do

something really amazing: Try being early. Go to the back."

Becca dropped her gaze. She looked at her notebook, which was crisp and new, and she could feel how much Jenn wanted to snatch it from her and rip off its cover. But instead, she stomped to the back of the room and flung herself into her seat. So much for safety, Becca thought. Obviously, she'd made an instant enemy out of this girl.

Next to her, Becca sensed Derric moving, and she glanced at him quickly. She saw him make the A-OK sign with his fingers. They were long and sensitive looking and the sign they were making was intended for her. *Don't worry about it*, his fingers were telling her, as if he knew what she was feeling.

Mr. Powder resumed his lecture. No one wanted to listen and who could blame them? He was boring, sounding the way cold oatmeal tasted. When the bell finally rang at the end of the class, Becca felt as if she'd been in the room for more than a week.

As the students began to leave, Derric spoke to her. He was over six feet tall, and he towered above her so he leaned toward her to say with a grin, "I'd tell you it's not always this bad, but it is. What's your next class?"

She looked at her schedule. "Physical Science," she said.

"Come on, then. I'll show you where it is."

———

LUNCH CAME AFTER second period, at eleven o'clock in the morning. Derric had told her to wait by the classroom door and he'd come for her and show her what the situation was in the new commons, so she stood outside the classroom and tried to look inconspicuous. But when he showed up, Jenn was with him, as if she'd heard his promise to show Becca where lunch was and had decided upon the best way to give her indigestion.

Jenn was shooting her looks that recommended she drop dead as soon as possible, and Becca heard her say, "I can't believe you're supposed to have *lunch* with her, too." She added a swear word that made her face shrivel when she said it. Becca felt Derric fend off the word, like someone holding up his hands against a rotten tomato, but he didn't say anything.

South Whidbey High School, Becca found, wasn't at all like the school she'd been supposed to attend in San Diego. There, two thousand five hundred students were enrolled, and they had to eat in shifts. Here, it seemed that the whole student body ate together, with about six hundred kids in a sprawl from a rec room that was the new commons, opening into another rec room called the old commons. She trailed Derric and Jenn to it, and she recognized it from earlier in the day. She raised the volume on the AUD box to block the secondary noise of hundreds of whispers.

Derric turned once to make sure she was following. Jenn turned him back, deliberately. Becca wondered if Jenn was trying to say the boy was her property. She wanted to tell her to go ahead and claim him. As long as she looked like a walking trash heap in makeup, there wasn't much chance he'd be interested in her.

Nearly every girl they passed said hi to Derric. A lot of the boys did, too. Only the boys didn't called him Derric. They said Nyombe or Big Math or Der. All of this seemed very odd to

Becca because if Derric was a freshman, everyone was supposed to ignore him.

They got into the food line, Jenn placing herself firmly between Becca and Derric. When it was her turn to get something, Becca knew she had to be careful. Debbie hadn't given her money for lunch—not that she'd expected it—and she had to use what she had as sparingly as she could. So she bought only a PBJ and ignored Jenn when she said, "Want to check my *money*, chick?" as they reached the cash register. But the remark was nothing more than throwaway nastiness because Jenn herself, as things turned out, had brought her own lunch from home. She'd only gone through the line in the first place to stay with Derric, it seemed.

As they were making their way to a table, the sense that everyone liked Derric altered. A boy leaned far back from his seat the second Derric walked behind him. He did it fast and hard so his body crashed into Derric's tray. He meant to knock it to the floor and spill the food, but Derric was too fast. He dodged easily. Still, the boy rose in a rush and said, "Hey, watch the hell *out*, asshole."

Becca recognized this boy from his spotty face and the ski cap rolled into a beanie on his head. He'd been with Jenn on the ferry, challenging her to cheat the cashier. He was sitting with a group of boys similarly dressed, with similar attitudes. Everything about them marked them as stoners. They slouched and smirked and waited for Derric to react.

Jenn said, "Grip yourself, Dylan," and shoved the boy out of the way.

"Oooh," Dylan said, "Big Der lets a *girl* protect him."

There was one of those silences in the immediate area as kids waited for what would happen next. Becca could feel the tension whip through Derric's body as he considered how best to react. It wasn't tough to see he could take the other boy down with his little finger. Dylan was as skinny as the handle of a shovel. He tried to hide this with baggy clothes, but he had the wrists of a ten-year-old.

"Hey, I let girls do my homework, too," Derric said. "You should try it, too, if you c'n find one willing."

"*That'll* happen when it rains frogs," Jenn remarked.

Dylan's eyes narrowed as his tablemates laughed.

Derric walked off. Jenn followed. Becca brought up the rear. She heard Dylan tell his friends what they could do to themselves as he sat down again, his neck red with fury.

<hr />

DURING THE REST of the day, as Derric showed her where her other classes were, Becca learned more about him. His full name, she discovered was Derric Nyombe Mathieson. She learned that he was from Uganda and that he'd been adopted as an eight-year-old by an island family. He revealed that he was sixteen years old and the reason he was only a freshman was that he'd not been able to speak English when he'd come to this country. He also added with an appealing honesty that he'd not been able to read or write or do math in *any* language at that point, which contributed to his problems. So his mom had taken a year off work to homeschool him, and then it was a matter of his catching up with everyone else.

"Never went to school in Uganda," he said. To Becca's question of what he did instead, he said with a shrug, "Got by," and that was it. She could tell he didn't want to talk more about the subject, although she heard the whisper *rejoice* coming from him as well and she thought that anything worthy of rejoicing about was surely something a boy would want to talk about.

At the end of the day, Derric walked her out to the parking lot. Jenn wasn't with them. This gave Becca a chance to thank him for hanging out with her, especially during lunch. He returned with, "It's cool. It's tough to be new. Especially here where everyone already knows everyone else."

Derric's name was called. Jenn was just coming out of one of the six double doors at the end of the school building, and as she approached, Derric said quietly to Becca, "Hey, don't let Jenn freak you. She's pretty much okay."

This was about the *last* thing Becca was ready to believe because it felt like quicksand all around her as Jenn came up to them.

Before she had a chance to make a comment, Becca asked the girl, "D'you know where the water treatment plant is?"

"Why?" Jenn inquired. "Thinking of finally taking a bath?"

"It's where I'm meeting my ride," Becca told her.

"At the water *treatment* plant? Whoa. Someone must not want to be seen with you."

Derric said kindly, "It's just across Maxwelton. We can show you if you—"

"No we can't," Jenn said. "*You've* got jazz rehearsal and I've got cross-country."

"S'okay," Becca said. "I c'n find it. Thanks."

"Mrs. Grieder picking you up?" Derric asked.

"Yeah. She said—"

"*Derric*. Come *on*." Jenn was clearly unhappy about any conversation between Becca and the boy.

Derric ignored her. He said to Becca, "Josh'll be with her. I need to say hi," and he added to Jenn, "See you later, okay?"

Jenn's face was stony. But she turned and walked off. Derric accompanied Becca to the truck. From a distance, Josh's voice cried out, "Hey, hey, hey!" as they approached. Debbie was standing next to the SUV, smoking a cigarette as she waited for Becca to join them.

Josh was out of the car in a flash at the sight of Derric. He yelled, "High fives!" and Derric laughed and obliged. Then he put his arm around Josh and rubbed his head. "You want to listen to some jazz?" he asked.

"Yeah!"

Derric said to Debbie, "Band practice. Can he come? Mom'll bring him back to the motel when she picks me up."

"Please, Grammer," Josh said. "I never heard Derric play sax yet."

Debbie agreed, casting a rare smile at her grandson and the Ugandan boy. "Maybe you can teach him something," she said.

"Like in the street band!" Josh cried.

Derric said he'd see what they could do about that, putting his hand on the back of Josh's head and giving it a playful squeeze.

Then he removed a small folded paper from his pocket and handed it to Becca.

He said, "I'll probably see you at Debbie's a bunch when I come over to hang with Josh, but here's my phone number if you ever have any questions about school."

Debbie raised her eyebrows with an expression that said *this* was an interesting development. Becca put the paper in her jacket pocket, said thanks, and turned away quickly, the better not to reveal her blush.

Once in the SUV with Chloe between them, Debbie said with a grin, "Aside from *that*, how did it go?"

Becca said it went fine. She told Debbie that Derric Mathieson had been her escort for the day. Debbie said, "Darlin', how'd you get so lucky so fast?"

"'Bout what?" Chloe asked. "Grammer, why's she lucky?"

"She got to spend the day with Derric," Debbie told her.

"Like Josh, you mean?"

"Not at *all* like Josh."

Becca knew Debbie was teasing, but it was okay. For she could see that Debbie felt lighter for once, with some kind of burden lifted from her shoulders.

Chloe wanted to know if Becca was going to be their permanent babysitter. She said, "Grammer goes to lots of meetings and she doesn't like to leave us on our own. Sometimes we go but we have to sit in the car and we *hate* to do that. Don't we, Grammer?"

"Sometimes," Debbie said. "That's how it is."

"Are you going to live with us for always?" Chloe asked Becca hopefully. "Where's your mom? We live with Grammer, see. That's 'cause our dad's in prison."

At this Becca felt the barrier come down between Debbie and her, just like one of those gates in a castle. Her previous lightness disappeared. Becca said, "I didn't know that, Chloe. That's too bad."

"Yeah," Chloe said. "He's got to straighten himself out or he's going to die, huh, Grammer? And our mom—"

"That's enough for now," Debbie said.

Chloe began to protest. "But you said—"

"Enough!" Debbie snapped.

Chloe shrank into her seat. She felt bad, Becca saw, like someone who'd made a serious mistake.

She was sitting right next to the little girl, so Becca reached for her hand. It was warm and damp and rather like the inside of a puppy's ear. She squeezed it lightly. Chloe looked up at her. She squeezed right back.

NINE

Becca never expected to hear from Derric or to see him outside of school hours, aside from the time he spent with Josh. There was also no way she intended to call him. It had been nice that he'd handed his phone number to her, but she understood that *nice* was actually all that it was. Reading anything into it other than just a friendly gesture would have been extremely dumb.

Still, he made it a habit during her first week to check with Becca and make sure that she was finding her way around the school all right. When this happened, Becca felt Jenn's baleful glare upon her.

Jenn kept making sure that she was by Derric's side as much as possible. So the only time Becca actually saw the boy at school without her was during Yearbook, which was the only class other than Eastern Civilization that they shared. In Eastern Civilization, too, Becca spoke to Derric occasionally. Although he talked to her in the same way he talked to everyone else, she could still tell Jenn didn't like it.

Becca wasn't sure why Derric continued to show her friendship. There was no way he was attracted to her, not with how she looked these days. She wanted to tell him he didn't need to keep a watch over her if that was why he was being so nice, but she didn't do that because she liked him, and she felt so strangely secure in his presence. Plus there was *rejoice* to consider. He said it over and over again, like a mantra.

Rejoice was practically his only whisper. He said it the way other people said to themselves *stay cool* or *don't blow it* or *keep a straight face.* The fact that he had to keep reminding himself to be happy was a puzzle, though. To Becca, it seemed to indicate he was hiding something. That, ultimately, made him just like her.

Laurel was Becca's secret. *Where are you, Mom* was her *rejoice.* She'd been phoning Laurel three times a day since that moment she'd learned that Carol Quinn was dead, but not a single one of her calls went through. She was trying very hard not to panic. Her mother, she knew, would *never* abandon her. She'd finally concluded that Laurel had purchased the wrong kinds of cell phones altogether when she'd picked them out at the 7-Eleven in San Diego. As Becca recalled, Laurel hadn't asked a single question about them. She'd just handed over her credit card and that had been that.

After school each day, Becca was keeping up her part of the bargain with Debbie. She'd been cleaning the motel rooms. Just ten days into her stay there, she found five dollars left on the dresser in one of them. She also found a sweater hanging behind the door in the bathroom, and she took it to Debbie as soon as her work was done. Debbie was supervising homework in the kitchen of her apartment. Josh and Chloe were at the table.

Becca showed Debbie the sweater she'd found and Debbie's

whisper in return was *have to send . . . more frigging . . . money . . .*
from which Becca figured she was going to have to send the
sweater back to its owner. This prompted her to hand over the
five dollars she'd found on the dresser as well. But to her surprise, instead of taking it, Debbie said, "No way. That's a tip for
you, darlin'," and not a single whisper contradicted that.

Debbie's whispers, Becca was finding, contradicted her words
a lot. Despite what she'd told Becca about lying, Debbie wasn't
always completely honest herself. Becca didn't know why this
was the case. She *did* know that it had to do with Reese, Debbie's
daughter.

When the phone rang, Becca went to join the kids at the table,
scooting Chloe over on the bench. She said, "Math homework?
Yuck," and Chloe agreed as Debbie answered the phone.

She said to someone, "Sure. She's right here. How's your
mom?" and listened for a minute. She went on with, "Tell her
not to work so hard," and then extended the phone to Becca. She
wiggled her eyebrows to communicate that someone special was
on the line, and in a second Becca found out who it was. Derric
Mathieson was calling her.

She figured it had to do with homework. Eastern Civilization
or Yearbook, she decided, and to her horror her mind went blank.
Did they have homework? What was it?

But it turned out not to be homework at all. Derric told Becca
that "a bunch of us are meeting at Goss Lake to do some bike
time trials. Want to meet us there? We're taking our bikes. Well,
obviously, since it's bike time trials."

Becca didn't know what he meant, but she could tell he was
a little nervous calling her, and she found this sweet. Then,

though, she heard the unmistakable snarky sound of Jenn's voice in the background, and Becca quickly said that she wasn't sure she could go. She needed to find out what else had to be done around the motel, so could she call him back in a couple of minutes?

He said sure and added, "You still got the number, right?"

She didn't tell him that she had it memorized. There was lame and then there was *lame*.

When she hung up, she said to Debbie, "Some of the kids are meeting at Goss Lake and—"

Debbie said, "*What* kids?" because her whisper wanted to know if *drugs . . . OxyContin these days . . .* was part of what was going on.

Becca could tell that *whenever* kids got together Debbie worried no matter who the kids were. She said reassuringly, "It's just some kids from school, Derric says," which wasn't exactly the truth but it wasn't a lie either.

Debbie asked how she was going to get there and her whisper added *don't ask me.*

To this, Becca accidentally responded, "Oh, I don't need a ride," before she realized what she'd done. To cover up, Becca added, "I'm riding my bike. That's what everyone's doing, Derric said. They're having time trials."

"Darlin', there's no way you can make it to Goss Lake on your bike," Debbie said. She went on to tell Becca it was miles and miles and the road was completely Whidbey Island. From this, Becca knew it was hills and curves all the way.

She said, "Oh," and she knew she sounded sad because she *felt* sad although she didn't like to think why this was the case.

It was, after all, just a bunch of kids riding their bikes around a lake, and the fact that Derric Mathieson had called to include her meant only that she was supposed to be part of the time trials herself. She knew she'd blow *that* in a very big way, so it was actually better she didn't go. Besides, although her bike riding skills were definitely improving since it was her only mode of transportation, she was still far away from being able to manage miles and miles of hills.

Good news for Jenn, Becca thought. She would hardly have been thrilled to see Becca King show up.

ULTIMATELY, BECCA WENT to the Star Store. It was a very short bike ride from the motel. Inside, she wandered a bit, with her five dollars in tip money asking to be at least partially spent. She snagged a large bag of Doritos for herself and two miniature pumpkins for the kids. She was at the checkout counter, getting ready to pay, when a voice said to her, "Those're sort of small for carving, wouldn't you say?" and she found Seth Darrow behind her. He grinned. "Thought that was you. How's it going? Still hanging around with dogs?"

This confused her till she remembered her first night in the doghouse and how she'd smelled the next morning. She said, "You were right. I'm staying at the motel. Debbie's great."

"I figured she'd help you."

When she made her purchases, Seth walked outside with her. He pulled his fedora out of his back pocket. He reshaped it expertly and put it on. He said, "Everything okay then? What're you doing with your time?"

"Nothing much," she said, and he looked disappointed for some reason. She didn't understand what he wanted to know or why, even, he might want to know anything. But she was grateful that he was a friendly-type guy, so she added, "Well, I was *s'posed* to go out to Goss Lake today to meet some kids from school, but I can't."

His face lit up. "Kids from school? Why can't you go?"

"Debbie said I probably wouldn't make it. On the bike. You know." She nodded to where her bicycle sat, this time next to the Dumpster.

Seth said, "Oh yeah. To get out to the lake, you definitely need a better bike than that."

"I guess. But I was sort of thinking Debbie worries too much and maybe that's why she didn't want me to go."

Seth said, "That'd probably be because of her daughter. That's how Reese died. On her bike."

"Oh." Becca hadn't known that. Only that Ms. Ward, the registrar from the school, had killed her. She wanted to know more, but Seth was saying that he'd just come into the Star Store to pick up his paycheck and, "Sammy and I can run you out to Goss Lake if you like."

She said, "Who's Sammy?" and Seth shot her a grin.

"Come and meet him," he said.

SAMMY TURNED OUT to be Seth's car. It was a Volkswagen, a vintage model from 1965. It was completely restored, with a paint job so shiny that Becca could see her face in it.

Before they left the Star Store parking lot, Seth pointed to a cottagelike building next door, mustard colored, with a garden in front. That, he told her, was South Whidbey Commons. "If you want to meet people—outside of the usual high school crowd—that's where you should go. After school and on weekends. I play chess there sometimes. Guitar, too, with my trio. It's a good hangout for people."

They trundled their way up Second Street as Seth explained there were several different ways to get out to Goss Lake, but Debbie had been more or less right about the ride. No matter the route, there were plenty of hills.

The way he chose was straight out Second Street and onto a road called Saratoga. This flashed in and out of the woods, passing meadows and wetlands, and curving high up along the passage between Whidbey and Camano Islands.

When they reached Goss Lake, Becca saw only a slice of it through the trees. It seemed protected from all wind, hidden away in a cavity of land.

There were kids everywhere. Most of them were whizzing in one direction on the road that ran around the lake. Others stood along the road with stopwatches, yelling out times. Becca said to Seth, "Wow. It's supposed to be a time trial for something. I didn't think there'd be so many kids. What d'you think's going on?"

Seth watched them for a minute, resting his hands on the top of the steering wheel as he idled Sammy at the stop sign just at the edge of the route the bicyclers were following. "Looks like they're getting ready for a race, doing laps around the lake," he said. "It's probably a fund-raiser." He went on to say that there was *always* a fund-raiser for one cause or another going on on the island. She'd get used to that.

They watched the kids for another minute, with Seth concentrating on every rider that went by. Becca finally said to him, "Are you looking for someone?"

He said, "Who me? Nah." He waved off the idea. "What about you? Who're you s'posed to meet?"

"Some kids," she said.

"That's helpful," he joked.

"Derric Mathieson," she told him.

Becca wasn't ready at all for what came next. The air in the car went completely dead, as if life itself had been sucked right out of the old VW. In its place Becca heard *prick . . . did not . . . oh yeah right . . . like I really believe . . .*

Warily, Becca glanced at Seth. She felt uneasy when she saw that his eyes had gone flat.

Finally, he spoke. His voice sounded careful and a little cagey. "Can't take you any farther than this. Too many bikes. Everyone's probably hanging around the boat launch. That'd be the logical place to start the ride." He pointed to the right. The launch was just along the road a ways, he told her. Someone would be there who could take her back into Langley later. "I can't stay," he said. "You'll ask someone for a ride, right?"

He sounded concerned, sort of sorry to be leaving her on her own. But *no way no way . . . just what I need . . . jerk-off buttwipe* was on his mind and his expression remained what it was. Becca had the feeling that she needed to get away from him. She needed to do it quickly, even if it meant that she would have to walk the entire distance back to Langley later.

———

BECCA MADE HER way along the narrow road in the direction that Seth had indicated. The bikes whizzed by. Kids along the road called out times and encouragement. As the riders flew by her, Becca caught some of what was going on in their heads. She couldn't, of course, attach the thoughts to anyone because the thoughts were like leaves in the wind. There were the swear words of someone getting tired of riding. Along with them were the words that told her some boys were admiring the butts of some of the girls as they rode. Someone was hot, and a whole lot of kids were thirsty. But it all felt friendly and innocent. Nothing like those final moments with Seth.

Becca found the boat launch. A table was set up at the top of the driveway down to a parking lot, and at the table there were three kids sitting with a stack of paperwork while two other kids were recording times being reported by stopwatch holders. One of these latter kids was Derric. He saw Becca and smiled and waved.

"You made it!" he cried. "Come on over. Watch out for the bikes."

As she crossed carefully, she saw him hand off a clipboard to one of the kids at the table. He came up to her and flashed his high-wattage smile.

He said, "How'd you get here? Manage to ride your bike? Pretty impressive . . . for a girl," and he grinned again.

She said, "I wish. Seth Darrow brought me. But he couldn't stay."

Derric said, "Oh, too bad," but Becca heard a whisper that said *close close close* and sighed from him the way clouds moved, darker ones lower than lighter because the darker clouds were heavier, containing the rain. He added, "Anyway, glad you're here," and *nice* was there, too, along with *way too close* and then *feels . . . rejoice.*

She wondered what all this meant. Did he think it was nice to have her around? Did he rejoice when she was near? But why would he when he barely knew her?

"Sort of the way it feels," he said with a shrug.

She felt herself get stiff, as if he'd answered her thought. She said, "Huh?"

He said, "It always feels too bad when someone doesn't want to be part of something, you know?"

"Oh," she said. "Seth."

"Yeah. Seth."

There were no swear words in Derric's thoughts and nothing nasty when he said Seth's name, but the dark clouds came again and with them the smell of smoke, as if a fire were burning five feet away. She said to Derric, "D'you know Seth? Well, I guess you do. I mean everyone knows everyone it seems. Around here."

"Oh yeah," Derric said. "I do know Seth," and his tone told Becca that something bad had happened between them. He took Becca's arm then and brought her farther off the side of the road. His grip on her arm was firm and she thought he intended to tell her something. But then he added, "We need to get more out of the way here. Someone loses control, and one of us gets hurt."

A FLURRY OF gutter whispers hurled at them. Becca knew without seeing who was approaching. She wasn't surprised when Jenn screeched up and braked in the dust at the side of the road.

"What the hell're *you* doing here? Get out of the way. Don't you *see* what's going on?" More gutter whispers followed but Becca could tell Jenn didn't want to say them in front of Derric although if Derric hadn't been standing at her side still with his hand on her arm, Becca knew Jenn would have let loose. "These're bicycle trials and you're in the way! What's the matter with you? Are you a retard or something? I thought you couldn't get out here anyway. Why'd you come? Worried there might be a *cash* register around?"

Becca fell back a step. The heat of Jenn's anger was far stronger than the smoke of Derric's whispers.

Derric's grip on her tightened. He said, "Seth brought her. It's cool, Jenn."

Jenn's eyes widened. She hooted. "Seth *Darrow*? Wow. You're a deep one, huh?" Her glance went from Becca to Derric to Derric's hand on Becca's arm. Then she seemed to catch sight of the bag from the Star Store that Becca was holding, the bag with the pumpkins and the Doritos inside. She said with a smirk, "So what's that, then? Your lunch or your score?"

Becca said in a stumble of words, "It's . . . well . . . there's pumpkins." She was too embarrassed to add that there were Doritos as well, all things considered. Jenn was as trim as a cheetah, and she didn't need to know there were reasons that Becca herself was heading on the fast track to l-a-r-d. She added, stupidly, "I got them for Debbie's kids."

Jenn rolled her eyes. "Aren't *you* the little saint. Like no one knows why you hang around those kids, Beck-*kuh*." She shook her head, gave a laugh, and took off again.

When she was gone, Becca realized Derric still had his hand on her arm, but his grip had loosened and now he was patting her and his whisper was *sorry . . . oh gosh . . . stupid*, although he didn't say anything. She was the one to speak.

She said, "Why's she hate me so much?"

Derric moved his hand briefly from her arm to her shoulder. "It's not you. Okay?"

"Who is it, then? 'Cause the way I see it, I haven't done a thing to her except see a ten and not a twenty."

Derric looked confused. "What?" he asked her.

"Never mind," she told him. "It's dumb. Forget it."

TEN

The first outside job that Debbie had for Becca in exchange for her room at the motel came on Saturday following the bike trials on Goss Lake. It wasn't too huge a job, Debbie told her that morning, but it was a bit dirty. Still it needed doing.

The job turned out to involve the entire front of the motel. There, flower beds ran along the two streets at whose junction the Cliff Motel sat, and they also formed a border between the motel rooms and the parking lot. Just outside the door to room 444, Debbie placed a bucket of tools, a huge container of bulb food, and two dozen bags crammed with bulbs. Autumn, she said, was the time for planting. She herself was heading out for groceries, along with Chloe and Josh.

Once Debbie and the kids had rumbled off, Becca got out the cell phone. So far, she'd continued to phone Laurel. So far, Laurel had continued not to respond. Unable to help it, Becca had begun to dwell on the unthinkable: that somehow Jeff Corrie had managed to track her mother. If he *had* found Laurel, then she would have ditched her cell phone as soon as she saw him. There was no way she'd want him to be able to trace

Becca, and that cell phone would have been one of the ways.

Once again when Becca tried, there was no contact. She told herself Laurel was okay, okay, okay, *okay*. She shoved the phone in her pocket and began with the bulbs. Each bag held more than a dozen, she saw. With two dozen bags to deal with, she was going to be at it for quite a while.

She'd never planted bulbs before because bulbs didn't do well in San Diego. So when she emptied the first bag, she picked up a bulb and tried to decide which way it was supposed to go into the ground. It seemed to her that the pointy end went down first, so that was how she began to plant them. She'd done the first four bags when a car drove into the parking lot behind her, and she stood up and brushed off her knees, ready to greet a potential customer for the Cliff Motel.

The car was a Volkswagen: Seth's. In the passenger seat sat a yellow Labrador. As soon as Seth opened his door to get out, the dog leaped over him and loped to Becca. His tail wagged so hard that his entire butt swayed. He was in among the bulbs before she could stop him. He started digging immediately.

"Gus!" Seth shouted. "Hey, cut it out! Sorry, Becca. He's just a pup."

Gus didn't look like a pup to her, but Becca figured Seth meant he was still very young. He certainly wasn't well trained because, despite Seth's words, he just kept digging.

Seth dragged him off, telling him he was a *very* bad dog. Gus didn't appear to be bothered by this. He leaped up and licked Seth on the mouth.

"Bleagh!" was Seth's good-natured response. He grabbed a

leash from the front seat and looped it through the VW's bumper. He attached the dog to it and then came over to see what Becca was doing.

She plopped a few more bulbs in the ground, telling him she was planting them for Debbie. Seth asked what she expected the bulbs to do.

"What d'you mean? They're supposed to be flowers next spring. Tulips and daffodils and . . ." She looked at one of the bags, "and hyacinths."

"Got it," he replied. "Except they won't grow as good as they would if you planted them right side up."

"What? Oh no!" Becca picked up one of the bulbs and looked at it. Didn't pointy ends always go down? she wondered.

Seth said, "How many'd you put in so far?"

"Four bags."

"Bummer." He scratched his head and looked from the dog to her. "What the hey," he said, "I'll help you. Fair exchange."

"For what?"

"Helping me out with Gus after."

"What're you doing with him?"

"Taking him to Saratoga Woods for a run. So we got to be fast here or he'll eat his way out of the leash."

Fast, then, was what they were, especially since Seth set about with the digging. They had just completed the job when Debbie returned with Josh and Chloe. Seth was sweeping the extra dirt back into the flower beds and Becca was picking up the empty bulb sacks and the tools. She heard the SUV and turned as Debbie parked it.

Josh and Chloe came tumbling out, crying, "Doggie! Dog!" at

Gus, and the dog responded by leaping, barking, and straining at his leash to get to the kids. The feelings that came from them felt like marshmallows to Becca: soft and sugary. But when Debbie got out of the truck and slammed its door, Becca felt her whispers, which were strong and angry. She heard *pothead* and *loser*, and she saw Debbie was looking poison daggers at Seth and Seth was turning from the flower bed farthest from Debbie's car. His expression grew wary.

Seth nodded and said, "Hey, Mrs. Grieder," and Debbie said, "What're you hanging around here for, Seth Darrow?"

Becca said hastily, "Seth helped me with the bulbs. This is *so* dumb. I was planting them sort of wrong."

To one side, Gus was still barking and jumping. The kids had knelt in front of him. He was licking their faces when he wasn't trying to jump onto their backs and Josh called out to Seth, "C'n we let him off the leash?"

"Heck no," Seth said pleasantly. "He'd probably make a run for it. But you c'n hold on to the leash if you want. His name's Gus. Here . . ." He strode over to the VW and unwound the leash from the car's bumper. He handed this over to Josh, who immediately got dragged around the parking lot and, ultimately, around the side of the motel in the direction of the vacant lot. Chloe followed, laughing. Becca felt their joy. It was as strong as their grandmother's anguish.

Seth seemed to feel it, too. Or, as Becca thought, he knew what it was about and where it came from. He quickly opened the door of the VW and flipped the driver's seat forward. He said over his shoulder, "I brought this by for Becca, Mrs. Grieder. It's better than what she has, and now I've got Sammy—"

"Who's Sammy?" Debbie's voice had an edge. "I thought the dog was Gus."

Seth said, "Sammy's the car." He ducked his head inside and began to wrestle with something in the back.

Becca couldn't see how he'd managed it, but Seth had somehow crammed a bike into the back of his Volkswagen Bug. He brought it forth and smacked his hand down on its seat. He said to Becca, "Road bike. Twenty-seven gears. A little old but it works fine, and I greased it up. I'll show you how to ride it."

"What, *now*?" Debbie glanced in the direction the kids had gone with Gus. Excited barking sounded. She said, "Is it safe for the kids to be around that dog?"

"Yeah. But I'll go get him." Seth leaned the bike against the car and jogged around the side of the building. He called, "Hey, you dumb dog!"

Becca looked at Debbie. Debbie was looking at the bike. *Not* was between them in the sunny autumn air. Becca couldn't tell exactly what the *not* referred to, but from what Seth had told her about Debbie's daughter, she figured it had to do with getting hurt while riding a bike. She said to Debbie, "I traded with him. I bartered."

Debbie tore her gaze from the bike and said, "What?" as she quickly pulled some cigarettes from the pocket of her jacket.

"I told Seth I'd help him with Gus in exchange for helping me with the bulbs."

"How's he need help with Gus?"

"Running him."

"Where?"

"Saratoga Woods."

At that, Becca could hear the alarm bells go off in Debbie's head. They might have been ringing all over town so loud were they. The bells were followed by *oh yeah . . . run . . . that's it*, which seemed to suggest that Debbie thought she was lying.

She said to Debbie, "I sort of promised him. He *did* help me, and I kind of want to pay him back. Anything else you need me to do first?"

Debbie said, "No," as Seth and the kids came back around the side of the building, this time with Seth in possession of the leash. "No, you go ahead to the woods. If that's what you want to do."

Chloe and Josh heard this and began to clamor to go to the woods, too. Seth said, "Sure. More the merrier," and looked to Debbie for permission.

She said, "Time for you to have lunch," to the kids.

Seth said, "I've got tuna sandwiches. Only two, but we could all share."

Debbie said shortly, "No way. The kids stay here. Have a nice time, Becca," and she went to the SUV, and started jerking grocery bags out of it.

———

THEY DIDN'T TALK about Debbie once they left the Cliff Motel. Instead, with Gus panting noisily in the backseat behind them, they rumbled down the slope of Second Street, where a cluster of people were sitting at tables eating and drinking in front of a coffeehouse called Useless Bay Coffee. Guitar music was coming from someone playing in a band shell there. It was fine and complicated. Just for a moment Seth slowed to listen.

He said to Becca, "That's me in six months. Gypsy jazz."

"You play guitar? Like *that*?" she asked him, impressed.

"Guitar," he told her, "is pretty much my life."

The day was bright, and the air was crisp, and it came to Becca once again how different this place was from what she was used to. There, if the sun was out, the day was probably going to be warm. Here, the sunlight meant only that the dawning autumn colors were going to be brighter and the sky was going to be bluer than blue.

Saratoga Woods turned out to be a couple of winding, tree-shrouded miles from the town, just across the road from Saratoga Passage, which glittered and heaved in the day's bright sunlight. The woods showed itself as a wealth of forest that climbed a hill across an expanse of meadow. A parking lot just off the road held five cars and a truck. The truck Becca recognized immediately. The woman who'd given her a ride on her very first night on the island, Diana Kinsale, was somewhere in the forest. Like Seth, Becca figured, she was probably there with her dogs.

Seth made sure Gus was on his leash, telling Becca that they'd let him off for a really good run once they got through the meadow and onto one of the trails. If he took off before then, Seth said, they'd be sunk because no way would they be able to catch him. He was too fast and the woods were too thick. They were vast, too.

Becca didn't have the AUD box with her. She'd not been using it while planting the bulbs, and she'd not dug it out of her room before setting off with Seth. So the first thing she heard as they crossed the meadow was the rustling of whispers, barely audible but definitely there. Along with those whispers came a subtle scent that she knew at once.

She looked around, back the way they had come. No one was nearby. There were only cars, the truck, and an information board beneath a sheltering roof that protected it from bad weather. Against one of the poles that held up this roof, a bicycle was chained.

Becca looked from that bike to the forest. A rush of warm sweet air came at her, which could have been the sunlight warming a breeze except here there was no breeze. What was there was that *scent* again, the fragrance of cooking fruit.

She looked at Seth, but he hadn't seemed to notice anything. He bent down when they came to a trailhead dipping into the shadows, and he unhooked Gus from his leash.

They began their walk. Everything went perfectly for about five minutes: They strolled into the woods along a path where the ground was springy and smelled richly of decomposing leaves while Gus dashed off, snuffled at the smells, lifted his leg against some huckleberry bushes, and came loping happily back to Seth for a treat.

Then some barking started, and things went south. Gus raised his head. He barked joyfully in return. And just as Seth read his intentions and yelled, "Gus, stay!" the dog took off. Clearly, there were canine companions to be had in Saratoga Woods. The yellow Lab shot up the trail and disappeared into the trees.

Seth said, "Oh damn! I've got to catch him," and he took off at a run as well. He was yelling, "Gus, stay! Stay!" as he dashed in the dog's wake.

Becca followed. Gus's barking grew distant and it wasn't long before she saw why. She came to a three-pronged fork in the trail and there were no indications which way Seth and the dog had gone.

———

BECCA STOPPED. THE air was cool under looming hemlocks, cedars, and Douglas firs. It was also teeming with whispers. They were oddly strong, despite no one being close by, as if people were hiding behind every tree. They spoke of longing and desperation. They seemed to reveal confusion, anger, and despair. They came from every direction at once.

Becca had had experience with whispers from the time that she'd been four years old. But these were too much for her to contend with. She felt a dizziness come over her, as if the whispers were an unseen hand that was spinning her around as she tried to distinguish them one from the other. Playing along with them like a constant undercurrent was Derric's sweet scent.

So he *was* indeed here. So was Diana, along with her dogs. And because of all the cars in the parking lot, there were other people, too. Somewhere, they were doing something. And they weren't terribly far away.

She had to choose a trail. She called for Seth. Then she yelled for Gus. In return came barking, but she couldn't tell which direction had sent it. So she chose the left fork, and within fifty yards she was climbing. She scrambled past the exposed gnarled roots of an ancient cedar and brushed against tall elderberry bushes.

She heard a yell then. It sounded like Seth. She yelled back and more dogs barked. The trail got narrow, climbed ever higher, made a hairpin turn, was broken by stones, and burst out of the trees. The sudden sun caused Becca to shield her eyes and stumble, and then she felt the assault of dizziness again. She fell back, a hand out. It made contact with a tree stump, and she lowered herself to this. She was out of breath from the climb. She was also dismayed from being what she was at the moment, which was completely lost.

She made herself try to ignore the whispers, to put some effort into thinking straight. But then there were dogs coming at her. They were barking with excitement, and one of them jumped and knocked her from the tree stump to the ground.

Snuffling ensued: dog noses everywhere. With the snuffling came a shout of, "Dogs!" and Becca knew immediately that Diana Kinsale was there. Had she not been, Becca would have recognized the dogs quickly enough, especially since the number one place they were sniffing was the jacket pocket in which she'd kept the sugar cookies she'd bought on the ferry. She was getting to her feet and pushing the animals to one side when the black poodle, Oscar, joined the pack, trailing his leash. And just behind him was Gus. She tried to grab him the second he got close, but he danced away.

Diana commanded, "All dogs come."

Just like that, they did as they were told, all except Gus, who trotted a safe distance from Becca and watched, eyes bright, tail wagging, and obviously waiting for more of the game called Chase. Diana said to Becca, "Did they knock you over? I'm sorry. They're harmless but they shouldn't . . . Why, hello. It's the girl with the bike. Becca, yes?"

Becca got to her feet, one eye on Gus to keep him in sight. "They didn't knock me over. I was sitting on the stump. I sort of slipped."

Diana said, "D'you need a leash for him?" meaning Gus. She took the one from the poodle's neck, saying, "Oscar doesn't really need it. You can use it. Is he your dog?"

"Gus? No. He belongs to Seth."

"Seth Darrow?" Diana spoke in a way that suggested she not only knew Seth Darrow by name but also by something else. "Which way did he go?"

It came to Becca as Diana asked the question that, as on the day she'd met her, Diana had no whispers at all. Yet she *should* have had whispers because the one thing Becca knew about whispers was that if you didn't have them, you were dead. But this woman Diana was clearly alive, she had no whispers, and she wasn't reciting *listen my children and you shall hear of the midnight ride of Paul Revere* or anything like that to prevent them.

Diana said again, "Which way did he go?"

"Seth? I don't know. We got separated."

"This is the trail over to Putney Woods and Metcalf Woods," Diana said, using her thumb to indicate the way she'd come. "Did he come this way?"

"I don't think so. I couldn't tell. There was noise and . . . Sorry. I'd better go after Gus."

"Here then," Diana said, "take the leash. You can return it later. You know where I live."

"You sure?"

"I'm sure."

Becca turned in the direction she'd last seen Gus lope. He was gone, of course, but she set off after him anyway. She went up one trail and down another. She called for Gus. Then she called for Seth. Finally she saw the dog lying in a mass of ferns up ahead of her, deep in the shadows but visible because of his yellow coat. He was panting, his paws were clotted with mud, and his fur was filthy. His expression was completely blissful.

He let her approach and for a moment she wondered if he'd hurt himself. But it was only exhaustion that had finally slowed him down. It was also exhaustion that encouraged him to allow the leash to be attached to his collar.

"Okay, let's go," Becca told him. "Game's over. Let's find Seth. Take us back to the car."

———

THEY WERE NOT far from the trailhead where they'd first come into the woods when Becca realized that the whispers had stopped. She paused and listened. There was no birdsong either. There was no barking, and there was no shouting. Every feeling on the breeze had died.

Worse than the silencing of whispers, though, was the matter of scent. Becca realized that there was none, where earlier there had been that sweetness to the air. What there was now was the absence of everything. Becca's stomach began to churn.

She said, "Derric." Then she said, "Derric?" And then because she knew without knowing what it was she knew, she cried, "Derric!" and she began to run.

She wasn't sure where she was going or why, but Gus seemed

to know that something was wrong. He also seemed to know where to go, because he took the lead. They tore down the trail and burst into the meadow at the edge of Saratoga Woods. But instead of pounding across the meadow to the parking lot, they veered to the right.

They raced along the edge of the woods toward a farm that began on the south side of the meadow. But before they reached it, Gus took a turn into the woods again. Another trail began here, at the far southeast edge of the forest. It was narrow and it rose at once, first climbing the hillside above the farm and then turning into the woods where it climbed again, quickly and steeply, higher and higher.

"Derric?" Becca called out as she ran. Gus strained against the leash. "Derric!"

Gus surged and barked and Becca couldn't keep up with him, so she released her hold on the leash and off he went. He loped a good fifty yards up the trail and just as she thought she might lose him again, he stopped and began snuffling on the ground in a frenzy.

It came to Becca that it might be Seth they were looking for, that Derric might be gone from the woods and this would be the reason that she couldn't hear or sense him. So she shouted, "Seth! Seth!" just as she'd called for Derric.

When she reached the dog, he began to take off, but this time he didn't continue to climb. He also didn't stay on the trail. Rather, he began to crash down a slope. As he did so, Becca saw what he'd been snuffling on the trail.

It was the very distinct print of a shoe with a strange-

looking sole. Right next to this was a huckleberry bush with broken branches. Below this bush was the sign of impact.

Becca didn't want to look. She certainly didn't want to know.
But then she heard the whining of the yellow Lab, and she knew
that something was wrong at the base of the steep slope.

It was a boy. He lay motionless, far down in the gully. He was
against a tree and his leg stuck out at an all-wrong angle.

She cried, "Derric!" for she saw immediately who it was,
although she didn't know why Gus lay next to him in the drop
position, with his yellow head resting on Derric's badly twisted
torso.

ELEVEN

Becca wasn't aware that she was screaming for help as she crashed down the slope to get to Derric. Later she would learn from others that her voice had echoed though the trees, causing the crows to chatter, the great barn owls to take flight, and several eagles to begin to soar above Saratoga Woods.

Somewhere in the distance she thought she heard Seth yell. Gus began to bark. He'd risen from his crouched position next to Derric, and his hackles were raised. She realized she was frightening him, so she stopped screaming, and just said Derric's name.

There was a lot of blood. This came from his head, and Becca knew better than to try to move him. But she had to touch him, so she bent and put her cheek to his. No whispers were present, but then how could there be?

All of this had taken less than a minute. But it seemed like twenty, and Becca knew time was of the essence. She rose and looked around. She needed help.

She remembered her cell phone and dug it out. No signal, she saw. Too many trees, too much cover, too far down in the gully, too deep in the woods. She had to get out. She had to find a signal. She said to Derric, "I'll be back. I'll get help," and she added, although she wasn't quite sure why, "Derric, don't *go*," before she started to climb.

On the path once more, she began to run. Gus followed her, but she couldn't worry about Gus. He was going to go where he was going to go. The important thing now was Derric.

She burst out into the meadow. She looked at her cell phone and finally saw the signal.

Becca dialed the number 9-1-1 and she could barely make her fingers connect with the buttons. A woman's voice spoke.

"Help us," Becca said to her. "We need help in the woods. An ambulance. A boy's been hurt. He's hurt bad and I think his leg's broken in a bunch of places and there's blood—"

"Name please?"

"His name's Derric Mathieson. He's on a trail—"

"I mean your name."

"But—"

"Your name and your birthdate, please. Your address as well."

Becca went with the last. "Saratoga Woods. We're in the parking lot. Across the street from the water. It's Saratoga Woods. D'you know where that is? On Saratoga Road?"

"I can see your location. I need your name and home address, miss."

See her location? Becca looked around frantically. Were there cameras or something? How could she . . . ?

"You're on my screen, miss. Your cell phone registers. I can see where you are. I need your name and address."

"You need to send an ambulance," Becca cried. "That's what you need and you need it *now*."

She ended the call and looked around frantically. She couldn't be here when the ambulance arrived. She had a feeling the police would be following. The strangeness of her 911 call was going to alert them.

Seth was coming out of the woods. Gus saw Seth and began to run toward him. Becca began to do the same.

Seth cried, "Hey! What's going on?"

She reached him, breathing hard. She said, "Nine-one-one. I called. Up in the woods. Derric's hurt. There's that trail—" She pointed to the trailhead at the far end of the meadow. "I had Gus and he started to run and . . ." She grabbed Seth's arm. "There's an ambulance coming and I can't be here, Seth. You've got to stay. Show them the trail."

Then she turned and ran because running was the only thing possible now. Questions were going to be asked when the ambulance got there. Names were going to be taken down. It was bad enough that she'd made a call from her cell phone because now that cell phone was going to be traced. Every cop show in the world showed that. You make a call from a cell phone, and they track you down.

She knew the worst in that instant. She had to ditch the phone. The *only* call she'd made on it other than to Laurel and now it could be what destroyed them both. As she pounded across the meadow and into the parking lot, Becca looked around for a place to toss the phone. She hoped against hope that she could come back for it later, so she needed a spot out of sight, where the rain couldn't touch it.

The information board, she thought. The same place where the bike that had to be Derric's bike was locked against a pole that held up the roof. The structure wasn't tall so it was a simple matter to stand on her toes and to put the cell phone on a rafter. She wiped off the cell phone first, however. Just in case.

———

BECCA WAS A long way from the Cliff Motel, and she knew she couldn't run the distance. She wasn't in that kind of shape. But she set off running and went as far as she could at a steady jog. She heard the wailing of the ambulance when she was about a half mile from Saratoga Woods. Here she found a thickly wooded driveway that split in two directions: One coursed up the hill and looked like access to someone's property and the other disappeared into the trees, this one posted as a means to get into Metcalf Woods. A sign said no one was supposed to park there, but someone had and this was just as well. Becca stepped behind a pickup truck with SMUG-GLERS COVE FARM AND FLOWERS on the driver's door. She crouched and was thus hidden as the ambulance tore past to go to Derric's aid.

When it was safe to do so, she set off again. She hurried along the road, and she began to pray.

Where Saratoga Road ended and Second Street began, Becca veered to the right. She paced quickly across the pebbly parking lot of the local Catholic church. This gave onto Third Street and a descent into the village.

A footprint meant nothing, Becca told herself. There were probably a billion footprints in Saratoga Woods. That the one she'd seen was fresh and perfect only meant that someone had hiked on that path. That the print was right above the spot from which Derric had fallen . . . ? Coincidence, pure and simple. And besides, Derric was going to be okay. He *was* going to be okay.

At the bottom of Third Street, Becca crossed a thick green lawn, and she climbed its slope up to Cascade Street, which ran east to west along the edge of the grass. A few fat rabbits were placidly chomping the lawn to bits along its left side, but they didn't scamper off as Becca surged past them. They were too busy getting themselves ready for the coming winter.

Just as Becca reached the parking lot of the Cliff Motel, a helicopter roared overhead. It was flying low, and she could tell it was heading in the direction of Saratoga Woods. She wanted to think this was just another one of those coincidences she'd been considering a couple of moments earlier, but she had a feeling that it had to do with the ambulance, Derric, and Derric's condition. She thought of that blood that had been seeping from his head. It was serious and she knew it. But she also knew that he was still alive or they wouldn't have needed a helicopter to get him out of there.

BECCA KNEW SHE had to tell Debbie she was back. Debbie hadn't liked her going to the woods with Seth. All her whispers had pretty much indicated bad stuff could happen, and it had. But this was something she didn't want Debbie to know, so she had to be careful. She tried to compose herself by taking a few deep breaths. Then she went inside.

She found them all in the kitchen. Debbie and the kids were at the table, and each of them had a paper in front of them. On the paper they had each drawn a pumpkin. On the pumpkins they were making designs.

Chloe cried out, "Becca's here!" and Josh said, "We're making plans. Check mine, Becca," and she saw that they were planning how they were going to carve pumpkins in advance of cutting them into jack-o'-lanterns at the end of October. "We get 'em up on Third Street, and we'll get you one, too," Chloe said. "Grammer said we c'n buy extra big ones this year. Josh wants one as big as this table, but Grammer says they all got to be the same size."

"They're from someone's garden," Josh confided. "So they're not perfect or anything."

"Which means they're cheap," Debbie said. She got up from the table and said, "Which one of you guys wants a quesadilla?"

Becca felt the tentacles of Debbie's suspicion slithering toward her. She heard the whispers that accompanied them: *all scratched up . . . brambles in your socks . . . where you been . . . up at the erratic, huh? . . . let me see your eyes . . . done to you*? Becca was scared of the suspicion and worried about the whispers and, more than anything, afraid because of the loss of that cell phone. All of this piled into her and made her hungrier than she'd ever been before.

She told Debbie she'd like a quesadilla very much and could she cut up the cheese for it or something? Debbie said no, just sit down and make a design for a jack-o'-lantern, darlin', because eventually they were going to have a pumpkin carving contest and the winner would be decided by Tatiana Primavera. Debbie started the quesadillas and for a moment Becca thought all was okay. But then as she had them heating on the stove, Debbie turned to Becca and said, "Seth bring you home, darlin'? I didn't hear that old Vee-Dub."

Becca said, "I walked from Useless Bay Coffee. Someone's playing guitar outside there," and she hoped from this that Debbie would conclude that Seth was still there listening to the music.

Debbie looked at her closely. Becca turned her head away and pulled some paper toward her. She studied it as if she was trying to decide on a design. But what she knew was that the topic of Seth Darrow wasn't finished between her and Debbie Grieder.

PART TWO

Saratoga Woods

TWELVE

When Seth Darrow watched Becca King run off toward the parking lot of Saratoga Woods, he didn't know what to think. Luckily, though, he knew what to do. He took Gus to Sammy, he put the dog inside, and he gave him a bowl of water. Had the car not been there, Gus would have been trouble. As it was, he'd stay right there in the passenger seat till Judgment Day waiting for Seth. He needed training to be free on the forest trails. When it came to the car, he was perfect.

Seth returned to the meadow then. Mrs. Kinsale was just coming across with her dogs. Seth met her halfway and told her what he knew: Derric Mathieson was hurt in the woods. He also told her an ambulance was on its way.

"Where is he?" she asked him.

"Didn't see him. All's I know is he fell up on Meadow Loop trail and it's bad."

Diana Kinsale didn't ask him how he knew this, although she looked at him sharply. "I'll go back," she said. "Send the paramedics when they get here." She ran to her truck and stowed her dogs in the back. She headed to the trail at the far end of the meadow.

A few minutes later the sounds of sirens in the distance grew louder as the ambulance approached. Because of the sirens and how insistently they shrieked, other people began to emerge from Saratoga Woods. Kids came down from above where an old landing strip had long overgrown a developer's dream of houses for rich people in possession of airplanes to fly them to the island for weekends. The local dopers stumbled down from a boulder the size of a house, an erratic buried deep in the forest and marking the Ice Age that had deposited it there from Alberta, Canada. Hikers came over from Putney Woods, connected to these woods by a winding trail that passed through acres of salal, ferns, brambles, and firs.

Among them was Jenn McDaniels, who blasted out of the woods at a run. She was sweaty from the top of her head to her ankles, and she was dressed for her training for the island triathlon. She ran and she biked in the woods, and Seth knew this. But she usually did this much closer to her home, which was at the far south end of the island. So why she was here didn't make sense to him, nor did it make sense to see the girl who emerged from yet another trail, off to the right, at a run.

This was Hayley Cartwright. This was Hayley who lived nowhere near these woods. This was Hayley whose family farm truck was not in the parking lot at all, so what, Seth wondered, was she doing here?

Seth didn't have a chance to ask her a thing although he looked at her and she looked away and the color in her face told him that she had more secrets from him than she'd had the day they'd broken up. They didn't say a word to each other because Jenn ran up first and said, "What's going on?" and the stoners sauntered over behind her.

He said to Jenn, "Someone fell in the woods." Deliberately, he did not tell her who.

"Heavy, man," came from among the dopers.

Someone snickered and Seth glanced their way. They were lit up like candles on a birthday cake, stifling grins and looking fully finished. He said to Jenn, "Ambulance is coming," which, of course, was obvious from the approaching noise. He added, "Mrs. Kinsale's up there. I'm waiting to tell them where to go."

"You the local traffic cop?" one of the dopers asked.

"*I'm* way impressed," another said.

"Shut up, Dylan," Jenn snapped at the latter boy. "Go back to your cage."

"Oh, baby, I'm scared."

"Come *on*, you guys," Hayley said. She was, Seth noted, not looking at him. The rawness of their breakup was still fresh and bloody. Six weeks past, and she'd cheated on him. He should have expected it, but he hadn't. He should have had brains to see it wouldn't ever have worked between them once he dropped out of school, but he had none.

The ambulance swung off Saratoga Road. Seth approached it as it sent up gravel and dust in the parking lot. One of the paramedics got out, and Seth told him the situation tersely. He pointed across the meadow to the trailhead, which was dimly visible from where they stood. The paramedic nodded, got back inside the ambulance, and they drove it straight across the meadow. They pulled to a halt right at the edge of the forest and took off at a run with a box of gear and a stretcher.

JENN FOLLOWED THEM, curiosity getting the better of her. Some of the people who'd emerged from the woods trailed after her. The dopers remained. So did Seth because, Hayley hadn't moved, and he wanted to talk to her. There was something strange about her being in Saratoga Woods by herself, and although Seth knew this wasn't his business, he also had a way to get her to talk, and he intended to use it.

He said, "So, Hayley, you still hooking up with—"

"Stop it." She'd been watching the ambulance and the people running after it. She turned back to Seth. He thought stupidly how pretty she was, how she'd always been pretty, and how the nicest thing about Hayley Cartwright was that she didn't know she was pretty. She said, "Okay, Seth? *Stop* it. Okay?"

He said, "Hey, just a friendly question. Isn't that what you wanted: you and me just being *friends*?"

"You don't know how to be anyone's friend," she told him.

"Oh, that stings, chick," Dylan Cooper said. He and his buddies had moved into a tight little enclave of whispered conversation.

"Shut up," Hayley said. "Why don't you go smoke another joint."

"I will if you will," Dylan told her.

"Can it," Seth snapped.

He took Hayley's arm. They moved away from the others. He said, "What're you doing here alone, Hayley?"

She said, "What're *you* doing here alone?"

"I'm not alone. Gus's in the car."

"Well, pardon me for not having a dog to walk."

"How'd *you* get here, anyway? Where's the truck? You come over from Keller Road or something?" Not that it was any of his business, but something was going on. Hayley Cartwright was a cautious girl. She never went into the woods alone.

She said, "Look, if you have to know, the truck's down at the Metcalf Woods entrance. I came that way. Are you satisfied?"

"The *Metcalf* entrance?" Seth wanted to add, "You mean the one with the big No Parking sign? The one that tells you to take your vehicle over to Keller Road if you want to go into those woods? The one that makes it *easy* to hide your truck from anyone passing by? Is that the entrance we're talking about, Hayl?" But he didn't say that because he felt queasy at the thought of Hayley hiding even more from him than she'd hidden already. So he repeated, "The Metcalf entrance? Why'd you park there?"

She said, "Gee, Seth, as if it matters right now," which was also her way of saying "as if it's your business."

He wanted to argue, but a sheriff's department car pulled into the parking lot then. At this, the collection of dopers beat a very quick retreat back into the woods. A deputy got out, observing their flight. He pulled some sunglasses from the breast pocket of his shirt, and he squinted over in the direction of the ambulance before he put the glasses on. He walked to where Seth and Hayley were standing.

He said to Hayley, "You make the call?"

Hayley said, "What call?"

The deputy said to Hayley, "Empty your pockets. Let me see your bag."

"What the *heck*?" Seth knew exactly what the deputy wanted:

Becca must have used a cell phone to make that 9-1-1 call. It was time to play dumb. "What's she supposed to have on her?" he asked. "This a drug bust or something? Come on, man. Why're you hassling her?"

Hayley said, "It's okay," and she handed over her bag. She said, "I don't get why—"

Seth said, "Leave her alone. She didn't do anything."

The deputy looked at him. His glasses were too dark to see his eyes but his mouth was like a ruler line drawn on his face, and Hayley said again but more cautiously this time, "It's okay, Seth." She waited for the deputy to do whatever he needed to do, which was find the cell phone, which of course she didn't have. Hayley didn't even own a cell phone. In her family that would have been a luxury.

The deputy did his business with the bag and handed it back. He said to them, "Stay put," and he set off across the meadow.

The paramedics were coming out of the woods with Mrs. Kinsale walking behind them. They had the stretcher between them. An IV drip was hanging from a pole attached to the stretcher, and just as the paramedics were about to load their patient up, the deputy reached them. Words were exchanged.

Then the oddest thing happened. The paramedics loaded the kid into the ambulance and one of them got inside with him. The other went to the driver's side and climbed in, but he didn't start the engine and they didn't take off. They didn't go anywhere. That could only mean one of two things. IV drip or not, either Derric Mathieson was dead and there was no big rush or he was so badly hurt they were radioing for a helicopter because they didn't want to risk the long drive to the hospital in Coupeville, midway up the island.

Hayley said, "Oh my God. Did someone *die*?" and Seth felt cold from head to toe. Dead in the woods would be very bad.

The deputy was coming toward them at a run.

———

SETH SAID TO him, "What's happening, man? What's going on?"

The deputy's name tag said that he was Deputy Picarelli, a squat individual who'd probably spent too much time eating the pies on sale at some of the farmers' markets. He shot Seth a look that said if any questions were going to be asked, the deputy was going to be doing the asking. Then he said, "Come with me. Tell the others," and he indicated the rest of the people within the meadow.

Seth did so, although the dopers he could do nothing about. They were long gone. He herded everyone else over to the patrol car, where the deputy was on the radio with someone, his privacy guaranteed by the rolled-up windows. When he was finished with the radio, he opened his door and from the car he started asking for names.

At each name, the deputy typed into a laptop that was attached to the dashboard and took up some of the space of the passenger's seat. He nodded with each one and said, "Okay. You can go. We'll be in touch," although no one knew what he'd be in touch about.

Then he got to Seth. Seth said his name. He didn't need to spell it because the island was crawling with Darrows, and the deputy was probably going to know some of them. Seth's grandfather had been one of five sons, and all of them still lived on Whidbey.

Deputy Picarelli nodded and typed Seth's name into his laptop. Seth hitched up his jeans and got ready to leave, like everyone else. But that was when things changed.

Picarelli got out of the car. He opened the back door. He said to Seth, "Get inside," and he wasn't offering him a friendly ride.

THIRTEEN

There was only time to take care of Gus. Seth said to Hayley, "Gus's in Sammy. Can you take him—" before the door was closed and he was in the back of the cruiser.

She nodded, but she cried, "Seth! What did you *do*?"

The deputy pulled out of the parking lot, heading south on Saratoga Road. Seth said to him, "Are you going to tell me what's going on?" but the only thing Picarelli said was, "Bench warrant, kid. Got to take you in."

Bench warrant? Seth was no expert on things related to the law, but he knew that *bench* meant a judge had been involved. A judge had ordered him arrested, but he couldn't come up with a single reason why. Still, he felt a tiny bit relieved because whatever he was being taken up to the jail in Coupeville for, it wasn't about this.

When they arrived at the sheriff's office some thirty minutes later, Seth expected the patrol car to stop in front. But that didn't happen. Instead a huge door yawned open in the building and they drove inside an enormous, tall, and decidedly forbidding parking bay. It was like a garage from which no one escaped, especially when its metal door crashed down with a sound of finality that did what it was intended to do: It scared Seth nearly out of his shorts.

He knew this place, not because he'd been here before but because it was part of Whidbey Island's history. Right beyond a thick metal door that he was looking straight at was a small room where a Breathalyzer sat on a table with a chair in front of it. There, anyone suspected of drunk driving was tested. Also right there in that very same room a kid just one year older than Seth had pulled out a gun from the crotch of his jeans and had shot two deputies dead.

Deputy Picarelli got out and opened Seth's door. He took his arm and heaved him up. Seth wondered if for some crazy reason the deputy thought he'd been driving drunk.

Things became clear when they walked past the Breathalyzer and finally got inside the booking area. This wasn't a place where people smiled and greeted the incoming losers, but at least they shared information with anyone who was being booked. Being booked consisted of having virtually everything on him taken off him. Being booked meant fingerprints. Being booked meant learning that he'd failed to pay two speeding tickets, one for doing seventy on highway 525 and one for doing sixty-three on Langley Road. In both cases, he'd been trying to get to the ferry on time. But they took this sort of thing seriously on the island. They didn't like speeding and they didn't like people who didn't pay their fines when they were caught.

Seth had completely forgotten the fines. He said, "Hey, I'll pay them now," although he had exactly five dollars and thirty-eight cents on him.

He was told politely that things didn't work that way when

other things got to this point and a bench warrant had thus been issued in his name. When that happened, bail was one thousand dollars, which of course he could pay if he wished to do so. Otherwise, he would be spending the night in Hotel Lockup and tomorrow morning he could explain via video to the judge up in the town of Oak Harbor why he thought traffic fines didn't apply to him.

"But I forgot, I forgot!" didn't get him far. Where it got him was locked into an interview room where he could "consider his options," as he was told.

The interview room was painted the yellow of dirty banana skins. It featured a table, a chair, a stool, and an enormous picture window whose view was of a bank of television monitors and the deputy in charge of watching them. That he was also in charge of watching Seth was something that became obvious when he waved hello from his perch at the monitors and made a no-no shaking motion with his hand and jerked his hand above his neck. From this Seth took it to mean that he wasn't to hang himself while he was in the interview room. No problem there, was what Seth thought. Unless he managed to do it with his socks, he didn't have anything he could use for the job.

He sat on the stool and not the chair because that was where he was told to sit. He put his arms on the table and his head in his hands and he wondered what was going to happen. Nothing about being where he was at the moment was going to impress his parents.

When he'd dropped the bomb on them that he wanted to leave South Whidbey High School, they'd thought Seth meant he preferred to attend the alternative school, lodged in an 1895 schoolhouse in a crossroads called Bayview Corner. When he'd dropped the *bigger* bomb that he was finished with going to school altogether, they hadn't panicked the way some parents might have. They understood his learning disabilities. They understood his talent and passion for guitar. They were artists themselves, so they'd just sat him down and named the conditions for the new life he was proposing for himself: a tutor to help him study for the GED, a part-time job, and consistent rehearsals of the trio with whom Seth had played the gypsy jazz of Django Reinhardt for the last four years. So far, he'd managed two of the three conditions with his job at the Star Store and regular rehearsals as well as gigs with the trio. He was having real trouble with the other one, though.

His parents didn't know this. They assumed his hours not at work were being filled with study as well as guitar strings. So Seth liked to stay under their radar, which meant that letting them know he was in the county jail was out of the question. As artists, they couldn't afford to spring him anyway, and they also couldn't afford to pay his fines.

The door opened in about twenty minutes. Seth looked up and said, "I get a phone call. I want to make it."

The deputy said, "Want a Coke or a sandwich?"

Seth said, "I want a phone call."

The deputy nodded and left. Seth waited. He ended up wondering if these guys were turning themselves into Alexander Graham Bell and *inventing* the telephone. Finally, another deputy came in, this one looking like he'd spent way too much time lifting weights in his garage.

Seth said to him, "I'm waiting to make a phone call."

He said to Seth, "Things have changed. The undersheriff is on his way. He's going to want to talk to you."

"Why? Don't you guys have anything better to do? We're talking about an unpaid speeding ticket. Okay, *two* tickets. But what is this? The biggest bust ever to hit Whidbey Island?"

"We've got a crime scene we're investigating, son," the deputy said. "He wants to talk to you about that."

A crime scene? Seth swallowed, hard. He said with as much bravado as he could muster, "I just came here from Saratoga Woods. Ask that guy Picarelli. He brought me in. How could I be involved in a crime?"

"That happens to be where the crime occurred," the deputy told him.

TWO MORE HOURS crawled by. Seth got out of the interview room once to use the bathroom. The only thing he knew for sure was that there was trouble coming.

Finally, he was allowed his phone call. He decided this was due to the fact that the undersheriff hadn't shown up. This allowed Seth a moment of relief. He couldn't be a suspect in a crime if the undersheriff wasn't interested in him, could he?

When it came to the phone call, Seth had made up his mind about its recipient. Since his parents couldn't make his bail, they didn't need the stress of thinking they'd have the choice of borrowing money or leaving their only son in a jail cell with a blanket, a pillow, and a thin mattress unrolled on a concrete shelf.

Instead, he made the call to his grandfather, Ralph Darrow. It would take him a while to get up to Coupeville, but Seth knew he'd come with the cash to bail him out of jail simply because that was who Ralph was.

It didn't take him long. He must have pushed his old Ford to its very limits, and Seth realized when he saw his granddad that he should have told him to take his time. But that wasn't Ralph's way when it came to family. It also wasn't his way to lecture, to blame, or to do anything other than what he did the moment he and Seth laid eyes on each other.

Ralph smoothed his graying Fu Manchu mustache and crossed to Seth. He cupped him on the back of his head. He said, "Favorite male grandchild, you make my life interesting. Got anything to say?"

"No," Seth told him.

<hr />

THEY DIDN'T TALK on the route from Coupeville back to Newman Road, where Ralph lived. It was dark, and he liked to concentrate on his driving. "Us oldsters," was the way he put it, "don't need to hit any deer in our declining years."

Ralph liked to talk like an old island hand, which he was in a way. But the rest of what he was he never spoke of: a graduate of Stanford University, a postgrad of Cal Tech, and a nuclear physicist. It turned out that he'd preferred working with his hands, not stuck in his head. A few years out in a world defined by rush hours on California freeways and work hours in the lab, and he was ready to return to Whidbey Island, where he'd taken up life as a master carpenter.

His house was on the eastern side of Newman Road, which created a semicircle that began on the highway and ended on the route into the center of the town of Freeland. A bumpy drive led up to the property. It was deliberately unpaved because Ralph hated paving. Had he had his own way in the matter, he wouldn't even have disturbed the land enough to build a house on it. But he'd been married then, long before his wife had passed on, and Seth's grandmother hadn't been a woman who would have considered living her married years and bringing up her children in a tent. So the house had been built, all of it with Ralph's own hands. At this point it had stood sympathetically in a dale on its huge plot of land for forty-two years.

When they got inside, Ralph lit a fire and pointed to one of the two armchairs that sat in front of it. He took the other and rested his feet on a hearth fashioned from river stones.

Seth joined him. He looked around this room he'd known as long as he'd known anything, and he realized that there wasn't a single object in it that had not been made by his grandfather's own hands, except for a picture frame on the fireplace mantel, in which Seth and his immediate family and Ralph all posed with Seth's sister at her graduation from South Whidbey High. It came to Seth as he looked up at this picture that Hayley had taken it. But that was as raw a spot inside him as was the fact that his sister Sarah was on a scholarship at Stanford while he was here, freshly minted as the family ex-con.

Seth sighed. Ralph glanced at him and waited. He could see what Seth was looking at, and he knew it was a sore spot in Seth's heart that the hand of cards he'd been dealt prevented him from being what his older sister was.

Seth finally said, "I guess the smart DNA all got used up by the time I got here."

"Meaning?" Ralph asked.

"Meaning Sarah. It's like all the DNA got worn out. It's like I'm the turkey sandwich and she's Thanksgiving dinner."

Ralph chuckled. "Most people like Thanksgiving dinner only for the sandwiches afterwards," he said.

"You know what I mean, Grand. I get tired sometimes."

"Of?"

"Of being the family loser."

"That's how you see it?"

"Definitely."

Ralph nodded and considered this for a few moments as the fire popped and crackled. Then he slapped his hands on the arms of his chair and got to his feet. "You come with me, grandson," he said.

Ralph went to the door, where he grabbed his old denim jacket and a flashlight. He handed a second flashlight to Seth. He went outside and began to walk in the direction of the forest.

Uh-oh, Seth thought. He needed to deal with Gus. He needed to get to his VW. But he also knew his grandfather. Ralph had an intention about something and when he had an intention, there was nothing Seth would be able to do to divert him from it. So he followed.

Ralph strode to the forest behind his house, to a trail that disappeared into the trees. The trail marked a narrow trek, hacked by Ralph through thick vegetation that grew like a contagion everywhere. They came to a secondary trail some way into the forest. They took this and then a third trail. At that point Seth knew where his grandfather was taking him although he didn't yet know why.

It was a clearing, perhaps the size of four parking spaces. In it, two ancient hemlocks had grown close together to form a V with their branches. In this V was a tree house. Across from the tree house and in the clearing stood an old log bench overtaken by lichen.

When they reached this spot, Ralph made for the bench and sat on it. Seth did the same, and together they shone the beams of their flashlights on the tree house, fifteen feet above the ground and accessed by a ladder.

This was no ordinary tree house. It had a viewing deck in front of its door. It had two glass-paned windows, and both of them opened. It had a metal roof and screen-topped metal chimney that spoke of a woodstove inside the place as well.

Ralph pointed to the structure and said, "Now that, grandson, is not the work of the family loser."

"I ought to use it more," Seth told him. "I put you to a lot of trouble not to be using it."

"Using it wasn't ever the point. Building it was. Just look at that thing, Seth. There's artistry in it, and you were the artist."

"No, I wasn't. You showed me what to do."

"That's how we all start. Knowledge is passed along. But at the other end of the knowledge has to be someone with the talent and skill to make something out of it."

Seth observed the tree house. It was a single room only, but he knew that, inside, it was worthy and perfect because that was how Ralph had insisted it be built. It was rainproof and snow-proof, and it was warm inside when you lit the small stove.

As they looked on the tree house together, Ralph spoke. "Where's Sammy, Seth?"

Seth told him that the VW was in the parking lot of Saratoga Woods.

"And Gus?" Ralph asked.

"Hayley's got him."

Ralph looked away. His lips curved down. He smoothed his mustache. "Hayley," he finally said, and he sighed. Then he murmured, "There's a kind of wood that won't take sanding, no matter how you go at it. It can't bear it, Seth." He meant by this that Seth had to let this one go, let Hayley go, let it *all* go and get on with his life.

"I know that," Seth said, "but I just can't do it."

"How's 'can't' been working for you so far?"

"Not at all," Seth admitted.

"Why'd you go out there, anyway?" Ralph asked. "Why Saratgoa Woods of all places?" and what Seth knew was that Ralph was asking because of Gus. He wanted to know why Seth had taken the lab out to Saratoga Woods, when the woods were vast and Gus wasn't yet trained well enough to run there.

"It wasn't the best idea," Seth said morosely. "I made the wrong decision."

"True enough and I'm glad you see that," Ralph told him. "So let's do something about it."

FOURTEEN

Something was getting Sammy first. Ralph said they'd go by way of Lone Lake, which shimmered like a silver coin in the moonlight, motionless water with a canopy of stars slung over it.

Seth could tell from his grandfather's silence that it weighed heavily on his mind that Seth felt like such a loser half the time. He knew it weighed doubly on his mind that Seth hadn't yet got past Hayley Cartwright.

They came upon Saratoga Woods from the direction opposite to the one Seth had taken earlier in the day. This route carved through a woodland of conifers that were black in the darkness, split occasionally by narrow driveways, overgrown with moss and ferns.

At Saratoga Woods, Ralph pulled the truck next to poor little Sammy. The VW looked sadly abandoned at this time of night. Seth thought his grandfather would just drop him off and head back home, but instead, Ralph shut off the Ford's engine and got out as Seth did.

Seth said thanks: for paying his bail, for coming up to Coupeville, for carting him back to the woods. Ralph nodded, but then he cleared his throat and from this Seth knew his grandfather had something to say.

It was this. "Not a good time for Gus, grandson."

Seth said, "Huh?"

Ralph said, "Best I hang on to the dog for a while."

This hurt, and Seth was surprised by how much. Ralph had given him the dog, and to have Gus taken away like this, with ten brief words, was a blow that felt like a fist smashing right below his heart.

Ralph, of course, knew all this, so he said, "It's the woods, grandson, that's all it is."

"What's that s'posed to mean?"

"You can't train a dog and be his friend at the same time, Seth. Training comes first. Friendship follows. The way I see it, you've got some things on your mind right now, things that need dealing with. Training a dog's not one of them. You take some weeks now and get yourself sorted out. Gus'll be fine with me."

"It's Hayley, isn't it?" Seth demanded bitterly. "It's the fact that I handed him over to Hayley and not someone else when the deputy took me."

Ralph shook his head. He was about to say that Hayley Cartwright was only part of what he was concerned about, but suddenly a telephone began to ring. He and Seth stared at each other and then looked around to find the source of the noise. Simultaneously, they headed for the information shelter.

The ringing stopped. Then in a moment, it began again. It was an easy matter to trace the sound then. Ralph plucked the cell phone from one of the shelter's rafters.

Seth heard only Ralph's end of the conversation, which began the way Ralph always answered the phone. "Ya*hoo* . . . What d'you mean 'Who is this?' Who the dickens is *this*? . . . I heard the ringing and followed the noise, that's how . . . Saratoga Woods, outside of Langley . . . You nuts, or what? . . . Ma'am I am seventy-two years old and so're my eyes and no way am I making that drive tonight. I've done it once already . . . You want it, you send someone for it . . . Ralph Darrow . . . I've got no problem whatsoever with that."

He flipped the phone closed and shoved it into his pocket. He said, "Cops. Someone used this thing to call nine-one-one today about some kid falling in the woods. You know anything about that?"

Seth shook his head.

Ralph evaluated him for a good thirty seconds. "I can't help you if I don't know," he pointed out.

"There's nothing to know," Seth declared.

<hr>

SETH'S GRANDFATHER WENT the way they'd come, which was also one of the routes he could take to get to Smugglers Cove Farm and Flowers, where Hayley Cartwright and her family lived. Seth, on the other hand, went into Langley to the Cliff Motel.

It came to Seth that he didn't know which room Becca King was staying in. Several rooms were lit, and he didn't think it would be one of his better ideas to knock on all the doors looking for her. This meant he would have to ask Debbie Grieder where Becca was.

He went to the office. The door was unlocked, and a bell rang to alert Debbie that a potential customer had just walked in. She came from the back where her apartment was, and when she opened the door, he could hear the television and Chloe and Josh squealing over something that they were watching.

Seth said, "Hi, Mrs. Grieder," in his most polite voice. "Came by 'cause Becca left something in my car, only I don't know which one of the room's hers."

Debbie gave him the kind of look a teacher gives to a kid when she suspects there are lice crawling in his hair. She said, "What?"

"Her cell phone. Must've fallen out of her pocket. I didn't notice till a while ago."

Debbie held out her hand. "I'll give it to her."

Seth said, "I sort of need to talk to her, too. I mean, just for a second. It won't take long." He wanted to add that it wasn't exactly Debbie Grieder's business what he was doing there since she wasn't Becca's mother or anything, but he didn't. He might not have been a scholastic whiz kid, but he wasn't stupid.

Debbie said, "You need to stay away from that girl, Seth Darrow. She's fourteen years old."

"I know that. I'm not interested in her in that way."

"Then *what* way are you interested in her?"

"No way, really. But we lost Gus in the woods this afternoon, and I wanted to be able to tell her what happened."

Debbie had an expression on her face that said she believed that story pretty much as firmly as she believed the moon was made of Limburger cheese. But she said, "She's in room four-forty-four. Make it quick."

Seth nodded and backed out of the office so that the daggers Debbie was aiming at him with her eyes wouldn't end up in his back. He went to Becca's room and knocked on the door.

When she answered, Seth was surprised to see that she was in her pajamas. It seemed early for that. She also didn't have her glasses on, and she wasn't wearing her usual mask of makeup, so she looked different to him. Her eyes were bloodshot, too, as if she'd been crying.

Seth wanted to feel some sympathy for her, but the sight of her brought everything back to him in a rush. Most of all what it brought back was the hours he'd spent in the jail, worrying about his parents and what they would say, thrashing over the mess he'd made of his relationship with Hayley, waiting for the cops' questions to begin . . . His mind went a little crazy with everything he wanted to say to Becca about the kind of trouble he was now in and the fact that now he'd even lost his dog and the hassle he had caused his granddad and—

Suddenly, Becca covered her ears. She cried out, "Stop it! I'm sorry! I'm *sorry*!" and she began to scramble around on the floor next to the bed. Seth could tell she was looking for something, but what she found made his vision go red. She grabbed an earphone and slammed it into her ear and turned up the volume on what looked like some kind of iPod. Seth thought, *What*? She's listening to *music*? And then he began to rant.

"What are you *doing*? Give me a break. We have to *talk*. I got taken to jail. You know that? They're asking questions. Then your cell phone started to ring, and my grandfather found it and . . . Would you take that stupid thing out of your ear and *listen* to me?"

She said, "It was ringing? The cell phone was ringing?" and unaccountably she began to cry.

Seth said, "It was the cops. They were trying to trace it. My granddad's taking it up to them. Or they're coming for it. Hell, I don't know. Will you *stop* listening to that music for a minute?"

"It's *not* music," Becca cried. "It's the only way I can hear you when you're mad like this. See for yourself." She pulled the earphone out of her ear and handed it to him. He received a blast of static that made him wince. Hell, who *was* this chick? was what Seth thought. Was she from another galaxy or something?

She was really crying now, Seth saw. She'd grabbed a pillow and she was clutching it. When she tried to talk, the words came out in big gulps of air.

From the gulps, Seth was able to piece together the story that Becca had no choice but to tell him. Without the cell phone, she'd lost her ability to phone her mother. Without the cell phone, she was so far into being on her own that she knew she would die without telling someone at least part of the truth.

Her stepdad had probably murdered his partner and *he* knew that *she* knew he'd done it. Plus he'd been using her to help him get money from old folks looking for secure investments, only Becca hadn't *known* how much money was involved and what Jeff Corrie was doing with it and how much more he wanted of it and how *this* was why he'd murdered his partner. But she couldn't go to the police about any of this because they wouldn't believe her because of how she knew it. And when it all became clear to her, she and her mom had gone on the run. Only Jeff Corrie was going to come after them soon. That was a given.

"I could tell what they wanted, see?" Becca gulped as she talked to Seth. "I could tell what they needed. I could see how . . . if Jeff said the right thing . . . I could tell what he *needed* to say to them and I thought it was *helping* them with their investments. Jeff said people sometimes are afraid of change so they don't do the right thing to help themselves when they start so I was the person who could guide him in what he had to say . . ."

Seth felt like one of those cartoon characters who needed to bang himself on the side of the head to make sense of all this. *What* was she saying?

The part he got clearly was the part about her mom. Her cell phone was the link to her mom, the cell phone was gone, and that was bad. But the way Seth saw, there might be something worse. This chick could be completely nuts.

"The phone," Becca said. "I need that phone."

"Cops are going to trace it," he told her. "If they get their hands on it, they're going to trace it."

He sat on the bed. Becca got herself up and sat next to him. Carefully, cautiously, Seth put his arm around her shoulders.

"I don't think they c'n trace it," Becca said. "We got the phones at a 7-Eleven."

"And how'd you pay for them? Did your mom use cash?"

"I think . . . She never used cash. It was her credit card." That was all Becca knew aside from the fact that when the phone was handed to her, her mother had programmed it with the only number she needed: the number that went with Laurel's own newly purchased phone.

"If she used a credit card," Seth said, "the cops'll find her."

Becca swallowed. She felt defeated. She'd let herself down, she'd let her mom down, and it even seemed that she'd let Seth down. She said to him, "What happened to *you*? I don't get how you ended up in jail."

Seth told her the CliffsNotes version of his adventure. This was the version that dealt with the unpaid traffic tickets and his grandfather making bail for him. He left out Gus and he left out

Hayley, and he left out a few other details as well. But then Becca asked a question that brought nearly everything into the open.

"You'll be able to pay the tickets, won't you? I mean, they won't lock you up if you pay them."

They wouldn't lock him up in the regular course of things, but there was something more that she didn't know. He said as carefully as he could, "I can pay the tickets. Grand'll help if I ask him. But there's something more."

"What?"

"Derric Mathieson. There's this thing between me and him."

"What thing?"

"A Hayley thing."

"Hayley Cartwright?"

"He's why we broke up. Her and Derric hooked up one night. I caught them at it."

Becca was silent for a moment as she took this in. She said slowly, "But he's only a freshman and—"

Seth shot her a scornful look. "Uh . . . like that's actually *important*? He's sixteen anyway. So is she. And big deal that she's a junior. It doesn't matter to Hayley. Lots of things don't matter to Hayley. Would it matter to *you* if that dude wanted . . . Forget it. Anyway, it's why me and her—"

The door flew open. Debbie Grieder stood there.

Seth dropped his arm from around Becca's shoulders. He put three feet between them as fast as he could. But he could see from Debbie Grieder's expression that this was too little, and it was way too late.

FIFTEEN

Debbie's face was flaming. Her forehead scar was a bolt of white. She came into the room like a tractor rolling over a field. She was talking in a fierce low tone because there was an occupied room to one side of Becca's, but there wasn't any need for her to shout because her expression was doing the shouting for her.

Becca had not returned the AUD box earphone to her ear, so she flinched from the assault of Debbie's whispers. They blended in with Seth's whispers and with what they both were saying aloud. The result was chaos in Becca's head. She dropped her gaze to the floor, which only made her look guilty.

"What's going on?" Debbie demanded. "I said no sleepovers."

You've been here . . . you think I don't know . . . how it starts and then . . .

"I said no boys."

Always happens like . . .

"You and I had an agreement and you're violating—"

Lying . . . they always lie . . .

"Mrs. Grieder, it's not what you think."

You've been here . . . who you are . . . you think I don't know . . .

drugs involved . . . like you he was . . . the struggle . . . not this time . . . boys get up to . . .

"How many more girls in this town are you going to try—"

"Me? Hey, I'm not trying anything. I just came by to—"

Totally bananas . . . whoa . . . control . . .

"Show me that cell phone. You show me that cell phone."

Control it . . . remember . . . God grant me . . . crazy . . . Saratoga Woods like always . . .

"You said you were taking that dog for a run. Well, where's the dog now? You tell me. Where is he?"

"Gus? He's with Hayley. When the cops showed up, I asked—"

My God . . . in the forest . . . that's where the drugs . . .

"Cops? Police? What've you been up to? Hayley didn't work out for you, so you're after *her*?"

"I'm not after anyone, Mrs. Grieder."

Stay cool, stay calm, she's flipping . . . not here . . .

"So why are you here? And why aren't *you* saying anything, Becca King?"

Because, Becca thought, because because. Because the words were flying around the room like banshees howling for someone's soul. Because she couldn't tell whose thoughts were whose. But most of all because she couldn't take her eyes off the floor, and the reason for this was that she couldn't move her gaze away from Seth's shoes. He was wearing the same sandals he'd had on each time Becca had seen him, but she'd never seen the soles before now. Now she saw them, though, because of how he was sitting, and the sight of them and what they looked like and what that meant froze her in place.

Becca couldn't look away and what she really couldn't do

was reply to Debbie's question. But then it didn't seem to matter because Debbie went back to Seth.

"So why are you here? And where's that cell phone you were so hot to deliver? Or is this a different kind of delivery? What've you brought with you? Show it to me." Then she began flying around the room, a witch looking for her regular mode of transportation. Only she was opening and closing drawers and doing the same to the closet and looking under the beds and—

Not here . . . oh man . . . not again . . . not like this . . . for God's sake . . . where it always ends . . . just like Sean . . .

"Okay, okay," Seth cried. "The cops have her cell phone. I wanted her to know. I figured she'd start looking for it, so I came to tell her. All right?"

But *cops* and *cell phone* and *this this this* and *what've you done* and *liars . . . liars just like Sean* were bouncing off the walls just like balls in a children's blow-up house. Becca felt them driving into her brain and knew that she was going to vomit if she didn't stop them.

She cried out, "It's Derric. It's *Derric*. He got pushed off a trail in the forest this afternoon, in Saratoga Woods. Seth was there and I was there and the dog got lost and Derric got taken to the hospital. It's Derric, okay? It's *Derric*. I thought he'd fallen but someone pushed him and that's what happened."

Then she looked at Seth. He was reading her face, and she *knew* he was reading it, and his expression was both wary and scared. But he didn't know what she'd seen in the forest along with Derric's broken body, and she couldn't tell him. Not here, not now, and possibly not ever.

Seth said on a breath, "I'm out of here." He made good on his word. A moment after the door closed behind him, they could hear the sound of Sammy roaring away.

In the void left by Seth's departure, Becca could hear Debbie breathing. Her whispers came like gasps, like her breath. She caught *no way out not again mess up they use it's the erratic where everything happens*, but only after Debbie turned away. She went for the door saying she had to tell Josh what had happened to Derric. But then she paused before she left Becca's room.

She said, "I'm not running the No-Tell Motel for a bunch of high school kids. No more boys in here. Is that clear?"

Becca nodded and Debbie left her.

———

BECCA REALIZED FROM that moment that her time at the Cliff Motel could be terminated at the least provocation. She had no clue where she could go if Debbie threw her out, but she had a feeling that she might need to start looking for a place. She was also worried that Debbie might betray her at South Whidbey High School, but she decided she had to let that one go. If things got hot over there, she would just have to leave school.

Monday morning after the scene with Debbie, Becca was rolling her bike off the motel porch when Debbie came out from the office. Becca hadn't yet put the AUD box on, since the ride to school usually had no whispers attached to it. But the sight of Debbie made Becca's insides quiver, so she fumbled for the AUD box and slipped the earphone into her ear as Debbie approached.

Debbie said, "I'm sorry about the other night. I shouldn't have done what I did. I shouldn't have talked like I did."

Becca tightened her hands on the handlebars of her bike. She wasn't used to adults apologizing. She said, "It's okay. I understand."

"That's just it, you don't. How could you?" Debbie glanced back at the office. Soon it would be time to take the kids to school, so they needed to keep their conversation out here brief. Still, there were things that had to be said and Debbie was the kind of woman who knew this since she'd had long experience of saying them, marked by the years since she'd taken her last sip of beer. "There are things from the past that I shouldn't let affect me. Sometimes I forget and they do. None of this is your fault. I shouldn't have unloaded on you."

"It's okay." Becca wished she *hadn't* put the AUD box on because now Debbie's expression told her that there were whispers here that might have helped her to understand what was going on. Something, for sure, because as usual when it came to personal stuff, Debbie lit up a cigarette.

She said to Becca, "You've got to stay away from Seth Darrow, darlin'. You just need to trust me on this. I *know* him. There are parts to Seth . . . You just need to stay away, okay?"

"Grammer!" It was Chloe at the door to the office. She saw Debbie and Becca in conversation and said, "Why'n't you come for breakfast today, Becca? We had pancakes and sausage. Why'n't you come?"

"It got too late," Becca called. "I gotta get to school."

"You'll be late too if you don't skedaddle," Debbie said to her granddaughter. "Why've you still got your jammies on?"

"Josh hid my undies."

"You tell your brother if he doesn't hand over your undies, he'll be wearing mine on top of his clothes."

Chloe laughed and darted back inside the office. They heard her calling out her brother's name as she went.

Debbie said to Becca, "I can get your cell phone back for you. I know the undersheriff fairly good."

Becca knew that couldn't happen. Debbie going after the phone would lead right back to Becca. A trail meant questions. Questions meant answers. She said, "You don't need to bother. It was a throwaway with only about one minute left on it. I was going to dump it in the trash, and I probably just dropped it in all the excitement."

"You want me to pick you up another?"

Becca shook her head. There was hardly any point. The phone she needed was the phone the cops had, which was the phone with her mother's number on it. It was also the phone that she couldn't allow near her at this point. Her eyes got blurry, but she blinked hard and fast. She said, "That's really nice of you, but it's okay. I don't really know anyone to call."

Debbie cocked her head. She said, "You know *me*, darlin'. What happened the other night . . . I'm really sorry."

BECCA RODE TO school as fast as she could. It was mostly level, so the going was easy, but she could still tell that she was getting better on the bike every day.

She was close to the first school on the route when she saw a flash of white to her left, across the road. It caught the corner of her eye, and she turned her head to see what it was, so buried in all the dark greens of the forest. Thus, she encountered the white deer. It was there for an instant, standing like a marble statue in the middle of a rutted driveway. Becca gasped at the sight and braked her bike. White deer. A buck. He was watching her.

Then he was gone, in a simple leap that effortlessly took him into the trees. So quick was he that Becca thought she might have imagined him. A bit of sunlight through the branches, perhaps. An old sheet hanging from a limb, maybe. On the other hand, she did *know* it had been the deer, and she recalled what Josh had told her about it. Seeing the white deer meant change was coming.

At South Whidbey High, she coasted into the parking lot. She heaved her backpack onto one shoulder and started for the six double doors that would put her next to the new commons.

A sheriff's car passed her. She ducked her head. A cop coming to the school could have meant just about anything, but after what had happened to Derric, Becca knew a cop's presence wasn't going to be good.

She turned the AUD box off and pulled the earphone from her ear. The whispers, she figured, might help her know what was going on. They were everywhere, prompted by what the other students—along with Becca—had just seen.

Cops . . . someone's in for it . . . out of it . . . do with Nyombe . . . homecoming dance . . . God he's so hot . . . what I want is . . . Aaron's got a bean . . . Courtney's having a cow . . . I would've if he'd asked . . . don't know his leg or . . . bummer . . . a chance with her now . . .

Becca pulled one of the six doors open. Inside, the spoken words and the whispers were pretty much the same. Six girls sat at one of the tables in the new commons, two of them crying. Four boys in letterman jackets walked by, talking earnestly to a coach. Students stood around gossiping, their expressions concerned. Then Tatiana Primavera walked by, heading in the direction of the administration office in her stilettos. She looked like someone with Important Things to do.

Then: "Were you there or what?"

Becca knew who was speaking before she turned to see Jenn McDaniels.

"Seth Darrow was there, so you had to've been, since him and you are so *tight*."

Jenn had come into the new commons behind Becca. For a girl so petite, she managed to make herself seem like a force of nature ready to do what forces of nature do: explode, howl, destroy, flood. Becca heard the gutter words in Jenn's whispers. She wondered how often Jenn said them aloud.

"He's in a coma." Jenn sneered, and added, "Make sure you tell Seth. Or did he tell *you*? Bet he's *totally* happy now."

Becca realized from this that Seth hadn't said a word to the police or to anyone else about her presence in the woods. Diana Kinsale had also known she was there, but there was something about Diana that suggested she wasn't going to betray Becca's presence either. She said, "A coma? Derric? What're you *talking* about?"

Jenn laughed harshly. "Oh like I don't *know* what you've been after since you saw him."

"Seth?"

"Don't be stupid, fattie. And have you looked in a mirror lately? Like you *ever* could have a chance with Derric."

Before Becca could answer, an earsplitting screech silenced everyone in the new commons and a voice came over the PA system. It said, "This is your principal, Mr. Vansandt," and he announced that all the students were to proceed to the big theater for an assembly. It would start in ten minutes.

The students began moving from the new commons into the big corridor where the six double doors marked the entrance to the school. They didn't go outside, but rather went left and were soon disappearing around a corner. Interestingly, though, Jenn McDaniels didn't go with them. Rather, she headed past Becca in the other direction. She gave a hard push upon her shoulder, saying, "Ex*cuse* me, Fatbroad," and she went the way Tatiana Primavera had gone.

INSIDE THE THEATER, the students jostled each other to get to seats. Up on the stage, a lectern stood. There were chairs on either side of this, four on one side, three on the other.

Becca became part of the jumble of people, but her mind was completely on what Jenn had told her. She didn't know what a coma meant exactly. She knew that people survived comas, but she also knew that sometimes they languished in comas for years and never came out of them at all. Or if they did come out of them, it was ten years later and they woke up to a different world.

She didn't want this for Derric. She wanted him well and

rejoicing, the way he kept telling himself to rejoice and the way his smile suggested to other people that he *was* rejoicing because they couldn't feel the rest of him, which was sunlight but which was sadness as well.

Becca thought about Seth and what Jenn had said about him, how he'd be happy to hear about Derric in a coma. She also thought about the fact that Seth hadn't mentioned her to anyone but especially he hadn't told the cops that she'd been there and that she'd made the phone call to 911. Then her thoughts switched to Diana Kinsale, her dogs, Seth's dog, and the *nothing* that came from Diana Kinsale when everyone else filled the air with whispers. And finally, because she couldn't avoid it any longer, not with Derric now lying in a coma, she thought of that footprint at the top of the bluff. It wouldn't have been there when the paramedics had finished with the site. Getting Derric up the bluff to the trail would have taken care of that. This meant that Becca was the only one who knew about that footprint unless Diana Kinsale had seen it as well.

But she couldn't think of this. She wouldn't *let* herself think of this.

She found a seat in the middle of a row. There, she ducked her head and dug in her backpack for her Eastern Civilization book. Mr. Powder had told them there was going to be a quiz, and even having one of his students in a coma in the hospital wouldn't stop Mr. Powder from holding firm to *that* plan. So she could study. It would occupy her mind.

She didn't get far. Someone tapped a microphone and said, "Is this on?" and she looked up to see Mr. Vansandt standing at the lectern.

He wasn't alone. There were six other adults on the stage with him, and since they were staring ahead into the audience of students who suddenly fell silent, there were whispers although they were very brief. Becca caught *one of these little losers* and *look at me, Dave* and *what was he doing there* and *my job my job* and *lawsuits come from this kind of* and *don't really care look at them*, but anyone could have been the owner of the whispers. One person, even, could have owned them all.

Mr. Vansandt asked them all to stand and pledge allegiance after which he made the grave announcement that everyone was expecting. He told them that one of their fellow Falcons had been badly injured in Saratoga Woods. Most of them knew him, he said. Derric Mathieson. He said that Derric was in intensive care at Whidbey General up in Coupeville. He was in a coma and he had a triple fracture of his leg, too.

At this, murmurs went around the room and a girl in the crowd wailed "Oh no!" dramatically. Becca focused hard on what was going on on the stage. Mr. Vansandt was talking about all doors being opened and extra counselors being brought on board and how they would be there for the entire week for any student who wanted to talk. He introduced them one by one. Tatiana Primavera was one of them, of course, but the other names were all new to Becca. She dismissed them as soon as she heard them because it was fairly clear that more was about to happen on the stage since the one person left to be introduced was a man in a deputy's uniform.

The principal was concluding his remarks by telling everyone where each of the new counselors would be stationed that week. He added that a classroom would be open each lunch hour for group talk. Then he concluded by saying that Derric's father would like to talk to them now about the part they could play in Derric's recovery because, he added, "Derric is a Falcon and this is one Falcon who's *going* to recover."

It was at this point that the man in the sheriff's clothes got up and went to the microphone. It was also the moment when Becca realized that Derric Mathieson's adoptive family was white.

SIXTEEN

Becca recognized the man. The lights shining onto the lectern were brighter than the lights on the chairs set around it, so while he was still sitting among the others on the stage, she hadn't given him any more attention than went with knowing he was someone from the sheriff's office because of his uniform. But when he walked into the fuller light on the lectern, Becca saw that he was the man Derric had been with on the ferry.

His face was like something carved. Becca knew in an instant that he was the source of the *what was he doing there* that she'd heard jumbled among the other whispers inside the theater. What seemed to be coming from him now sounded like *please God . . . punish . . . I swear . . . not because . . . black black black . . .*

His expression was so hard that it hushed the crowd of kids, especially those who were still reacting to the news about Derric's injuries. The silence that fell over everyone made their whispers soar upward. Becca caught snatches of them only, disjointed words like *what's with . . . scary . . . is there . . . ever . . . does he think . . . like dead? . . . coma . . . Derric Derric . . . something new . . .* Along with these whispers came a flutter of feelings, like birds high up near the ceiling among the lights. All of this made Becca look around her. What she noted gave her pause. For unlike her schools in California, there didn't seem to be a single kid in the entire assembly who wasn't white.

Then she understood at least part of the whispers. Derric's father was wondering what sort of mess he'd created in bringing a black son to a place where he would probably never fit in. *Raisin on Wonder Bread* was what his whisper actually seemed to call it.

Becca wanted to stand up in the audience, then. She wanted to tell Derric's father that he was wrong. She wanted him to know that that wasn't even what people were thinking, that the only whisper in the theater declaring *black black black* was coming from Mathieson himself.

He began to speak. He said that Derric's mom was with him at the hospital and he was getting very good care but he sure could use everyone's good thoughts and prayers. Then he went on in a different tone, one that was firm with a meaning that he didn't need to make explicit. He said that there were things that had happened in Saratoga Woods while Derric had been there, things that needed to be looked into. He said he was hoping that *anyone* who had been there that day would be willing to come forward at the end of the assembly and sign a sheet so that they could be talked to individually.

"No one's in trouble." Mathieson peered over the lectern into the audience. "*No* one's in trouble." But his whispers said *only you and when I know who you are I swear to God* while he concluded by telling them that the sheet would also be available in Ms. Primavera's office for anyone wishing to sign it privately. Then he shifted his weight with a shift in his topic. He said, "I know a lot of you also want to do something to help Derric. Here's what it is."

Then he nodded to someone sitting in the front row in the audience. Jenn McDaniels rose and walked up the steps and onto the stage.

———

JENN WAS CARRYING a clipboard. She strutted to the lectern. She seemed to be enjoying her moment of importance. To Becca, she was exactly like a high-tension wire, filled with energy but lethal if you got too close.

Jenn said into the microphone, "Okay, here's the deal," as if they were talking about a business transaction. "We need people up in Coupeville with Derric as much as possible because, like, the doctors are saying that one of the ways to bring him back is going to be to talk to him and to read to him and to play him music and whatever else. And this is where this comes in." *This* was her clipboard, which she held up for the other students to see. "I'm organizing our part of the deal to bring him back, and here's how it'll work."

A little buzz went around the theater as students spoke quietly to one another. Jenn kept talking. Up there, Becca figured she wouldn't be able to hear them. What she also definitely wouldn't be able to hear was the louder buzz that accompanied the students' murmurs. This was their whispers, and they were mostly about what Derric's father had said versus what he probably meant. These whispers began to fight with their murmurs, which made a whirlpool out of the air. Everything seemed to switch, to be about Derric and Jenn and Jenn and Derric and what it meant that Jenn was up there on the stage ordering everyone around because *who's she think . . . what's the story . . . geez you can only tell . . . so obvious . . .* The very atmosphere in the auditorium became hot and swirling for Becca as the real murmurs and the accompanying whispers were joined by questions from the audience, which then were joined by *sue the whole place . . . on my watch . . . Dave Dave please . . . job on the line . . . you made this happen . . .* And then one of them came through so loud that it might have been shouted on a megaphone and this was *know when we trace that cell phone to whoever used it . . .*

Which was the last whisper that Becca heard before she fainted.

THE NURSE'S OFFICE turned out to be just down the hall from the registrar. Two senior boys carried Becca there, which was more embarrassing for her than having fainted in the first place.

The nurse had seriously bad coffee breath, but at least she was nice. She told the boys to set Becca down on the narrow bed and she put her hand on Becca's forehead. She said, "You're burning. We'll need to call your mom. I don't think I know you. What's your name?"

"Becca King. But I'm okay. I've got a test this morning and—"

"Nervous about that?" The nurse plopped a digital thermometer into her mouth.

Becca didn't want her temperature taken. She didn't feel hot. On the contrary, she was so freezing cold that her teeth were chattering. She said, "I'll be okay in a minute. I freaked out because of the stupid test."

The nurse tucked a blanket around her and said, "Sit tight. Keep that in your mouth. I need to get your information." Then she left the room and went in the direction of the registrar's desk.

Becca felt panic on its way. There was *no* information to be gotten from the registrar. Beyond that little problem, she'd been meant to keep her head below the radar on Whidbey Island, and so far she was failing at this. First making that cell phone call from Saratoga Woods, then running away from the woods when the cops were on their way, and now this. Feeling light-headed was one thing. Fainting in the presence of the entire student body of South Whidbey High School was another.

She wanted to leave the nurse's office, but she knew that could make things worse. She decided she had no choice but to wait, see what would happen next, and plan how to bluff her way out of trouble. What happened next surprised her, however.

The nurse returned. Shaking her head, she said, "Ms. Ward says she's got the lock stuck on her K filing cabinet, if you can believe it. She should have filled out a card for you, but she's behind in her work. Well, aren't we all?" She went to a desk. She took out the slim volume that was the island phone directory and said, "You're lucky you happened to faint today. I get shared with the middle school, so if you'd fainted tomorrow you'd be flat out of luck." She flipped the phone book open. "You're Debbie

Grieder's niece, I understand from Ms. Ward. I know Debbie. You belong to her brother?"

"Sister," Becca said, recalling Debbie's words to Ms. Ward.

"Oh!" said the nurse and knotted her eyebrows thoughtfully.

"Anyway," Becca said quickly, "I'm feeling okay now. I c'n go to class." She took the thermometer from her mouth. The nurse came over, took it from her, carried it back to the light. She studied it and said, "Uh-huh. Looks like you're fine. You were awful hot, though."

"Yeah. I didn't eat breakfast this morning. I think it was that, the test, and the heat in the theater."

"You *need* to eat breakfast. You girls. Always trying to lose weight." The nurse's face got altered to an assessing look. "Is that what you're doing? Are you avoiding breakfast because you're losing some weight?"

Becca only wished. She said, "As if."

"What d'you mean?"

"Look at me. I know that I'm fat."

The nurse set the thermometer down on her desk. *What the heck* was in her movements even if it hadn't burst between them. She came back to the bed and told Becca to stand. She eyed her, held her wrist, circled her fingers around it, delicately pinched the flesh of her arm. She said, "Where on earth did you get the idea that you're fat? You've just got a big frame. It's called being full bodied. Believe it or not, it's the way women were *intended* to look at one time. All you need to do with what you've got is to distribute things. You exercising, dear?"

"Riding a bike every day."

"So give that a month. You'll be in fine shape. Meantime,

here. Take this." She brought an energy bar out of her pocket and handed it over. "And don't skip breakfast again, okay? Hang on a second. You'll need a pass back to class."

The pass in hand, Becca headed out. The way took her past the school's main reception desk, where Hayley was once again seeing to phones. Jenn was there, too, with her clipboard in hand, and she was giving the sign-up list to Hayley. This prompted Becca to pause and to say, "I'd like to sign up to visit Derric, too."

Hayley looked up. She smiled and said, "You're Becca. I remember from your first day. That's real nice of you to want to help out. Because you're new here, and everything."

"Derric showed me around. I have Eastern Civilization with him. And Yearbook."

"*And* she's totally hot for him," Jenn added with a roll of her eyes. "As *if.*"

Hayley handed the list to Becca and Becca signed beneath Hayley's name. She avoided looking at Hayley, recalling what Seth had said about her and Derric. All the time, she tried to ignore the gutter whispers that were coming from Jenn. It was difficult to do. They were stronger than ever.

She handed the list back. Jenn snatched it like someone who's having their kidnapped baby returned. She stalked off while Hayley said quietly to Becca, "He's a nice guy. I can understand why you like him."

It was a kind thing to say, and Becca could tell that Hayley was sincere in saying it. The words made her wonder, though. Was Hayley hooked up with Derric or was she not? Becca wanted to talk to the older girl, even though, like before, a strange form of sadness came off her like the scent of fading violets. But she had to get to class because the teacher was Mr. Powder, who was going to look at her pass from the nurse and do the math on how long it would have taken her to walk from the nurse to his classroom.

Jenn waylaid her just outside the administration office. She said, "Let's walk together to class, okay, Beck-*kuh*?" She accompanied this with more gutter whispers about Becca's size and the clothes she was wearing.

On top of everything else that morning, this was finally too much for Becca. She fumbled in her pocket for the earphone to the AUD box, and she shoved it into her ear. The AUD box was where it always was, on the waistband of her jeans, and she felt for the volume nob and turned it up full blast. The static obscured what Jenn was thinking, but it did nothing to hide what she wanted to say.

"Thought I'd fill you in on something before you buy your wedding dress, Beck-*kuh*. I hope that's okay with you 'cause I hate to destroy your dreams."

"Whatever," Becca said.

"Good. Smart, too. 'Cause one of the cheerleaders—a chick called Courtney—is after Derric and everyone knows it. And between her and you, who do *you* think he'd choose?"

SEVENTEEN

Jenn McDaniels or no Jenn McDaniels, Hayley Cartwright or a cheerleader called Courtney, Becca was determined to get to Coupeville in order to see Derric.

School wasn't the same without him. She missed the safety she felt when he was near. She missed the warmth coming off him and the scent that seemed to hang in the air around him. She missed the way that he was special to her in a manner that other boys had never been special.

The intense interest in Derric's condition faded after a few days at the high school. Other things rose to take the place of what had happened in Saratoga Woods. Football games and pep rallies distracted the other students. Homecoming was hanging out there in the near future as well. But these things didn't concern Becca. She didn't expect to be asked to homecoming, not with how she looked. She wasn't exactly dating material these days.

She hadn't seen Seth Darrow since the night that Debbie had come upon them in room 444. Ever since then, Becca had done what she could to soothe Debbie's concerns about her hanging around with Seth. She'd gone to school, come home to the motel, done her homework, played with Chloe, tried to reassure Josh about his Big Brother's condition, and cleaned the rooms of departing guests. But having committed herself to helping Derric in his recovery, she had to get to Coupeville where the hospital was, and she figured Seth was her best way to do that.

She remembered what he'd told her about the place called South Whidbey Commons: It was where kids from Langley tended to hang out.

Some days after Derric's father had spoken to the assembly, Becca went in search of Seth. She'd finished her work cleaning the rooms of departed guests, and she popped into the motel office to tell Debbie what she was off to do. Debbie wasn't there, so she left a note. She was careful to tell her the full truth of the matter: She was finding Seth Darrow to see if he could take her up to Coupeville and show her where the hospital was. He could also show her where to catch the bus so that when it was time for her to sit with Derric during his recovery, she'd be able to get up there to do so. Then she left the motel.

South Whidbey Commons sat on Second Street, a converted cottage that did quadruple duty as a coffeehouse, a secondhand bookstore, and an art gallery, as well as a gathering place for young people. It was painted the color of mustard, with tables and chairs in its front garden.

Inside, Becca found Seth in the farthest back room, playing guitar. He was accompanied by another boy on the mandolin. A third played bass. They were very good, creating a complicated kind of music similar to that which Becca had heard that day on her way to the woods with Seth. It was a cross between jazz and flamenco, and she hung back listening. Seth saw her and nodded hello. When their piece was finished, the three boys talked, their heads together. They scribbled a few notes on their music and then agreed "to meet at Mukilteo Coffee tomorrow for another session." They high-fived each other and packed up their instruments.

Becca sat down next to Seth. Some of his hair was loose from his ponytail, and he shoved this roughly behind his ear. He said, "Hey. What's happening?"

"You guys are *good*."

Seth looked pleased. "It's Django Reinhardt," he reminded her. "Gypsy jazz. What're you up to?"

She told him what she needed: a ride to Whidbey General Hospital and someone willing to show her where to get the bus that would take her there later on and bring her back to Langley. She asked him if he had the time to help her out, and he said, "Sure. Give me a couple minutes."

She said, "I've got money for the gas," and she brought a crumpled five-dollar bill from her pocket.

He said, "No big deal. Put your money away."

She said, "Where's Gus?"

He shook his head. "My granddad's still got him."

Seth packed up his music and folded the music stand. He put his guitar in its case and slid the room's furniture back into place. When he got up to do this, Becca saw that he had on his feet those sandals that he always wore, and her insides lurched a little at the sight of them. She still hadn't seen any sandals like them on anyone else's feet. This worried her, but she shoved the worry aside.

They went to the parking lot of the Star Store, where Seth's

ancient VW stood in well-polished splendor. On their way to
the car, Becca told Seth about the school assembly although all
the time she was thinking about what he had said about Hayley
and Derric. She kept waiting for him to add more to what he'd
already told her, but he said nothing. There were whispers coming from him, to be sure. Unfortunately, they seemed determined to be about Gus. Seth missed Gus. He wanted Gus back.
He didn't know how to convince his grandfather to hand Gus
back to him.

They were about to get into the VW when Becca heard her
name shouted joyously. She turned and saw Debbie Grieder
approaching, with Chloe hanging on one hand and Josh on the
other. Chloe had been the one to shout. Debbie released her, and
she danced over to Becca.

She said, "We're going to Sweet Mona's! We get to choose ice
cream or a chocolate, don't we, Grammer?" She turned to Debbie.

"You do." Debbie eyed Becca, then Seth, then Becca again.

"We got our flu shots over at the clinic," and here Chloe waved
vaguely in the direction of the public library, "and Grammer said
after we'd get to go to Sweet Mona's. You want to come?"

Becca was having a difficult time tracking all this because of
the flood of everything else she was hearing. Sharpness was all
around her in the form of *he's used that's what . . . stop to this
before things get worse . . . playing a head game . . .* which smashed
against *messed-up chick* and *Sean* and *what's her problem* and
out of luck. She couldn't contend with the whispers and the talking, so she broke into both by telling Debbie about the note she'd
left her at the motel

When she mentioned Derric's name, Josh's eyes grew large.

Could he go, too? he wanted to know. "I want to see Derric," he told his grandmother. "Please? *Please?*"

"Too young, Joshua," Debbie said not unkindly. "They wouldn't let you in, darlin'. But Becca'll tell you how he is when she gets home. Tacos tonight," she added to Becca. "Hope you can make it."

Becca said that she'd definitely be there. She didn't expect to be gone that long, just up to Coupeville and back. She added, "What if I stop and get something for dessert?" as a try at firming up Debbie's opinion of her.

Debbie said, "Sure, that'd be nice. We'll see you later, then."

Debbie didn't move off with the kids, though. She seemed to be waiting for Seth to get into the car. When he did, she spoke again, her voice low so that only Becca could hear her. "Just be *careful.* Please. You don't understand who this boy really is."

———

THEY WERE ON the main highway and heading north toward Coupeville before Becca decided to say something to Seth about Debbie's final words to her. She asked him directly why it was that Debbie Grieder didn't like him.

He reached down for the heater knob of the old VW and he cranked it open. The days were getting colder now. This one was also looking like rain.

"Drugs," he said. "She thinks I'm into them. Because of Sean, her son. I used to know him. He taught me chess. He also dropped out of school like me. So . . ." Seth shrugged.

"He's the one in prison," Becca said. "Josh and Chloe's dad."

A quick glance from Seth. "Debbie told you *that*? That part about prison?"

"The kids said something. Isn't it true?"

"It's true all right. Makes sense that it came from the kids and not Debbie. It's pretty rough stuff for a mom to talk about."

"What'd he do?"

"Flipped out on meth and assaulted a cop trying to get him into a patrol car. Practically strangled him. Went down for attempted murder. He's doing hard time." Seth slowed the car as someone ahead slam-braked for three deer crossing the highway. They'd emerged out of a mass of bracken, where the forest grew right up to the edge of the road. "That's another side of Whidbey Island," Seth said.

For a moment Becca thought he was talking about deer and their sudden appearance in front of a car. But then he went on.

"Sean got into meth a year after high school. Before that, he was fine. He did some weed and he drank a little, but nothing serious. Till meth. Made him someone he completely wasn't. Well, that's what meth does."

"How'd you find out? I mean, about the meth?"

"Told you before. Sean taught me how to play chess. At South Whidbey Commons."

Becca wondered about this relationship that had existed between Seth and Debbie Grieder's son. She wondered what it meant about Seth as anyone might have wondered when a connection to a methamphetamine addict is brought up in casual conversation.

She said to Seth, "Did he . . . did Sean want you to do drugs, too?"

He frowned. "I'm *not* a meth freak, if that's what you're thinking. I may *look* stupid to you, but I'm not an idiot. And I don't do drugs."

"Sorry. I didn't mean . . . It's only that when someone drops out of school . . ."

Seth punched the steering wheel lightly. "Learning disabilities, okay? I've got them from A to Z and school was hell. Dropping out had nothing to do with anything else." He shook his head. "Let me tell you, I do *not* get why people think . . . Forget it."

Hayley . . . Hayley was present the entire time he spoke, though, and the soreness of her name was a bruise of sound.

This reminded Becca of what Jenn had said. There were scores of things to be found out here in this car with Seth Darrow, and because of *Hayley Hayley* Becca wanted to know them. She wasn't sure how to go about this, though, so she began with, "I saw Jenn McDaniels the first night I got to the island. She was on the ferry. I think she was with some stoners."

"Like I'm surprised about that? There's one chick with serious issues. She needs to get a life."

"She said something the other day . . ." Becca went for the truth in a rush. "She told me that one of the cheerleaders has a thing for Derric and that everyone knows it. So I sort of wondered if what you said about Hayley and Derric hooking up . . . ?"

Utter silence. Not even a whisper. Becca went on. "Anyway, I remember you told me that you and Hayley broke up because she and Derric . . . ?"

"What about them?" *This your business, chick?*

Becca swallowed. That one whisper came through loud and clear. She nearly answered him. "So I was wondering something." Becca hurried on before he could say anything in reply to that. "Maybe they never hooked up at all. Could you have been wrong?"

His head jerked in her direction. His eyes were narrow. "And exactly why do you want to know this stuff, Becca?"

Seth usually sounded laid-back, but with this question he sounded rough. He sounded sinister, in a way. Becca looked out the window at the passing scenery. She thought about the sandals he wore and the soles of those sandals, and she thought about what she had seen and what the sight of a single footprint in soft earth could mean about the boy she was with.

She finally said, "I don't know. I s'pose it doesn't really make any difference. Just that sometimes people make a big deal out of stuff that turns out to be nothing."

Seth shifted in his seat. "Yeah? Well, this wasn't nothing to me."

Becca wished that he had said something else.

EIGHTEEN

Whidbey General Hospital was on the main street of Coupeville, which dipped down toward the waters of Penn Cove. Becca discovered from Seth that it would be a two-bus ride to get to the place from Langley, and including the wait for the buses and the stops along the way, she knew it wasn't going to be easy to see Derric as often as she would have liked. That was one of the reasons she asked Seth for yet another favor when they arrived.

Would he give her a few minutes to run inside the hospital? She wanted to see how Derric was doing. Was that okay?

Seth said, "I'm easy," with a shrug.

She said, "You sure?"

He said, "Yeah. I'll wait for you here. The door's over—" He'd been pointing in the direction of the hospital, but something had caught his attention.

Becca looked to see what it was. As she did so *Hayl* brushed against her hair like her grandmother's fingers. She searched for Hayley Cartwright, but she saw that what Seth was looking at was a pickup truck. She recognized it from the logo on its door: SMUGGLERS COVE FARM AND FLOWERS.

As Becca got out of the VW, so did Seth. He said, "I think I'll go inside with you. Want something from the cafeteria?"

Becca didn't need a whisper to tell her he wasn't going into the hospital to get a snack. He was going in to find Hayley. She didn't see how anything good could come out of this, especially if Hayley was at the hospital because of Derric, but she didn't say anything except, "Think they have fruit? A banana or something? Here's some money." She handed over the cash she'd tried to give him for the gas, and this time he took it. Her hope was that he'd go to the cafeteria and not go on a search for Hayley.

Inside the hospital, there were too many people, which added up to too many whispers. Becca winced at the unexpected assault of noise and she set herself up with the AUD box.

She and Seth went to the reception desk, where they asked a heavyset woman where they could find Derric Mathieson's room. The woman put a hand on her heart, and she smiled at them winningly. She said, "I have just *got* to say it. This is a real fine thing you kids're doing for that boy and his family." She shook her head with one of those looks that said wonders would never cease, and she picked up a clipboard and handed it over. She said, "Just check your name off. The undersheriff wants to keep track."

Becca saw that the clipboard held a copy of the sign-up list that Jenn McDaniels had devised. She also saw that the next name on the list was Jenn's own. That told her that her visit to Derric was going to have to be very brief since the last thing she wanted was to be there when Jenn showed up. She'd chosen her own particular visiting day precisely because Jenn McDaniels *wasn't* going to be there.

She checked off Jenn's name and handed the sign-up sheet

to Seth. He glanced at it, glanced back at her, then checked off the name beneath Jenn's. It was Terry Grove, a convenient AC/DC name. He flashed a smile at the receptionist and handed the clipboard back to her. She told them where they could find Derric, and she said she hoped they'd brought something to read to him. "Reading's best," she said. "The sound of voices is what's important, but sometimes when people get with a patient who's unconscious and hooked up to machines, they run out of things to say pretty fast."

"We'll do okay," Becca said. "We've got lots to tell him."

They were on their way to Derric's room when they saw Hayley. All three of them stopped in their tracks. Hayley got sunburn red, and Becca heard Seth swallow something that sounded like a piece of concrete going down his throat.

"Hi," Hayley said. She looked from Seth to Becca to Seth.

Seth said, "What's happenin', Hayley," and drove his fists into the pockets of his jeans.

Becca said hello and reached for her AUD box to turn it down. If any whisper was going to help her know what to do next, she wanted to be ready to hear it. But all she got was *more lying . . . nice . . . Hayl* and then *understand is what* before Hayley spoke.

"Going in to see Derric?" She was looking at Seth but Becca answered.

"How is he? Is anyone else here?"

"His dad just left to talk to someone. You want to go in?" Like the receptionist, Hayley gave the room number. Still she looked at Seth, so he was the one to reply this time.

He said, "I'll wait. You go ahead, Bec."

Becca knew he meant to talk to Hayley. She didn't think this was the best idea in the world, but she also knew there were times when you couldn't stop people from doing things no matter how crazy you thought their plan was. So she left Seth as he was approaching Hayley and Hayley as she was holding up a hand as if to tell him to keep his distance.

Becca didn't turn the AUD box back on as she entered Derric's room. Because of this, as the door silently closed behind her, what she noticed at once was music. At first she thought it was coming from a speaker in the ceiling. Then she realized that it felt like something surrounding her because it was actually inside her head, just like a whisper because it *was* a whisper, a swelling of sound that was coming from Derric.

As she approached the bed, the music got louder. It was brass music, Becca thought. Saxophones, trumpets, trombones, a tuba, drums. All of them were hesitantly playing but the sound grew more assured the closer Becca got to the boy in the bed.

Derric was perfectly still, a contrast in hues. The sheets, the pillows, the blankets were white. The bandage on his head was white. But his skin was bittersweet chocolate, and this single color was broken only by the muted pink of his fingernails, clipped short to his fingertips and smooth like the inside of seashells.

He was hooked up to an IV drip, its connection taped down to his arm. He had a tube through his nose and a monitor attached to his chest to keep track of his heartbeat. But he was breathing on his own.

His lips were chapped. They looked painful. Becca wished she'd brought some lip balm with her. She knew he probably couldn't feel the hurt of them, but she didn't want him to suffer anything that she could do something about. She hated to be so useless to him. At least, she thought, she could talk to him.

She said hello. She said, "It's me, Becca King, from school." And then she understood the receptionist's point. What *do* you say to someone who was somewhere between life and another place?

She cast about for something to say. She looked around the room. That was when she first became aware of the flowers, the balloons, the cards, the stuffed animals, an old letterman's jacket hanging on the back of the door, the map of Africa pinned to the wall.

She went to this. She saw that Uganda had been highlighted in blue marker and that three little flags were pinned to the country. One stuck out of Kampala, with "Derric" written on it. One said "Mom" and the other said "Dad." These two were close to each other but some distance from Kampala, and Becca figured they marked the places where Derric's African mother and father had been born.

She went on to look at some of the cards strung around the room. She pulled on the strings of the balloons. She read the messages attached to the flowers. She wondered what it was like to be so popular. She'd had a small group of friends in San Diego, but nothing like this. Finally, she realized that she'd come empty-handed to see Derric, with nothing at all to leave him that would show her affection for him on the chance that he would suddenly awaken.

She realized that, despite her feelings for him, she had no actual place in his life. She was the new girl at school and the rest of the kids represented by the cards and the flowers and the balloons all shared a long history with Derric. But still she wanted to be a *part* somehow, and she wished she had something. . . . She drove her hands into her jacket pocket to see if she had anything, even a stick of gum.

Her fingers made contact with a piece of paper. She brought it out. She saw that it was the phone number that Derric had given to her on her first day at school: his name, the number, and that was it. She turned it over and grabbed a pencil from the bedside table. "Give this back to me when you're well," she wrote. Instead of signing her name, she put the letter B. Then she reached for his hand to place the slip of paper into his palm.

Something strange happened as her fingers touched his. The music altered. It became fast and high and it suddenly sounded like a whole band of professionals playing. Along with the music came *rejoice rejoice* and Becca knew this was Derric's whisper as his mind expanded over that one word.

She felt a surge move from his hand to hers. It was like a wave, but unlike a wave it didn't recede. It remained just there, sweeping between them, and Becca recognized it as joy. Pure happiness, she thought, and because she felt it, too, she didn't want to let go of Derric. It had been so long since she'd felt so flooded by peace.

She looked at his face. She searched it for some kind of meaning to attach to what he was feeling, and she was sure she found it in his sweet chapped lips. For they moved slightly and he seemed to smile, and she looked from his lips to the crescent of white where his eyes didn't close completely.

She wanted to enter there. It would be so pleasant to drift

for a while inside his head. But the whispers didn't give her that kind of access. Only this brief contact of her fingers with Derric's would do that for her.

But there was also a problem. No matter what he was feeling and no matter how much she wanted to feel it as well, Becca knew that Derric was in the dark place of coma. He needed to emerge from this, returning to the world of the people who loved him. Yet she knew for certain that he didn't want to. And without wanting to return, he would remain where he was.

"No," she said to him. "Derric, you can't."

Will was the whisper. *Rejoice. Will.*

———

BECCA WENT TO find Seth. She wanted someone to tell her what to do with what she'd learned in Derric's room, but she knew the only two people who could do that were the two people unavailable to her. They were out of range in the most profound way. Her grandmother was buried and Laurel was in possession of a cell phone whose number Becca did not have.

She found Seth in the lobby of the hospital. He was talking to Hayley. From across the room Becca could see that their conversation was heated. They were sending out no whispers. This was because they were saying their whispers, which was bad in the extreme. "That's what we mean when we refer to thinking *before* speaking, hon," Becca's grandmother would say. "Don't ever do both at once."

Well, Seth and Hayley were doing both at once, and that wasn't going to lead anywhere good.

Becca went over to them. It was time to save Seth, even if she couldn't save Derric. She said to him, "Hi. I'm ready to go," pretending that she didn't have a clue that he and Hayley were arguing.

He said, "Give me a minute, okay?" and then a whisper came from one of them. It sounded like *don't make me* and Becca wanted to say, "Don't make you what?" but she didn't. Instead she said, "Okay. I'll wait over there," and she pointed to a plastic philodendron across the room, a safe distance from them. Seth didn't answer and neither did Hayley. They were too intent on each other.

Becca went to the chair next to the plastic plant. But then the worst thing happened. Derric's father came into the lobby. He wore his undersheriff's uniform, and he wasn't alone. Jenn McDaniels was with him. They saw Seth and Hayley, and they walked over to them, and that was Becca's one piece of luck.

The last person she wanted to be known to was the undersheriff of Island County, no matter that he was Derric's father. She couldn't afford to be on his radar while Jeff Corrie was an unresolved problem in her life.

She couldn't leave the lobby without being seen if she tried to make it out the front door of the hospital. So she ducked back into the bowels of the place. There had to be another way out, she told herself. All she needed to do was to find it as quickly as she could.

She ended up in the emergency room, bursting through the

doors like someone being chased. All of sudden, sounds came at her. They were whispers and words. They were everything at once.

Someone was howling behind a curtained cubicle. Someone else was shouting "My head, it *hurts*," a loudspeaker was asking for "Dr. Shapiro, Dr. La Rue," and with all of this flying at her like paintballs being shot from a gun, Becca could barely breathe and she certainly couldn't think. She only knew she had to escape, and she saw a glass door in the distance. She dashed for this and made her way, thankfully, outside.

———

THERE, SHE FELT like someone having an asthma attack. It took a while before her chest loosened enough for her to get sufficient air. When she felt somewhat normal once again, she looked for the bus stop. She couldn't rely on Seth to take her back to Langley. With the undersheriff there, with Jenn probably causing trouble, with Hayley on his mind . . . Who knew how long it would be before it occurred to Seth to look around for Becca and wonder what had happened to her.

The bus stop was across the busy main street that dipped down into the center of Coupeville. Becca made for this, hurrying across in advance of an oncoming vehicle. This was a pickup truck, and it honked twice sharply, as if whoever was driving it was expecting to run Becca over if she didn't get out of the way. The truck pulled to the curb, too, and for a moment Becca thought the driver would get out and lecture her about the dangers of jaywalking. But then Becca saw the dogs moving in the bed of the truck and the shape of another dog in the passenger seat, and at that same moment the driver opened her door, and she got halfway out.

Diana Kinsale called, "Hello there, Becca King. I've seen you more often in the last few weeks than I've seen people I've known for thirty years. What are you doing in Coupeville? You didn't ride your bike here, did you?"

Becca approached the truck. The dogs in the bed all crowded over the side to greet her, a mass of wagging tails. Inside the truck Oscar blinked a dignified poodle hello. Diana said, "Do you need a ride to Blue Lady Lane again?"

Becca told Diana she wasn't going to Blue Lady Lane but she was indeed going to Langley. Diana told her to hop in. "You'll have to share the space with Oscar again." The poodle was belted in as usual. Diana unhooked him and moved him over. "Where to, then?" she asked as she pulled back into the traffic.

Becca told Diana that she was staying at the Cliff Motel with Debbie Grieder. She thought about adding the fiction that Debbie Grieder was her aunt but she stopped herself. The first night she'd met Diana, Becca had been heading to Blue Lady Lane. It wouldn't make much sense that she would have been heading there if Debbie Grieder was her aunt.

Because she was alone in the truck with Diana and because she didn't have the AUD box turned on, Becca should have picked up at least part of a whisper from Diana in reaction to what she'd just told her. But as before, she picked up nothing. Becca considered what this could possibly mean beyond what she'd learned from her grandmother, which was that no whispers meant someone was dead because *everyone* had whispers. "Even the Buddha had whispers," her grandmother would say. "The Pope has whispers, even Jesus Christ had whispers."

Yet her grandmother had been able to control them. So Becca looked at Diana in an entirely new way, wondering if she *knew* there were listeners in the world, people like Becca who would sense the thoughts of others.

Diana said, "How's that working out, then?" and for a moment Becca thought she meant "How's listening to whispers working out?" But then Becca remembered they'd been talking about Debbie Grieder, so she answered, "It's okay 'cause I help out around the motel. I like the kids a lot. Debbie doesn't like one of my friends, though."

"Which friend would that be?"

"Seth Darrow. He's who brought me up here this afternoon."

"Did he just drop you off?"

"He got involved in a conversation with this girl. Hayley Cartwright?"

"I know Hayley."

"They were talking in the lobby of the hospital—"

"Hospital? What were you all doing there?"

"I came to visit Derric Mathieson. I guess Hayley was there to see him, too."

"I see." Diana looked thoughtful. Becca could tell Diana knew something about something, but she didn't ask her what the somethings were. She thought about doing so, but it seemed impolite and none of her business. She looked out the window, instead, and she saw that the plains of Coupeville were fast giving way to forests as the pickup sped along the narrow highway.

Inside the truck cab, it was warm. The rhythm of the road was pleasant. Diana reached for the knob of the radio and turned on some music. Soon, Becca felt lulled. Oscar was so toasty against her shoulder, and because of all this, she grew quite drowsy. Soon she was asleep.

NINETEEN

A bump in the road awakened her. It was dusk now, but Becca could see they were pulling off a narrow lane and entering an even narrower gravel track that ran between two brick pillars shadowed by fir trees. Diana had switched her truck's lights on, and in their glow, Becca saw they'd come to a cemetery. There were tombstones aplenty, shadowy beneath enormous trees.

The little track curved, and they followed this curve to a section of the cemetery where there were fewer trees. Here, Diana Kinsale parked her truck. She said to Becca, "Got to make a quick visit to Charlie. Are you okay with cemeteries? Some people aren't."

Becca was more than okay with cemeteries. Since her earliest childhood, she'd been taken to them, once it had become obvious to her mother and grandmother that the whispers had skipped a generation in Laurel's case and had descended with double force into Becca. "She'll calm down here," was how her grandmother had put it as she'd hoisted Becca out of the car. "You just think that Paul Revere poem, and she'll ignore it and I'll go blank and she'll be fine." Off Becca would go among the graves, then, and she'd hear not a single whisper for once.

Becca said to Diana, "I like cemeteries."

Diana said, "So do I. So do the dogs. I'm letting them out for a run."

She lowered the tailgate of the pickup and the dogs scrambled out and away among the graves. Diana took a couple of potted white chrysanthemums from the truck bed, asking Becca to bring along a small metal tool case as well. Then she walked over to a grave where a stone bench faced a granite marker with CHARLIE KINSALE, BELOVED LIFE'S COMPANION carved into it. He'd been dead a long time, Becca saw from the date, but his stone looked new. She saw why this was when Diana set the potted plants down and opened her toolbox. From this she took rags and polish. She set to work.

When she had finished, Diana fixed the chrysanthemums on either side of the stone. She went over to a spigot for some water and watered them thoroughly afterward.

She said to Becca, "I'd plant them, but they'd never last. Took me a while to understand they're not intended to. Here. Sit with me on the bench for a minute." She went to the stone bench and patted it. She called, "All dogs come," and from various points in the cemetery, the animals came running.

The dogs milled around her feet, nosing her pockets for treats. She dug out some kibbles and handed them out. Tails wagged encouragingly. Diana said, "Charlie's been gone for years, but I still miss him. You do, you know, when someone dies."

The idea of missing someone was like the swooping of a bird too close to her face. Becca felt a kind of agony along with it. She longed for her mother so strongly that her eyes filled with tears and she knew they'd spill over, and she'd have to explain them if that happened. She got to her feet abruptly and walked out into the cemetery, just to the point where Diana's headlights ceased illuminating the graves.

Diana came after her. She put an arm around Becca's shoulders. "I've upset you. I didn't intend to," and at her warm touch Becca felt unburdened for the first time since she'd futilely phoned Laurel from Blue Lady Lane.

She said, "It's okay. I'm fine. I better get going, though."

"Let me show you something first. It won't take long."

She led Becca back the way they had come on the gravel track, dipping into some cedar trees at the far edge of the cemetery. Here, there was another grave and its stone had an angel perched on it. It was the kind of gravestone that a picture can be fit into, and Becca could just make out this picture along with the words on the stone—TERESA GRIEDER—and that she'd been fourteen years old when she had died.

Becca said, "Oh," and next to her Diana said quietly, "This is the source of everything that Debbie feels. It's the one thing she would change in her life if only she could."

"Seth told me she was killed on her bike," Becca said. "But Debbie told me Ms. Ward over at the high school killed her."

They both gazed at the stone. From the dates upon it, Becca could see that Reese Grieder had been dead for fifteen years.

Diana said, "They're both telling you the truth, Seth and Debbie. But like everything else, there's more to it than a bicycle, Reese, and Ms. Ward. There's a deer, too. It leapt out into the road in front of poor Reese and in front of the car. Ms. Ward veered to avoid the deer. And Reese veered to avoid the deer, too.

But they veered toward each other and Reese was hit. She wasn't wearing her helmet."

"How terrible," Becca said.

"If Debbie could do anything in her life differently from what she's done, she'd go out after Reese. She thinks she should have been able somehow to make things different."

"No one can do that really."

"That's the truth of the matter," Diana agreed. "There are no do-overs in life. We can't change what's happened, no matter what we do."

Becca saw that the grave was unkempt. The gravestone had lichen growing on it. This filled her with even more sadness, and Diana said as if realizing this, "Debbie can't bear to come here, and no one wants to mention to her that the stone's going bad because of the weather."

She linked her arm with Becca's. They turned and headed back toward the truck. Diana said, "Sometimes, we can't see a reason for what happens, so we try to find one because it's easier to do that than to go through the pain of recovering. That's one of the things that people do."

PART THREE

The Dog House

TWENTY

Hayley Cartwright knew that Seth Darrow would never be able to understand their breakup. He made it all about Derric because of his own insecurities. But the truth was that their breakup had very little to do with Derric at all.

Seth thought otherwise because of a night when he was supposed to be playing a gig with his trio over in Lynwood. He'd gotten there only to discover with his friends that they'd been double-booked with a Seattle group called Paranoid Amber, and this had put him into a mood. Hayley couldn't blame him. He'd bought a ticket for the ferry, gone over town, showed up as scheduled with the other members of the trio, only to find out someone had made a mess of things.

On his return to the island, then, he ducked into Langley's performing arts center. The marquee out in front said that a troop of Rwandan dancers and musicians would be performing, and since Seth was all about music, he had decided to peek inside.

The usual suspects were there. These were South Whidbey's ageing hippies who came out of the woodwork any time music and dance were involved. Derric and Hayley had been among them, dancing. They'd gone to this concert for reasons having nothing to do with dating. Instead they'd gone for reasons having to do with what Hayley wanted to do with her life and with where Derric's own life had begun. Not in Rwanda, of course, but in Africa. From the expression on Derric's face during that evening, Hayley could see a happiness that she'd never seen in all the time she'd known him.

But Seth had witnessed none of this. All he took note of was Hayley with Derric, who was tall, nice looking, incredibly built, sexy, an A student, and an athlete. Aside from the mutual interest they shared in music, Derric was, in short, pretty much everything that Seth was not. He was also pretty much everything Seth thought that every girl wanted and that *he* ought to be.

At the end of the dance, she and Derric were laughing because they were both wretched dancers. But so was nearly everyone else on the stage, except the Rwandans. She and Derric swayed in a hug, the way people do when they're having a wonderful time. Then they kissed. It was a spontaneous thing, with Derric's hands cradling her face and her arms around his waist.

Seth saw this, but he didn't confront her. Instead, he took off, and she hadn't even known he was there until the end of the evening when Derric walked her out to the farm truck in the parking lot. They stood there talking, and they kissed again, and she liked the kiss. But that was the extent of it: She liked kissing Derric Mathieson. Period.

What she didn't know was that Seth was watching from his VW. Dimly, she heard a car start, but until it pulled up next to her, the truth was that she hadn't thought about him at all. But then a voice said, "Great going, Hayl," and Seth shot Derric one of those looks that tend to suggest someone has just stepped in someone else's vomit. After that, he gunned the motor and took off.

She'd phoned his home the next day to explain and asked his mom to have him call her. When he didn't, she called him three more times. The third time being the charm, she'd caught him still in bed and she'd asked his mom to wake him up. When he was finally on the line, she said, "So are we finished? Is that what this is about?" and he'd said in his typical Seth way, "Whatever, Hayley."

How lame, how stupid, how totally weird, how completely insane had been her immediate reaction. She'd kissed Derric Mathieson. She liked kissing him. She might kiss him again if she had the chance. Big deal. End of story. But it was a story Seth Darrow didn't even want to hear.

She told herself that if that was the case, Seth Darrow wasn't worth the time spent thinking about him. She turned to school for comfort and she found that comfort in the jazz band, in the marching band, and in hanging with Derric. They weren't boyfriend and girlfriend but they were close friends and mostly they talked about Uganda and what he remembered of Uganda. They did this because of Hayley's plan: the Peace Corps in Africa.

Her mother didn't agree with the plan. Her father didn't know about it. There were far greater worries than where Hayley was going to go as soon as she was old enough to do so, and her father was worry number one. So as far as her mother was concerned, it was a case of, "We aren't going to talk about it, Hayley," and that was life at the Cartwright farm. There was so much that they weren't going to talk about that most of the time what they did talk about amounted to the weather and who was going to do what to keep the farm going another week while pretending everything was A-OK.

Hayley was tired of all this. Seth, of course, didn't know about any of it. So when she'd run into him at the hospital up in Coupeville, things had gone from bad to horrible.

They were broken up, so it was *none* of his business that she was there, and she figured her being there in the first place was what he wanted to talk to her about. So she'd prepared herself to say that, as far as she knew, they weren't together any longer so if she wanted to drive up to Coupeville, it wasn't up to him to ask her about it. But it turned out he'd wanted to talk to her about Saratoga Woods because she'd told him about parking the farm truck down the road at the entrance to Metcalf Woods where no one was supposed to park at all. Unless, of course, they had a *reason* to park there, that reason having to do with not being seen.

What Seth had known was what everyone knew. To get from Metcalf Woods to Saratoga Woods involved a complicated hike. You had to know where you were going or you had to have a map, but in either case it didn't make sense to go into Saratoga Woods that way.

So what Seth said to her at the hospital that afternoon was, "Why'd you hide your truck by Metcalf Woods? You were meeting him there, weren't you? Is this supposed to be some big secret between you two? Because it *isn't*, okay?"

She said sharply, "I don't have secrets, Seth," and of course this was an outright lie.

Their argument went on from there. It became about Derric. It went on to Seth's dropping out of school for his music. It shifted to his grandfather taking Seth's dog. Then it made its way to whether Seth had even *bothered* to get a tutor yet to help him study for the GED since he'd been out of school since the previous January. It was one of those arguments that turn out to have no real starting point and no real ending point, just a lot of pain generated and a lot of forgiveness needed to get past it.

But there was no time for forgiveness, because in the middle of their argument, Derric's dad came into the hospital along with Jenn McDaniels. Jenn went over to the reception desk to check in on the list while the undersheriff came over to Hayley and Seth. He said hello to Hayley and he nodded to Seth, who mumbled something about being really sorry he hadn't paid his speeding tickets on time. The undersheriff couldn't have cared less about speeding tickets, and Hayley felt like telling Seth this, but then Jenn McDaniels came over to them, said, "That stupid list is *already* screwed up and I'll have to fix it," and then took the temperature of the Seth/Hayley/Undersheriff Mathieson moment and knew in that Jenn McDaniels way of hers that something somewhere was wrong. Jenn cast a shrewd look from Hayley to Seth to Hayley to Seth. For sure, she knew they'd had a fight. That could mean trouble, Hayley realized.

———

SETH PRETTY MUCH disappeared after that, which was fine with Hayley. She didn't want to talk to him any longer, since talking to him was pointless. Instead, she went with Undersheriff Mathieson to Derric's room while Jenn went back over to the reception desk to rescue her all-important list of visitors and to figure out how it had gotten messed up.

In Derric's room, the undersheriff approached the bed with something like reverence. Hayley held back respectfully. The undersheriff touched Derric's forehead in a tender way and said, "Come on, little man. Time to wake up now," and the term *little man* seemed strange to Hayley because Derric was not only over six feet tall, he was also taller than his father. Still, she could tell it was a term of affection and Dave Mathieson had probably called Derric that from the first moment he'd seen him.

Then the undersheriff bent and kissed Derric's forehead, and he took up his hand to hold it. He uncurled Derric's fingers and something fell out. From where she was standing not too far from the door, Hayley saw it was a piece of paper.

Dave Mathieson read the note aloud: "'Give this back to me when you wake up. B.'" His lips curved and he said, "Ah, kids," and he put the note back into Derric's hand. What Hayley thought was that B would be Becca. Give *what* to Becca? was what she wondered.

Then Jenn McDaniels came into the room. She said, "Someone came here actually *pretending* to be me, if you can believe that. It was right after you, Hayley. Did you see anyone?" and she acted as if a crime had occurred.

Hayley figured that Becca had been the one to do the pretending. Once again, who else could it have been? But she wasn't about to tell Jenn McDaniels that. She didn't know what *any* of it meant, that Becca hadn't signed her own name, that she'd come more or less on the sly, and that she'd put a strange note into Derric's hand. But one thing was for sure: She intended to find out.

The undersheriff said to Jenn, "Sounds like the kids are enthusiastic about coming up to see him. Let's hope they stay that way. Meantime . . . I'd like to talk to you girls about that day in the woods. Come with me, okay? Let's have a Coke."

———

"EITHER OF YOU have a cell phone?" was what the undersheriff asked them. He'd taken them to the cafeteria where instead of Cokes he'd bought an enormous brownie for them to share, along with three small cartons of milk.

Hayley thought Dave Mathieson wanted to make a call. She knew that there was virtually no way Jenn would have a cell phone. Her family was so poor that they were lucky to have shoes. So she reached for her purse.

She said, "I have one. My mom just got it for me because—" But the *because* of it all couldn't be spoken: the need to contact Hayley because something bad might happen on the farm. The undersheriff didn't know that and he didn't need to know.

"Where is it, Hayley?" The undersheriff sounded a little sharp and this took her by surprise, but Hayley dug the cell phone out of her purse. She said, "Mom decided she'd like to be able to get in touch," which was not a lie. Lots of mothers liked to be able to keep tabs on their kids.

Undersheriff Mathieson took the cell phone from her and turned it over in his hands. He said, "This wouldn't be a replacement phone, would it?"

She said. "No. Why?"

"Because we're tracing a cell phone that was left in Saratoga Woods, in the information shelter at the edge of the meadow."

"Someone must've lost it," Jenn said.

"Someone hid it. Ralph Darrow found it. It's a throwaway phone, but we're on its trail. People don't generally know how easy they are to trace."

He was watching Hayley's face as he spoke, but Hayley was stuck on *Ralph Darrow found it* and how Ralph Darrow led to Seth. Thinking this, she didn't say anything but she didn't have to because the undersheriff went on, his eyes plastered to her face.

"Those phones all have serial numbers, Hayley. Serial numbers lead to the stores that sold them. Stores that sold them lead to the days they were sold. Days they were sold lead to credit card receipts or to the closed-circuit films of buyers. It takes some research but it's only a matter of time, which is all that police work is, really. A matter of time." He cocked his head at them. Still, he kept his gaze fixed on Hayley. He said, "So eventually we'll find out who bought the phone because that's the girl who made the call to nine-one-one about Derric. She knows something about what happened. And what happened is what I want to know."

What happened that day is Derric falling because he slipped somehow, was what Hayley wanted to say to the undersheriff. But she could tell that he thought it was something else. The only other thing it could be was Derric was pushed, shoved, or thrown from the path. She didn't want their conversation to head in that direction.

Undersheriff Mathieson said, "What do you two know about that day in the woods? What were you doing there?"

Jenn went first. She said she'd been there for a run with some other kids who were getting ready for the South Whidbey triathlon. They'd been over in Putney Woods where there were more trails and a circuit had been marked, but when they heard the sirens they crossed over on Coral Root Link. She added that they'd parked on Lone Lake Road and started their run from there. It was easier because there was a parking lot there, whereas if they'd gone in another way, like on Keller Road, they'd have had to park on the shoulder, and since they liked to hang out after the run, the parking lot on Lone Lake Road was . . .

Hayley wondered if Jenn knew how guilty she sounded. She was determined not to sound the same way. She prepared herself mentally to respond to the question that came her way in about one minute: "What about you, Hayley?"

She'd taken her little sister Brooke to dance class in Langley, she said, and rather than drive all the way back to the farm, she'd just gone to the woods for a walk till the dance class was over. She could've walked around the village for ninety minutes, she supposed, but she'd been in the shops about a thousand times so she decided to go to the woods for a while.

The undersheriff said, "Were you there to meet Derric? You can tell me, Hayley. I understand how things are with boys and girls sometimes."

She could feel the fire on her skin, turning her red. Her answer was the only one she could give without ending up unraveling most of her life. So she said, "I was alone because it was only ninety minutes," which, of course, didn't mean a thing at all. She just felt she had to add something more, and the only other thing to add would have been a full explanation. For Hayley, a full explanation was out of the question. No one knew what was going on, and she fully intended to keep things that way.

TWENTY-ONE

Diana Kinsale drove Becca back into Langley in the kind of silence that old friends travel with. This felt good to Becca.

The ride wasn't long. When they pulled up to the motel, Debbie came out of the office. But she did it so quickly that it was clear she'd been waiting.

She came off the porch just as Becca opened the pickup's passenger door. Becca caught *what in God's green earth . . . this is how you repay*, but she heard nothing else because Diana got out and spoke.

"I've brought your assistant back from Coupeville," she said. "How are you, Debbie? I haven't seen you for a while."

Debbie didn't answer Diana. Instead, she said to Becca, "You've been gone for hours. You said Seth was taking you to Coupeville just to show you the bus routes and the stops."

"Yeah. He did. Only he got into a conversation with his old girlfriend and I could tell—"

"So he just *left* you to fend for yourself?"

This, Becca knew, was another black mark against Seth. She said, "It wasn't like that. I saw Mrs. Kinsale while Seth was talking and she offered me a ride."

"But you've been gone ages. I was worried about you. Anything could have happened," and the whispers that came in a rush with this were *with him . . . drop out . . . happen when drugs are . . . pain takes such . . .*

Becca wanted to cover her ears. She wanted to say to Debbie that she—Debbie—was not her mom, so she needed to stop worrying about her. She also wanted to say that Debbie didn't really know Seth so she had to stop thinking such bad stuff about him, but on the other hand the truth was that Becca didn't really know Seth either.

"I'm awfully sorry," Becca said. "I guess it was a little dumb of me."

Diana said, "It's part my fault, Debbie. We stopped at the cemetery so I could visit Charlie. I do apologize. Anyway, it's good to see you. I'd love to get together with you sometime. Useless Bay Coffee, maybe? When you have the time?"

Debbie said, "Sure," although *not a chance* was as obvious from her expression as it was from her whispers. As was *think . . . bring her back . . . oh right*, which came through the air like pellets from a BB gun.

It all made Becca very tired. She said thanks to Diana and took a few steps toward room 444. But Debbie's words stopped her as Diana pulled out of the motel parking lot.

"I get that you didn't bring dessert. But you forgot about the tacos, too? Chloe and Josh have been waiting for you."

BECCA WENT BACK with Debbie to her apartment. She found Chloe and Josh on the sofa, shoulder to shoulder, watching an old video of *Survivor*. "Grammer has them all on tape," Chloe announced. "We like it best when they have to eat bugs."

"Or snakes," Josh added. "We like it when there're snakes, too." Then he scooted off the couch and asked anxiously, "Did you see Derric? Is he coming over to play?"

Becca touched his shoulder and gave it a squeeze. "I saw him for a minute, is all," she said. "He was pretty much asleep, but I think he'll be over to play again. Just not yet."

"Oh," Josh said, and his voice was small.

"I thought you wanted tacos with Becca," Debbie said to him. "She's here now. Don't you want to eat? What about you, Chloe?"

"Tacos!" they cried at once. They dashed toward the kitchen with a "C'mon, Becca!" which gave Debbie a chance to ask quietly, "How is he, then? I wasn't sure what to tell Josh."

Becca said, "He's still in a coma," and when Debbie nodded sympathetically, Becca felt a little better about things. But then *serves him right . . . what did he think* came right after that nod, and Becca felt those whispers like a slap against her cheek. She blinked and turned away. But *then* Debbie said, "Poor kid. I'm really sorry to hear that," and the strangest thing to Becca was that Debbie sounded completely sincere. So she was either lying or *serves him right* referred to someone else. And that, of course, was the problem with whispers.

Then Debbie sighed. She said, "Well, I don't know how you feel about cold tacos, darlin', but if you want 'em, we got 'em," and when Becca approached her on the way into the kitchen, Debbie put her arm around her shoulders and gave her a quick hug.

That hug made Becca want to say something to Debbie about having seen her daughter's grave, but she knew this was dangerous territory. Still, she felt bad that maybe Debbie was stuck somewhere, waiting to change the fact that her daughter had died when that was the very last thing that would ever be possible for her to do.

She said, "Mrs. Kinsale stopped at the cemetery on the way back to her house. She wanted to put flowers on her husband's grave. She had the dogs with her. They were running all over the cemetery."

"Those dogs of hers." Debbie sounded cautious, but she wasn't angry. Becca figured it was safe to go on.

She said, "I was chasing them around to catch them. I saw your daughter's grave."

The wall *whooshed* into place. Becca's ears were hit with what felt like a pressure change of *that helmet* . . . and *she knows.* Then *no no no* came like the wind, the way it blew off the desert into San Diego, that ruthless and dry Santa Ana wind that withered everything in its path.

Becca said, "That's a really pretty picture of her. The one at her grave."

Debbie said, "We can heat the tacos in the microwave."

TWENTY-TWO

Seth Darrow brooded about his argument with Hayley for almost a week before he finally decided that he had to talk to someone about it. In that time, he did what he always did. He worked his early-morning job at the Star Store, he rehearsed with the trio, and he hung out at South Whidbey Commons. He avoided his parents and the potential for questions about what he was doing to find a tutor for the GED. But none of this took his mind away from Hayley.

"Got to move on, favorite male grandchild," was what his grandfather would have said. But Seth was finding it completely impossible to do that. So after a week of brooding, he was ready to talk. To someone. About anything.

The best person for this job was his grandfather. Plus, Ralph still had Gus, and Seth was ready to get his dog back. So he drove over to the property on Newman Road.

Ralph was out in the garden up on a stepladder. He was deadheading his massive collection of rhododendrons, dropping the dead flowers onto the soil beneath the enormous shrubs.

Gus had been snoozing on the front porch of the house, but he'd obviously heard the car and recognized it. For as Seth began his descent into the garden, Gus bolted in his direction. He barked and leaped and licked Seth's cheek.

Ralph said nothing during the reunion between Seth and his dog. They rolled on the lawn together, and they ran in circles, and Seth brought Gus's ball out of his pocket and he began to throw it.

Ralph said, "You're undoing his training. That tendency of his to bolt . . . ? It'll be trouble if you don't stay consistent with him, Seth."

"He's good if there's a ball involved. Or food. He'll do anything for food."

Ralph shook his head. "Leave him for now. Make yourself useful. Move this ladder for me."

"Where d'you want it?"

"Grandson, where d'you think I want it? In front of the next rhodie, for God's sake."

Ralph sounded irritated, but Seth knew he wasn't. Fighting with the garden was part of his joy. Still, Seth said to him, "Don't you ever get tired of doing all this?" in reference to the size of the place and its wealth of plants. "I mean, everything here just keeps getting bigger and you keep getting taller ladders and where's it going to end?"

"With my death, I guess," Ralph responded. "Tough to outlive a good rhodie." He shoved his hand into his pocket and brought out a Butterfinger. He broke it in half and handed part over to Seth. "Love these things," he said. "They get stuck in your teeth and you can enjoy them for the rest of the day."

They worked on their candy for a few minutes while Gus snuffled around their feet. Ralph gestured over to part of the garden hill where boulders formed a retaining wall and greenery tumbled. He said, "Those wretched old plants over there didn't bloom all damn summer. I've been babying the things for five years now and there's not a single bud on them. Damned if I know why."

Seth looked around. "I don't know why any of this blooms, to tell you the truth."

"It blooms because I take care of it. I do the same darn thing to that stuff on the wall, but nothing happens. Which is the story of gardening in a nutshell, I guess. Sometimes you win and sometimes you lose and most of the time you don't have the slightest idea why."

Seth reached down and scratched Gus's ears, but he glanced at his grandfather. He knew Ralph wasn't really talking about the garden. He said, "Grand, I did everything I could to show Hayley love, and she *still* picked him over me. She disrespected me—"

"Not a verb, grandson. Let's not make it one just because the rest of the world's trying to."

Seth sighed. "She *showed* me disrespect by wanting to be with this guy who'll *never* care about her like I do. It makes me . . . I need to do something about it and I don't know what."

Ralph took another bite of his Butterfinger. He looked not at Seth but at one of the rhodies. He said, "You sure about all that? You have the measure of all other people, Seth?"

"Didn't say I did. But what I need right now is for Hayley to be on *my* side, Grand, and she's not."

"And your side is what?"

"I need her to be okay with what I decided to do. About school, I mean. She *said* she would be when I dropped out. She said she understood how hard it was for me and how music was more important to me and how I wanted to make it with the trio and how *if* I could publish some of my pieces . . ." Seth kicked at the lawn. Gus, at his feet, rose in an instant. He dropped the ball and barked. Seth threw the ball as far as he could. It disappeared over the edge of lawn, heading in the direction of his grandfather's pond.

"That dog goes in the water and you'll have a mess on your hands," Ralph said. He used his tongue to move the Butterfinger around in his mouth, the better to enjoy it. He said, "Go on, then. What's this girl done to tell you that she's not on your side?"

"What d'you mean 'What's this girl done?' I just said. She's with *him*. We're finished, and when I show up at the hospital, she acts like . . . like whatever. Hell, I do *not* know."

Ralph nodded. He was wearing a baseball cap with his long gray ponytail sticking out the opening in the back. He took the cap off and made an adjustment to how it fit. Without the cap, his hair was flat against his skull. Seth could see the age in him when he was exposed like this, with deep lines in his forehead and around his eyes.

Ralph said, "That's just it, Seth."

"What is?"

"What you said at the end. You don't know. It's like that plant on the wall over there. I've done what I can do to make that plant bloom and it won't for now and I've got to accept it. Maybe it will bloom someday and maybe it won't and that's how it is."

"Hayley's *not* a plant."

Gus came running back into the garden, the ball in his mouth and his paws muddy. He'd been near the edge of the pond, but he hadn't gone in. There was a mercy in that.

Ralph said, "Grandson, you can't force love out of Hayley. You can try but, trust me, you're going to fail." He picked up the clippers he'd been using on the plant and shoved them into the back pocket of his jeans. He nodded at the ladder and said, "Catch that for me. I think I'm done out here for the day."

They carried the ladder to the gardening shed, which was tucked behind Ralph's house close to a grove of alders. It was too tall to fit inside the shed, but an overhang protected it and others from the weather. Seth set it there. Gus investigated it for interesting smells. Ralph spoke again.

"So why'd you really go to that hospital, Seth? You tracking this girl?"

"I didn't know she was there." Seth told him about Becca: who she was and how she'd needed to see where the hospital was and what buses to take to get to Coupeville. She'd asked him to take her, and he'd agreed. He hadn't known that Hayley would be there.

"So what happened to this Becca while everything was going on with Hayley?"

Seth dropped his gaze. "Damn," was his answer.

"'Damn' happened to her?"

"I don't know what happened. I forgot about her. I felt so wrecked after talking to Hayley that I took off."

"Hmm." Ralph took out an old cowboy neckerchief and wiped his hands on it. "Sounds like you were pretty darn miserable." When Seth nodded, Ralph said, "Got it," and headed toward the house.

Seth followed. Ralph paused and then did something unexpected. He put his arm around Seth's shoulders and guided him forward. He said, "Grandson, not everything in life is about you. If you can learn this now when you're eighteen years, you've got one of life's big lessons mastered."

"Fine. Okay. I know that, Grand. But I don't get what that has to do with Hayley."

Ralph chuckled. Then he did something more unexpected than putting his arm around Seth's shoulders. He kissed him on the side of his head. He said, "Throw that ball for Gus for half an hour. Wear him down so he'll give me some peace. Then take yourself over to the Cartwrights' place and say hi to Hayley's little sister, Brooke. I expect she's missing you."

"She's twelve years old!"

"I didn't say to marry her, grandson. I said to say hi. You can manage that."

———

SMUGGLERS COVE FARM and Flowers was a sweep of farmland north of South Whidbey State Park. Decades earlier, it had been carved out of a massive forest. When Seth reached the place, he didn't turn into the long driveway at first. Instead, he pulled to the side of the road and looked at the farm.

He'd always liked it. To him it was like something out of the nineteenth century, representing an ideal of what a farm should look like, with rolling hills, a pond behind the house, all the red buildings, a tractor parked somewhere, and four cords of wood stacked in a wood shelter.

As far as Seth was concerned, it was perfect. But Hayley had always pointed out that it was perfect to him because he didn't have to live there and do any of the work. She also thought it was completely ridiculous to have everything on the farm painted the same color of red. "More economical that way, my dad says," she'd said. "But gosh, you'd think we could at least make the *house* a different color."

Seth thought the house was fine as it was. He liked the way it sat off the road on a rise of land with the forest trying to creep up behind it. He also liked the fact that the long low chicken house was close to the road and across the side of it SMUGGLERS COVE FARM AND FLOWERS had been hand-painted in white a long time ago. The words were fading, and he liked that, too. The fading suggested permanence to Seth, and he liked to know some things would always stay the same.

He turned into the drive, which, like so many driveways on the island, was unpaved. Years and years ago, a hard pack of pebbles had been laid down, but over time the movement of cars and other vehicles over the hard pack had created tracks. Between these tracks and along their edges grew moss in the winter, creeping buttercup in the spring, and wild grasses in the summer. Autumn was a transition period. The rains began, and the ground waited for something to leap from it anew.

Seth jounced in the direction of the house. He passed the field where Mrs. Cartwright's horses grazed. He glanced over at them, but then he frowned. There were no colts or fillies with the mares, and at this time of year there should have been because part of the farm was used to raise horses.

The farm truck wasn't visible on the property. Nor was the family's old SUV. The truck was usually kept by the barn and the

SUV had a spot next to the house near a huge old maple, but now in the place of the SUV was a pile of wood. This consisted of the four cords that would see the family through the winter.

Usually the wood was stacked in the shelter. Mr. Cartwright always made a point of that, as soon as it was delivered. He also made a point of planting the enormous vegetable beds for autumn, but Seth could see that that hadn't been done. Along with the absence of colts and fillies and the pile of wood, Seth wondered what this meant. Mr. Cartwright's desertion of the family was the first thing he thought of. That would be bad.

It didn't look like anyone was at home, but Seth got out of the VW anyway. He went up the stone path to the front porch, and when he mounted the steps, he saw the shifting light and dark against the sheer curtains that told him someone was inside watching television. So he knocked.

Hayley's sister Brooke was the one to answer the door. She didn't hold it open for him to enter, though. She opened it only the width of her body and looked out at him to say, "Hi, Seth."

Seth said, "Hey. I was in the area. I came by to say hi."

"No you weren't," Brooke said. "No one's just in the area."

"Okay." He looked around, feeling caught. He said, "Hi, then," and added with a gesture over his shoulder, "Why're there no colts or fillies this year?"

"Mom didn't breed them. She didn't want the trouble."

"Why?" The trouble was the stud fees and the bill for the vet but after that . . . ? The Cartwrights needed money, and horses meant money.

"I dunno," Brooke said with a shrug.

"So's anyone home?"

"Just me and Cass."

"No Hayley, huh?"

"She's at special practice for jazz band."

"No Mom and Dad?"

"They're over town."

"Shopping or something?"

"I dunno. No one tells me anything." Brooke looked back into the house.

Beyond her, Seth could hear the television racket. Some sort of corny music was playing. He could hear Cassie laughing, so he figured she was in there glued to a cartoon, and Brooke was supposed to watch it with her.

She seemed really changed from the Brooke he'd known while dating Hayley. That Brooke had been a bubbly pest, a skinny twelve-year-old always wanting a ride in Sammy. This Brooke? One thing Seth knew for sure: She wanted more than anything to close the door on his face, but she'd been too well brought up to do it.

He said, "Hey, Brooke. Is something wrong around here?"

She turned back to him. "What d'you mean?"

"The wood's not stacked like usual. The vegetable beds are looking ragged. So I wondered . . . Everything okay? Nothing's going on, is it?"

She said, "Nothing's going on. I'm just watching Cassie, and Hayley's not home. Okay?"

He said, "I didn't come to see Hayley. Look, are you going to talk to me? Are you going to let me in or what?"

"Or what," she said. "I gotta go." She closed the door softly. It clicked like a sigh.

TWENTY-THREE

What with waiting for the two different buses to Coupeville as well as the stops they made along the route, Becca had time to do all her math and English homework before she reached the hospital. She was impatient to see Derric. This made the ride tedious, but the fact that the island buses were free made up for just about anything.

The sun was shining, but the temperature was plummeting on this particular day. As Becca approached the hospital entrance, across the parking lot a bank of trees tossed some of their leaves into the wind. Winter came early to this part of the country, with frost arriving hard on the heels of the last fallen leaf.

Inside the hospital, Becca raised the volume on the AUD box to block painful whispers hanging from the ceiling like bats. At the reception desk, she learned that the sign-in list for Derric wasn't there. "That little bit of a girl took it off somewhere with her," were the receptionist's words, telling Becca that Jenn McDaniels was here at the hospital, too. She didn't want to see Jenn, but she wanted to see Derric. She was going to have to put up with one in order to make the other happen.

Jenn was sitting outside Derric's door. Her face was screwed up into a knot, and she was copying the sign-up list neatly onto a new schedule. She said without looking up, "You're not *supposed* to write anything on this except your name. Then *when* you come, you're *supposed* to check your name off to show you were here." At that, she looked up and saw Becca. Her face grew more knotted. Becca was grateful that the AUD box prevented her from hearing Jenn's whispers.

Jenn said, "Why d'you keep coming here? It's not like you really *knew* him or anything."

Becca didn't answer. Jenn had said *knew* instead of *know* and for one sick moment, Becca thought Jenn meant that the worst had happened. She said, "He's okay, isn't he?"

"He's in a coma, stupid. I don't think that means he's *okay*."

When Jenn said this, her features looked like a coiled snake, and Becca thought this was too bad because Jenn was actually a pretty girl, otherwise. But she couldn't let herself be pretty because of rage, which rose inside her and filled her head, and Becca could feel it sweeping toward her. So she ducked into Derric's room.

Inside the room and away from Jenn, Becca pulled the AUD box's earphone out of her ear. She approached the bed. It was quiet in here, with only the sound of the monitor that told the doctors Derric's heart was beating strongly. Becca had heard at school that Derric was passing all the tests that proved he was alive and well inside his head. He simply wasn't waking up, and no one could account for that. She'd also heard that a specialist had come from Seattle, but they'd learned nothing more from him than they'd learned from anyone else.

She reached for his hand, with its long smooth fingers. She

enclosed his hand in both of hers and she gripped it tightly. She closed her own eyes and whispered, "Please, Derric," and then what came to her was sounds: the rustle of clothing, children's laughter, and a high voice calling Derrrrrrrrr-*ick* like a chant, over and over. More laughter followed and with it came the music from a brass band.

But there was nothing more, nothing for her to see or to understand. After standing at his bedside for several minutes, Becca finally released her hold on him, sat down as close to the bed as she could, and took a book from her backpack. It was the only book she'd brought from San Diego, something that she'd sneaked into her things. It was a clear and present danger to her because it was inscribed with loving words about imagination, words her grandmother had written to "my sweet Hannah" when she'd given it to her five years earlier.

Becca opened it and began to read to Derric, just as the other kids were doing when they came to visit. "'Mrs. Rachel Lynde lived just where the Avonlea main road dipped into a little hollow,'" she read, and she found herself doing what good books always made her do. She sank into the story of an orphaned girl named Anne Shirley and her life in a place called Prince Edward Island.

IT SEEMED TO Becca that she'd read for a long time when she heard someone enter the room. *Lucky boy* accompanied a nurse, who bustled to the IV drip and changed the bag, shooting

Becca a smile and murmuring, "Hope you all keep coming. It's important, you know."

Becca stretched and set the book on the bedside table. She saw, then, that something new had been added to the flowers and the silly stuffed kiwi bird that had been by the phone the last time she'd visited. A framed photograph faced Derric's pillow, and Becca picked this up. As the nurse left the room, Becca studied the picture.

The setting wasn't Whidbey Island. As far as Becca knew, there was no community of African children on Whidbey and certainly no group of African children who were in a brass band. But that was what the picture showed: a small brass band whose musicians were all children, and among the children was an unmistakable, grinning little Derric with a very large saxophone in his hands. The band was surrounded by laughing, smiling, clapping children, much younger than the band members. One of them had her arms around Derric's waist and another was perched on his shoulders. This was the case for the other band members as well.

Derric looked about seven years old, and his face was filled with so much joy that Becca reached for him, smoothed her fingers against his cheek, and grasped his hand in hers another time.

Rejoice . . . rejoice . . . rejoice. Becca understood what his whisper meant. His rejoicing came from the music he made and from the children who listened to it. She wondered if anyone was playing music like this—big brass music—when no one was there to read to him. She could *hear* it clearly, so she knew how important it was to Derric. She wanted to tell someone but there was no one present, so she let herself be taken by the music as he himself was, and with his hand in one of hers and the picture in another, she listened.

"He's all right, isn't he?"

The words made her jump. She dropped the photo instead of dropping Derric's hand as she had intended to do. The picture hit the floor and the glass shattered. She cried, "Oh no!" and she turned to see a woman in the room she'd not seen before.

The woman had long salt-and-pepper hair done up in a pony-tail, with wisps escaping from it and framing her face. She wore jeans, black-and-white Converse sneakers, and a hooded sweat-shirt that had MARINERS on its breast. She hurried over and picked up the picture. She said, "Whoops," and Becca said, "I'm *sorry*. I got freaked. I wasn't all here."

"No harm done," the woman said with a smile. "I can get another frame, and the picture's fine. I'm Rhonda Mathieson, Derric's mom. You must be Becca." *Strange for Derric* accom-panied the words but Becca didn't have time to think what the whisper might mean because "Oh yeah, she's Beck-*kuh* all right" came from the doorway.

Jenn entered the room. Her gaze went to the broken glass on the floor and she said, "Great. What'd you do *now*?" A string of nasty words made up the whispers that accompanied the ques-tion along with *string beans* and *minutes on the tanning bed* for some reason, which Becca assumed had to be coming from Derric's mom. She fumbled for the AUD box earphone and put it into her ear. Jenn's lip curled when Becca did this. Her eyes nar-rowed in speculation.

"Just an accident, Jenn," Rhonda said. "It's a picture frame. That's all."

But it didn't seem "that's all" to Jenn. It seemed like a major crime. Becca looked away from what was coming off the other girl's face, and she saw that Rhonda had turned to Derric. She wore such an expression of love as she gazed at him that Becca wanted to tell her that when she'd held Derric's hand, she'd been able to hear and feel what was happening with him. "He's totally *there* inside," she wanted to tell Rhonda Mathieson. But she didn't want to say that in front of Jenn.

Rhonda picked up the book that Becca had left on the bedside table. She said, "Were you reading *Anne of Green Gables* to him?" When Becca nodded, Rhonda said, "What a nice choice."

"I didn't really choose it," Becca said. "I mean, it sort of chose me." She glanced at Jenn and saw Jenn roll her eyes. She made a move to take the book back from Rhonda and stow it in her backpack, but the move came too late. Rhonda opened it and read the inscription. She looked up and, handing the book back, said, "Who's Hannah?"

"Dunno. The book was secondhand," Becca said, although she felt her face beginning to flame when she told the lie. But she was saved from any further questioning by the arrival of the next person on Jenn's sign-up list.

This turned out to be one of the cheerleaders from the high school, a perky girl with a Bible in one hand and a bunch of balloons in the other. She said, "Oh! Hi there!" And then she seemed to take a reading from the room, probably from the expression on Jenn McDaniels's face, which was no more welcoming to her than it had been to Becca. She said to Rhonda Mathieson, "I'm the leader of the prayer circle? Courtney Baker? I have sixty-seven kids in it?" in that way of talking that kids tended to use when they're nervous about something. "We meet at school and pray for Derric?"

"Rah, rah, rah," Jenn McDaniels muttered. She sauntered to the door and left the room.

The cheerleader got busy with the balloons and tied them to the end of the bed. Becca took the opportunity to say good-bye to Derric by touching his hand. The heart monitor raced suddenly. She looked from it to Rhonda.

Rhonda's expression said what her voice did not. *Who are you really and why is my son reacting to the touch of your hand?*

———

BECCA WAS STRUGGLING into her backpack out in the hospital corridor when Rhonda came out of Derric's room. Jenn had resumed her position by the door, where she had returned to the work of copying the sign-up sheet. Rhonda looked from Jenn to Becca and said, "Would you like to go into town for an ice cream?"

Becca looked toward the door of Derric's room. Rhonda said with a kind smile, "I think she'll be in there for a while. She said she's planning to read the whole book of Gideon to him. Jenn, you come, too, okay? It's time for you to take a break."

Becca saw that Jenn was looking like a girl who'd rather take strychnine than have an ice cream with Becca King. Becca eased the earphone from her ear in time to catch *has to that's what . . .* before the other whispers in the corridor from people passing began to overwhelm her. She replaced the earphone quickly and said, "That'd be great. Thank you, Mrs. Mathieson."

"Rhonda." Rhonda looked at Jenn and said, "Come, too, Jenn."

Out in the parking lot, Jenn made for the front passenger's seat, and Becca let her. She could tell it was important to Jenn to ride shotgun, and she herself was happy enough to climb in the back where she could go unnoticed and where the seat was cluttered with old copies of the island's newspaper as well as fly-ers for fund-raisers: a group supplying food to the unemployed, an animal shelter, an orchestra, a playhouse, a land conservation organization . . . Everyone on the island was looking for money. Good causes crawled out of every corner.

Becca had not yet been to the downtown of Coupeville, which sat on the far west end of Penn Cove. Like Langley, the downtown comprised only two streets, and cottages and Victorian houses climbed a hillside behind them. The buildings were quaint and colorfully painted, interrupted by a pier that stretched into the harbor with a wharf building sitting at the end of it, with the white letters C-O-U-P-E-V-I-L-L-E above a wide double door.

Rhonda parked in front of an old tavern called Toby's where a screen door was banging in the wind. She said, "Over there, girls," and she pointed across the street to four wooden steps. These led to an ice cream parlor. Inside there were three tiny tables, all of them vacant. It was getting rather cold to be eating ice cream.

Rhonda said, "Order up, ladies. I'm going for a banana split myself."

Jenn ordered a tin roof parfait. Becca wanted a strawberry sundae. But old habits are the most difficult to break and her old habit was "In through the lips and onto the hips," so she settled for a biscotti, only to see Jenn scowl as if her choice made her a goody-goody or something. Rhonda added a scoop of strawberry ice cream to Becca's order and said she wouldn't feel so bad herself if she had a partner in her own crime.

They were quiet for a bit as they ate their ice cream, and Becca couldn't help noticing that Jenn seemed content for the very first time since she'd met her. She took note of ice cream, chocolate syrup, and peanuts perhaps being the answer to appeasing the anger that coursed through Jenn's whispers like poison.

Rhonda dipped into her banana split and said, "*Anne of Green Gables* was one of my favorite books when I was a girl, Becca. It's perfect to read to Derric because, obviously, he was adopted just like Anne."

"He told me you came to his orphanage in Uganda," Becca said.

Rhonda explained that she had gone with her church group to help out at a mission that took street kids in. She said that there were thousands of children homeless on the streets of Kampala because so much of the adult population had been devastated by AIDS. She said, "We *think* that's what happened to Derric's birth parents but no one knows for sure. He was only five when he was found by the mission. He'd been living behind a bar in the city, with eight other children. They'd cobbled together a little shelter from cardboard and tin. The oldest child was ten. The youngest was not quite two."

Gently, Becca pushed the rest of her strawberry ice cream

away. Jenn continued with her tin roof parfait as if she hadn't heard what Rhonda Mathieson had said, but perhaps, Becca thought, Jenn knew the story and was used to it. She herself couldn't imagine becoming used to it. He'd been five years old, on the street, alone.

Rhonda said, "When I first saw Derric . . . Well, who could resist that smile? We adopted him, and it all worked out. Just like Anne Shirley being adopted by the Matthew and Marilla in your book, Becca."

"Except Marilla didn't want her at first."

Rhonda said nothing. She was thinking, obviously, but Becca couldn't pick up her whispers because she had the AUD box's earphone in her ear. Then Rhonda said with a quick smile, "No. Not at first. She didn't want Anne, did she? I'd forgotten that part."

Rhonda got up to go to the counter, where she said something about buying more biscotti "to take home to Dave." Becca then looked at Jenn for the first time since Rhonda had begun telling her story. Jenn, she saw, had finished her ice cream. She'd begun to simmer. Loathing was emerging right out of her eyes and Becca could feel its intensity.

She looked down and saw her own ice cream had become a bit soupy and the biscotti remained uneaten. She wondered if Jenn was thinking what a waste of food and money Becca King was turning out to be, and she said to her, "I'm not too hungry. D'you want my biscotti?" as a way to explain why she hadn't been able to finish either.

Jenn whispered fiercely, "Are you crazy or something? Why would I want your leftovers? What's *wrong* with you?"

BECCA WAS DOING some homework for Eastern Civilization when Debbie knocked at her door and popped her head inside. She said, "I've got to go to a meeting." She tilted her head in the direction of the little cottage on Second Street where she and Becca had first met. "Can you watch Chloe and Josh? Just for an hour or so? There's a woman who needs me to be there . . . ?"

She meant one of the ladies she helped in Alcoholics Anonymous. Becca understood this because time and again she'd come in on Debbie having a phone conversation with someone she was trying to help stop drinking. Becca said she was happy to help out. She was falling asleep over her homework anyway.

In the apartment behind the motel office, Josh was working on his Social Studies, while Chloe was supposed to be listing all the adjectives she could think of that could be used to describe the picture on a postcard that her teacher had given her. Two adjectives were required for every noun, and Chloe was finding this a stupid assignment.

Becca couldn't disagree. "But if you get through it, we can do something fun," she said.

"Like what?"

"We'll have a drawing contest."

"What's the prize?" Josh asked shrewdly.

"Sweet Mona's for a treat. Winner's choice."

That was all Josh needed to hear, and wherever Josh went, Chloe followed. The kids finished their homework in record time and were ready for the drawing contest before Becca had a chance to get into the English homework she'd brought with her. Act 1 of *The Merchant of Venice*. It was proving as tough to get through as the Eastern Civ.

She set the play aside. She said, "Okay. Here's the contest. You draw me, and the best drawing wins."

Chloe protested that she couldn't draw Becca. Josh would win too easily. But Becca said that wasn't the contest. The contest was to draw Becca in her favorite place in the world and they had to guess what it was. Whoever guessed closest would win. "It's not about the best drawing," she told Chloe. "It's about the best guess."

This was acceptable to Chloe, and both of the kids settled into their drawing while Becca settled back into figuring out what was going on in *The Merchant of Venice*. But she was tired and it was warm, and soon enough she fell asleep.

She woke with a start when the motel's office door snapped shut. She was about to swing herself to her feet, when she recognized Debbie talking to someone. They came into the apartment's living room.

Debbie's companion was Tatiana Primavera, the counselor from the high school. Debbie said, "Look who I found walking home from choir practice," and to her grandkids she said, "You guys finished with your homework? What're you doing?"

"Contest," Josh said.

"Drawin' Becca," Chloe said.

Debbie said, "That right? Well, Becca looks wiped out. You can finish tomorrow. She needs to go to bed and so do you."

"No! We can't!"

"Grammer!"

"Hey, you guys, listen." Debbie and Tatiana Primavera exchanged the kind of look that passes between adults when their plans have just undergone a change that they didn't anticipate.

Becca said, "I c'n stay. I think they're almost done anyway. You guys almost done? What d'you say? Ten minutes?"

"Ten minutes, Grammer!" Chloe cried.

Debbie huffed, said, "No more than that," and took Tatiana Primavera into the kitchen. The running water and banging around suggested she was making some coffee. With this came some whispering, the real kind and not the kind that floated to Becca on the air.

She could hear it well enough. She might not have even listened had it not been said in whispers. But whispering suggested adult information, and adult information suggested something she might need to know. So she sat quietly and picked out from the hushed conversation what she could.

Tatiana was talking. ". . . and now Dave wants to come to the office to *look* for her. I keep *telling* him that it's nothing. Just some kid on a cell phone who got unnerved by the accident and didn't want to hang around. But he doesn't believe that. He's sure it has to do with why Derric was in the woods. I can't convince him otherwise. Then when he had the phone traced and told me the name—"

Debbie said, "You *sure* that's the name you heard? I mean, it was a while ago, wasn't it?"

"Sure. Right after she died. But I remembered it because I thought I *knew* all of Carol's friends, and this one . . . someone called Laurel. I'd never heard of her."

Becca froze. Every muscle that she could feel in her body went tense.

"Maybe it was Laura, not Laurel," Debbie said.

"It was Laurel. I know that's the name I heard," Tatiana was saying. "I'm sure of it. Evidently she called that evening when Carol collapsed, and with everything going on, Pete didn't pick up the phone. Her message was still on the machine. He played it for me because it was so odd. 'Carol, this is Laurel. Just wanted to make sure you two made contact. Remember, it's not Hannah, okay?' Pretty strange, huh? But that was it. And that was the name. And Laurel's not that common so Dave's convinced it's *got* to be this Laurel Armstrong person he's looking for. So *now* he wants—"

"I'm done!" Josh shouted. He jumped to his feet and waved his drawing in the air in front of Becca's face.

"Me too, me too, me too!" shouted Chloe. "You got to decide!"

Deciding anything was the last thing Becca wanted to do. She wanted to know what else Tatiana Primavera was going to say. She looked at the pictures: herself in the forest reading a book and herself on the sofa reading a book. She said, "Amazing! Both of you win. Yea!"

"No fair!" Josh shouted.

"You got to choose," Chloe cried.

"But you've both got it," Becca said. "My favorite place is anywhere I can read a book, and you've both got that. So you're both the winner. We'll go to Sweet Mona's on Saturday, okay? You each pick what you want. Let's put the crayons all back in the carton now."

That got them relatively quiet for a minute or so, long enough for Becca to ease closer to the kitchen door where she was close enough to hear Tatiana say, "I told him that the voice on Carol's machine didn't sound like a kid to me. But because of the connection to that stupid cell phone . . . You know how Dave is. He's fixated on finding her. If Carol were still alive, she'd be able to tell him, but as it is. . ."

As it is, Becca thought. She looked down at the two pictures she was holding: herself in the forest and herself on the sofa. But she had in her mind another picture altogether and that was of Becca King at Carol Quinn's house on Blue Lady Lane the very first night she had been on Whidbey Island. Exactly *when* had Laurel phoned Carol Quinn, Becca wondered. And why hadn't she come back to Whidbey to look for her daughter when Carol Quinn failed to return her call?

TWENTY-FOUR

It hadn't taken long for Hayley Cartwright to discover Seth had been to the farm. Brooke told her. She said he'd come by to say hello and he'd *claimed*, Brooke said, that he was there to say hi to *her*. But *she* knew he'd really come because he wanted to know what Hayley had been doing.

"He was looking all around," Brooke added carefully. "He could tell everything's not good here, Hayley."

Hayley said in response, "Everything's *fine*," but Brooke just looked at her with that sad, wise look she had. She said, "Whatever," and wandered off.

Now at school, Hayley was worried. If Seth had come to the farm, then Brooke was right in what she was saying. It had to do with Hayley. And if it had to do with Hayley, it also had to do with Saratoga Woods. She and Seth weren't finished talking about that.

She was working her hour at the reception desk when Derric's father showed up at the school again. The undersheriff looked really bad. His eyes were bloodshot and his face looked jowly with weight loss. Dave Mathieson had always been the kind of man that people referred to as "robust," which Hayley translated to mean full of health. But he didn't look like that now.

She said, "Hi, Sheriff Mathieson. How's Derric doing?"

The undersheriff shook his head. "No change. The signs are good, but he's not waking up. The doctors're making noises about more tests. They want to take him into Seattle to Children's Hospital and bring in a specialist team from Ohio." The undersheriff scrubbed his hands over his face.

Hayley said, "I *know* he's going to wake up. It's just a matter of time."

Dave Mathieson said, although she didn't know why, "Sometimes you do the wrong thing," and then he took a deep breath and altered his course with, "I'm meeting with Ms. Ward and the A-to-L counselor. That's Ms. Primavera, right?"

She said, "Sure," but before she could pick up the phone and call them to say he was here, he said to her, "Laurel Armstrong, Hayley. Is she someone from the school?"

Hayley shook her head slowly, as she thought about the name. "I don't know. It could be a younger kid, I guess," she said. "One of the ninth-graders? Why?"

"She's who bought the cell phone that made the call to nine-one-one, that day from the woods."

Hayley's eyes widened. "How'd you find that out?"

"Like I told you, these phones have serial numbers," he said. "That took us to a 7-Eleven in southern California."

"And that took you to Laurel Armstrong?" Police work was amazing, Hayley thought, just like on television.

"It took us to her credit card. Not likely that the card belonged to the kid who made the call, but we've got to check everything. The cops down there are helping out, going to the address associated with the card to see if it was stolen or if the phone was stolen. It's a loose end that needs to be tied up." He looked around, and his eyes seemed dim, like eyes not taking in what they were seeing. He finally said, "Anyway . . ." which reminded Hayley that she was to phone Ms. Ward and Ms. Primavera. She picked up the phone and did so.

But she could see that there was another reason the undersheriff had come to the high school. She just hoped it had nothing to do with her.

WHEN HAYLEY WAS walking out to the farm truck after school that afternoon, she saw that the undersheriff's car was still in a guest spot in the parking lot. As she watched, he came trudging out of the administration building. The expression on his face suggested that he'd had no luck in finding someone called Laurel Armstrong.

He wasn't alone. Ms. Primavera was with him. She was talking to him, but her expression indicated she was feeling impatient with Derric's dad. Hayley figured she was probably telling him he was wasting his time looking at South Whidbey High School for someone who wanted to hurt Derric because no one there *wanted* to hurt him, and no one ever would.

Or maybe, Hayley thought, all of this was just wishful thinking on her part.

She continued toward the farm truck. But she heard the undersheriff call her name, so she turned back. She did this in time to see him say something to Ms. Primavera, to see Ms. Primavera frown and roll her eyes, and to see them part ways. The undersheriff came toward Hayley.

When he reached her, he said, "Looks like you were right. No Laurel Armstrong. There's a Cindy Armstrong in ninth grade, but she's no relation." He smiled in a tired way. "Back to square one. Have to wait and see what else the cops in California come up with."

"Gosh." Hayley waited for more. She figured that the undersheriff had something else on his mind or he wouldn't have called her name.

He began with, "You and Derric have been pretty tight this year, huh? You know him pretty well."

"We're not boyfriend and girlfriend or anything."

"Sure. I know that. But what I don't know it this: What the *hell* was he doing in Saratoga Woods, Hayley? You say he wasn't with you. Okay. I accept that. But he had zero reason to be there. It wasn't like him to go out for a hike alone, and even if he did on that day, why ride his bike all the way to Saratoga Woods when Putney Woods is closer?"

Hayley shook her head, drawing her eyebrows together. "I don't know, Sheriff Mathieson."

"Things go on in the woods," Dave Mathieson said. "I know that, Hayley. Up there by the erratic, things go on. That's always been the case."

"Derric's not a stoner, if that's what you mean," Hayley declared. "He never even *talks* about drugs. Besides, he doesn't hang with stoners at school and he probably would, wouldn't he, if he was using. I mean, it's not like he's nasty to them or anything. It's just he's not interested. 'Cause if he was . . ." Hayley's voice drifted off as she saw the undersheriff was looking at her oddly. She'd been talking aimlessly, she realized. That was stupid.

Dave Mathieson said, "What were you *really* doing in the woods that day? You, Hayley. Not Derric."

"Sheriff Mathieson, I'm not a stoner either."

"Were you there because of this Laurel Armstrong?"

"I don't know her. Really."

"But something was going on. I know it and so do you. It had to do with what happened to Derric, and it's why he rode his bike all the way from home instead of going to a closer woods to hike. My guess is that it's also why you parked your truck over by Metcalf Woods. None of you kids wanted to be seen. Right?"

"No, really. That's not how it was."

The undersheriff shook his head. He said, "Hayley, I'm going to get to the bottom of this eventually. You might want to pass that message along to everyone else who was there."

TWENTY-FIVE

S eth was walking back out to Sammy after paying for gas at a highway strip mall called Casey's Corner when he saw Mrs. Cartwright come out of the Goose, a grocery store on the other side of the parking lot. She was carrying what looked like seven or eight reusable shopping bags, heading to the family SUV. As she walked, the bags started to get tangled up. He drove over quickly and rolled down his window, saying, "Hang on and I'll help you."

She was trying to untangle the bags and find her car keys in her purse at the same time. She said, "Thanks, Seth," and she shot him a smile. When he'd parked and jogged back over to her, she said, "This stuff'll have to go in the backseat. Hold on a sec," and she put the bags on the ground along with her purse, which she opened and fished her car keys out of. Seth saw that she'd been running errands. She'd filled the back of the vehicle with boxes of canning jars, two huge sacks of barley and oats, and three big bags of chicken feed.

She opened the passenger's door and leaned across the driver's seat to unlock the driver's door and the other doors, too. Seth went to the driver's side with some of the bags and she joined him there with the rest, saying, "Got to get that door fixed. It doesn't open any longer with the key. You can lock the darn thing, but you can't unlock it. Even when it's unlocked, you can't open the door with the outside handle. I swear. Everything's falling apart."

"My granddad could probably fix this door lock for you," Seth told her. "I can ask him to if you want."

Mrs. Cartwright said, "Let me think about that," and then she said, "Brooke told me you stopped by to say hello."

He said, "Yeah. I did," but thinking about his trip to the farm and the condition of things there made him feel the need to say something altogether different. He went with, "Hey, thanks for watching Gus that night. You know, the night that my granddad came for him?"

Mrs. Cartwright looked confused for a moment. Then she said, "Oh! That night. Not a problem. Hayley kept Gus in her room."

Hayley. There. Her name was out between them, so it was a good time to say something about her and ask how she was and what she was doing and whether Mrs. Cartwright knew how serious Hayley was about . . . But Mrs. Cartwright was getting into the car. She said, "Thanks for the help, Seth," and she patted his hand.

She started the car, which took on her second try. Black exhaust belched out of the tailpipe. Seth said, "Someone wants an oil change," when he saw this. "Better tell Mr. Cartwright. You don't want to let something like that go for long."

She looked flustered. Then she said, "Yes, yes. I'll tell him," and she put the car into gear. It jerked.

Seth thought the transmission or the clutch could use a look, but he didn't like to say that after already mentioning the exhaust. So instead he said, "How *is* Hayley?"

Mrs. Cartwright looked at him in much the same way someone looks at a lost puppy. Seth didn't like this, but his words were out, so he had to listen to her response. She said, "She's been busy. I don't see much of her. She's at the hospital a lot because of Derric Mathieson. You know Derric, don't you?"

"Yeah. I know him," Seth said. "Everyone knows him."

Mrs. Cartwright nodded and cocked her head. She smiled at him tenderly and said, "We all like you, Seth. Every single one of us likes you."

He said, "Whatever," and she backed out of the parking space. He watched her, heavyhearted, as she drove off.

He felt completely alone in that moment. He kicked his toe against the tarmac, and that was when he noticed that he'd left Mrs. Cartwright's purse behind the SUV when he'd picked up the grocery bags and carried them around to the door of the vehicle. She'd backed up and had been lucky not to run over it, but there it stood, with all her stuff inside.

He went to it and scooped it up. Best to return it. At least it would save her another trip to Casey's Corner from the farm.

⸻

SETH GOT STOPPED by both of the traffic lights on the highway before he got to the route that would take him to Smugglers Cove Farm and Flowers. So he was a couple of minutes behind Mrs. Cartwright and when he reached his destination, the SUV was parked and the grocery bags had been taken inside. The stuff from the back was still within the car, so with Mrs. Cartwright's purse slung over his shoulder, he opened the back of the SUV and grabbed the cartons with the canning jars in them. As he went toward the door, he passed the woodpile. It still hadn't been stacked.

Mrs. Cartwright seemed surprised to see him. Then she saw her purse hanging from his shoulder. She said, "My heavens. I didn't even miss it," and she held the screen door open.

He went to the kitchen, where she'd set the grocery bags on the floor. One of them had spilled out and the family cat was sniffing a cherry tomato that he proceeded to bat around.

Seth set the boxes of canning jars on the counter and asked Mrs. Cartwright if she'd like him to stack the firewood. She said, "Oh, that's so sweet of you, but don't bother, Seth. Bill just hasn't gotten to it yet."

Seth said, "No trouble. I sort of like the work. It's a nice day and . . . I got nowhere I need to be."

Mrs. Cartwright cast a look in the direction of the barn, which could be seen in part from the kitchen window. She said, "All right then. Thank you, Seth. That's very good of you."

"No worries." He went back outside and approached the woodpile.

The wood had become fairly heavy from the rain. It should have been stacked in the covered woodshed right after it had been delivered. Seth wondered if they'd have to buy another cord of it to use until these four cords dried out. He doubted they could afford it.

He set to work. It was the kind of labor he enjoyed, making

order out of chaos. That, his grandfather liked to tell him, was always pleasurable to the human mind.

Seth worked steadily for about twenty minutes, at which point he paused and took off his flannel shirt. He turned back to the pile and picked up another load, and he heard a man's voice call out, "Don't tell me that woman's put you to work."

Seth looked up to see that Mr. Cartwright was coming in his direction from the barn, carrying a bottle of water in his hand. He was walking slowly, in the way people walk when their feet are tender and bare and they find themselves suddenly treading on pebbles. Only Mr. Cartwright was wearing tough work boots and Seth wondered if he was breaking them in or maybe had blisters from wearing them too long.

Mr. Cartwright said with a nod at the wood, "I would've gotten to that sooner or later, but I appreciate the help. I been working like a dog with a bone." He jerked his thumb in the direction of the barn, although Seth couldn't imagine what he'd been doing there. He also laughed for no particular reason. "Anyhoosy, I brought you this." He extended his hand, holding out the bottle of water.

Seth reached for it, saying thanks, but before he made contact the bottle dropped between them. It was one of those weirdly perfect falls. It hit a piece of wood just right and burst, sending its contents out over the bottoms of Mr. Cartwright's jeans.

Mr. Cartwright began to laugh, but the sound of the laugh was high and strange. Seth saw that it wasn't a laugh of humor because there was nothing like humor in either his face or his eyes. Seth also saw that Mr. Cartwright's hands were shaking, and he realized that Hayley's dad had probably been drinking.

Mr. Cartwright dug a handkerchief out of his pocket and wiped his eyes. He said, "What the whoosey, let me help you here, Seth," and he bent and picked up three pieces of wood. But he wasn't able to carry them to the woodpile without dropping two of them, and the third he just dumped on the arranged wood in such a way that two of the pieces that Seth had stacked neatly ended up rolling off. Mr. Cartwright laughed that strange laugh again. He said, "Oops. Sorry about that."

Seth wanted to tell him that he would do the work himself. But it was Mr. Cartwright's farm, and he figured Mr. Cartwright could do whatever he wanted. Even if he was making a mess of things, Seth could hardly tell him that.

He was saved by the fact that Mrs. Cartwright came out of the house, then. She was carrying two bottles of water and an old faded blue canvas stool. She said cheerfully, "You boys are working too hard," as she opened the stool. She added, "Have a seat here, Billy boy, and take a load off for a while."

Seth said thanks for the water and drank his down while Mrs. Cartwright urged her husband to use the canvas stool. He cooperated well enough, but he groused, "You're making me soft, Julie," and he didn't open his water.

Seth went back to work. But he could feel that Mr. Cartwright was watching him, staring at him, really, and so hard that the force of the look seemed to bore into Seth's back like a drill making a hole. He thought he might be doing something wrong, and he glanced over at the man. Mrs. Cartwright was rubbing his shoulders, her head cocked and her gaze affectionately resting on Seth. Mr. Cartwright made an irritated face, and pushed her hands off his shoulders. "I *said* you're making me soft," he told her. "Cut it the blazes *out*, Julie." She dropped her hands and pressed her lips together, and Mr. Cartwright said to Seth this time, "Man slows down a bit and ends up with a bunch of women hovering over him like he's an invalid."

"Bunch of women?" Seth said with a smile. "Sounds sort of nice to me." He was thinking that he would settle for one woman, that woman being a girl-woman, and that girl-woman being Hayley, when something like a snort came from Mr. Cartwright. He looked over to see that Hayley's dad was crying. He was making no other noise beyond that single snort, but the tears were streaming down his face. Seth turned away and stacked wood like crazy and waited for someone to say or do something, but no one did.

"*Well*, now." Mrs. Cartwright finally spoke. She clapped her hands as if to get their attention. "*I'm* going to go in the house and make you two some *sand*wiches. You're growing boys. You need to be fed."

Seth wondered if she hadn't noticed her husband was crying. That was surely possible because she'd been standing behind him. But the way she sounded and the way she gave Seth a sharp glance told him that she probably knew and was signaling Seth not to say anything about it. This was fine by him because asking a grown man why he was laughing and crying and stumbling and dropping things was pretty much the last thing Seth wanted to do.

So he said, "Thanks. That would be nice."

"Good," she said. "I've got leftover ham."

She reached to help her husband to his feet. He jerked away from her. He said, "Julie, do I *look* like I need your help?"

Her eyes got bright, but she stepped away and waited for him to struggle to his feet. Then she headed toward the house with him, close at his side. She was very careful not to touch him, but she kept glancing at him as if expecting him to fall.

Something was definitely going on with him, Seth thought. Something was going on with Mrs. Cartwright, too.

WHEN SETH GOT to his grandfather's property later that day, he found Ralph lobbing tennis balls with an old wooden racket. He was serving the balls up the slope in the direction of the parking area, and Gus was tearing up the path to retrieve them. His tongue lolled goofily out of his mouth.

He charged past Seth and knocked him off balance. Seth toppled into a large stand of Oregon grape. A few branches snapped off and a few sharp leaves scratched his face. He said, "Hey, watch it, Gus," but taking care not to knock people over wasn't on the yellow Lab's mind. Seth got to his feet and brushed himself off.

Seth called to his grandfather, "What in heck're you doing?"

Ralph called back, "Trying to wear that dog out so he'll sleep tonight without getting up and chewing on your grandmother's rocker is what I'm doing." Ralph watched the Lab come tearing back down the hillside, ball in jaws. He said, "We've been doing this for an hour. Any chance I'm close to wearing him out?"

"Give it another hour," Seth said. "Here, I'll do it," and he joined his grandfather on the lawn.

"Change directions, then," Ralph told him as he handed over

the tennis racket. "Hit it toward the pond. I think he's done enough damage to the shrubbery and there's not much chance you or he can hurt anything else if you aim toward the pond. Or lob it into the forest, if you like. That'll keep him looking for a while."

Seth chose the forest and whacked the ball in that direction. Gus hurtled after it, crashing through the bracken. In less than a minute he came running back, the tennis ball in his mouth. He chewed it energetically before dropping it at Seth's feet.

Ralph watched all this and then said, "So. What's on your mind, favorite male grandchild? I'd like to think this is a social call, but lately you show up when it's talking you want."

"Talking's social," Seth pointed out.

"I think you know what I mean."

So Seth told his grandfather about the Cartwrights: how he'd gone out there on Ralph's suggestion but had seen the place didn't look quite right, how he'd gone again to take Mrs. Cartwright her purse, and how Mr. Cartwright had acted while he was there. He ended with, "Grand, I think he was drunk. Really blitzed. He couldn't walk right. He couldn't even put wood on the woodpile without dropping it."

Ralph considered this as Seth wacked the ball into the forest again. He said, "Drunk doesn't sound like Bill Cartwright. I used to see him having a beer at the Dog House when it was open, but he never got drunk that I can recall."

"He's drunk now," Seth said. "And I was thinking that maybe that's what's been going on with Hayley. Like she doesn't want me to know her dad's drinking. Like she's embarrassed I might find out."

Ralph said, "Seth . . ." in that way people speak when they're disappointed. This made Seth remember what his grandfather had said to him about this kind of thinking, and he added quickly, "I know, Grand. Everything's not about me. I know you're thinking that *I'm* thinking—"

"Now, that's where you're wrong, grandson." Ralph took the tennis racket from Seth and lobbed the ball for Gus once again, this time toward the pond.

"What d'you mean?"

"You're thinking Bill Cartwright's a drunk because of what you've seen, right? But that's just like people thinking you're a druggie because of how you look, isn't it?"

"Totally unfair," Seth protested. "Just because I'm not in school, just because my jeans are loose and my hair's long and I got ear gauges—"

"You take my point. That things aren't always what they seem. That could be the case here." Ralph waited as Gus came dashing up from the pond. He'd found an old rubber rain boot in lieu of the ball. This was a delicious diversion and the dog set about chewing on it. Ralph said, "Get that darn thing away from him before he chokes," and as Seth went to do this, he said, "Seth, you want some advice on this matter? I ask because people rarely do want it and I'd rather save my breath to throw that damn ball for another hour or two if you're not going to listen."

"I'll listen," Seth said.

"Then hear me. Don't rush to judgment on this matter of the Cartwrights. And don't say a word about what you've seen to Hayley."

TWENTY-SIX

Becca was sitting in the new commons, around the corner from the lunch line. On the other side of the room, Jenn McDaniels was waylaying kids on their way in and out of lunch. She had her sign-up sheets with her, and she was taking names of anyone willing to go up to Coupeville.

Jenn was worried about Derric. Becca could hear this in her whispers whenever she talked about him. Becca knew that the doctors were worried, too. On one of her own visits to Derric, she'd managed to hear one of them quietly talking to a nurse about some kind of brain bacterium that could put its victim into a deep sleep for years. But she refused to believe this was what had happened to Derric. Regardless of Jenn's dislike of her, Becca figured the other girl felt the same way.

As if knowing she was being watched by Becca, Jenn looked in her direction. She lifted a hand as if waving to her and half-rose from her seat. Becca was startled, thinking Jenn's attitude toward her had undergone a massive change, but then she experienced a jolt of reality as the undersheriff passed right by her. He'd come into the commons from the opposite direction, behind Becca's back. She ducked her head and pretended she needed to get a book from her backpack. He passed her table and went to the one three tables away, where he sat down with the kids and started to talk.

Across the room, Jenn had picked up her clipboard with its sign-up sheets. The undersheriff looked intense, and Becca could tell that Jenn was worried that Derric's father was telling the kids something that she *herself* ought to hear. She'd pretty much dominated Derric's recovery, after all, letting everyone know that *she* was spending more time than anyone at his bedside, riding the bus up to Coupeville practically every afternoon. She'd been filled with stories of her visits to Derric, which Becca had overheard in Eastern Civilization and English: how she'd been in the room when Derric's father had come to see him; how he'd cried that time after talking to one of the doctors. He'd confided in her about being scared, she'd declared, and he felt terrible about not having been there for Derric all the time. Wow, he'd even told her about having had his doubts about adopting a kid from Africa in the first place and bringing that kid to lily-white Whidbey Island and expecting him to fit in. But *that* had happened a long time ago, which was what Jenn explained that she'd said to Dave Mathieson, and he sure didn't need to worry about it now.

To Becca, it had all sounded like a girl declaring her territory. She felt strange about it, so she kept her distance even while she picked up what information she could about Derric's condition.

Becca saw Jenn leave her table, clipboard pressed to her chest. Jenn started to come across the new commons in the direction of the undersheriff. The students being talked to by him all shook their heads with a solemn-looking *no* to whatever questions Derric's dad was asking them.

Undersheriff Mathieson rose. Jenn picked up her speed and raised her hand in a wave. He didn't see her, or he didn't care. He moved on to the next table, where he sat and started his questions again.

Becca wished she could hear what the undersheriff was asking because once again the students were shaking their heads no. She figured when he reached the table directly next to hers, she'd have a chance as long as Jenn didn't get in his way.

Jenn's expression said she wanted to, though. Becca had the AUD box plugged in because of the noise inside the commons, but she didn't need it to hear Jenn's whispers since her face was so easy to read. It said *I'm the one* and *Why aren't we talking?* and *What about me when I've done so much?* But the undersheriff noticed none of this. Instead, he left the table where he was sitting, came to the table closest to Becca's, and asked a question that felt like a hand grenade placed in the center of Becca's life.

"I'm looking for someone called Laurel Armstrong," he said. "Is that name familiar to any of you?"

Becca felt herself turn into a block of concrete with a pounding heart. She knew the need for instant escape, but nothing about her body worked except her eyes and her ears. The kids would say no, of course, and then the undersheriff would be at her table, and she didn't know how she would keep her face from broadcasting everything she was trying to hide.

But then a little miracle happened. Halfway across the new commons, a table of stoner boys started to give Jenn McDaniels a bad time. Clearly, they hadn't noticed the undersheriff's coming into the room because one of them grabbed Jenn by the arm and made kissy faces at her while another wailed at top volume,

"Derric, oh Derric, be tah-*roo* to me *now*," as if he was singing a country song, to which he added, "For Jenn misses you like a calf misses a *cow*," and the rest of the boys began laughing like hyenas.

Becca recognized the boy with a grip on Jenn's arm. She'd been with him on the ferry. He'd hassled Derric during lunch one time, too. Dylan, Becca thought. His name was Dylan.

Jenn jerked away from him. She snarled, "Get a grip, Dylan," to which Dylan replied, "Hey, *you* get a grip."

Another boy said, "What a dyke," as a third said, "Grip *what*? Bet we know, freak."

Undersheriff Mathieson saw all of this. Most everyone heard it, too. The undersheriff got up from his seat and went over to the boys. He said, "What's this all about?" and the way he said it told everyone that he meant business of the you're-in-trouble kind.

Dylan turned the color of eggplant. The other boys started to stammer. The undersheriff leaned over their table and got right into Dylan's face. He said in a loud voice, "I asked you what this was about. You were singing about Derric, so how d'you know him? What're your names? Were you there when he was injured in the woods?"

Dylan went instantly from eggplant to white. Jenn sneered, "Yeah, Dylan. Were you *there*?"

This set the undersheriff off even more because he said, "Was Derric meeting you there? You better damn well tell me if you—"

"Hey. Chill, dude," one of the other boys said.

Dave Mathieson made a move toward him. That was when Ms. Primavera intervened. Becca didn't know where she'd come from, but she put her hand on Undersheriff Mathieson's arm, and she said something to him in a very low voice. Then she said to the boys, "You have some place to be, I think," and she ignored Jenn McDaniels altogether.

The boys got up like kids with their pants on fire. The undersheriff put his hand briefly on Ms. Primavera's where it still rested on his arm. Becca saw their fingers interlock, and then Ms. Primavera dropped her hand to her side. The undersheriff said something to her and, just like that, they left the commons. Jenn remained, a lone figure with the stares of the other students resting upon her. She spun around and left by the doors that led to the theater corridor and the band rooms. No one said another word to her.

***

THE BAD PART was that Jenn had chosen to leave by the very same door used by the boys who'd been giving her a bad time. Becca saw this and knew what it probably meant. There was unfinished business in the air.

She had a moment of indecision. Jenn was a real piece of work, and Becca owed her nothing. But she'd been trying, at least, to do *something* to help Derric. That was a mark in her favor, wasn't it?

Outside in the corridor, Becca saw that the boys who'd been confronted by the undersheriff had gone no farther than the doors that led to the band rooms. These were close to the girls' lavatory, and she could see that Jenn was headed there. But the boys saw this, too. They approached her and surrounded her.

"What's *with* you anyway?" Dylan demanded.

"What's with the clipboard?" another added. "You some kind of school *official* now?"

Jenn said to them all, "Why don't you guys shut up and do something useful?" and she tried to push through them.

"With *you*?" Dylan laughed. "Good idea!"

Two of the other boys grabbed her arms and her clipboard fell to the floor. Dylan started to chant, "She wants it, she wants it. Do it to me, do it to me, Derr-*rick*!" as the other boys moved their hips suggestively.

Becca threw her backpack to one side. She shouted, "Hey! You guys leave her alone!" because she could see from Jenn's face that she was perilously close to crying.

"Ohhh! It's the dyke's *wife*!" one boy yelled, and another boy cried, "Bacon Grease Hair with legs!"

They laughed stupidly. But the diversion of Becca's interference was enough. Jenn twisted away from them and dashed to the restroom.

The boys went for Becca but the band instructor came out of his classroom at that moment and his sharp "What's going on out here?" was enough to send them scurrying like rats off a sinking ship.

Becca watched them go, only dimly hearing the band instructor say to her, "You all right?"

She nodded, but the truth was something else. For as the boys made themselves as scarce as possible, Becca had a glimpse of something that made her breath catch in her throat. The boy Dylan was wearing a pair of sandals. The sandals were exactly the same as Seth's.

THERE WAS NO real time to process this, not with the band teacher standing there waiting for Becca to respond to him. So she said thanks and grabbed up Jenn's clipboard and her own backpack. She ducked into the lavatory to find the other girl.

Jenn was bent over one of the washbowls. She swung around in a flash. She was crying and Becca knew instinctively that this wasn't good. A tough girl like Jenn McDaniels crying? Everything, Becca knew, was about to get worse.

She wasn't sure what approach to take, but it didn't matter. Jenn spoke first.

"What d'you *want*?" she snarled. "Why are you *following* me? God, you're such a *pathetic* piece of trash with your ugly glasses and your stupid dyed hair. You don't *belong* here. You don't fit *anywhere*. Why'd you come here, *anyway*?"

The force of Jenn's words stopped Becca from saying what she wanted to say: about Dylan, about his sandals, about the forest and the footprint she'd seen and Saratoga Woods itself. So she merely extended the clipboard to Jenn. Jenn didn't take it.

"What?" Jenn cried. "*What*? You think I need you to fight my battles? Leave me *alone*. You butt in everywhere and *no* one wants you around. Don't you get that, fattie?"

Becca set the clipboard on the floor. She knew the best course was to get away. But Jenn wasn't about to have this. As Becca turned to go, Jenn raced around and planted herself squarely in Becca's path.

"Why'd you follow me? What do you *want*? I know what you're trying to do, you know. It's only obvious to everyone."

Becca drew her eyebrows together. Finally she was able to speak. She said, "I don't get—"

"Oh, yeah right. You don't *get* it. You just go up there and read your stupid book to him and act like you're not trying to do anything at all except practically get into the bed with him and we *both* know what that's all about, don't we?"

"That's not . . ." Becca began to back off.

This, apparently, was just what Jenn wanted. She shoved her. She grabbed Becca's backpack and began to go through it. She said, "Where is it? Where's that stupid book?" She dumped the backpack's contents onto the floor.

"What book?"

"Oh *right*. You know exactly what I'm talking about. You play dumb but it's all an act. When you have a chance—"

"You're crazy," Becca said. She bent to gather her things.

Jenn shoved her again. Unbalanced, Becca fell to her side. The earpiece to the AUD box was dislodged from her ear onto the floor. Jenn grabbed this. She jerked it hard and along with the earphone came the AUD box itself. Jenn hurled it viciously at the opposite wall.

"You're a loser," she shrieked. "You and your *books* and your music and your . . . your . . ." Tears sprang to her eyes. She ran from the room.

TWENTY-SEVEN

Becca was able to make it through the rest of the school day, but it wasn't easy. When she rescued the AUD box, she found it badly damaged. It wasn't broken altogether, but it didn't work right. It offered only intermittent static.

As soon as school was over, she shoved the damaged AUD box into her backpack and got off the campus as quickly as she could. Without the box, she knew she was going to have trouble on her hands because during both Integrated Algebra and Yearbook there had been so much whispering flailing around in the air that she could barely concentrate on the teacher and she understood why her grandmother had said, "Cemetery time," when she'd start howling and covering her ears and banging her head as a little kid.

So Becca knew where she had to go in order to be able to think about what she was going to do without the AUD box working right. She rolled the bike away from the rack and set off down Maxwelton Road toward town.

When she reached the cemetery, Becca left her bike at the edge of its main lane. She crisscrossed among the old monuments and markers, and she made her way over to Reese Grieder's grave. It was covered by leaves from the maple and sycamore trees nearby, and Becca sat on a pile of them so that she could lean against the side of the stone.

She took the AUD box out of her backpack and examined it more closely. The back of it was smashed in. Three of the interior wires were loose and were going to need to be soldered back into place. The earpiece wasn't wrecked, but the amount of work that it was going to take to make the device usable again felt, for a moment, insurmountable. Becca sighed and tossed the entire AUD box to one side, into the deep grass. She lowered her head to her upraised knees.

Truth was, she didn't understand why Jenn McDaniels hated her so much. It wasn't like Becca had done anything to her. She was just trying to wait for Laurel's return, and in the meantime she was just trying to stay in school and be Becca King, someone completely different from the girl who'd left San Diego and all her friends to be on the run from Jeff Corrie. But now with Derric's father in possession of Laurel's name, Becca didn't know what might happen.

More than anything, Becca wished she had someone to talk to about all of this but particularly about Jenn McDaniels. She tried to find something positive in what was going on, but the only thing she could come up with was that *if* Undersheriff Mathieson was on the trail of Laurel, he might actually find her and bring her back to Whidbey Island and protect her and Becca from Jeff Corrie once they told him the truth. *If,* of course, he even believed them. On the other hand, though, now that he had Laurel's name, he might just go down to San Diego. He might find Jeff Corrie that way or he might just phone and ask him about

Laurel, in which case Jeff Corrie was going to want to know why an undersheriff in the state of Washington was calling him about his runaway wife. If *that* happened, Jeff Corrie would turn up on Whidbey Island eventually. And if *that* happened, he was going to find her. Maybe he wouldn't find her at first, but he would in the long run because he wasn't going to rest, Becca knew, till he had found her and had dealt with her.

Everything felt black to Becca. Everything felt hopeless. She shifted her position and looked at Reese Grieder's gravestone as if there might be an answer or two there.

Poor Reese, she thought. Her grave was sad. The stone had lichen growing on it. Her picture had mildew at its corners because the cover on it had sprung a leak. The grave itself was full of weeds. It was all so dismal. It seemed unfair that Reese would be left alone and forgotten like this.

Becca cleared the leaves from the site and began to pull at the weeds. When she'd completed this job, she rustled in her backpack and found a ruler and started to use this against the lichen. She was going at this industriously when a hand touched her shoulder. She shrieked. Diana Kinsale jumped backward, a hand at her heart. She said, "Lord! I'm *sorry*."

Becca looked beyond her and saw Diana's truck in the other, newer part of the cemetery, parked near her husband's grave. Diana said, "They're not with me this time," in reference to her dogs. "I just stopped to say hello to Charlie." She looked down at Reese Grieder's grave. She said, "Are you cleaning it? That's very kind of you."

"It looked sort of sad."

"It needs a plant or two, I think," Diana said. "Even some

greenery would help, if you put it into the flower holder. Shall I get some for you? From over there?" She took a few steps in the direction of the trees at the cemetery's edge, where ferns grew in a rich profusion. But this put her on a direct line to the AUD box, and Becca cried, "Wait!"

Diana's expression was startled. Becca dashed over to where she was standing and scooped the AUD box from the ground where it had been half-hidden in a clump of the overlong grass.

Diana said, "Yours?" and she reached for it, turning it over in her hand so that the damage Jenn had done to it showed. "What is it?"

Becca said what she'd learned to say about her hearing problems. She embellished a bit with Diana Kinsale, adding, "I had ear infections all the time when I was little. . . . My hearing's not right because of that. It's a sound spectrum problem."

Diana looked at her quizzically. "You sure this isn't a radio, Becca?"

"I wish. All it does it help me equalize sounds. It blocks background noise so I c'n focus." It was the spiel she'd heard her mother give teachers and other adults so many times that she could say it from memory.

"It looks broken now."

Becca lied without thinking about why she would bother to protect Jenn McDaniels. "I was riding up the hill, on the road by the fairgrounds? It fell out of my pocket and my back tire went over it. I've got to figure out a way to fix it because without it, I'm hopeless if there's more than one person around me talking."

What she didn't add was that right now without the AUD box

working, she should have been picking up whispers from Diana since Diana was the only person around and Diana clearly *had* to have something going on in her head. But as before, nothing came off the woman, not a single whisper, not even a word.

Diana said, "I know someone who can probably fix this if you'd like me to take it to him."

"I was sort of figuring that maybe I could take it to the metal shop at school . . . ? I was hoping they could solder it or something?"

"Perhaps," Diana said, "but it's probably not quite like anything they've dealt with in the metal shop." She waited a moment. A few drops of rain fell. She looked at the sky and then at Becca and said, "I *can* help you, you know, my dear."

Becca hesitated. She didn't know about accepting help because the only people who could really help her were gone. She said, "I was just thinking . . . I mean, I need it back pretty fast because of school."

Diana said, "I'll have it back to you before you begin to worry about where it is."

She walked over to Charlie's grave then. She sat on the little bench there and bent her head and for the very first time, Becca caught a whisper in the air that had to have come from her. It was *the one, Charlie? . . . how will I know . . .*

Becca looked away quickly, back to Reese's gravestone. She returned to cleaning the lichen from it.

ONCE BECCA DECIDED to allow Diana Kinsale to see to the AUD box, she tried not to worry about whether she'd get it back. It was tough enough just to concentrate without the device.

She spent a lot of time in the town library as a result. She also did her work for Debbie. Plus, she went out to the cemetery to continue fixing up Reese's grave, and she tried to keep away from Jenn McDaniels as much as possible. She also kept clear of any place where she might be seen by the undersheriff and get confronted with some of the questions he appeared to be asking everyone he encountered. This meant, unfortunately, keeping away from the hospital in Coupeville. That meant not seeing Derric.

He filled her thoughts, anyway. Particularly she thought about the picture on his bedside table, with him and his band and his saxophone. She thought of him with those little children hanging on him and his bandmates. She thought of the music that filled the air when she touched her hand to his. Becca sent him every good wish she could, but she knew she couldn't risk going to see him.

Yet Becca knew she *had* to talk to someone. For always at the back of her mind was the sight of that footprint on the trail where Derric had fallen. Not saying a word about it meant not getting to the bottom of what really had happened that day in the woods. But saying a word meant getting the information to the undersheriff, and when she thought about *that*, she always reached the same conclusion: He was going to want to talk to whoever had seen that footprint. And she couldn't have that.

Several days after she'd handed over the AUD box to Diana Kinsale, Becca was in the Langley library working on a paper for her English class. She was using one of the library computers, but the challenge was enormous because of the whispers she was picking up on. Whereas most of the time, the whispers were general buzzes of useless information that she couldn't even apply to a particular person, there was something about the silence in the library that allowed her to pinpoint where the whispers were coming from, which made it more difficult for her to concentrate on her work. The worst at the moment was coping with the whispers coming from the man at the computer next to her. He was looking at Match.com and his whisper of *what kind of book she might think I like* was something Becca was itching to reply to. The man was about a million years old and he'd been looking at women who appeared to be about twenty-five. Becca wanted to tell him that it wasn't *exactly* going to matter to them what kind of book he might like if he wasn't rich, so he'd be better off thinking *how much money she might think I have* and go from that angle rather than trying to discuss *Huckleberry Finn* with them.

Becca wanted to giggle when this came to her mind. She knew she'd reached the point of having *nothing* more to write on her English paper. So she used the rest of her quarters to print up what she'd written so far about *The Merchant of Venice* and its relevance today and she left the library.

She crossed the street so that she could walk along the bluff on her way back to the Cliff Motel. She looked out into the passage. It was late afternoon, so the sun was behind her, casting long shadows from the overgrown bluff out onto the golden water.

What she saw then in the passage brought a smile to her face. The surface of the water was broken by a fin. Then another broke the water, followed by a third. All of them were huge. They were also black. As she watched, she caught a glimpse of flukes as well.

"Orcas!" she cried. She took off at a run for the Cliff Motel. The kids would want to see this, she thought. So would Debbie.

She dashed into the office, crying, "Hey, you guys, there's—" but Debbie was on the phone and she held up her hand to stop Becca and said to someone on the other end of the line, "Just don't touch that bottle. You want me to come over?" and covering the mouthpiece of the receiver with her hand, she said to Becca, "I need you to clean room twelve-sixteen."

Becca dropped her backpack and said, "Sure. Where are the kids? There's at least three orcas—"

"Room twelve-sixteen, Becca. There're people on their way from Tacoma."

Josh, though, had come into the office from the family apartment. He said, "Orcas! Where?" as Chloe ran into the office as well.

Becca said to Debbie, "This'll only take a sec. I promise," and to the kids, "Quick, come with me."

She took them around the side of the motel to the back. It was easy to see Saratoga Passage here and the direction in which the orcas had been swimming.

She helped the kids edge through tall ocean spray bushes at the top of the bluff, holding each child by the hand. Chloe was bouncing with excitement and Josh was listing everything he knew about orcas, which turned out to be quite a lot. They were killer whales, he told Becca, because they were carnivorous, and they hunted their prey, and they were really, really big. They didn't kill *people*, but only sea creatures that they needed for food. They were apex predators and—

"There!" Becca pointed out the fins. There were seven of them now.

"Whales, whales, whales!" Chloe cried.

She bounced on her feet while Josh shouted with delight, and Becca thought about how free they all were in that moment: she and the kids and especially the orcas. No one hunted them any longer. They were safe in Puget Sound.

When the whales were finally out of sight, it had grown nearly dark. Becca said, "I've got to clean room twelve-sixteen or I'll get my butt kicked by your grammer."

"We'll help," Chloe said, as they crossed the grass at the back of the motel.

Becca didn't think that having the kids help was what Debbie had in mind, and she knew they would probably just get in her way. So instead of accepting Chloe's offer, she said, "Here's what you can do to help. Chloe, we'll get the sheets and towels and you take them to the laundry room. Josh, you get the cleaning cart and wheel it over to the twelve-sixteen. I'll meet you there and—"

They'd come around the corner of the motel. Becca stopped in her tracks and pulled the kids quickly back out of sight. The undersheriff's car was just pulling into the Cliff's parking lot. Laurel, San Diego, and the cell phone, Becca thought. It had finally happened. Jeff Corrie was next, no doubt about it. Her day of reckoning was upon her.

TWENTY-EIGHT

"New game," Becca whispered to the kids. "Cops and robbers. Be real quiet."

The kids squealed. Chloe covered her mouth and bounced from foot to foot.

"Here's how it works," Becca said. "You go to the office without anyone seeing you."

"Even Grammer?"

"Even Grammer. You get my backpack. It's just inside the door, okay? You bring it back to me without being seen."

"What about room twelve-sixteen?"

"That'll come later," Becca told them.

"Is there a prize if no one sees us?" Josh whispered.

"There's always a prize. But later, not now, okay?"

"'Kay!"

Becca watched as they slinked along the porch. Then she faded back out of sight and hoped for their success. Even if the undersheriff beat them into the office to talk to Debbie, there was still a chance that they could get in there and snag the backpack without being seen.

They managed it. Or at least Josh did because Chloe, he said, was "creating a version. She pretended to fall. We had to do it 'cause Grammer was still on the phone."

"Great," Becca said. "Now you head back and I'll see you later. After the undersheriff's gone, okay?"

"But the undersheriff's not—"

"Just go back and don't mention me to anyone. I'll be back sooner than you think."

This last was a lie, and Becca hoped she'd be forgiven for it eventually. She grabbed Josh and kissed the top of his head. Then she cut through some bushes and emerged on Cascade Street.

She crossed over and dashed behind a long, shingled building that was the Saratoga Inn. This put her out of sight of Cascade Street, where there was little doubt the undersheriff's car would come cruising the moment he had finished talking to Debbie, which would *also* be the exact same moment after he was told about the fourteen-year-old girl who was staying at the Cliff, waiting for her mother to show up.

Becca hunkered down against a Dumpster at the edge of the inn's property. She was out of sight of the inn's windows, and that was how she wanted it because she needed to think.

She could handle seeing the undersheriff. She could even, perhaps, bluff her way through a real conversation with the man. But if Jeff had reported his wife and daughter as missing and if he'd said in his smooth Jeff Corrie way, "Say, let me e-mail you a picture of them so you know who you're looking for," there was still a chance that her looks weren't changed enough and the undersheriff would recognize her, and she couldn't risk that.

Becca hit her fists gently against her forehead, as if this would help her know what to do. She rested her cheek on her knees and she saw the lights of the library go out for the end of the day. Next to the library was the tiny brick city hall, also the location of the police department. So she could hardly stay in her present position because surely the undersheriff would check in with the local police and share her picture and tell them whom to be on the lookout for.

She got to her feet. She crossed Second Street. She made her way quickly to South Whidbey Commons. If anyone on earth was left to help her, she figured it had to be Seth. She didn't believe in him completely. She couldn't believe in him completely. But there was no one else.

He wasn't there. She looked around in all of the rooms. She finally had no choice but to ask if anyone knew where he was, and she had luck. It turned out that Seth had scrounged money from everyone there and had gone over to Village Pizzeria for a large one with pepperoni and mushrooms.

Becca felt the panic of having to go outside again, but she made herself do it. The pizzeria was on First Street, at nearly the highest point of the bluff overlooking the passage. Next to it and behind a picket fence and a hedge, there was a little garden filled with wrought-iron tables where, in the summer, tourists ate their pizzas. Becca waited here anxiously, but when Seth didn't emerge as soon as she thought he would, she steeled herself and went inside.

He was just paying. Becca approached, but the noise assailed her. The place was filled with a combination of music, talk, and whispers, and for a moment she fell back a step because it felt like something was clawing at her eyes.

Seth turned, as if he could feel Becca's panic. He said, "Hey. Happenin?" as the pizza was handed over to him.

She said, "You've got to . . . Seth, I need help . . . I don't have anyone—"

He nodded at the door and said, "Outside."

"I can't! They might see!"

"What's going on? Alien invasion? Come on," and he led her out the door but not onto the sidewalk. He went into the little garden at the pizzeria's side and Becca told him the undersheriff was at the motel.

He said, "So?" and a single whisper broke through Becca's panic. *Paranoid*, it claimed.

"You don't understand." She babbled about the undersheriff's appearance at the school, about the questions he'd been asking, about the cell phone, about tracing the cell phone, about her mother's name coming up and the fact that the undersheriff now knew it. She said, "They've probably talked to my stepfather by now. They *have* to have talked to him. I can't go back to the motel because if the sheriff sees me and my disguise isn't good enough and he tells my stepfather . . . The undersheriff's going to lead him right to me, Seth. He'll kill me then. Do you get it? He'll *kill* me."

"What the heck . . . ?" Seth looked at her strangely. She could hardly blame him. The more she told him, the more insane the story sounded. He said, "Want to tell me what's *really* going on?" and all that she could hear beyond that was *careful, careful* accompanying this. He trusted her about as much as she trusted him, and she didn't know what to do about this.

She said, "I can't. Seth, please. *Please.* I don't know anyone else who can—"

"Okay, okay." Seth shifted his weight as Becca watched over his shoulder for the lights of the undersheriff's car to come cruising along First Street. He finally said, "You wait here. I got to take this back over to the commons. You hungry? Here. Have a piece of the pizza. Go ahead. No problem. It'll be my piece."

Becca took it although her hands were shaking. She could hardly hold the pizza, and lifting it to her mouth was something of a joke. Seth closed the box and told her to sit in one of the wrought-iron chairs at the far end of the garden. He said no one would see her there, and this was the truth for it was shrouded in shadow.

When he was gone, Becca made her way to the far end of the garden. From here, the noise from the pizzeria was muted. She could hear the sound of water in the passage slapping against the shore at the bottom of the bluff. But aside from that, it was only a car passing that she heard, and she couldn't tell if it was the undersheriff because behind the shrubbery at the garden's edge, she could see nothing.

She thought about Jeff Corrie and what it would mean if he showed up. He'd be able to grab her, and what could she do to stop that? He wasn't her father, but she didn't even know who her father was. All he had to do was to produce the marriage certificate to prove he was married to Becca's mother. He'd think ahead the moment he got the phone call from the undersheriff. He'd lay his plans. He was good at that, and she knew he had a plan for what to do with Becca when he found her. And how was she supposed to prevent this: tell the sheriff that she'd read her stepfather's mind and knew he was a murderer? What a great idea.

"Okay."

Becca jumped. Seth had come into the garden and she hadn't heard him.

He said, "Come with me. I know a place you can stay. You'll have to be careful and keep out of sight, but if you do that, you'll be okay" and he headed back toward the street.

Becca whispered fiercely, "I can't go back out there!"

"We won't be on the street for long. It'll be all right."

She felt the sting of frightened tears. "Seth, I *can't*."

He said patiently, "Becca . . ." and then he seemed to reconsider because he altered to, "Okay. There's another way, but it's not easy and there's gonna be blackberry bushes if we miss the jump. You okay with that?"

"*Anything.* Just not the street."

He led her back to the pizzeria, but rather than turn toward its front door, he turned toward the bluff. There at the end of the building, a picket fence blocked the entrance to a bed and breakfast built into the bluff below the pizzeria. Here, bedrooms opened off a balcony that gave them each a view of the water. Seth climbed over the picket fence to stand on the balcony and at first Becca thought, despite his words about a jump, that he intended to break into a room as a hideout. But he motioned her to follow him over and once she'd joined him, he took her to the balcony's edge and said, "That's where we're going," and she saw he meant that they were going to drop from the balcony into the bushes below.

These grew wildly everywhere, holding back erosion. They comprised blackberry brambles with thorns the size of a child's thumb, ivy, salal, ferns, and ocean spray. The plan, Seth told her in a whisper, was to lower themselves from the balcony as far as they could and then make the drop into the bushes. With luck, he explained, they'd hit ocean spray and not land in the middle of the blackberry brambles.

At the bottom of the bluff lay Seawall Park, a grassy walkway that ran most of the length of First Street high above it. Lights along it made it accessible at night, but few people used the place after dark when summer ended, and there was not a soul in Seawall Park now.

"Ready?" Seth asked her.

Becca licked her lips. She said, "Okay," and she watched him slide between the top and middle of the balcony's rails. He held on to one of the posts and lowered himself. When he'd gone as far as he could, he said, "Here goes," and made the drop to the bluff. She heard him cursing. He'd hit the brambles. She winced and said, "Seth, I'm *sorry.*"

He said, "Damn! I got one in the butt. Toss your backpack down first. Then use the next post over, and you should be okay."

She was. The drop was at least ten feet, but the bushes formed a living mattress beneath her. She made her way through them like a jungle explorer, descending to the bottom and out into Seawall Park. Seth was waiting.

He led her silently along the grassy walkway. When he came to the end of the park, he stopped and said, "Here."

Above them hung the backs of the shops on First Street. Next to them was the water of Saratoga Passage. Becca looked around and said, "Where?"

Seth indicated the backs of the shops, particularly the last one in the row. It had a concrete base built into the cliff, and it rose above them three stories. It was painted a bleak and faded red. It was completely dark inside.

Along the west end of this place, a tarmac slope gave service vehicles access to Seawall Park. It was to this slope that Seth next headed. Fear shot through Becca. At the top of the tarmac was First Street once again.

Seth hadn't gone five feet upward, when a city police car pulled onto the tarmac, its lights shining out at an angle over the water. Seth dodged into the darkness at the side of the building and whispered fiercely, "What the *hell*? The local cops after you, too?"

This was the nightmare Becca had anticipated. She said, "Oh my God!" But then the police car backed up to finish a three-point turn, returning the way it had come along First Street. Becca waited for a moment, then joined Seth in the shadows.

He said, "This way," and he led her to the back side of a staircase that rose above them, along the side of the building with the concrete base.

"What is this place?" Becca asked him.

"The Dog House," he said.

"That old tavern?"

"Yep. Been closed for years. No one wants it torn down, but no one can figure out what to do with it." He grinned at her. "Good thing *I* can, huh?"

As she watched, he approached a small door of plywood, perhaps four feet high. It had a simple hasp closing it, and from this a padlock hung. Seth jerked the hasp and it loosened from the wood, which had long ago rotted in the rain. He opened the door just wide enough to slide inside and he said to Becca, "Come on."

It was completely dark inside. The smell was of mildew, dust, and old stones. It was as cold as a witch's heart and what little light there was came from outside on the tarmac. Becca could see piles of sagging cardboard boxes. She could also hear the skittering of rat feet nearby.

She backed up. "I *can't—*"

Seth said, "Just wait here. It's not as bad up above. But I can't take you up there without some stuff."

"What stuff?"

"Stuff I'm going to get. I'll get your stuff, too, back at the motel. It'll all take a while. Couple of hours. But I'll be back."

"C'n we leave the door open?"

"No way. The cops check it. It has to stay closed, but don't worry. Like you saw, the hasp's broken so you won't be locked in and all they'll do is shine a flashlight on it. It'll look locked to them. Long's you're quiet, it's cool. Okay? Look, don't worry. I'll be back. I got to go to my granddad's. That's where stuff is."

"What stuff?" she asked again.

He sounded patient when he replied. "The stuff you'll need. Okay?"

She nodded. And then he was gone, with the door closed in place behind him. The last thing she heard him say from the other side was that she could trust him. In the dark and the cold, with the rats skittering around her, Becca desperately needed to believe just that.

IT SEEMED TO Becca that days passed while she waited for Seth in the basement of the Dog House. There was a sketch of light around the door leading to the tarmac slope, but that was the extent of it.

It was an odd sensation. Becca realized that there were no whispers. The only other times she'd experienced this was when she was too freaked out by something to hear them clearly—as she'd been with Seth—or when she was in a cemetery or with Diana Kinsale. That was it.

When the little door to the basement finally opened, Becca held her breath for a moment, thinking about the police. But then a duffel bag was crammed through the opening, followed by a sleeping bag, followed by a pillowcase filled with something, followed by Seth's grunt, followed by Seth himself. He said, "Whew, *that* wasn't easy. Grand moved a bunch of things."

Becca said, "Seth! Did you tell your grandfather—?"

"Chill. He didn't see me. He was doing something in his shop. Now lemme see . . ." He rustled inside the pillowcase and found what he was looking for. He pulled closed the plywood door and flicked on a powerful flashlight. He shined its beam around the basement, highlighting cobwebs, spiderwebs, and a few tiny rat eyeballs "Sheesh. Let's get outta here." He grabbed the duffel bag and the sleeping bag. Becca picked up the pillowcase and followed him.

The stairs were in the far corner, toward the front of the building. They climbed up to another door, this one regular sized and unlocked. Seth pushed it open, and they were in a commercial kitchen. It was small and smelled of grease. It contained a stove with a massive griddle, a large refrigerator, and a bathtub of a sink.

"Don't use *anything* in here except the water," Seth advised her. "You light that stove, and the whole place'll probably explode. Come on."

From the kitchen, they went through swinging doors and here Seth extinguished the flashlight, for this part of the Dog House looked out onto First Street. The room they were in contained a bar, a pool table, small tables, chairs, and a huge mirror reflecting it all. The windows had been soaped over, but muted light still came through them. Outside, the winter bulbs on a restaurant across the street twinkled in the cavity of its porch.

At the back of the building, the windows overlooked the water, and here there were dusty tables and chairs that gave evidence of the place once serving food. But Seth didn't put the duffel bag down here. Instead, he opened another door, this one to a stairway leading to the second floor of the building.

The room above was large. Here, Seth said, was where she was going to set up shop. He began to unpack the duffel, and Becca saw that he'd brought her camping supplies. A small propane stove, cooking utensils, collapsible water bottle, some packets of dehydrated food. He even put together a stool from various parts that toppled from the bag. From all this Becca realized that her stay in the Dog House was not intended to be a single evening's affair.

She said, "Seth, no! Am I gonna have to stay *here*?"

He looked up. "No place else. You go to someone's house and their parents are going to ask questions. Maybe not the first night, but after that? Oh yeah, they're gonna want to know what you're doing there. You want that?"

"But what'll I do for food when I run out? What'll I do for . . . It's *freezing* in here." Becca could, indeed, even see her breath. She wondered how much colder it was going to get as the night wore on, not to mention how much colder it would get as time itself went on. She thought about going to Diana Kinsale and asking for her help, but how could she? She would have to tell Diana Kinsale about everything, including the whispers and how the whispers had caused the trouble she and Laurel had been fleeing in the first place. Becca couldn't do that. She absolutely couldn't.

She swallowed. "I guess I'm here, then." Then she looked around for the rest of her belongings, the things she had left at the Cliff Motel, but none of them was among what Seth had brought.

She said, "But my stuff . . . the motel?"

Seth shook his head. He was blowing up an air mattress that he'd taken from the pillowcase. He said, "Couldn't get it. I'll try tomorrow. The undersheriff was in the parking lot talking to that Primavera chick from the high school. No way did I want them to see me going into your room or *any* room."

"Ms. Primavera?" Becca said. It was worse and worse. For Tatiana Primavera had heard the phone message from Laurel and she would now tell the undersheriff and then the final connection would be made. It would *have* to be made. People weren't stupid. "What was she *doing* there?" Becca wailed.

"Heck d'I know." Seth finished with the air mattress and then unrolled the sleeping bag on it. He said, "I'll try to get the rest of your stuff tomorrow. Meantime, don't sweat it. You'll be okay here. There's even a bathroom. I'll bring you soap and a towel.

I'll bring some shampoo. Just hang tough. You can do that, can't you?"

Becca didn't see that she had a choice. It was hang tough or nothing. For better or worse, the Dog House was going to be her new home.

PART FOUR

The Meadow Loop Trail

TWENTY-NINE

Hayley Cartwright was driving the farm truck out of the school parking lot when she saw Becca King pushing a bike with a flat tire in the direction of the school. It was the end of a school day, though. Becca was going in the wrong direction.

Hayley recognized the bike. It belonged to Seth. Because of its crazily painted psychedelic handlebars, there couldn't have been another bike like it on the island. Hayley wondered why the dowdy-looking girl with the thick-framed glasses had it. Obviously, Seth had handed it over to her, but Hayley didn't know what this meant. She *did* know it shouldn't be important to her. But it was, somehow. Just as it was also important to Hayley that this girl Becca had put a note into Derric's hand at the hospital. "Give this back to me when you wake up," it had read. That message suggested more than one thing to Hayley, and one thing it suggested was confidence. Confidence in Derric, confidence in his condition, and confidence about other things as well. Hayley told herself she could use some of that confidence. So she rolled down the window and called Becca's name.

"You need a ride? You're going in the wrong direction, you

know." She smiled. "School's over. You aren't just getting here, are you?"

Becca blinked owlishly behind those weird glasses. She had so much black around her eyes that she looked like a panda. She said, "Oh. Hi," and she added with a glance down at the bike, "Got a flat. I needed to get some stuff from my locker."

"Well, if you want, I c'n give you a ride after you get the stuff. There's a tire place up on the highway. I c'n take you there."

"'Kay," Becca said. "That'd be good. I thought I'd fixed this stupid thing yesterday, but I guess I didn't do such a good job." She waited till Hayley had pulled to the side of the road and she handed the bike over to her. She said she'd be right back and she hurried in the direction of the school building. She looked around a little furtively as she walked.

When she returned, her backpack was crammed. Hayley said, "Wow. Impressive. You've got the homework, huh?" and Becca said, "I had to miss school a couple days. Makeup work. You know."

Hayley knew that much, at least the part about Becca missing school. For she had been on the reception desk when Debbie Grieder had phoned in a panic. Where was Becca King? she'd demanded. Could Hayley tell her if she was in school? She was missing from the Cliff Motel, but her belongings were still in her room. Debbie Grieder didn't want to *think* what this might mean. Please, please tell me she's in school, she'd cried. Hayley had put her through to the attendance clerk. Beyond that, she didn't know how to help.

She opened the tailgate of the farm truck and loaded up the bike. They set off in the direction of the highway.

Hayley said to Becca, "Debbie Grieder called the school. She said you were gone but your stuff was still at the motel. She's really—"

"I got my stuff," Becca broke in quickly. "Well, Seth got it for me. I was staying with Debbie but things didn't work out."

"Oh." Hayley cast around for something else to say to the girl. Seth seemed the logical subject at this point, but she didn't want Becca to get the wrong idea. Another good subject would be "Where are you staying now?" but—

"Debbie doesn't like Seth," Becca announced out of nowhere. "If you see her, don't tell her he helped me, okay?"

Hayley glanced at her curiously. Becca was looking down at her fingernails, which were dirty. So was the rest of her. She smelled pretty bad. Hayley wondered where on earth she was staying if she wasn't at the Cliff Motel. She looked like someone who'd been sleeping in a car. Seth's car, maybe, but that hardly made sense. Wouldn't Seth just take her home to his parents or to his grandfather's house if she needed a place to stay?

"Course, he's not my boyfriend or anything," Becca went on suddenly. She was looking intently out of the side window. Her face was completely hidden from view.

"Huh?"

"Seth. He's not my boyfriend. He's just . . . I met him right when I came to the island. Him and Diana Kinsale. Well, I met Diana Kinsale first 'cause I was riding my bike—my other bike?— on Bob Galbreath Road and I didn't know how bad it was there. I had to stop. She gave me a ride. I met Seth the next day at the Star Store."

How weird, Hayley thought. Something wasn't right in all

this. She could sense it. Seth, Becca, Diana Kinsale, the Star Store, Debbie Grieder, the Cliff Motel, Becca leaving it, Debbie Grieder not knowing, and now Becca talking about it all with no apparent reason. It almost seemed like—

"It's drugs, see," Becca said in a rush. They'd come to the end of Maxwelton Road and were at the light, waiting to go onto the highway. "Debbie thinks Seth's into drugs."

"Seth doesn't do drugs."

"That's not what Debbie thinks."

"Wow. Not fair."

"That's what I thought. So . . ." Becca shrugged.

She was making it sound as if she'd cut out on Debbie due to loyalty to Seth, Hayley thought. That was nice, but it didn't seem exactly probable. How long had she known Seth, after all? No. There was more here than met the eye. She was about to ask Becca what was really going on, but Becca spoke first.

"How's Derric?" she asked. "I haven't been able to get up to see him."

"The same," Hayley told her. The light changed and they pulled onto the highway, heading south. "I saw that note you put in his hand. Seems like you're sure he'll recover. That's nice."

Becca finally looked at her, then. Her forehead furrowed. She said, "I just . . . It was dumb, but I wanted him to have something. I didn't have anything else with me, and I saw all the balloons and flowers and stuff. It just seemed like something . . . It didn't *mean* anything. I don't expect him . . . I mean, it's not like I'm after him."

"What if you are? He's a great guy."

"Gosh," Becca breathed. "That's sort of . . ."

"What?"

"Aren't you guys . . . You and Derric . . . ? You know."

"Seth told you that, didn't he?" That figures, Hayley thought. "He doesn't know what he's talking about."

"Oh."

"He *doesn't.* Plus, he acts first and he thinks later. If you hang around him much, you'll see him in action. You'll do something and he won't give you a chance to explain and he'll lose his temper and—" Hayley stopped herself. She *heard* herself. Acting without thinking and there Derric was in a coma from which he would not emerge to point a finger at whoever pushed him over that bluff. If he was pushed, Hayley told herself. *If* he was pushed.

Becca said nothing in reply to Hayley's words. Hayley went no further with them. But it wasn't a friendly silence that hung between the two girls at that point. It was a silence heavy with thoughts and suspicions.

So much for learning about the source of her confidence, Hayley thought. So much for thinking she had confidence in Derric's recovery at all. For if she was thick with Seth Darrow, chances were good that she knew more than she was saying about everything. For all Hayley knew, she'd been at the hospital with Seth for a sinister reason, not an act of kindness toward Derric at all but rather a threat.

"Give this back to me when you wake up" had an entirely different meaning, then. It was the same as saying, "Call me when you come to because you and I have stuff to talk about."

It was too horrible to contemplate where all of this was leading. Hayley wanted Becca King out of her truck. Mercifully, the tire store was in view. Hayley sped up to get to it. When they arrived, she braked the truck, hard. She waited for Becca to climb out, get her bike, and get away from her. But instead Becca said the strangest thing of all:

"You know Seth's sandals?"

"Huh? What about them?" Hayley wanted to push her out of the truck, but it didn't seem she was in any hurry.

"I saw that kid Dylan had a pair like them. I never saw sandals like that before."

Hayley stared at her. "So?" *What a weird chick* was what she was thinking.

Becca turned red. "I was just wondering . . . Do you think they came from around here? They're sort of cool. I'd like to get—"

"There's no shoe store around, if that's what you mean. They're probably from some place over town. Seattle, maybe. And anyway, why d'you want a pair of sandals this time of year? It's going to get too cold to wear them."

"I guess," Becca said. "I never saw . . . I mean, no one else has them."

Hayley wanted to yell, "And this is important *because* . . . ?" but she kept quiet, thinking furiously. She could make no connections among Becca's shifts in topic except the obvious one. And the obvious one had everything to do with Seth, Derric, and what Becca knew about Saratoga Woods.

Hayley said shrewdly, "Are you protecting Seth?"

"From what?" Becca asked her. At last she had her hand on the door handle. At last she was going to get out of the truck. But not before Hayley found out what she knew because she did know something. It was written all over her.

"Come on," Hayley said. "You know what I mean. Are you *protecting* him, Becca?"

She shook her head.

"You're lying, aren't you?" Hayley asked her.

Becca looked at her squarely then. Her gaze was steady and it chilled Hayley from her head to her feet. "Not any more than you are," she said.

———

HAYLEY'S BRAIN WAS whirling once Becca left her. Seth, Derric, Diana Kinsale, Saratoga Woods, Dylan, a pair of sandals. Becca King was a girl who talked in riddles, and Hayley couldn't work out the answer to any of them. By the time she got home, she was in a state of strung nerves. That state got immediately worse when she saw the SUV was gone.

Her stomach clenched hard. If the SUV was gone and her mom was gone, there was always the chance that something had happened with her dad.

She got out of the truck. But then she heard the sound of the rototiller's motor. The fact that the sound of it was coming from the direction of the vegetable beds meant her dad was actually working there.

It was such a pleasure to think of her father finally back out on the land again that Hayley hurried in the direction of the massive beds. But there she saw it wasn't her father at work at all. Rather it was Seth. Hayley looked around for Sammy, but the VW was nowhere in sight.

Seth made the turn at the end of one of the beds. He looked up and saw her. He jerked his head in hello and she waved him over. He turned off the motor of the rototiller and strode across the beds, meeting her by the deer fence.

She said, "What're you doing here? Where's my dad? Where's your car?"

Seth looked startled by the onslaught of questions. He hiked up his loose jeans in that way he had and said, "Hi to you, too, Hayley."

"*Answer* me."

"What*ever*, Hayl. Your mom needed to take Brooke and Cassidy to the dentist. Your dad was working on the SUV so I loaned them Sammy."

"So where's the SUV now?"

"What's with the third degree?"

"*Where's* the SUV, Seth?"

"Th' heck should I know? Your dad said he needed to get something from the gas station over in Greenbank. I don't know what. Spark plugs maybe. Oil. He didn't say."

"And you just let him go?" Hayley backed off from the deer fence. "What's *wrong* with you?"

"What's wrong with *you*? It's his SUV. He can do what he wants."

"You don't—" Hayley made herself stop. It was all *right*, she told herself. She was just scared. She wasn't thinking straight. She was worried about Derric, she was worried about her dad, she was worried about how her mom and her sisters were going to keep the farm running, and now she was worried about a pair of sandals. Because Seth wasn't wearing his at the moment and what did *that* mean?

She said brusquely to Seth, "Funny. You don't even ask how he is."

"Your dad? Hey, I was thinking there's something wrong with him. D'you—"

"I'm not talking about my dad! I'm talking about Derric. Why don't you even mention him? Why don't you ask? 'Is he alive? Is he dead? Is he still in a coma?' Why aren't you asking? Don't you even want to *know*?"

Seth came the rest of the distance to the deer fence and put his hands on it. He said in a quiet voice, "Hey. What's going on?"

"Where're your sandals, Seth? Why aren't you wearing them?"

He looked at his feet and then at her. He said, "Hayley, you're all over the map. What's the big deal if I'm not wearing those sandals?"

"You *always* wear them. You never wear anything else."

"Wrong."

"No. Right."

Seth had his fedora on, as usual. He pulled on its rim in a way someone would to hide their face. He said, "What's it to you what I have on my feet? What's it to you if I want to walk around in my socks? What's anything I do got to do with you, Hayley? Way I remember stuff, I'm nothing to you anyway. So quit with the questions." He turned away from her, as if to go back to the work he'd been doing.

She cried, "What're you *doing* here, Seth? Why're you working on the vegetable beds? Why'd you stack all that wood? Mom told me you did it. What d'you *want* from me?"

"I'm just trying to help out, okay? I fixed the rototiller motor, too, and it seemed—"

"Oh, what could be cooler than that? You *fixed* the rototiller.

How totally great. What's *wrong* with you? Why don't you at least wear a size of jeans that fit? Why don't you get a decent job? Why don't you study for the GED? Because you're *not* doing that, are you? You haven't even begun. D'you think you can just show up here and stack some wood and work in the garden and I'm not going to figure out what you did?"

"*Did?* What the heck?"

"You pushed him, didn't you? You were in the woods. You argued with him about me. We were kissing and so *what*, Seth, and I tried to tell you that but no way did you want to listen to me. But then you saw him and you saw your chance and—"

"Hey, hey, hey!" Seth shouted. "This is all about *Derric*?" He turned to the fence and banged his fist on it. Then he shoved his way off it. He started to walk away. He swung around and walked back. He walked away again. He kicked at the dirt. He came back to her and punched his fist on the fence post. "Great," he said. "Wonderful. Why don't you just call the sheriff and turn me in?"

"Do everyone a favor," she said. "Turn yourself in."

That said, she left him and headed for the house. Her mother rumbled into the driveway in Sammy.

THIRTY

Seth wanted to smash his fist into the deer fence another time, just to do *something*. More than that, he wanted to follow Hayley and shake her by the shoulders until her head bounced around. But everyone was getting out of the VW, and Cassidy was crying and shouting, "It's not fair! She *said*!" and Brooke was yelling, "I was sitting in the front seat! I couldn't share! Mom, *tell* her!" and Mrs. Cartwright looked completely done. Cassidy went on about the dentist telling Brooke she was supposed to "share that stupid comic book with me" and Brooke continued to argue that she couldn't share it from the front seat, so "here it is, dummy, why don't you just *eat* it," as she threw it at her sister and then slammed her way into the house, with Cassidy following.

Hayley had already gone into the house, too, and Mrs. Cartwright started looking around, her face confused. Seth figured that here was another person about to ask him where that stupid SUV was, so he decided to go over and let her know that Mr. Cartwright had taken it to Greenbank for spark plugs or oil or something.

When he told her this, she cried out, "*What?* When did he leave? *Greenbank?*" She said the last word as if Greenbank was

Portland and not the nearest place to find a gas station and a general store. She cried, "We have to find him. *Now*," which was something of a mystery since Seth couldn't figure out why they had to find a man who'd gone about five miles down the road.

But he had no time to remark on this. Mrs. Cartwright threw him the keys to Sammy and said, "You drive. I'll look," as if Mr. Cartwright had probably crashed the SUV into a ditch.

Seth took the keys and climbed in the VW, but what he was thinking was that there was something seriously wrong around here.

In less than two miles, they saw the SUV. It was parked neatly enough along the roadside, in a pull-out beneath a patch of big-leaf maples. Mrs. Cartwright was out of the VW before it came to a full stop. She ran to the driver's door and tried to open it. She pounded on the window, too. Seth realized she'd forgotten that the door didn't open from the outside any longer, and he dashed over to the passenger's door and got inside.

Mr. Cartwright was just sitting in the driver's seat, not doing a thing, not even looking at the window where his wife was pounding. He turned his head slowly when Seth said, "Mr. Cartwright, you okay?"

"Yeah, son," he said with a smile. "I just can't push the damn clutch all the way down. Something's wrong with it."

By this time, Mrs. Cartwright had come around to Seth's side of the car, and she started to pull on Seth's legs to get him out of the passenger's seat. Her reaction was so extreme that Seth was beginning to wonder if she was a little crazy. He was more than happy to vacate the car.

Mrs. Cartwright crawled inside. She said, "It's okay, baby. It's okay, honey," to her husband, and then she turned to Seth. "I'm going to need your help getting him over the console."

Seth wanted to ask her why she just didn't ask Mr. Cartwright to crawl over the console himself, but she didn't look like a lady in a state to receive that kind of question. So he said, "Sure," and she told him to get in the backseat and help with Mr. Cartwright's shoulders while she took his legs.

Mr. Cartwright said, "I c'n manage, Julie," and his wife said, "Bill, let us get you into the other seat, honey."

As far as Seth could tell, Mr. Cartwright couldn't manage a thing. He was dead weight, and getting him out of the driver's seat, across the console, and into the passenger's seat was no easy feat. Seth didn't see what good this was going to do anyway because of the SUV itself, and he said to Mrs. Cartwright, "He says there's something wrong with the clutch. Maybe we should leave the car here so—"

"There's nothing wrong with the clutch." She strapped the seat belt around her husband. He lolled to one side, and she cried, "Bill! Bill!"

Mr. Cartwright said, "I'm okay. That darn clutch . . ."

Seth could see that something was seriously wrong, and it didn't have anything to do with the car. He said, "D'you think we should take him up to the hospital?"

"He *said* it was the clutch!"

"But you just said—"

"Seth, stop it. Please."

Seth could see she was near tears. He said quickly, "Okay. I'll drive this car, you take Sammy."

She said, "I'll drive him home," but Seth pointed out that it was going to be easier for him just to climb over the backseat and into the driver's seat than it was going to be for her to crawl over her husband, and if there *was* something wrong with the clutch, it was better to let him deal with it.

She agreed to this. She swiped at her cheeks and said, "Bill? Seth's going to drive you home. I'll be right behind. You just close your eyes."

Mr. Cartwright murmured, "Couldn't push that clutch in," and Mrs. Cartwright told him that everything was going to be okay.

But Seth knew one thing above everything else. It wasn't going to be okay at all.

———

THE WAS NO question about it as far as Seth was concerned: He needed to tell his grandfather. When he arrived at the property on Newman Road, the lights were on in Ralph's shop behind the house. He made his way over and looked through the window. There he witnessed a miracle of sorts, and it cheered him up at once. For Gus was sitting on an old army blanket about five feet from where Ralph perched on a stool in front of his workbench. The Lab's eyes were fixed on Seth's grandfather in a manner that might have suggested utter devotion had there not been a small pile of dog kibbles next to the project Ralph was working on. As Seth watched, he heard Ralph say, "Good stay, Gus," and then "Come. Sit," which the dog did obediently. Ralph said, "Good," and gave him one tiny kibble.

He didn't look at the dog as he did this. Instead his attention was on what he was doing, which was fiddling with something that lay in pieces on the workbench. Without a glance at the dog, Ralph said, "Bed," and Gus returned to the army blanket. "Stay," Ralph told him, and he stayed. "Down," and down he went and there he remained. It was, Seth thought, the eighth wonder of the world.

He figured things would change when he opened the door and entered the shop, but when he did this, Gus merely raised his head, wagged his tail, and lifted his ears slightly. Ralph looked over his shoulder and, seeing Seth, said to Gus, "Okay," and to Seth, "He jumps, you turn your back. I don't care how much you want to love him. You do like I say. We're *going* to train that dog."

It took three tries, but Gus finally stopped jumping to greet Seth with typical Lab enthusiasm. Seth was able to pat his head and rub his ears, and when his grandfather handed him two kibbles, Seth said, "Good dog, Gus. Good, good, *good*!"

"Last thing he needs is to be a victim of too much positive reinforcement, grandson," was Ralph's growled comment. His back was turned, as he continued his work. "One 'good' is enough. Now tell him bed."

Seth did so. Gus looked as surprised as a Lab could look, receiving a command from someone who previously was considered his number one playmate. But the dog cooperated, heard himself pronounced good, and received one kibble for this feat of greatness.

Seth joined his grandfather at the workbench. He saw that Ralph had taken apart the hearing box that belonged to Becca

King. He said, "Where'd you get that, Grand?" And he added, "What is it?" to hide his own knowledge of its ownership.

"Diana brought it by."

"Mrs. Kinsale?"

"You know another Diana?" Ralph was separating the wires and frowning down at them.

"Guess not," Seth admitted, but he wondered how Mrs. Kinsale had gotten hold of Becca's hearing device. He also wondered how Becca was doing without it. She hadn't mentioned losing it or breaking it. But then, she'd been in a panic anyway when he'd taken her to the Dog House, so she probably had bigger worries on her mind.

He was thinking about this when his grandfather spoke. "Seth, you ready with an explanation?" He paused with what he was doing and looked at Seth, and Seth could see there was an unusual droop to the corners of his eyes.

"Explanation for what?"

"Not like you to be less than direct with me," was Ralph's reply.

"I wouldn't be if I knew what you were talking about." Gus gave a whine, and Seth looked at the Lab. He was eyeballing both of them, like a kid at a tennis match.

"My camping gear's missing, Seth. You left a bungee cord dangling from the rafters."

Seth dropped his gaze. He looked up again as Ralph changed positions at the workbench, putting his face in shadow as he leaned against it. The strong task light was behind him then, and it made a halo around his head. His hair was loose, and it glowed in the light.

"Did you need money for some reason?" Ralph asked quietly.

"What d'you mean?"

"I mean did you sell my camping gear?"

"Why would—" Seth stopped. He peered at his grandfather and saw on Ralph's face an expression that he'd never expected to see: suspicion. He said, "No, Grand, I didn't sell it," but his voice had an edge to it and he knew the edge sounded like a defense being raised. "I needed it for a friend. You'll get it all back."

"It's not like you to borrow things without asking me," Ralph noted. "Was I here when you took the stuff?"

"No!" Seth lied. "I would've asked if you'd been here. A kid I know's been couch surfing, and he was out of places to sleep. I figured he could use the stuff. I know where to find him. You'll get it all back."

Ralph said nothing, but Seth could tell by the way his mouth curved downward that his grandfather not only doubted him but also thought Seth might really have sold the gear, despite his words. There would be only one reason for Ralph to reach that conclusion, too. Drugs.

Seth *never* used, and his grandfather was supposed to know that. But the fact remained that he had once been a protégé of Sean Grieder. The fact also remained that Sean Grieder was sitting in a prison cell because of meth, among other things. And these two facts amounted to a single damning point being made.

Seth wanted to yell, "He taught me to play chess! He *didn't* get me into drugs!" But in everyone's eyes it was a case of guilt by association. Seth had known Sean, *and* he'd dropped out of school, just like Sean. *Everyone* drew a conclusion from that. Except his own parents. Except his own grandfather. Until now.

Seth felt as if something was slicing into his heart. He said, "Okay, then."

Ralph said, "'What's that mean?"

"Just 'okay.' See you later."

"You came by for something, didn't you? What was it?"

"To talk. But I guess we've done that, huh?"

"Seth . . ." His grandfather's voice was gentler now, but Seth didn't want gentleness from him.

He walked to the door and opened it. He left the shop but Gus came as well. He said, "Stay, Gus," but the dog didn't obey. Instead he leaped up as if begging Seth to remain, to play, to be his pal-above-pals. Seth started to stride off, but Gus followed. Seth headed to the path leading up to his car, but Gus hurtled by him. At the top, the Lab leapt eagerly and Seth staggered backward, nearly losing his footing. He said, "No! *No!*" and shoved Gus away.

Gus gave a yelp of surprise. Then Ralph was at the door of the shop down below. He said sharply, "Gus. Come."

The dog obeyed at once.

THIRTY-ONE

Becca had thought the worst part would be the Dog House at night. But the really bad part turned out to be missing school in order to stay away from the undersheriff during his search for Laurel Armstrong. She had all of her books, so she tried to keep up with what she imagined the schoolwork would be, but the integrated algebra was slaying her and there was nothing she could do about her yearbook class.

Despite the camping food that Seth had given her, she didn't use the Coleman stove. It worried her that she might cause a fire, so mostly she darted down to the Star Store in the darkness of early morning when Seth was at work. She was quickly running out of what little money Debbie Grieder had paid her for helping out at the motel though. Soon, she knew, she would have no money at all, aside from her San Diego funds, which she didn't want to spend. She didn't know what she'd do then except rely on Seth to pass her food throwaways as he'd done on the first morning she'd met him.

At first Becca had thought that, without the AUD box, she'd be able to sort out truth from lie when she was around Seth. She thought she'd be able to get to the bottom of that footprint she'd seen where Derric had fallen. But inside his head Seth *never* dwelled on Saratoga Woods, and he certainly never thought about his sandals. Whenever she saw him in those early mornings, the only whispers she was able to hear clearly from him concerned the Cartwrights. If he wasn't mulling over Hayley Cartwright, he was onto Hayley's father for some reason, and then onto her mother, and *then* onto their SUV. It was as if he knew Becca could pick up on his thoughts and was keeping them fixed in a place that was safe.

At least he had managed to get the rest of her things from the motel. He'd hung around the missionary alliance across the street from the place, he said, till Debbie had finally gone to one of her meetings. He'd sneaked into room 444 then, and he'd collected everything he could find. He brought her his bike as well, and this they'd stowed in the Dog House cellar. Just in case, he'd told her.

The bike provided an outlet for Becca, the only way to escape worries that ranged from her mother's continued absence, to Jeff Corrie pulling into town, to the undersheriff's showing up at the Dog House. When she couldn't handle one more second of solitude and breathing the musty air of the ancient abandoned tavern, she slipped outside for no more than an hour and tore over to the Langley cemetery. There she took at least a little comfort from continuing to work on Reese Grieder's grave.

That was what she was doing the next time she saw Diana Kinsale. On her knees and working on the gravestone, Becca heard her truck this time, and even if she hadn't, soon enough the swarm of dogs encircled her. She swore at herself for having left the Dog House in the first place. She only hoped Diana hadn't heard she'd taken off from the Cliff Motel.

Diana had parked where she always parked, near her husband's grave, but she didn't pause there. Instead, she came across the lawn toward Becca, carrying something in a lunch sack.

The dogs bounded about, snuffling and lifting their legs against the shrubbery. Becca said to them, "Don't you dare pee on this grave, you guys," and she heard Diana's warm laugh.

Then Becca heard something more. *Can you hear what I'm thinking, Becca King?* came to her distinctly, every bit as distinctly as she'd ever heard her mother's whispers of *listen my children and you shall hear of the midnight ride of Paul Revere.* Becca stopped what she was doing and swallowed down a lump of pure terror. She thought of many things at that moment, but central to everything was Jeff Corrie and what it had meant once someone other than her mom and her grandma had learned about the whispers.

She said, "Hi!" as brightly as she could manage and she went back to cleaning Reese's gravestone.

As if she hadn't sent out a whisper at all, Diana said, "I *thought* I might find you here. I've brought this back for you."

She extended the lunch sack, and Becca opened it to see within it the AUD box and its earphone, all repaired. She felt a surge of relief. She said, "Who fixed it?"

"Ralph Darrow. Seth's grandfather. The man can fix anything." Diana smiled and added, "Almost anything. He can't fix broken hearts." She stood next to Becca and looked down at Reese's grave. "You've done a nice job with this. All you need is a new picture of her." She moved to the other side of the grave where she could face Becca directly. There she spoke again. "Debbie's worried about you, Becca. She phoned me."

To this Becca said nothing, although she considered what kind of answer she could make.

"My dear, why did you leave the motel?"

"It was time."

"Was Debbie still going to her meetings?"

Odd question, Becca thought, but she said, "Far as I know."

"I'm glad to hear that." Diana squatted. She brushed some of the newly fallen leaves to one side of the grave. "She misses you. So do the kids. It's double for Josh, I think, because of Derric being in the hospital."

Becca felt a little stab at the thought of Chloe and Josh. "They okay?"

"When Debbie's there."

"Is she going out places and leaving them alone?"

"No. But there's being there in body and there's being there at the same time as your thoughts."

"Oh." Becca knew her voice sounded as small as she felt. Chloe and Josh had done better when she was with them, and she knew that.

As if she'd heard what Becca was considering, Diana said, "I think Chloe and Josh did a little better when you were at the motel."

"Maybe." Becca knew she sounded miserable, because she *felt* miserable about those two kids.

Diana said quickly, "I didn't say that to get you to go back. I wouldn't want you to think that. Whatever I say to you . . . Please don't think it's anything more than *exactly* what I'm saying. Do you understand?"

"Guess so," Becca said.

"All I meant is that you provided them with the extra thought thing that Debbie can't give them right now."

"Why not?"

Diana patted the grave. "Because her mind is on this."

"Where's their mom, then? Debbie never said."

"She's gone."

"Dead?"

"Disappeared. She went to Arizona a long time ago, when the kids were still with Sean."

"Why didn't she take them?"

"Because she was using. More than Sean was, in fact. It wasn't a good situation."

Becca looked away. She shifted her gaze from Diana to three monoliths that marked the part of the cemetery where people's ashes were spread, their names left in the form of carvings on the three huge stones so that they wouldn't go unremembered.

She felt very bad for Chloe and Josh. She knew Debbie loved them, and she knew they were better off with Debbie than with their mom. But it was true that Debbie wasn't always *there* completely. Becca had seen this herself although she didn't know why Debbie couldn't move on from Reese's death.

Diana said, "Losing a child is the worst that can happen to a woman, Becca, with one exception."

"What's the exception?"

"Being the person responsible. That's the worst."

THEY WALKED AWAY from Reese Grieder's grave. Becca went toward her bike, which she'd left leaning against a sweet gum tree that was a haze of red and gold in the afternoon light. Diana was heading toward her truck, but she paused and asked two questions Becca had been hoping to avoid.

"Where are you staying now? Why aren't you in school?"

To avoid answering the first question, Becca went with the second one. "I couldn't go without the AUD box. Now that I've got it back, I'll go. Thanks for getting it fixed."

This constituted the first time that Becca had actually lied to Diana Kinsale. The part about the AUD box was true, and so were her thanks. But the part about going back to school now that her AUD box was repaired was as false as a plastic Christmas tree.

Diana said again, "Where are you staying, Becca?"

"At a friend's."

"Seth's family?"

"Seth? Nope."

"Don't want to tell me?"

Becca sent Diana an agonized look.

"Okay." At the truck, though, Diana didn't get inside, although she opened the back of it to let the dogs leap into its bed. They all cooperated except Oscar, of course. Diana opened the cab door for him but still she didn't climb in. Instead she said to Becca, sounding thoughtful, "I've got to go up to Coupeville for an appointment. Would you like to come with me? Have a chance to see Derric?"

Becca thought how much she'd like to do just that. It had been so long, too long, since she'd been willing even to take the risk of seeing him. And now there seemed an added risk because of that single whisper she'd heard so clearly from Diana. Still, Becca wanted to go. So she said yes. Derric was more than worth any risk.

They put her bike in the bed of the pickup and set off. Diana made the turn onto Fairground Road, and she didn't say anything more until they reached the bottom of the steeply curved descent. What she said then caused a shiver of consternation to run through Becca's veins.

"May I tell Debbie Grieder that I've seen you and that you're all right?"

Becca hated to disappoint Diana, but she still had to say it. "Please, can you not?"

"Becca, what's wrong? Can you believe in me enough to tell me?"

But how *could* she tell her? Becca wondered. Telling her anything meant ultimately telling her that the undersheriff had been looking for Laurel Armstrong and, on the path of Laurel, he'd come to the motel. This meant he'd been a mere few yards from Becca's room and a mere few minutes from discovering her. To tell Diana this would mean telling her about Jeff Corrie and San Diego as well. It was just too much. So she said, "I can't. But it's not like I've done something bad. It's just that . . . I can't."

They were at the stop sign, facing Langley Road, and Diana didn't move the truck forward. Instead she said, "Do you know that Seth Darrow might be in trouble because of you?"

"*Seth?* Why?"

Diana explained that Tatiana Primavera had seen Seth Darrow driving off from the motel just before Debbie Grieder discovered that Becca's belongings were missing from her room. To Debbie this meant that Seth had taken Becca's things and to Debbie *that* meant that Seth either knew where Becca was or had done something to her. "Debbie thinks she knows which one is the case," Diana told her. "I'm worried she'll talk to the sheriff about Seth."

Becca let her head fall back against the headrest of her seat. She couldn't *believe* she'd caused Seth more trouble. Now she'd have to warn him about this. But how could she? There'd been signs all around Seth that were making it tougher and tougher for her to find safe footing with him. His obsession with Hayley Cartwright and the Cartwright family was one of those signs. The footprint she'd seen in the woods was another. His admission that he didn't like Derric was a third. Becca felt dizzy with not being able to decide what she ought to do about him.

They listened to the Dixie Chicks for the rest of the drive to Coupeville. When they reached the hospital, Diana pulled into the parking lot. She said her appointment was across the street. A doctor's visit, but she wouldn't be long. She'd come by Derric's room when she was finished. She'd like to look in on Derric, too.

"Doctor?" Becca asked quickly. "Are you sick?"

Diana smiled. "When you get to be my age, you become that line from the poem: 'Things fall apart / The center cannot hold.' I'm in the 'things fall apart' stage of my life." She shouldered open her door and told Oscar and the other dogs to stay. "See you in a bit," she said to Becca.

NO ONE WAS in Derric's room in the middle of a school day. So in place of people reading to him, music was playing. It was cheerful marimba music, and it came from an iPod set up on the bedside table. Next to the iPod, Becca saw, the picture that had fallen from her hands now had a new frame. This one was chrome, but there was a smudge of stickiness on it where the price tag hadn't come off completely. So as Becca sat next to the bed, she picked up the picture and worked her thumbnail against the remains of the glue. She also reached for Derric's hand to tell him what she was doing. She said she hadn't brought him anything to read, but she could tell him what was going on around him, if he would like that.

The music altered in the time it took for two heartbeats. Suddenly there was no marimba music at all but rather a jazzy kind of tune played by saxophones, trumpets, a tuba, and drums. Along with this music came children's laughter and a voice crying *Derric! Derrrrr . . . ic!* And over that crying rose the word *rejoice*, and the jazzy music increased in volume. But none of this was coming from the iPod.

Derric's fingers moved in Becca's hand. They curved around hers, and they held on tightly. Becca gasped and looked at him. His eyes were open. He was looking at her.

She thought, Oh my God, and she looked around frantically, knowing she had to get someone to come at once. But she was afraid to let go of his hand because she knew, somehow, that letting go would break a connection that had been established between them.

Becca couldn't tell if he really saw her, but as she watched, tears came into Derric's dark eyes. They slid down his temples and began to wet the pillow on which his head lay. Between his hand and hers flowed an immensity of heart pain. He seemed to struggle for breath.

She said, "Derric, can you see me? Derric?"

She wanted to hold his hand in both of hers, so she put the framed picture back on the table. She took his hand in her palms.

Instantly, everything stopped: the music, the laughing children, the *Derr . . . ic!* the *rejoice!* and most of all, Derric himself. His hand went slack in Becca's, his eyes closed, and his breathing returned to normal. Only the faint trail of tears on his temples and the damp spots on his pillow indicated he'd undergone a change at all.

"No!" Becca sank back in her chair. She looked from Derric to the picture of him, the band, and the children. And she understood.

It was all so simple. He was just like her. He wanted to go home to Uganda. He was no more a Whidbey Islander than she was.

She saw the solution to his deep slumber. Somehow, she thought, they needed to make him understand in his unconscious state that he *could* go home to Uganda. And if they were able to make him understand that, he'd return to them. He'd have a reason to return.

Becca knew she had to get this information to Derric's parents. But how to do it? And who was going to believe her anyway, when it came to revealing what Derric was trying to communicate?

The door swung open. Diana Kinsale came into the room. She took one look at Becca and came to the bed. "He wants to go back to Uganda," Becca whispered.

She moved away from the bed. She paced to the far wall and

back to the bed and back to the wall where she looked at the map of Africa with its tiny flags.

She turned back to the bed. Diana stood there with her hand on Derric's forehead. Her eyes were closed.

The door to the room opened again and Derric's father walked in. He looked neither right nor left but rather directly at the bed in front of him and at Diana Kinsale, who stood next to it. Becca froze as Undersheriff Mathieson crossed the room to stand at Diana's side.

She turned to him. She removed her hand from Derric's forehead and extended it to Dave Mathieson. As he bent to kiss his son, Diana nodded at Becca and then at the door. Becca was leaving soundlessly when she heard Diana's voice as she spoke to Derric's dad.

"He'll be back," she said. "You can trust that, David."

BECCA HAD KNOWN the risk when she'd left the Dog House and sneaked up to the cemetery. She'd also known the greater risk of going to Coupeville in order to see Derric. Those risks had seemed worth it at the time: fresh air and a chance to touch Derric's hand again. But she had to rethink the value of both as she crept back to First Street and the ancient tavern. For it was late in the day, her approach took her right in front of the Good Cheer thrift store, and as she was coasting by, intent only upon the slope that would take her to the Dog House's cellar, Jenn McDaniels walked out of the store.

"Hey!" got Becca's attention, followed at once by a torrent of foul language, whisper language but perfectly clear to her. She became immediately queasy at the sight of Jenn. With the small, tough girl was a sandy-haired woman carrying a plastic bag of secondhand clothes. Jenn said something to her and jumped into the street.

"Where the *hell* have you been?" she demanded of Becca. The woman moved off toward a line of cars and got inside one of them. She didn't start it.

"Oh hi," Becca said casually. "Is that your mom?"

"*I'm* asking the questions, *Beck*-kuh," Jenn replied.

"You are? Is this a cop show or something?"

"Very funny. Do you *know* exactly how much trouble you're in because of school?"

"So? Are you the truant officer now?" Becca asked her.

"You've dropped out, haven't you?" Jenn demanded. "Just like that loser boyfriend of yours. And *he's* in bigger trouble than you are. Everyone who touches you gets into trouble. Why don't you leave this place and take your trouble with you?"

"Nice to see you, Jenn." Becca began to move off.

Jenn grabbed the handlebars of the bike. "Nothing happened to *anyone* before you got here, Beck-*kuh* King. We were all just fine. Then you show up and Derric gets told to take care of you and the next thing we know, he's in a coma."

"Like I had *anything* to do with that," Becca said.

"Yeah, just *like*," Jenn countered. She shifted her weight from one muscled leg to the other. She thought for a moment and then made a shrewd guess. "You were there that day, weren't you? You knew he'd be there so you figured you'd just show up. Only he wasn't as happy to see you as you thought he would be and you took care of him for that, didn't you?"

Becca said nothing. She was so close to her place of escape, the Dog House a mere thirty yards from where they were standing. She wanted to shove Jenn McDaniels out of the way and run to its safety. She *also* wanted to smack the other girl right across the face, however. But that was exactly what Jenn wanted, too, because *come on come on come on just do it* whipped from Jenn's mind into Becca's and she could see the other girl balling up a fist in preparation for what would follow. Her mom might be waiting in the car, Becca thought, but here was unfinished business and Jenn intended to complete it. Great way for me to stay anonymous, Becca thought. Great way to stay unnoticed by the undersheriff.

She said to Jenn, "You don't know what you're talking about."

"Think I don't? Well, let's see if Derric's dad agrees with you."

Alarm shot through Becca, although she tried not to show it. "What's that supposed to mean exactly?"

"Ex*act*ly? It means he's gonna want to know you were there that day, chick. The cops took down names, see, but they didn't get yours. What d'you think they'll do when I drop the bomb on them?"

"They'll probably ask you if you pushed him yourself. I know I would," Becca told her. She jerked the bike away from Jenn's grasp on it. She headed up First Street, away from the Dog House. It was a long hill, upward, but Becca was more than a match for its challenge now.

THIRTY-TWO

Given time to cool off and think about things, Seth decided there was nothing he could do about whatever his grandfather believed with regard to the camping equipment. To explain who had it would put Becca at risk, and he wasn't willing to do that. On the other hand, it came to him that there *was* something he could do about Hayley. He could see now that they were broken up for good, but he wasn't about to let Hayley Cartwright get away with outright lies. Whether they were lies she was telling someone else, telling him, or telling herself, Seth was going to put a stop to at least one of them and that was the lie about her father. *Something* was wrong with Mr. Cartwright. The sooner his family admitted that, the sooner they could do something to help the poor guy.

When he drove into Langley several days later and parked in front of South Whidbey Commons, it had just begun to rain. The afternoon was cold, so he dashed inside the building and grabbed some cider steaming from a Crock-Pot near the espresso machine. He took his cup into the farthest room. The computers were here.

The connection was slow, like trying to pour cold syrup onto pancakes. Finally, the Internet showed on the monitor. Seth googled "dropping things" because he thought about that water bottle that had fallen from Mr. Cartwright's hands as well as the logs he couldn't manage to carry. But he found there wasn't much to work with so he went with "muscle weakness" next, although it took him several tries to figure out how to spell *muscle*. That silent *c* killed him.

A decent primary list popped onto the screen, everything from "muscle weakness causes" to "muscle weakness symptoms." Seth worked through this painstakingly. He finally chose "muscle weakness in legs" because of the way Mr. Cartwright had been walking and because of that clutch, which he hadn't been able to push down, and most of all because he—Seth—could read the four words "muscle weakness in legs" without any trouble. When he clicked on this topic, though, he was horrified to see forty-two pages of sites flash onto the screen.

This, he realized, was going to be a real problem. He glanced at the computer next to him. A young girl sat there, gazing at her Facebook page. He thought about asking for her help, but he just couldn't do it. She looked twelve years old, and he wasn't about to admit to some little kid that he couldn't read well enough to choose a Web site. So he began to fight through them.

There were sites for fatigue and muscle weakness, there were sites for causes of weakness in legs, there was something called "fibromyalgia symptoms," there was something about musculo-skeletal disorders. Seth's eyes ached with what he was trying to do, and he finally put his cheek in his palm. He stared at the screen and thought about how someone with a brain that didn't misfire like his would have been able to read through this in twenty seconds flat.

Then his eye saw something that his brain recognized without a struggle. In one of the sites, the first line of an article appeared and in that line were two words Seth didn't even have to read because he'd been seeing them all his life: *Whidbey Island.*

He clicked on this. What he came up with was an article about Lyme disease. He managed to get through it by sounding things out as he'd been taught in elementary school. What he learned was that Washington had the highest occurrence of multiple sclerosis in the country but the lowest incidence of Lyme disease.

Seth thought about this for a moment. He knew that Lyme disease came from deer ticks. He knew that Whidbey Island was jumping with deer. Sometimes it seemed there were more deer than people, and he wondered for a moment how deer had gotten to the island in the first place. Had they swum? he asked himself. Did they just evolve? They sure hadn't sauntered across the Deception Pass Bridge. Of course, they could have—

Seth slapped his forehead. This was *exactly* what his brain always did. He'd be reading and then one idea would lead to another and before he knew it, he wouldn't be reading at all any longer. He forced himself back to the matter at hand.

The story was about a man on Whidbey Island who'd been diagnosed with multiple sclerosis. He'd been treated for MS for years, only to find out he had Lyme disease. Seth read through the symptoms of both diseases. He felt a ball of excitement inside of him.

It all seemed obvious. There had, after all, been nothing wrong with the SUV's clutch. Whatever was wrong, was wrong with Mr. Cartwright.

Seth knew he had the answer he was seeking. He knew he

needed to tell the family about this. He left the computer and headed out of the game room. He was striding to the door of the commons when it opened. The undersheriff of Island County walked in.

———

THE FIRST THING Seth thought when he saw Dave Mathieson was that Hayley had called him and turned him in for pushing Derric off the bluff in Saratoga Woods instead of waiting for him to act on her suggestion and make the call himself. As things turned out, though, Dave Mathieson didn't want to talk to Seth about Derric and Saratoga Woods.

He said to Seth, "You're just who I'm looking for. Debbie Grieder's reported her niece missing. Becca King. What do you know about that?"

Seth said, "Becca King?" as he rapidly assessed what he could tell the undersheriff without telling him anything useful. This was the trail of bread crumbs that Becca was terrified of, the one that would ultimately lead her stepfather right to the Dog House to find her.

"Debbie says that you and Becca are friendly," the undersheriff said. "Just like you and Sean were friendly, as a matter of fact."

"Hey, I *knew* Sean," Seth declared. "He taught me to play chess. So put me in jail."

"Don't get smart with me. You were seen leaving the motel after Becca's disappearance."

"Who supposedly saw me?"

"Don't worry who saw you. Just know someone did and that person reported you to me. Do you want to tell me about it? We've got a missing girl whose belongings were left behind but now are missing, too. For the moment, I'm assuming she's a runaway. I'm going to continue assuming that unless you give me a reason to assume something else. So, were you at the motel?"

That question told Seth that the undersheriff *didn't* actually know for sure, no matter what he'd been told. So he replied by saying, "Not since Becca left."

"So you know she left."

"You just told me she was a runaway, man," Seth said. "Look, what's this about? You think I did something to her? Why would I? Why would I do something to anyone?"

The undersheriff just let Seth's questions hang there. He just let their implications grow. He watched Seth closely, like a book he was reading. The silence dragged on.

Seth finally said hotly, "I don't know *anything* about Becca King. I don't know anything about anyone else. Or any*thing* else for that matter."

"Oh, I bet you don't," UnderSheriff Mathieson replied. "But keep this in mind: I'll be watching you, Seth."

AFTER THAT CONFRONTATION, Seth nearly didn't go to Smugglers Cove Farm and Flowers. Instead, he nearly went to the Cliff Motel to point out a few choice things to Debbie Grieder. For Debbie might have known a lot about alcoholism from her years in AA, but there were lists of things she either didn't know or just felt like ignoring.

It was hard to believe, for example, that she hadn't known Sean had been using drugs from the time he was fifteen years old, right when Reese died. It was also hard to believe that she hadn't known he'd grown weed on the sunniest part of the bluff, hidden in plain sight among the ocean spray. And how could she not have noticed when he started on speed? Seth might have been ten years younger than Sean Grieder, but even *he* had known when things began to go south in Sean's life.

Well, he thought, as he coursed north up the highway, there was nothing he could do about Debbie Grieder. There was nothing he could do about Sean. There was practically nothing he could do about Becca King except help her out a little. But there was something he could do with the information he'd just gathered off the Internet.

When Seth pulled into the long driveway of Smugglers Cove Farm and Flowers, he took note of the remains of the wild summer grasses along the edge of it. These were long dead now, but he couldn't help thinking how the grasses were a magnet for Lyme disease ticks. So were people's socks, legs, feet, and toes. If people weren't careful, a tick could be on them for days without their knowledge.

It felt good to Seth to be doing something useful for the Cartwrights. Obviously, they were worried sick about Hayley's dad, and he had the answer to what was happening to the poor guy. He smiled when he thought about being able to help them. He was still smiling as he drove up to the house and beep-beeped the VW's horn.

Hayley came out into the rain in a flash. She started waving her hands, and when he got out of the car, the first thing she said was, "Shush! Be quiet! Don't honk that horn!" before he could even get the door closed. She sounded furious.

Seth said, "Chill, Hayl. I wanted to see how your dad—"

"What about my dad? Nothing's *wrong* with my dad. That stupid SUV broke down."

"That's what I wanted to talk to you guys about because when I drove it back here, there was nothing wrong with the clutch."

"So what? So *what*?" Hayley's face was scarlet, even in the rain.

"So nothing," Seth said. "Look, can we go inside? Or at least on the porch?"

"No, we can*not*."

He turned up the collar of his flannel shirt and pulled the rim down on his fedora. He said, "Okay. Whatever. But, Hayley, listen, I was looking on the Internet because of how your dad's—"

"You leave my dad alone!" Her voice grew louder, and Seth could see that along with the redness of her face, her eyes were teary. It seemed as if the tears made her even angrier, though, because she clenched a fist and said, "What's the *matter* with you? You act like you're not going to end up in jail in a few days."

"Hey, I got no idea who supposedly saw me at the Cliff Motel, but even if I was there—and I'm not saying I was—I got *no* clue why Becca King ran off, okay?"

"What are you talking about?"

"The undersheriff. What else? I just got through being accused of—" Seth eyed her more closely then. He realized they were talking at cross-purposes. He said, "Whoa. Saratoga Woods and

Derric. You weren't just blowing smoke, were you? What you said the other day about turning myself in—"

"What were you doing there that day?"

"Like it's any of your business?"

"Tell me!"

"Hey! I was taking Gus for a run, okay? What were *you* doing there?"

"What were you wearing? Did you have on your sandals?"

Seth's jaw dropped. He snapped it closed. "What the *hell* . . . What's this all about, Hayley?"

"You're not wearing them. You've stopped wearing them."

"Uh . . . it's raining? In case you haven't noticed?"

"You *always* wear them. Do you still have them? Did you give them away? Did you give them to Dylan Cooper?"

Seth swore then. She was crazy and he was crazier for having come over to this stupid farm. It was over, over, *over* between him and Hayley. But he couldn't let go, not of Hayley, not of her family, not of the farm, not of anything.

She said, "*Answer* me! Because Becca King was talking about those sandals and that doesn't even make sense. She knows something. And so do you. And I swear, Seth, if you don't tell me . . ."

Seth's head felt like something about to explode. He sank back down on the driver's seat of Sammy. He put his head in his hands. Her thoughts. His thoughts. Accusations. Truth. A balloon was being inflated in his brain and he couldn't begin to deal with the pain.

Hayley said, "Yeah, that's right," in reaction to this. "You've got a lot to think about, don't you? And the first thing you might want to think about is why you just can't leave me alone, leave *us* alone, leave our whole family alone. What do you want, anyway? You can't just walk away from school and forget all about taking the GED and *then* get jealous and *then* hurt someone just because he's my friend and he kissed me and I kissed him and I *liked* kissing him. Okay? I *liked* it. And then you get the girl Becca King involved in your plan to—"

Seth jumped up. He put his hand over Hayley's mouth. He cried, "Stop, just stop! I can't even *think*."

She whipped her head away from him and said, "You've got *that* right. You can't even think."

The front door opened. Mrs. Cartwright stepped outside. She hugged herself and called, "You two need to get out of the rain. What are you up to?"

Hayley said, "Nothing."

Mrs. Cartwright smiled a little cautiously. "It didn't look like nothing from here. Are you okay, Seth?"

Seth managed to say, "Yeah. I'm okay. I'm good." Then he remembered why he'd come. "But I've been noticing that Mr. Cartwright isn't doing too good," and he told Hayley's mother about Lyme disease, about the man on Whidbey Island who'd been misdiagnosed with multiple sclerosis, and about Lyme disease on the island itself. As he was talking, he heard Hayley hiss his name and he saw Mrs. Cartwright's hand climb to her throat and rest there. He couldn't stop, though, till he got it all out, because forget about Hayley, this wasn't about her. This was about one thing that he could do right. He explained how Mr. Cartwright might not have noticed a tick on his body. He explained how he—Seth—found ticks on Gus occasionally. He went on to say that Lyme disease could make someone pretty sick and it needed to be dealt with and—

Tears were streaming down Mrs. Cartwright's face. She said, "Thank you, Seth. Thank you for coming, dear," and she went back into the house.

Seth saw Hayley watching him. She was soaked from the rain, but her face wasn't red any longer, and her expression was odd. She said in an entirely different voice, a completely calm voice, what he would think of as the old Hayley voice, "What happened in the woods that day, Seth?"

But Seth didn't know what her expression meant, and he didn't know why the old Hayley voice was suddenly the one asking the questions. So he replied, "What the hell difference does it make?" and he got back into Sammy and drove away.

THIRTY-THREE

A lot of things were messing with Seth's head when he left the Cartwrights' farm, but the subject of his sandals was front and center. If Becca had mentioned them to Hayley, she had a reason for doing it.

He was almost sorry he'd bought those sandals. They were all-weather and all-terrain. They were in-the-water as well as on-the-land. Provided your socks were warm enough, you could wear them year-round anywhere except in the snow. And that's what he'd intended when he bought them: to wear them every-where, all the time.

He wasn't wearing them now because . . . because he wasn't wearing them now. End of story. It wasn't Hayley's business why. It *also* wasn't Hayley's business to ask him questions about them. Or about anything, if it came down to it.

At this point, she was stressing him out. At this point, just about everything was starting to stress him out.

Part of this was his own fault. He'd had a deal with his parents and he wasn't upholding his end of it. Hayley was right when she'd accused him of doing nothing to make the GED happen. There was no tutor and he wasn't studying. And why was that?

Because he couldn't handle flunking the test and knowing for all time that he was a loser.

When he reached the highway and came to Freeland, Seth realized that there was *one* thing he could do to prove to himself that he wasn't a hopeless case. He took himself to the farmers' supply store.

He parked not far from some hay bales. They were covered with tarps against the weather, but you could still make out their sharp rectangular shapes. He went inside the building and prowled down the aisles till he found the dog food.

He heaved a forty-pound sack of it to his shoulder. Then he looked for something that Gus might like and might also not destroy in three minutes flat. He settled on a real bone with gristle attached, a huge thing that Gus would gnaw on for days.

Seth grabbed this bone and headed for the register. He was being rung up when a hand descended heavily on his shoulder and a voice he knew and loved more than anything said, "I'll be paying for that. This, too."

He looked up to see his grandfather. Ralph had an identical bag of kibble on his shoulder. Seeing this made Seth's throat close because he knew that along with everything else he was supposing, Ralph was *also* supposing that Seth would forget to buy the food for his dog.

Seth said to the cashier, "Absolutely no frigging way," and he handed over the money. He scooped up the food along with the bone and he strode outside. He went to the bales of hay, but he ran out of the gas of his indignation there. He dropped the bag of kibble and sank onto a bale. He turned the bone over and over in his hand.

He heard a *thump*, and someone sat down next to him. Then that beloved voice said to him, "I did you a grave wrong, Seth. I want your forgiveness. I hope you'll give it."

Seth said to his grandfather, "You even thought I'd forget to give you food for Gus."

"I did. And I was wrong in that, too. I'm asking you to forgive me for that, too, Seth."

"Grand, I didn't steal your stuff," Seth said. "And I *don't* use drugs. My brain's so scrambled anyway . . . C'n you think how much worse it'd be, if I used drugs?"

Ralph sighed. He took off his hat, scratched his head furiously, and reset the hat on his head. He said, "I know that. I had a moment of doubt, but doubt's a human thing and I hope you know I'm human. But here's the real heart of the matter: No matter what I think or what I thought, I never for one instant stopped loving you, boy."

Seth thought about this and what it meant to be so wrong, to draw a conclusion without waiting for the facts that would constitute an explanation. He said, "I thought I had good reasons for taking your stuff without asking. I needed those things and someone needed my help. I'm sorry I didn't ask you. But I thought if I did that, you'd ask questions."

"So?" Ralph asked. "What if I had?"

"You can't, Grand. Not about this. I need to help a friend and you need to have some faith in me."

Ralph looked at him squarely for a very long time before he nodded and said, "I see." He was quiet for a moment, during which he seemed to be studying the bone Seth was holding.

He took one of his cowboy handkerchiefs from his pocket and honked loudly into it. He balled it up, eyed Seth again, and said, "C'n I ask you a question? How much of what's going on these days has to do with Hayley?"

That was the real question, Seth thought. He hadn't come close to answering it for himself, let alone to his grandfather.

"I don't even know anymore."

"Ah," Ralph said. He leaned back against the hay bales. He looked up at the gray and angry sky. He blew out a long sigh and muttered, "Love sucks."

Seth had to chuckle. "You got that right."

"You ask me, the worst part of love is the not knowing part," Ralph said.

"Not knowing if someone loves you back?"

"There's that," Ralph said. "There's also not knowing what'll happen next. Seems to me that there's always one helluva big picture involved when a man and woman love each other. Problem is, no one can really see it."

"I sure can't," Seth said.

"Believe me, you're not alone in that." Ralph put his hand on the back of Seth's neck, and his hand was warm, calloused, and familiar. "Can I give you some Granddad information, Seth? It's probably hogwash, but I'd like to say it."

Seth wasn't sure he wanted to hear, but Ralph's apology had made things easier between them so he told his grandfather to go on. Ralph was glad to do so. He said the big lesson about loving someone was coming to understand that when love ended for one person, it ended for both people. He said the important part of this was recognizing *when* it had ended and not fighting against that. "Now, I'm not saying Hayley doesn't love you any longer," Ralph added. "All I'm saying's you got to wait and see and not *push* so hard to make something where there might be nothing. Because I'm getting the feeling you're pushing with Hayley. Would I be right?"

"Maybe," Seth said. "I don't really know. I mean, I *think* I understand why I'm doing what I'm doing. But then, sometimes I turn out to be wrong."

"Meaning?"

"Meaning I go over there because something's wrong with her dad—I swear it, Grand—and I think I know what it is. I want to tell her and to tell her whole family, but she thinks I'm there for something else."

"What d'you think?"

"I think," Seth said slowly, "that it's somewhere in between."

"What is?"

"The truth."

"Ah."

"See, she thinks I'm jealous. She thinks everything I've done—and everything I do—is because I'm jealous."

"And are you?"

"I guess. And I *know* it's totally stupid to be jealous," Seth said. "What good is it doing me? I can see that. But I got to say that so far . . . Grand, I haven't been able to *help* how I feel. It's just *there*, asking me to do something about it."

"That's the kind of thing that can get you off course," Ralph noted.

"I know that for sure. Like, is it helping me get a tutor? Is it helping me work on my music with the trio? Is it helping me at *all*? Hell no."

"Good you see that." Ralph sighed again. "Me, I like to stay away from the unproductive feelings in life if I can. Jealousy's one of them."

"So far it's not done a heck of a lot for me," Seth admitted.

"Glad we agree on something. Beside the importance of feeding that dog of yours." Ralph slapped his hands on his thighs and got to his feet. He heaved the sack of dog food to his shoulder. Seth did the same. They walked to Ralph's truck, which, Seth saw, was parked next to his own VW. Gus was inside. Seth opened the door and the yellow Lab leapt down and then leapt up, paws on Seth's shoulders.

Ralph let this go on for a minute before he said, "Inside, Gus," and the dog obeyed. Then he said to Seth, "I want to ask your permission to do something, Seth."

Seth's eyebrows rose. *This* was certainly different. "What?"

"I want to talk to Hayley."

"Hell, no, Grand. No way. I mean—"

Ralph's raised hand stopped him. "Not about you and her. At least not directly. But there're matters she and I need to discuss and I want your okay. Say the word, and I fade away like a shadow. But if it's okay . . . ?"

Seth thought about this. When had his grandfather meant anything but the best? He said, "I guess. Okay. But c'n I give you some advice?"

"Always welcome."

"Don't mention her father."

Ralph considered this as he smoothed his mustache. "Seth," he finally replied, "if I've learned nothing else in my life—and God knows I've learned precious little—I do know one thing. The things you shouldn't mention to people are the reason you should talk to them in the first place."

THIRTY-FOUR

When Hayley quietly swung the door open, she saw that Rhonda Mathieson was in her son's room. She was shaving Derric's head, devoid of bandages now. It was smooth and round, without a single mark on it that Hayley could see. She'd asked him about this once, teasing him about shaving his head in order to show off his perfect skull. He'd laughed at this, his boisterous, joyful, Derric laugh. It was just the custom in Uganda, he'd said. He liked it this way.

Rhonda turned the electric shaver off and said, "There now, darling." She turned from the bed to see Hayley standing near the door. "I didn't expect to see you, Hayley," she said.

"I'm not on the list to visit. I just wanted to see how he is."

"The same." Rhonda forced a smile. "And how are you, dear?"

"I miss him."

"Well, let me tell you, I completely understand that."

"How are you and Undersheriff Mathieson doing?"

Rhonda turned back to the bed. She made a little fuss over Derric's top sheet and his blanket, straightening the first and rearranging the second. As she did so, she said, "We don't see too much of each other right now. We spell each other here, so it's mostly at breakfast. He's in Langley a lot. He wants to find out who hurt his boy. He wants to know what Derric was doing in the woods. Me, though? I just want Derric back." She touched her son's cheek as she said this.

Hayley thought there was something more to be said between them, but she didn't say her part, and Rhonda didn't say hers. Hayley looked around the room and saw that the most recent balloons were deflating and needed to be replaced. Rhonda saw where she was looking and went to unfasten them from the foot of the bed.

She said, "I'll give you some time with him, Hayley. It's always nice to see you. Thanks for coming."

Hayley said, "Sure," and approached the bed as Rhonda left the room. At Derric's side, she saw that his lips were dry, so she dug a small tin of salve from her purse, and she smoothed some of it on his lips, and then with what remained on her fingers, she smoothed onto her own. It was like a kiss, and she thought about the night they *had* kissed each other after the Rwandan dancing. She couldn't get her mind around everything that had changed in that moment and everything else that had happened since then.

He was such a friend. He was so special.

Look, I'll give you Africa till you can have it yourself, was how he'd put it, and he'd pulled out the first of dozens of pictures he'd shown her from the orphanage where Rhonda had first seen him. *Check out this van we used in Kampala,* he'd said with a laugh. *Good thing there wasn't much rain there or the thing would've fallen apart. See this village, Hayl? We went there for a soccer game once, only instead we played music. See that*

thing there? It's like an African xylophone. See, this is Warren.
He learned to play it when he was seven. For me, though, it was
always the sax.

It hurt to imagine she could hear his words. Hayley put her
head close to Derric's on the pillow. She closed her eyes and whispered into his ear. "Please, come back, Derric. You're the only one
who knows, and I can't do this alone. You've got to come back."

When she opened her eyes, though, his were still closed, still
with that slight crescent of white showing at the bottom. She
said to him, "We're here at the hospital, Derric. Mom, Dad and
me. Derric, things are getting worse."

———

WHEN SHE LEFT him, Hayley went to the imaging center at
the back of the hospital. Her father was inside, having an MRI.
Her mother was sitting in the waiting area, with a magazine open
on her lap. She wasn't reading it. Instead she was sitting with her
head lowered and her eyes closed. She was praying. Praying was
what her entire family did. Praying was what they'd been doing
for months, but they all did it privately, and none of them admitted it to each other.

When she sat, her mother looked up. Her eyes were watery.
Hayley said quickly, "Did they tell you something?"

"No, no. I was just thinking about that lighthouse in California.
You remember the one with all the steps?"

Hayley nodded because she'd heard the story. It was her parents' honeymoon and, on a bet, her father had run up all three

hundred steps from the lighthouse out on a peninsula back to the top of the cliff. He'd not even been breathing hard when he finished.

"Anyway," her mom said as she fished in her purse and found a tissue, "he's not out of the machine yet. Listen. You can hear the pounding it makes. They wanted to give him a Valium before he went into it, but you know your dad. He said no. Then he said . . . He said, 'I think I should get used to confined spaces.'" At that, her mother's tears spilled over and she pressed the tissue to her mouth and said, "Sorry. Sorry, dear."

Hayley knew what he'd meant by *confined spaces*. She felt her own tears coming and got hastily to her feet. "I'm going outside for some air," she said. When her mom nodded, Hayley hurried away.

Outside, the cold made her gasp. A parking lot was the only thing out there, and she looked around, blinking hard. She noticed how beautiful the sugar maple was at the far side of the parking lot, its leaves crimson against a true-blue sky. She walked over to it, something beautiful and uplifting in a day when everything else was grim.

She saw there was a bench beneath the tree and she sat upon it. She tried to remove her father from her mind, and after that she tried to remove Derric. But neither would leave her thoughts and when she closed her eyes she could see them both, and that made things worse.

Someone sat on the bench next to her. She looked up to see Seth's grandfather looking at her. Ralph Darrow was wearing an Indiana Jones kind of hat, and his hair was out of its ponytail for once. He looked like a cross between an outlaw and a mountain man, but he smiled and said to her, "I'd like to join you if you can bear the company."

"Guess I can," she said.

For a moment they were silent together before Ralph said, "You know, I sure like autumn. Some people think of it as the herald to winter and the long dark days to come. But I like the chance to be inside the house with a fire roaring and my feet on the hearth and me pretending to be reading a book."

"I remember your place in autumn just like that," Hayley said. "Only I remember playing poker with you and Seth."

Ralph looked at her with a smile. "And you were one hell of a player, miss. Never saw anyone keep a poker face like you."

Hayley found a Kleenex in the pocket of her jeans, and she blew her nose on it. Ralph looked out at the parking lot, where there was nothing to see but cars, and he spoke to them, it seemed. "I stopped by the farm," he said. "Brooke told me you all were up here."

"Mom asked me to come. I should really be inside with her, I guess. My dad's . . . He had an appointment." Hayley knew that she'd said too much with that, and she also knew that she belonged inside the hospital with her mother. But there was comfort in sitting at Ralph Darrow's side. She could understand why Seth loved spending time with him. She said, mostly out of politeness, "How's Seth?"

Ralph smoothed his mustache in that way he had. "Well, I've got to say Seth's not too good. But he's coming along. He's got his worries, though."

"What about?"

Ralph shot her a look that clearly said, *Hayley, I think you know.*

Hayley said nothing, but she stirred on the bench. She really should get back inside the hospital, she thought.

Ralph said, "Now I'm not one to interfere in the affairs of the heart between two individuals. But I've thought some things over left, right, and center, Hayley, and I can't work out the answer to something."

"What's that, Mr. Darrow?"

"Time was, you called me Grand. I kind of liked that."

"Grand," she said.

"Thank you. C'n I go on?"

"Guess so."

"Okay, then. I can't work out why you aren't telling Seth the truth."

"I *did*," Hayley cried. "I *tried*. He saw me with Derric and *he* was the one who wouldn't call me back when—"

"Except I'm not talking about Derric," Ralph said. "Didn't even know about him and whatever. I said I don't interfere in affairs of the heart and I meant that, Hayley."

"But you asked me why—"

"Why you won't tell him the truth. Yes, that's what I asked. And if you and I set Derric aside for just a moment here, I think you know what truth I'm talking about."

Hayley made no reply. She wanted to tell him. She wanted to let everything come pouring out. But at that moment, she saw her parents walking out of the hospital, and the wall that was her promise of silence—that point of family pride—came up between Ralph Darrow and her.

Her dad was moving slowly with that foot-dragging problem of his, and her mother's arm was around his waist. Hayley could tell from her dad's expression that he didn't like this help from his wife. She could tell from her mom's expression that she was determined to help him anyway.

Hayley pressed her lips together to keep from blurting out everything. She was so desperate to talk to someone. But with Derric in a coma and with Diana Kinsale having explained that things with Hayley's father *had* to play out to the end, Hayley had no one. Certainly she didn't have her mother or her father, who wouldn't talk about *anything*.

Ralph said quietly, "What would you like me to do, Hayley?"

Hayley tore her gaze from her parents and looked at the old man. She saw that he was watching her dad. She said in a low voice, "Grand, it was never about Seth."

Ralph took one of her hands. He held it enclosed between both of his, and there was enormous comfort in this. "Guess I've known that all along," he said.

She said, "Please don't tell him."

"Course not. That's something for you to do."

"I can't. I promised."

"Understood. But sometimes you have to bend a promise. Thing is, no one can tell you when the right sometimes is. And I don't intend to. He needs you, though."

"I don't want to be needed."

"Don't mean it like you're thinking," Ralph said. "What I'm saying is it's time to help Seth get out of a mess he seems to be in. I can't do that helping because I don't see all the parts clearly, and if I intervene in some way, Seth's not going to like that and I don't blame him. He's not a child and I can't treat him like one. So the way I see it, I need your help."

Hayley looked at him. She knew he wasn't telling the entire truth to her because the last thing Ralph Darrow would do was fail to see things clearly once he had the information he needed, and the second to the last thing he would do was not intervene to help Seth. So she knew he was asking her to help his grandson in order to help herself. And this was fine with her. God knew she needed the help.

She said, "Okay, Grand." She got to her feet.

Ralph Darrow did likewise. "Thank you," he said. "Now let me go say hi to your old dad."

THIRTY-FIVE

It was three evenings later when Seth startled Becca at the Dog House. She'd hidden in a corner of the library for as long as she could, working through some questions in her Eastern Civ book. But when the library closed, she had no choice but to make her way down to Seawall Park where she'd be safe from sight as she returned to the tavern.

It was icy cold. She knew it would be only slightly warmer inside than outside the place, but at least she had a down sleeping bag there. She could crawl into that and wait for the hours to pass.

The flashlight was where she'd left it when she departed the tavern, right inside the plywood basement door. She climbed up to the first floor. The old oak bar with the mirror behind it reflected her appearance like a ghost, and here, as usual, she could see the lights from across the street. They were dimmed because of the soaped windows, but they gave enough illumination that, as Seth had done when he'd first brought her here, she switched off her flashlight before she stepped into the room.

That was when Seth materialized from behind the bar. He rose like the undead. Becca yelped in fright.

He said, "Cool it. It's *me*. Hell, I've been waiting for . . . like two frigging hours or something. *Where've* you been?" *Dumb-ass chick* was pretty much crystal clear, like a thought balloon over his head.

It wasn't quite right to be angry at someone because of their thoughts, which she wasn't supposed to know anyway, but *dumb-ass chick* was too much for Becca. "I can't stay in this place twenty-four hours a day," she retorted tartly. If she sounded a little snappish, he'd have to put it down to her being tired.

"So where *were* you? I thought your big deal was to stay out of sight."

"I was at the library if you have to know."

"And what? Like your stepfather *isn't* going to check the library and every other place in town if he shows up? How about the undersheriff? I thought you were worried about him, too." *Lying . . . what she thinks is just what . . . Hayley might have . . .*

Becca desperately wanted Seth's whispers to be clear. She needed them to be complete, to tell her what to believe at this point. She said, "I *am* worried about both of them. What? You think I was lying to you?"

"I didn't say that. Did I say you were lying?"

"You were thinking it, Seth."

"Oh, you know that, do you? You can read minds now?"

"It's written all over you." They were so perilously close to the truth about whispers that Becca knew she had to change directions as quickly as she could. She was cold, she was hungry, she didn't see how she was ever going to get out of the Dog House, but she couldn't let any of that provoke her into revealing something she wanted no one to know. So she said, "Where's Sammy, anyway? You know, if someone sees that car and *then* sees you heading down the slope to the basement door—"

"I'm not an idiot," Seth countered. "I parked in the lot at the bottom of Third Street. I brought you something to eat." He shoved a recycled grocery bag onto the counter toward her.

Becca looked at him curiously. She asked herself what it meant that he'd brought her food: that she could trust him or that, like Jeff Corrie, he was merely adept at playing a role. She approached the sack on the bar, concentrating as hard as she could on Seth's whispers. She was determined that they were going to tell her who he really was. But she had to hear them first and understand them second. Still, what she netted were only the usual maddening fragments. *Maybe . . . even . . . no one . . . Grand . . .* They amounted to less than nothing and left her only wondering even more about him: who he was and what he might have done.

She had to see if he had on those sandals. She strode the rest of the way to the bar, went to the other side, and picked up the bag. She drew out a panini along with a take-away cup. She lowered her head to show Seth her embarrassed gratitude, but what she was really doing was looking at his feet. Boots, not sandals, were what she saw.

Time of year, she told herself. Rain, snow, sleet, whatever. This wasn't southern California. People didn't wear sandals year-round in this place. But she wasn't convinced.

Seth said, "Tea'll be cold."

She said it didn't matter and thank you and she would pay him back for the food when she had the money. Then she added carefully that he hadn't needed to wait. He could have put the panini upstairs next to her sleeping bag.

He said, "I wanted to talk to you." And then his whispers came in some force and they were all about Hayley Cartwright. *Hayley . . . what she told her . . . why did she say that . . .*

Hearing this, Becca wondered if Seth knew she'd taken a lift from Hayley on that day her bicycle tire had gone flat. If he knew that, it was a short jump to conclude that he also knew she'd mentioned his sandals to Hayley. She said, "Go ahead. Talk away."

He said, "Let's go to the back."

She evaluated this. It seemed safe enough. There were unsoaped windows but they overlooked Saratoga Passage not the town. So she said fine and she followed him down a hall from the bar into what had once been the restaurant. The lights from Seawall Park down below gave the room illumination enough to see that their shoes left footprints in the dust.

Becca looked at hers. She looked at Seth's. The sandal print came into her mind once again. It was like a yellow caution sign. Until she got to the bottom of why it had been next to where Derric had fallen, she knew she couldn't believe in Seth completely. And when she *did* get to the bottom of why it had been next to where Derric had fallen, chances were still good that she'd know she couldn't believe in Seth at all.

"Aren't you going to eat the sandwich?" he asked her. He was looking at her as if she smelled bad, and that look plus his whispers told Becca that, panini or not, he hadn't really come as a friend.

She knew right then that she couldn't continue to live like this and expect Seth Darrow—or anyone else—to keep coming to her aid. She was going to have to do something to change her circumstances, and she was going to have to do it soon.

He said, "I need to talk to you, Becca. Hayley thinks—" and Becca heard nothing else for a moment because the force of Seth's whispers when he said *Hayley* actually pounded against her eardrums along with *Hayley came . . . why can't you . . . no I didn't, why would I . . . know me, KNOW ME . . . something special . . .*

Actual words accompanied the whispers. But the whispers themselves overpowered everything. Becca flung her hands up. She put her palms over her ears and cried, "Stop it!" before she realized what she was doing and how all this would seem to Seth.

His surprise at her reaction abruptly stopped both the whispers and the words. After a moment she was able to hear him say, "Stop *what*? I'm not accusing you of anything. *I'm* the one getting accused. So if you've got some reason for asking Hayley about my sandals, I want to know what it is."

She said, "*What* sandals?" She wasn't playing dumb with him. For the moment she was only trying to regain her footing in the wake of his words and whispers.

Seth didn't understand that. How could he? He pushed his chair back with a scrape against the old wooden floor and he snapped, "Oh that's just *great*! So *you* think so, too. I *can't* believe it! Well, let me tell you: I *didn't* touch that dude! I wouldn't have touched him! Who the hell do people think I am?"

He jerked away from the table, then. He strode over to the large plate-glass window and he banged his fist against it once, so hard the glass quivered the length of the room. His shoulders heaved. He gulped loudly.

Becca stared at him. She felt momentary wonder. Oh my God, she thought. Seth was trying not to cry. And then she heard *what's the point . . . total joke.* And then, quite simply, Becca knew.

Sometimes whispers weren't random thoughts. Sometimes whispers were also signs. And these whispers of Seth's were telling her something about what was real and what was not. He hadn't done a thing to hurt Derric Mathieson. He hadn't lifted a finger against him.

Becca got out of her seat. She was hesitant, but she still approached him. She put her hand on his shoulder and she felt him flinch. He swung around, and she flinched, too.

Before he could speak, she said, "I saw your footprint in Saratoga Woods, Seth. It was right above where Derric fell. I asked Hayley about your sandals because I thought maybe a lot of people around here wear them, maybe it wasn't your footprint at all."

Seth was staring at her. She was staring at Seth. *What to do . . . what to do . . .* was heavy in the air, and she knew why. It was because they both were thinking it, not just Seth. And to her *what to do* she was adding What to do to help Seth, who hadn't hurt anyone. But someone had, and she thought she knew who.

She said, "That kid Dylan has a pair of sandals like yours, Seth. Maybe other people do, too. I haven't seen any but—"

"He was in the woods that day," Seth said.

"Dylan? I wondered. Hayley said kids meet up at the big rock . . . Could the stoners have been on Meadow Loop Trail, too? Where Derric fell? Could Derric have been meeting one of them there?"

"Dylan, you mean?" Seth rubbed the back of his neck. "Maybe. I don't know. I mean Derric's not a stoner, far as I know. Some of the athletes do drugs, but even they don't *hang* with stoners."

"Do they buy from them, though?" Becca hated to think it. It didn't seem possible. But Derric had been doing something that day in the woods and this had to be ranked among the possibilities.

"Did he buy from Dylan, you mean? Did he owe him money, even?" Seth thought about this and blew out a breath. "Could be. But if that's the case, he's sure put on one hell of a performance as Mr. Straight. I dunno, Becca. It's hard to believe and I don't even like the guy."

"Were you on that trail, Seth? Can you remember?"

"Meadow Loop Trail? Who knows? I was all *over* the woods that day. So were you. You were looking for Gus, too. Did you keep track of where you went? I didn't. Why would I? Why would anyone? I mean, everybody and his brother and his sister and his dogs and his cats were in the woods that day. At least I had a *reason* to be there, but no one—"

Becca held up her hand to stop him. She realized suddenly that his words and his whispers for the very first time were so identical that they melded together. It came to her that she'd made a step in understanding the power of whispers. When everything matched—words and whispers—she was on the path to people's truths.

But there was something Becca had learned from sitting in

Jeff Corrie's office once she'd passed around refreshments, and that was that sometimes what people understood to be the truth was only what they wanted to believe was the truth.

The reality was that there was more truth out there, and she was going to find it. Finding it was the only way to help Seth and to free him from the burden of everyone's suspicions about him.

THIRTY-SIX

W hen the undersheriff showed up, Hayley was in her favorite class. This was AP U.S. History, and she was listening
to her fellow students debating the moral and ethical issues connected with advancing upon the land of indigenous people.

Ms. Stephany, the teacher, left for a moment. When she
returned, her face was grave. She said, "Hayley, you're wanted . . .
I think you might need your things . . . ?"

The tone of her voice made Hayley's mind start whirling with
possibilities, all of them having to do with her dad. She grabbed
her backpack. Outside the classroom, she found Undersheriff
Mathieson waiting.

He looked as grave as Ms. Stephany had. He said as Hayley
closed the classroom door, "You and I need to talk."

Hayley said, "Is something wrong?" although she didn't really
want an answer to her question.

"It's time for you to be completely frank with me about
Saratoga Woods, Hayley. You haven't told me the whole story
and I want it now."

Hayley sagged against the wall. The relief she felt over *not*
hearing something about her dad was so intense that she thought

she was going to melt right there in front of the undersheriff. She understood then how scared she'd been, how long she'd been scared, and how scared they *all* were that her dad might hurt himself because of how his body wasn't working.

Undersheriff Mathieson grabbed Hayley's arm and walked her down the corridor away from the classroom. He said to Hayley, "*Very* good. So you see there's no point to lying to me, don't you?"

Very good? Hayley furrowed her brow. But then she understood. He was taking her reaction of sagging against the wall not as the relief of knowing her dad was okay but as an admission of guilt. She wasn't sure what he thought she was guilty of, but the set of his face made her see him differently from how she'd always seen him in the past. Before he'd been Derric's dad, the great guy who'd done things like drive them to Seattle to see an exhibition of Congolese art. Now . . . Hayley didn't know who he was.

"Am I going to have to bring your parents in on this, Hayley?" the undersheriff asked her, giving her arm a tug. "Or are you planning to answer me? I've spoken to the other kids who were on that list. I have their stories. Now I want yours. All of it this time."

At this, Hayley realized she hadn't yet replied to anything he'd said. Still, she felt a tightness inside of her at his tug on her arm and at the thought that he'd even *bother* her parents about her presence in Saratoga Woods when they were already dealing with more than they could possibly handle. She felt the tightness within her morph into anger, and she decided then and there that she was not about to help this man. She said firmly, although her heart was slamming inside her chest, "There were lots of kids in the woods that day. Not everyone got put down on that list of yours."

He said, "I see," but his lip curled in a nasty way and he added, "And was this Becca King I've been trying to find one of those kids?"

Hayley said, "I barely know who Becca King is," which was hardly an answer to his question.

"She's disappeared from the Cliff Motel," he told her. "She's also been out of school for weeks. What do you know about that?"

"Not a single thing," Hayley replied. "Since I didn't notice her when she was here, I don't think I'd notice if she was gone." She saw at once that this was the wrong thing to say. The under-sheriff took a step closer. She thought he might drag her to the dean's office, then, or to the jail in Coupeville, in order to force her to tell him everything.

He was so close she could see a patch of whiskers at the corner of his mouth that he missed when he'd shaved. She could smell his breath, and it wasn't pleasant. He said, "You listen to me. You were in the woods and you're the only person on the list who hasn't explained what you were doing there. Now someone hurt my boy in that forest and I'm not leaving this school till I know who. So let's get back to the question you haven't answered and let's hear the answer. Why were you there?"

Hayley's heart-slams got worse. *My boy* reverberated in her mind. Not *my son*, but *my boy*. Like *my bike, my car, my refrigerator.* She recalled Derric telling her how the undersheriff never referred to him as his son. He'd say "This is our boy, Derric" or "This is our Derric," and what did it mean that he never used *son* in reference to him?

She just snapped, then. "Why do you *call* him that?" she demanded. "Why do you say 'my boy'? Why don't you ever say he's your son?"

The undersheriff's whole body stiffened. His mouth formed a line like a scar on his face. "Who the *hell* do you think you are?"

"I'm Derric's *friend*. And no, I wasn't meeting him there, if you still think I was. I was meeting Mrs. Kinsale. And why I was meeting her is none of your business unless you think we pushed him off the bluff together."

Hayley had never in her life talked to an adult like this, but she went on, believing that the upper hand was hers. She said, "You know, Sheriff Mathieson, there were stoners in the woods that day, too, and they *all* ran off before their names were taken. Why don't you concentrate on them for a while, because you're wasting your time hassling the kids who actually *liked* Derric."

"He doesn't do drugs."

"Did I say he does? But *he* was there and *they* were there and people run into each other in the woods all the time. Have you even thought about that?"

The undersheriff reached in his pocket. He brought out a small leather notebook and a pen. He flipped the book open and gazed at Hayley meaningfully, and Hayley saw the trap that she'd just walked into.

"Names," he said.

She didn't really know. They'd all run off too fast, and she'd been caught up in talking to Seth. But she did have a piece of information that she could give Dave Mathieson to get him off her back. "Dylan Cooper," she told Derric's father. "I think he was there."

"Student here?" the undersheriff asked as he took down the name.

"Yes. I guess so. I mean, yes."

But Hayley felt the misery of naming *anyone*. She didn't know anything, after all. The only detail connecting Dylan Cooper to what had happened was a pair of sandals, and *that* information had come from Becca King. Hayley didn't even know what it meant, whether it was important, or whether Becca had just thrown it out to muddy the waters. She *thought* Becca King had been there that day in Saratoga Woods, and she figured the girl had run off before the ambulance arrived. But why she'd done this . . . Hayley didn't know. She only knew that doing so had kept Becca's name away from any involvement with Derric's fall.

Undersheriff Mathieson was closing his leather notebook. He had a name now, but Hayley saw that he didn't look triumphant about it. He looked miserable. He looked like someone living a bad dream. It was a dream of not knowing.

The last thing she'd expected to feel was sympathy for the man, considering the way he'd been talking to her. But Hayley did feel it, then, just for an instant. She understood the bad dream of not knowing. Better than anything, she understood it.

———

WHEN THE UNDERSHERIFF left her, Hayley started breathing normally again, but she was shaken. Not only by having the conversation with him, but by naming Dylan Cooper to him. Across the corridor was the girls' restroom, and she headed for it. The door hit someone as she entered. It was someone who'd been standing behind it, listening to her entire conversation with Derric's father.

This turned out to be Jenn McDaniels. Who else? Hayley thought with resignation. Jenn had probably slithered into the restroom while the undersheriff had stood at the door to Ms. Stephany's classroom waiting for Hayley to join him.

She brushed past Jenn and went to the washbowls. She took off her glasses and turned on the water although she could see her hands were shaking.

Jenn obviously saw this, too, because she said, "What's the problem? You got *Parkinson's* or something, Hayley?" She went behind Hayley and strolled over to one of the translucent windows. She cracked this open.

Hayley splashed water on her face while behind her she heard the *snick* of a match being lit. She smelled the tobacco burning because the cold breeze from outside was blowing the smoke right back into the room instead of taking it away. Hayley kept splashing her face, ignoring the other girl.

Jenn said, "Uh . . . I think you're clean now, Hayley."

Hayley turned off the water. She grabbed some paper towels from the dispenser, and she dried her face. She put her glasses back on, which gave her a much better look at Jenn's smirking face.

"So," Jenn said. "You and the undersheriff had *quite* the talk. Maybe you should be more careful when you start accusing people of stuff."

Hayley ignored her. She turned to walk out of the restroom, but Jenn was away from the window in a flash. She tossed her cigarette onto the tiles of the floor and let it lie there burning. She blocked Hayley's path.

Hayley said, "Excuse me?"

"You're not excused."

When Hayley tried to get by her, Jenn was a wall. Her small body was entirely muscle. Hayley realized that the other girl looked like something the wind could blow away, but she was a rock.

Jenn said, "I never figured you for a snitch, *Hay*ley. One word from me, and Dylan's going to know all about what you told the undersheriff. So . . . you want to do something to stop me?"

What Hayley wanted to do was to slap her silly. She wanted to punch her right in the face. But although she was taller than Jenn McDaniels, she knew she wasn't a match for her. Jenn was as tough as uncooked beans, and she was just the kind of girl who itched in places only a brawl could scratch.

She said, "Here's what I'm figuring out about you, Jenn. You sort of *like* having Derric in that hospital bed. You sort of like feeling important to him, to his parents, to his recovery even. But the deal for you is that he has to *stay* in that coma for you to be important, doesn't he? Because if he wakes up, you go back to being just Jenn McDaniels, the girl everyone tries to ignore because she's such a pain in the butt."

Jenn's face drew together like a fist. Hayley knew she'd hit her mark. But she hated herself for descending to the other girl's level. That wasn't who she was.

"You," Jenn said, "don't know the first thing about me. Fact is, you don't know the first thing about anyone, Derric included. You think him and you have some special relationship that's all about *Aff*-rick-a, but here's the deal: That's just your excuse for getting your hands on him. You want to hook up and here's the way. 'Oh, Derric, tell me all about Uganda.'"

Jenn clasped her hands beneath her chin and fluttered her eyelashes sarcastically.

Hayley's lips parted but at first she didn't speak. The other girl's ability to see things and twist them, to make something seem dirty when it was nothing of the kind . . . It was incredible. Hayley said to her, "Why're you so hateful? How d'you think life's going to work out for you, when all you do is look for every weakness in people so you can hurt them?"

"I'd rather know who people are than let them pretend they're someone else."

"I don't pretend," Hayley told her.

"As if. Everyone pretends."

"No. They don't. Your problem is that you make guesses about people. But that's all they are: guesses."

"Yeah? Want to hear my guesses about you, then? Want to hear my guesses about Seth? Want to hear my guesses about Beck-*kuh* King?"

"What I want is not to talk to you for another second."

"Good, 'cause all you have to do is listen," Jenn sneered. "So listen to this. Becca King pushed Derric off that bluff, not Dylan Cooper. She came on to Derric. He said no. That's when she shoved him. That's what happened. This whole thing's her fault, and I'm going to help the undersheriff find her."

"You make me sick," Hayley said.

Jenn nodded toward one of the stalls. "Well, there's the toilet."

HAYLEY HAD TO admit that she hardly knew Becca. Most of the kids at South Whidbey High School she'd been around since preschool, but Becca King . . . What *did* she know about this girl? Nothing, really. But she knew someone who did.

Early the next morning she drove directly to the Star Store. She banged on the door. She rattled the handle. She went back to banging until Seth appeared. He was carrying a mop over his shoulder like a rifle and when he saw who it was, he stopped dead. Hayley shook the door handle again and called out, "Seth, open up. I need to talk to you."

He put the mop to one side, but when he unlocked the door, he didn't let her in. After their last encounter, he was wary of her and Hayley could understand this since she'd been going off mentally in all directions for months now.

"Yeah?" Seth spoke in a way that was not unfriendly, but it certainly wasn't the welcome mat. He didn't act surprised to see her. He *did* act like someone waiting for the next weird outburst from her to come his way.

It came to Hayley that she had a lot to apologize for, and the first thing she needed to say "I'm sorry" about was her failure to see how mismatched she and Seth had been from the first. She'd thought music would be enough to bind them because he was a brilliant musician and no one would ever be able to deny that. She'd thought his essential goodness would add to that. But music and Seth's core decency hadn't been enough, and she saw that now. But she couldn't get into that at the moment, so she said, "I need to talk to you about Becca."

"What about her?"

"The undersheriff thinks she pushed Derric off the trail. Or at least he's going to think that because Jenn McDaniels is going to tell him."

"Why the hell would Jenn do that?"

"Why does Jenn do anything? All I know is that she's convinced herself that Becca was trying to hook up with Derric and Derric wasn't interested, so Becca shoved him off the trail. Course, she's also convinced herself that just about everyone was trying to hook up with Derric. Except her, of course. She's completely innocent of everything."

Seth seemed to consider all this carefully. He finally said, "No way. I was there. Me and Gus were there and . . ." But then his voice faded and Hayley could tell something had come to him.

She said, "What?"

"Nothing." But he said the word too slowly. *Nothing* meant *nothing I can tell you.*

She said, "Seth, Becca was there and you got separated from her, right? Everyone got separated from each other and—"

"You were there that day, too," Seth said. "Who'd you get separated from?"

"Not from Derric. Seth, this isn't about me and Derric. There *is* no me and Derric. We were always just friends and . . . We might have been kissing but it was *just* kissing and . . . Oh, that doesn't matter now. What matters is Becca and what Jenn's going to do."

"I don't get why that's so important to you."

"Because it's *wrong*. Do *you* think Becca hurt Derric?"

He shook his head. "She was acting all weird but—"

"So she *was* there."

"Yeah. But we were looking for Gus."

"Together?"

"No. Like you said, we got separated. I don't know where she went. I don't even know where *I* went. I was just trying to find the dog. So was she, far as I know. I can tell the undersheriff that if it comes to him thinking Becca did anything."

"But the problem would be, you don't know for sure, right?"

"Right."

"So think of how everything'll look to him once Jenn shoots her mouth off. Becca was there that day. Becca has disappeared. Becca hasn't been in school. Jenn wants to hurt Becca because hurting people is what she does best. So she's going to help the undersheriff find her. You know where she is, don't you?"

Seth looked cagey. "I'm not saying that."

"You don't *have* to say it. I know you, Seth. If she came to you for some reason, you'd help her. That's who you are. So help her now."

Seth examined her, chewing this over: not only her words but what they meant. He said, "I didn't push him, Hayley."

She said, "I know. I'm sorry I ever said or thought . . . Look, we have stuff to talk about, you and I, but we can't right now. Right now the important thing is protecting Becca. You've got to keep her away from the undersheriff and away from Jenn. Will you do that, Seth?"

He nodded slowly. She turned to leave. But she could tell he was watching as she walked back to the truck.

THIRTY-SEVEN

It was still early in the morning when Becca ducked out of the Dog House and pedaled toward the edge of town. She took a shortcut she'd discovered and ended up on Sandy Point Road, a route that would have destroyed her weeks earlier. But now she had no trouble with it, in part because of Seth's bike and in part because of the shape she was in. Soon, she knew, she'd be able to do twenty miles with no problem.

She made quick time to Diana Kinsale's house, where the lights were on in the kitchen and the porch as well. Diana met her at the door. She was dressed for the day. She said, "Becca. Come in," and she led the way to a sunroom. Her house was filled with warm autumn colors. Walking through it felt like falling into a hug.

In the sunroom, all five dogs were lying on the warm concrete floor and tea was laid out for a visitor. Diana said, "All dogs stay," as they raised their heads. Tails wagged, but they obeyed as always.

Becca said, "They got to stay inside last night?"

"No. They just wanted to say hello to you this morning."

Becca felt a tingle go over her as she understood from this

that Diana had known she was coming. And she heard quite distinctly *It's just between the two of us, Becca*, but this frightened her. She knew when she heard a whisper from Diana that Diana was making the choice to be heard. She just didn't know what this meant.

She remembered her grandmother saying to her, "Sometimes you've got to take the leap, hon, and this is going to be tough for you. See, when most people leap, they leap in darkness, but until you learn to *master* the whispers, you'll always be leaping in half-light." Becca finally realized how this applied to her: The whispers as she received them at this point in her life told her something, but they didn't tell her everything, and with Diana this was one of those half-light moments.

The half-light was duplicated outside the sunroom because dawn was breaking over the Cascade Mountains. It was making of the sky an unfurling banner in which the color rose was transforming into apricot, then into pearl gray, while above them both the arc of black night still hung.

She said to Diana, "I need to trust you, Mrs. Kinsale."

Diana sat and gestured for Becca to do the same. She poured some tea. She said, "I think you're in the midst of trust now. You wouldn't have come here otherwise." She looked out at the still, dark water that even now was just beginning to reflect the sky. She said, "It's going to be beautiful today." And then after a pause, "How can I help you, Becca?"

Becca looked at Diana and felt her complete acceptance. This seemed to flow from Diana, like a river that Becca could plunge into if she wanted to. So she said what she'd been longing to say for weeks upon weeks, which wasn't at all what she'd come to say.

"D'you know where my mom is, Mrs. Kinsale?"

"Safe is what I know," Diana replied. "Safe is what I see."

Becca's vision blurred. "I miss her."

"It's a hollowness inside your chest. I know that feeling." And when she spoke, the peace that came from Diana was a pool of calm.

Becca said impulsively, "Can I live here with you? With you and with the dogs?" Then before Diana could answer, the rest poured out of her like a flood that sought to join that pool, as water always will. "The undersheriff is looking for me. I had to run from the Cliff Motel. I've been in the Dog House and I've missed school and I want to take a bath or a shower and I want to go *back* to school and have a place to live and—"

Diana rose and came to her. She knelt in front of Becca's chair and placed her hands on Becca's knees. Becca looked down at them. She saw they were rough from gardening and rough from a long and useful life. She said, "*Will* you finally trust me, Becca?"

At this, Becca felt something heavy and painful release from inside her. The sensation was like parts of her body lifting and dissolving and being washed away. "Yes," she said.

"Good. I want you to trust what I say to you. Here, this house, the dogs and I . . . these things aren't what you need right now. Eventually they will be and when that time comes, I'll know and I'll tell you. But the time isn't right."

Becca's heart sank. "Why not?"

"Because there are things you need to resolve first."

"I don't know how."

"You *do*. It doesn't seem like it. But you have the wisdom to move forward and do what you need to do."

Wisdom? It didn't feel like wisdom, Becca thought, whatever it was that was churning inside her. What it felt like was being caught in a maze where at every dead end loomed something else that she either didn't understand or didn't know what to do about: Derric, Seth, the sheriff, Jeff Corrie, her mom, hiding out at the Dog House, missing school all this time . . . It made Becca desperate for someone to rescue her.

But there was no rescue that she didn't bring about herself. That, she realized, was Diana's point. She said, "I wish I'd known Derric better before everything happened. I wish I'd known *everyone* better. I'd be able to do the right thing then."

"Which is what?"

And here was the point of departure. The road forked here, and Becca knew she could choose which route to take. She'd chosen so badly in San Diego with Jeff Corrie's gleaming smile upon her. To choose badly again . . . Becca didn't see how she could cope with that. There was too much at stake. But Diana was waiting—just as Jeff Corrie had waited—and Becca had to decide if she wanted to know what this woman before her was really made of.

She finally swallowed hard. "I'd have to tell the undersheriff what I saw in the woods."

Diana rose. She moved an ottoman over to Becca's chair and she sat on it, close to her instead of across from her. She put her hand on Becca's arm and said, "The undersheriff's caught up in this as much as you are. Your worries match his because they're centered on the same situation and the same group of people."

"Except I'm *part* of that group because he wants to find me. So if I talk to him—"

"He's turned all around, Becca. Just like you. It's no different, really, except that he's an adult. He's trying to sort through the same doubts and fears. He's trying to help Derric. Same as you."

"I get that, but I can't go to him, Mrs. Kinsale. Not only because of the Dog House and everything but because he'll go after someone if I do."

"Isn't that the point?"

"Not if that person didn't *do* anything." Becca cast an agonized glance at Diana, whose faded blue eyes watched her so kindly, whose fingers were so warm on her arm. She fought with herself for a moment, trying to reach a decision. Then she said on a sigh, "Seth."

"Ah."

"He doesn't like Derric, but he didn't push him."

"No?"

"Dylan Cooper probably did."

"Are you sure of that?"

"Which part?"

"Let's start with the Seth part. Are you sure that he didn't push Derric?"

Becca considered what she knew about the boy, and her mind filled with images: Seth and his dog, Seth giving her his bicycle, Seth handing her a sandwich from the Star Store on her first day in Langley, Seth driving her to Coupeville just to see Derric, Seth helping her find the Dog House.

Diana said quickly, "Yes. Yes. I see."

Becca stared at her. Diana cocked her head. Becca said, "You . . . you *see*?"

Diana smiled. "I do."

Another fork in the road, Becca realized. Another decision for her to make. She plunged on. "Seth's always helped me. I want to help him now."

"That certainly makes sense. Let me think a minute." Diana looked back out at the water, where dawn was coming on quickly now, stretching fingers of light up into the sky. She said, "I remember you that day, in the woods. You were looking for a dog, and I gave you Oscar's leash. Let's go back to the moment when you arrived in the woods. Close your eyes and tell me what you see in your memory."

Becca did as Diana asked. She allowed her mind to fill with the images of that day as it unfolded: heading across the meadow with Seth and Gus, walking toward the opening in the trees that marked the trailhead into the woods, huge fir trees overhead, more trails opening off of the one they were on. But she didn't have time that day to learn the names of the trails because the moment she stepped into the woods—

Becca opened her eyes. She looked at Diana and was very afraid of revealing more. It was a half-light moment. *Go on, hon.*

Diana said nothing. She took a sip of her tea. She waited.

Becca spoke, "All right. I could hear mind whispers in the air so I knew the woods were full of people. Usually I have to be with people to hear their mind whispers, but this was different. I don't know why. And there was a scent, and I knew from this that Derric was there. Then Gus heard dogs barking and he ran off. Seth had to run after him. I tried to follow, but I got lost."

"You've been lost ever since," Diana murmured. "Not just you, but all of you. You, Seth, Hayley Cartwright, Jenn McDaniels."

"Jenn thinks I'm 'after' Derric. She wants to get me into

trouble. She was how the AUD box broke. She threw it against a wall. From the day I got to school, she's been a complete—"

"Yes," Diana murmured. "But let me think a moment."

They sat in stillness. Diana's eyes were closed. When she opened them, she said quietly, "We need to take a drive. It won't take long. I think it'll allow you to resolve one thing of all the concerns you're trying to deal with."

***

DIANA DROVE THEM in the direction of town, but at the end of Sandy Point Road, she didn't head into Langley. Instead of right, she turned left, and soon enough they came to the main highway. They crossed over onto Cultus Bay Road, which led to the other side of the island.

The way began with forest, deep and dark, where conifers grew in abundance and alders wore their seasonal crowns of yellow leaves. When the forest ended, farmland spread out for half a mile or so, and then they were in the trees again, and the road carved a path south until, finally, they began to curve downward, and the scent of salt water grew strong as they approached the water.

They crawled along a hairpin turn and then another. After a third, a rutted driveway to the right displayed a crusty hand-painted sign reading LIVE BAIT with a faded red arrow pointing in the direction of the water.

Diana pulled to the shoulder here. She nodded toward the driveway, saying, "We must walk from here."

The pebbles crunched loudly beneath their feet as Diana and Becca walked along the unpaved lane. Their breath was misty in the air, which itself was damp and held the scent of seaweed and smoke. Some two hundred yards along, the lane fanned out to a lumpy parking area and here stood several ramshackle buildings.

One of them was a wretched rusting trailer, a single-wide with threadbare curtains and drooping steps leading to a porch-less front door. Another was an unpainted shack with LIVE BAIT lettered across its side. The last was an ancient gray house whose roof sagged ominously and whose rain gutters were so choked with debris that they looked like miniature garden planters with weeds growing from them.

Like the single-wide trailer, the building had precarious-looking steps that climbed to a narrow porch and a door, one with a screen in poor repair. Also like the single-wide, the house had windows with threadbare curtains, although it was easy to tell that these curtains had been fashioned from bed-sheets long ago.

The house stood near the water, and stretching out from it was a pier. To one side a clothesline extended from the house to the bait shack, and on it hung clothes, although how they were supposed to dry in the cold, damp weather was anyone's guess. Piled here and there with no apparent sense of order were mounds of fishing nets, floats, crab cages, buckets, wheelbarrows, and life rings. Farther off a toilet lay on its side, with a rotting hammock draped over it. An aluminum boat sat on a boat trailer near the toilet, a huge dent in its bow and a tarp thrown over a hump that was its motor.

The woodsmoke they'd smelled as they'd walked along the

lane was coming from the house. As they observed it, a light came on. The door opened, and Diana drew Becca out of sight but not so far that she couldn't see a man come outside. He was coughing wetly, and he headed down the pier to hack and spit and pee into the water. A gull sat sleepily on a piling at the end. He picked up a shell and threw it at the bird. He spat again, this time on the boards of the pier. He ground his foot into the spit and headed back toward the house.

Diana touched Becca's arm. Becca looked at her. *Let's go, my dear.*

They didn't speak until they were back in the truck and Diana had driven farther along to the end of the road, where a boat launch identified the area as Possession Point. Then Diana braked the truck for a moment, looked at Becca, and said, "You know why I brought you here."

"Jenn lives there," Becca said.

Diana put her hand on Becca's shoulder. Becca felt the same tingle she'd felt before at the woman's touch. "People usually hate because of a despair they can't let themselves feel."

Becca swallowed and looked out the window. She nodded.

They said nothing else until they had returned to Diana's house. Then she said to Becca, "There are always answers to questions. To Jenn, to Derric, to Seth, to everything. The point of struggling through the questions is to recognize the answers when you see them and not to give up until you find them."

She got out, and when Becca did the same, she faced her over the hood of the truck. "You can do this, Becca," she said firmly. "Trust me in this. I know that you can."

THIRTY-EIGHT

Seth was heading out to his car in the morning darkness when the Star Store's manager zoomed into the parking lot and pulled up next to him. Jake cranked down the window of his Toyota and said, "Glad I caught you. Got a call this morning, and Trevor can't restock. Truck's showing up any minute. C'n you stay?"

Seth said sure. He always needed the money. He went back to the store and was swinging open its door when the delivery truck pulled into the parking lot off Second Street. The guy slid open the back and the smell of vegetables wafted out. Broccoli, cauliflower, cabbage . . . Seth went back inside to the storeroom, where he took a knife from the holder and sharpened it.

He was ready when the delivery man rolled the first stack of boxes into the vegetable area at the front of the store. There, the windows looked onto First Street and the streetlights were still shining on sidewalks empty of people. Seth set to work, slicing the dirty ends off the broccoli. He'd been doing this for less than five minutes when he saw the sheriff's car rolling toward him from the direction of city hall.

Seth looked to see who was driving, but he pretty much knew

it would be Dave Mathieson. The undersheriff locked eyes with him and pointed in a way that said Don't move an inch. But Seth wasn't planning on moving. He was planning on doing his job.

In three minutes Derric's father was standing in front of him, one hand resting on the gun on his hip. The undersheriff said, "I want to talk to you." Seth thought *that* was pretty obvious but what he said was "How's Derric doing?"

The undersheriff ignored this question, but Seth was ready for what he had to say in place of reporting on Derric's condition. "I want you coming clean about this Becca King," he said, which allowed Seth to see that Hayley had been right. Jenn McDaniels had shot off her mouth.

"What d'you want to know?" Seth asked.

"The nature of her relationship with Derric."

"Absolutely no clue."

"Then where she is. Everyone says her name. No one knows where to find her. There isn't even a picture of her at the high school. Unavailable for photo on the day they were taken. There's nothing about her on Facebook, either. If she's not on Facebook, I have to wonder if people are just making her up, if she even exists."

"I'm not on Facebook."

"I rest my case."

Seth dropped his gaze. He understood perfectly what the undersheriff meant. To Dave Mathieson, he was just some drop-out kid waiting to be arrested for breaking into the second home of a dot-com millionaire at Useless Bay. He said, "Yep, that's me, Sheriff. Start to finish."

At that, Dave Mathieson seemed to realize he'd crossed the

line for a supposed officer of the law talking to a kid holding a head of broccoli. He said, "Look, Seth, I'm just trying to find this girl. I want to know what happened to Derric, and I think you understand that. Everything I'm hearing now keeps taking me back to Becca King when it's not taking me back to this other name—Laurel Armstrong—who apparently isn't anyone either, at least not anyone on Whidbey Island. So I want to talk to this Becca. But she's like a ghost around here."

As the undersheriff was speaking, Becca herself materialized exactly like the ghost he thought she was. Seth saw her over the undersheriff's shoulder, crossing First Street from the Dog House. He saw her heading toward the Star Store, and he knew that she was probably looking for him, for it was too early for her to be seeking anyone else because there *was* no one else out and about other than himself, Jake, and the undersheriff. He tore his gaze away from Becca as the sheriff said, "What does she look like, at least?"

Seth said, "Like a girl. Whatever."

"Seth. *What* does she look like?"

Seth called to Jake, who was behind the deli counter, "Jake, you know Becca King, right? What's she look like?"

Jake raised his head from a platter of meat. He said, "Uh . . . darkish brownish hair, chubbette body. *Major* thunder thighs. Butt like a bronco. She wears weirdo glasses like something from nineteen fifty-two, and she dresses like shit, but hell, I'd do her."

Seth said to Dave Mathieson, "I wouldn't. She's fourteen years old."

Jake leered and winked. "Start 'em young." And then with his gaze flicking to the window and back to Seth, "Hey—"

Seth cut in quickly. "I bet the undersheriff here'd like to talk to you about doing fourteen-year-old girls, Jake."

Jake ducked his head. "Just *kidding*, Darrow."

Outside, Becca had seen the undersheriff and had executed a neat turn. She was walking swiftly back up the street where, Seth hoped, she would duck out of sight. The undersheriff wasn't going to hang around the Star Store forever. It was pretty clear that he was in town to prowl around, looking for her.

Mathieson said, "Very amusing, you two. I'm just peeing my pants, you two guys are so funny. But my boy's in a hospital bed hooked up to IVs and a heart monitor, with his leg in traction, and someone put him there. So you listen to me and you hear me good." He eyeballed Seth. "You find this Becca King and you bring her to me for questions. You got that?"

"I got it fine. But I don't know where she is."

"That's not what I've heard."

"Look, she's just some kid who came in once looking for grease for her bicycle chain. Sometimes she buys a sandwich here. That's all I know, and that's all Jake knows."

The undersheriff looked at Seth long and hard. He took his hand off his gun and he pointed at Seth again. He said, "Don't play me. We can always go up to Coupeville to the jail and have a conversation there. How'd you like that, Seth?"

"Do what you need to do," Seth replied. "I've had worse things happen lately than taking a ride to Coupeville."

BUT SETH WASN'T happy about having made it through his talk with the undersheriff when he clocked out of the Star Store several hours later. His time had been elongated. Restocking vegetables had become working one of the registers when two more people failed to show up for work because the sun was out and they'd probably decided that a day windsurfing at the beach was better than eight hours working in the Star Store.

Manning the cash register had been like every bad dream Seth had ever experienced about being in his history classroom and being mistakenly handed a calculus test by the teacher. His grandfather's old friend Mrs. Prince had been pretty nice about being charged $2,100 for a newspaper, a six-pack of beer, a loaf of Dave's Killer Bread, a jar of peanut butter, and a pound of green beans. But once Seth had cleared *that* little mess up, he was pretty stressed, and the rest of the morning was downhill from there. When it was over, he climbed into Sammy, put his head on the steering wheel, and said to the car, "I wish you could drive yourself because I am *finished*."

"You can't be," Becca remarked as she rose from the backseat from beneath an old beach towel. "You gotta get me out of here."

Seth jumped a good six inches. "What the heck!"

Becca shed the towel. "This thing smells awful."

"It's Gus's. What d'you expect it to smell like? Roses?"

"Don't you ever wash it?"

"It'll just get dirty again." He fired up the car and headed out of the parking lot. He pulled into Second Street, and he began to drive up the hill that would take them to the north edge of town. Where Second Street changed its name to Saratoga Road, he pulled into the parking lot of the local Laundromat.

Becca climbed over the seat and dropped down next to him, and it came to Seth that Jake's description of her was no longer apt. She still had the weirdo glasses and the bad brown hair, but she wasn't a chubbette any longer. If she deep-sixed the glasses and owl-eyes makeup she would almost look good. She said, "I saw the undersheriff talking to you. I didn't know where to go but I figured he wouldn't look for me inside Sammy."

Seth said, "Good thinking. And you're a suspect now." He explained his visit from Hayley, what she'd said about Jenn's promise to her.

Becca listened to all this and shook her head slowly. "So I'm supposed to have . . . what? Like, I pushed Derric off the trail because he didn't want to be my boyfriend?"

"That's about it." Seth looked away from her. Across the street was a vacant lot, for sale as long as he could remember. At the moment it hosted a doe and three fawns. Triplets, he thought. You didn't see triplets often.

Becca said, "*Seth . . .*" as if to get his attention. "You don't think I did that, do you? You don't think that *I* pushed Derric?"

"I guess not," Seth said.

"Well thanks. *That* sounds real positive."

He turned back to her. "Hey, I can't help what it sounds like. *I* didn't push him. Someone did. I don't know who. Maybe it was you."

"Great." Becca threw herself back against her seat and stared out the window and into the Laundromat. She sighed.

It looked to Seth as if he and Becca had come to a crossroads in their friendship, and one of them was going to have to move across it. But he didn't want to be the one who did the walking.

As he was thinking this, Becca turned her head and looked at him. "At some point," she said, "we're going to have to trust each other or we're not getting out of this."

"What's that supposed to mean?"

"I guess it means you need to tell me why you stopped wearing your sandals. Dylan's still got his on, so I'm thinking it's not the weather that made you stop wearing them."

Seth swore. Then he said, "Those sandals. Crap. I wish I never bought them."

"Okay. Whatever," Becca said. "But d'you see how it looks that you stopped wearing them pretty fast after Derric fell?"

"And do *you* see how it looks that you disappeared after Derric fell? *And* how it looks that you left that stupid cell phone in the parking lot of Saratoga Woods?"

"Yeah. Matter of fact, I see it. But those were things I had to do."

"Yeah? Well, I had to do some stuff, too."

"Like what? Push Derric over the bluff?"

"Hey, come *on*."

"Okay, okay." Becca watched him for a moment in a way that made Seth feel she was trying to delve into his brain. She finally said, "Like I said, at some point we're going to have to trust each other, so here's the deal: I saw a footprint of those sandals on the trail where Derric fell *and* I'm saying that you didn't hurt him."

"Good. Because that kid's over six feet tall and built like a linebacker, and I'm not stupid. No way would I put a hand on him. What about you?"

"I don't push boys over bluffs. No matter if they tell me the sight of me gives them the runs. Okay?"

He smiled. "The runs, huh? Okay. So what now?"

"So now you tell me about the sandals."

Seth rolled his eyes. "The *sandals* again. Hell, Becca, they're being repaired. I had to send them to Seattle. Probably a week after Derric fell. The sole started to separate and they cost me over one hundred fifty bucks and they're guaranteed for life."

"That's *it*?"

"Yeah. That's it. Period. They're all-weather and the whole nine yards and when the sole started to come off, believe me, I was pretty pissed. So they're being fixed."

"Why didn't you just say?"

"Say what? To who? 'Hey, world, I'm getting my sandals fixed'? I didn't even know why anyone *cared* about them."

Becca shook her head, but Seth could tell it was in wonder now and not in disbelief. Her expression said it was such a simple answer and one that made perfect sense.

She said, "I think we've got to talk to Dylan Cooper then."

Seth said, "Looks like. If you saw that print and if anyone knows anything, it's going to be that dude."

"Know where to find him?"

Seth looked at his watch. "This time of day? No problem."

THIRTY-NINE

When Seth took Becca back toward town, she felt trepidation. She hadn't been out in broad daylight in weeks other than to whip up to the cemetery for an hour or to sneak to the library via Seawall Park. So she slouched in her seat as they coursed down Second Street, and she ducked her head altogether when they passed the Cliff Motel.

She couldn't believe it when Seth headed up Maxwelton Road. It seemed to her that South Whidbey High School had to be his destination. All she caught from his whispers was *Dylan . . . stoners always . . . like Sean said*, so she figured he *was* sure about where to find Dylan Cooper. Her only terror was that his idea was to find Dylan by marching into the administration office of the school and demanding to see him.

But he made a left turn just before the school, and they curved up a road behind it. They went past a baseball diamond and ended up tucked into a parking area where two trailheads branched into a woods that Becca hadn't seen before.

She said, "Where are we?"

Seth said, "South Whidbey Community Park. Part of it backs onto the high school. *Very* convenient for the stoners. Come on."

He led the way into the trees. It was a broad path, but it soon got narrow. There weren't additional trails breaking off it as in Saratoga Woods, though. It was all straightforward for quite some distance until a single fork appeared. Seth didn't hesitate. He veered right, heading vaguely back in the direction of the high school. They were far behind it and up above it, though. Dimly in the distance, a bell for changing classes rang.

This path was narrower than the other. Salal and ferns grew so thickly along the way that Becca knew she would have missed the third trail leading off from the path they were on, had Seth not pointed it out by a young, arching alder that marked it some fifty yards into the trees and brush.

He said, "This way," and ducked into the shrubbery. Becca followed. Soon enough she smelled, rather than saw, what they were looking for. The scent of burning weed was unmistakable and what accompanied it was the murmur of voices and the additional whispers of *oh man heavy . . . where'd this stuff . . . drag man . . . lid of this all right*, which told the tale of the state they were about to find the dope smokers in.

There were three of them, and they were blitzed. Becca recognized them all as she emerged into a small clearing behind Seth. Dylan Cooper was there—wearing those sandals—and his two companions were the boys who'd been with him the day he'd harassed both Jenn and her just outside the new commons. Beyond them and below, Becca could see the school. It wasn't so far away as to make sneaking into the woods a problem for kids who wanted to dope up.

"S'happenin'?" Dylan was the one to speak. "Seth, cool. You here for a toke?"

"God. It's that skank," one of the other boys said, pointing to Becca. "Whew, you're one ugly chick."

"Or you buyin'?" Dylan asked as if the other boy hadn't spoken. "I got three beans for later but I c'n sell you one."

"We need to talk to you," Seth said to Dylan.

Dylan drew in on the joint he was holding and smiled a slow and knowing smile. "Bet I know about what. Also bet I don't care."

Becca rolled her eyes. This, she saw, was not going to be easy. She said, "You dope up in Saratoga Woods sometimes, right? On weekends, I bet, most of all."

"At the erratic at the top of the woods," Seth added. "Everyone knows it."

Dylan shrugged. "So what?"

"So that day when Derric Mathieson fell, you were there," Becca said.

Dylan's eyes looked as guarded as they could, considering how lit up he was. One of the other boys said, "That dude Mathieson again. *When*'re we goin to stop *hearin'* about him?"

Dylan smiled. He said to Becca, "Mayyyyyyybeeeee. Or mayyyyybeeeee not."

"I saw you, Cooper," Seth said. "You took off when the cops showed up, but I saw you and so did everyone else who was there."

Dylan hadn't considered this, obviously. Or at least not in his present condition. He said nothing, but Becca could see that he was attempting to make a few calculations in his head. She heard *fuh . . . gotta . . . wow . . . damn . . .* all bouncing around him, but that was it. Her hopes of somehow wrestling some sense out of this boy were pretty well dashed. But she had to try.

"Were you meeting Derric in the woods?" she asked him.

"Th' hell would I be meetin' *him* for?" Dylan asked.

"You tell us," Seth said. "Because you left your footprint on Meadow Loop Trail right where he fell and if you don't want the sheriff to hear about that—"

"Hey hey hey!" Dylan was on his feet in an instant, in a way that belied the extent to which he was doped up. "What you *saying*, dude?"

"That you were there and you know something and it's time to cough it up," Seth told him.

Dylan approached. He and Seth were matched for size, but with his friends present—no matter their condition—the odds weren't good. He got in Seth's face and sneered, "And what about *you*?" as his two friends rose to their feet. "*You* bein' there and *him* bein' there an' you such a fug of a loser an' him such a fug of a winner . . ."

Seth put a hand on Dylan's chest to keep him at a distance. He said, "When it comes to losers, dude . . ."

Dylan's friends were up and circling the two boys in an instant.

Becca said, "Come on, Seth. If these guys know anything—"

"Nope," Seth said. "Dylan's going to talk. Because if he doesn't, I'm going to punch his lights."

"Uh . . . Seth?" Becca said, for one of the boys had spied a fallen branch and had decided to arm himself with it.

Seth gave it a glance. He looked at Becca. "He couldn't hit a dead turkey with that," he said.

The boy took this as a challenge and swung, but Seth was quick. One move and the branch was his. He twisted it and its wielder was on the ground. Seth threw the branch to one side and said, "Come on. You guys are way too strung out to fight. We can go that way but even Becca here's going to be able to take you on. So you want to answer me or you want to throw punches?"

Dylan wanted punches. He landed one, but in his condition it was a glancing blow. One blow from Seth and he was on the ground. Seth sighed. "Guys," he said. "Get real."

"Fug. Loser."

"Fat 'n' ugly."

"Yeah, dude. And all the rest," Seth said. "So what happened in the woods or do I have to sit on your face to hear it?"

"*Nothin'* happened in the woods, okay?" Dylan said. He was on the ground still, but his concern now wasn't Seth so much as the roach he'd dropped. "Didn't know that dude was there. What's *with* you? We heard the fuggall noise. That's *it*. Next thing we know the cops're there. Like we're goin' to want to talk to *them*?"

Becca listened hard to this and to everything else, but there was nothing more. Particularly there was nothing in the air among the boys to suggest that Dylan was lying. He was a piece of work, but it seemed that he was telling the truth. And if his condition now was anything like the condition he might have been in at the erratic in Saratoga Woods, he wouldn't have been able to push anyone anywhere, least of all Derric Mathieson, who probably outweighed him by forty pounds and definitely outsmarted him by forty IQ points.

She said to Seth, "That's it, then."

"You think?" he said.

She nodded. "Let's go."

ALL THE WAY to the car, Becca thought furiously. She wanted answers and she wanted them *now*. But the whole idea of having answers handed to her took her back to the words that Diana Kinsale had spoken to her when they'd returned from their look at Jenn McDaniels's house: The point of struggling through the questions was to recognize the answers when you finally had them. She'd struggled through her questions about Jenn McDaniels and Jenn's dislike of her, and the answers had lain in that place where Jenn lived, in its grinding poverty and its sense of hopelessness. Here, now, she was faced with more questions, and while Dylan Cooper hadn't provided the answers, she had a feeling they were staring her in the face.

She said nothing as they made their way back to Seth's VW. She felt that they had a partial picture of what had happened that day in Saratoga Woods but how to finish it? She'd thought talking to Dylan would do it. She'd been wrong. So she had to seek another way.

She leaned against the VW when they reached it. Seth climbed inside and drummed his fingers on the steering wheel. She pictured Saratoga Woods once again, much as she had pictured it for Diana earlier. So many people had been there. But how many of them could have taken the trail that Derric was on when he fell? It was by itself. It was far to one side of the meadow, tucked out of sight. True, it connected to other trails high up in the woods, but there were far easier ways to get to them, both from the parking lot and from within the forest itself. So for Derric to have been there . . . for anyone to have been there . . . there was going to be a significant reason, and it wasn't going to have to do with a day hike. For a day hike just didn't make sense. Not that trail. Not where it was. Not how you got to it.

She leaned into the VW and spoke to Seth. "I think we've got to do it all again."

"What? Talk to those losers? Not hardly."

"No. I mean go into Saratoga Woods. Seth, I think we need to relive that day because we're missing something and it's right in front of us."

"What makes you think that?" he asked her.

"Because answers always are," she told him.

FORTY

They needed Gus. If they were going to replay the day as it had occurred for the two of them, Gus had been part of it. Seth wasn't sure how his grandfather was going to take his request for the return of the dog, though. So he left Becca at a place near the highway called Bayview Corner, a congregation of restored and repurposed buildings.

He didn't give her time to argue. Instead, he shoved open the car door and led her to a bigger-than-life chessboard fashioned out of a lawn between a group of clapboard shops and a gardening center. He pointed to a spot on the chessboard and said, "Knight to king's bishop six. Wait there. I'll be back with the dog."

She sank to the ground, where she leaned against one of the chessman. She said, "Don't need my help?"

"Not for this," he told her.

He cruised along and thought about what he would say to his grandfather. They'd parted well the last time they'd seen each other at Skajit Farmers' Supply, but Ralph's intention had been to speak with Hayley. Seth didn't want his grandfather to think he was showing up to pump him for information about that encounter.

He needn't have worried about where to begin his conversation with Ralph, however. As he turned to drive up the hill to Ralph's house, an oxidized red Mazda was coming toward him down the slope. He pulled to the side and saw, to his chagrin, that Mrs. Prince of the $2,100 bill at the Star Store was just leaving. She waved at him merrily and grinned and Seth waved back gamely. He wondered how Ralph had reacted to the news that his grandson had managed to screw up running the Star Store's cash register. He could easily imagine Mrs. Prince's words: "Ralph, I hate to ask, but can that boy even count?"

Seth drove the rest of the way up the hill. When he descended to the house, he found Ralph standing at the kitchen counter with Gus sitting under the table. Ralph was leafing through a recipe book, a six-pack of beer on the counter next to him and Gus watching his every move, hoping food was going to be involved eventually.

The dog yelped a greeting when he caught sight of Seth. He began to rise. Ralph said, "Cave, Gus," as the Labrador started to come out from beneath the table, tail wagging furiously. Gus hesitated, his brown eyes going from Ralph to Seth to Ralph again. Ralph repeated, "Cave," and the dog retreated back under the table, where he hunkered.

"Pretty cool," Seth said. "Can I say hi to him?"

"Course you can. He's your dog."

Seth bent under the table and put his cheek on Gus's head. The tail swept the floor faster.

Ralph slapped the recipe book closed. "Fran Prince tells me they got you on the cash register at the Star Store, favorite male grandchild."

Seth groaned. "I saw her leaving just now. I didn't think she'd stop by and tell you, though. She must think I'm a dolt."

Ralph frowned. "Why?"

"I charged her twenty-one hundred dollars for her order. She didn't tell you?"

"Nope."

"What was she doing here, then?"

Ralph nodded toward the six-pack of beer. "She brought me that. Fixed her back door yesterday and damn fool woman thought she needed to give me a thank-you for it."

Seth said, "Oh." He wondered what his life might be like if he *stopped* jumping to conclusions the moment he saw someone doing something. "Anyway, I was only on the register for about twenty minutes. They wouldn't put me on it permanently. That'd just about drive them out of business."

Ralph didn't answer at first. Instead, he stowed the beer in the refrigerator one bottle at a time, and Seth could tell by his expression that he was thinking hard. He finally said, "Enough of this. You come with me, Seth."

Seth thought, Uh-oh, but he followed his grandfather into the living room. Ralph went to a cabinet with open shelves crammed with books, framed photos, and keepsakes. He took from these shelves one of the pictures and a small wooden box.

He said, "You look at these."

Seth said, "Grand, I just came by to ask—"

"Oh hell, boy, I know you're here for a reason. I didn't fall off the truck this morning. But you and I have business to finish up and finishing that business begins with you looking at these."

Seth knew what they were, of course. The box was his first

effort in wood, a crude container made in a summer craft class when he was between third and fourth grade. The picture was of him standing on the deck of the forest tree house, grinning proudly, a few years ago.

Ralph said, "There's knowing what you have in here"—he indicated his head—"and there's also having the sense to use it. You're a fine musician and an equally fine craftsman, Seth, and I'm damned if I'm going to watch you wishing your way into a state of failure because you think the rest of the world wants you to be something else. The world doesn't *care* who you are, grandson. *You're* the one who's supposed to care about that."

He removed the box and photo from Seth's hands and replaced them. He went back to the kitchen where he leaned against the counter, arms crossed, facing Seth who followed him. "So what's up?" he asked.

Seth sighed. He looked back into the living room, at the box replaced upon the shelf. He looked at that picture, too. He said, "I haven't done one single thing to get a tutor for the GED."

"Now that's a real problem, isn't it?"

"Considering I promised Mom and Dad . . . yeah, it's a real problem."

"Figured out why yet?"

"Why I don't have a tutor?" Seth leaned against the counter, matching his grandfather's posture. "I *want* to say because the whole GED thing is a load of crap. I'm a guitarist, and I'm a *good* guitarist. What difference does it make if I take the GED?"

"That's what you want to say, eh?" Ralph said. "Is the truth something different?"

Seth blew out a breath. "I'm starting to think so."

"And?"

"I'm scared I won't pass. *And* I don't want some tutor seeing how lame I am."

"Lame? For God's sake. Consider that tree house."

"So I built a tree house," Seth said. "So what? I couldn't have done it without you standing there telling me where to pound the nails."

"That's just the point, grandson. That's how you learned. I set you loose in this forest now and tell you to find a spot and build another tree house, you think you could do it?"

"Now I could. Sure." Seth looked at his boots but what he saw was his grandfather's point. He had to *start* somewhere in order to *finish* somewhere else. What he didn't see, though, was how this applied to a test that would serve him nothing in his life.

Ralph said, "I'm not going to disagree with you about whether that damn test is important or just one hell of a waste of time. That's not really the issue."

"What *is* the issue then?"

"It's keeping the bargain you struck with your parents. You don't do that, you're going to keep feeling the way you've been feeling. I've been watching you thrash around for months now, Seth, and I got to tell you that until you finish doing what you promised to do, you're going to keep thrashing. And all the Hayleys in the world—"

"It's not *about* Hayley, Grand."

"*All* the Hayleys in the world," Ralph persisted, "are not going to make up for what you haven't done to take care of business."

Ralph pushed away from the counter, then. He shoved his fists into the small of his back, and as Seth watched him do this, it came to him that his grandfather wasn't a young man any longer. He wasn't going to live forever. He saw then that it was all about time and time was passing. His own time would pass as well.

Ralph said, "This whole damn test? This tutor? Passing, failing, whatever? This is something you owe yourself. You promised your parents, true. But you keep the promises you make for yourself."

"I guess so." Seth looked from his grandfather to Gus. The Lab was still patiently waiting beneath the table. Seth said, "Grand, c'n I have my dog back?"

"Course you can, favorite male grandchild," Ralph replied. "He's your dog."

Seth pushed away from the counter as well. He said, "Come, Gus," and the dog got to his feet. Seth said, "Grand, there's one other thing."

"What's that, Seth?"

"You always call me 'favorite male grandchild,' and I like that. I do. But fact is, I'm your only male grandchild."

Ralph looked at him, blue eyes sparkling. He smiled. Then he laughed out loud. "Details," he said. "Mere details, Seth."

FORTY-ONE

"I don't know why we have to start with the motel." Seth was idling the VW at the stop sign that marked the end of Sixth Street across from the Cliff Motel. "What's the point? Nothing happened here. It was all in the woods."

Frigging . . . hates me . . . total bull . . . like Sean . . . told Becca he probably didn't want to see Debbie Grieder, and she couldn't blame him. But she said it was just a feeling she had. They needed to walk back through that day in order to see it from another angle, and the Cliff Motel was where the day had begun. In the backseat as she spoke, Gus whined and thumped his tail.

Seth said, "At least *that* part's the same. He whined all the way. He wanted a run." He proceeded through the intersection and signaled for the turn into the motel's parking lot. "How're we going to do this without running into Mrs. Grieder?"

"It's one o'clock," Becca said. "She's still at her meeting. The kids are in school. We'll be okay."

Seth pulled in and parked. He said, "Tell me we don't have to dig up all those bulbs and replant them."

Becca laughed as she opened the car door. Before she could answer, though, Gus had shot through the opening. He'd seen a squirrel and he was barking like mad.

Seth said, "*Excellent* way to begin." He dashed after the Lab, yelling "Gus! Stay!" He disappeared around the side of the building.

At that, the office door opened and Debbie Grieder stepped outside at the same moment as Becca noticed what she hadn't seen before, which was Debbie's SUV tucked along the side of the motel. Chloe came storming out right behind her shouting, "Is that Gus?" She ran off in the direction of the barking while Debbie stopped short at the sight of Becca.

Thin . . . like Sean . . . oh God fractured the air but along with Gus's barking and Chloe's cries, Becca heard nothing more because Josh, too, came out of the motel, only in his case he stumbled and a hot water bottle that was strapped to his head by means of a scarf came loose, fell to the ground, and spilled, splashing water over his slippers.

Becca went to him. She said, "Hey Josh, what *happened* to you?"

"Earache," he said. "Grammer says it's an infection so I get to stay home and so does Chloe. How come you left?"

Debbie said sharply, "Go back inside, Josh. The cold will make your ear hurt worse."

He looked from beneath his eyebrows at his grandmother. He said, "'Kay," which told Becca that he truly *didn't* feel well, so quickly cooperative was he.

Becca got to her feet. Debbie observed her with *lost so much weight . . . what that means* the flittering message in her whispers. For Laurel, Becca thought, it would have been cause for celebration. For Debbie it meant something different. Debbie looked from Becca to the VW to the side of the building where Gus's barking was coming from. As she did this, Seth came around the building with Chloe and Gus, but he slowed down at the sight of Debbie and he hustled the dog back into the car.

Debbie said to Becca, "So it's ended just like I warned you. I told you to keep clear from him. I told you it would lead to nothing good. Who're you running from? His dealer?"

Becca blinked in surprise. *His dealer* meant only one thing in this context. She said, "Seth's been helping me."

"I'm sure that's what he wants you to think. That's what they always say. Meantime, what's really going on is that *you're* helping him. The only question is how. Want to tell me?"

"It's not whatever you're thinking. Without Seth, I'd be—"

"Without Seth you'd be here in room four-four-four. Without him, you'd be in school. Without him I wouldn't be sick with worrying about where you are and what's happened to you."

"I'm sorry. I didn't mean to worry you."

"Why'd you run off then? You must have known I'd worry."

Becca thought hard about what she could tell Debbie: what was safe and what was also true. She said, "Remember at the start when I needed a place to stay and a way to get into school and you helped me? And I was so grateful and you never asked me a single question? Well see, there were things I *couldn't* tell you or anyone else, like where my mom is because I don't know or why she left me here, which I *do* know but can't explain because it wouldn't make sense. I mean, part of it would but a big part wouldn't. See, she told me to find a friend of hers only the friend had just died when I got there and I couldn't get my mom on her cell phone to tell her that. So I ended up going to the AA building where I met you but when the police came here that night, I had to run away because—"

"Wait. Wait." Debbie scratched her badly scarred forehead. She dug in her pocket and brought out her cigarettes. Before she lit one, she said, "*What* police came here? When?"

"The undersheriff came when I was outside with Josh and Chloe. That time I showed them the orcas? I couldn't let him take me away, Debbie. Especially not in front of them."

"Are you talking about Dave Mathieson?"

Becca nodded. "I figured someone must've reported me. He was looking for me anyway because of my cell phone and where I had to leave it. I figured that if he found out that my mom had left me on the island—"

Debbie blew out a lungful of smoke. She said, "You thought Sheriff Mathieson was here at the motel because of *you*?" and she put a hand to her forehead. Then she said to Chloe, "Darlin', you go inside and see if Josh's all right."

"But I want to play with Gus and Becca," Chloe protested.

"I'll come back and play later," Becca told her. "I promise."

The little girl shuffled to the door, albeit reluctantly. When it had closed behind her, Debbie said, "Becca . . . the undersheriff wasn't here for you that night. He's got . . . He does some other business at the motel from time to time with someone else. That's all."

Becca frowned. "What business?"

Seth coughed loudly. Debbie glanced his way. *Knew it . . . life is . . .* went between them, and from that look they shared and out of Debbie's whispers came a fleeting memory of something Becca had seen: Tatiana Primavera's fingers on the undersheriff's arm in the commons that day. The undersheriff's fingers interlocking with hers. So quick had the gesture been, it would have meant nothing by itself. But like so many other occurrences on this island, it did not stand alone.

Becca said, "Oh."

Debbie said to her, "It was never about you, that night. Later on he came back, when I reported you missing. But that night? You were the farthest thing from his mind. So where did you go?"

"I went to find Seth. He helped me. Like before."

"'Like before?'"

"He was the one who told me to find you at that meeting up Second Street where I met you. He said if I went and waited there, you'd find me. He told me you'd help me. He said you always help people."

"Seth said that?" When Becca nodded, Debbie looked at Seth and kept looking at him while she said, "He didn't hurt you? He didn't bother you? He didn't . . . give you anything? Or encourage you to . . . do something?"

"Like what?"

Debbie looked back at Becca, studying her. She said, "Like drugs. Like weed. Like pills. Like meth. Like anything. He didn't give you anything?"

Becca shook her head. Then she added, "Except camping equipment and some food."

Debbie murmured, "God." Then she said, "He's been taking care of you? He's given you a place to stay?"

"Yeah. I mean, he's my friend."

Debbie seemed to droop with all the information she'd been given. She was like a woman who'd been loaded up with bricks to carry upon her shoulders. *Sponsor . . . wrong . . . what sort of fourth* were a few of her whispers but they seemed to combine with others about *Sean . . . years of his life . . . what's it really*, and even these were clogging the air with others that seemed to come from Seth because they dealt with *time for people to stop thinking . . . how stuff looks . . . Sean but not me . . .* until Becca could bear no more. She fumbled for the AUD box, brought it out, plugged it into her ear.

Debbie said, "The kids have missed you, Becca."

"I'll come back and see them."

"What about school?"

"I've been keeping up with the work, sort of. I'll be going back."

"Want to tell me when?"

"Really soon. I hope."

"What's this all about, then? D'you want to tell me? Either one of you?"

Becca shot a glance at Seth who made a gesture of lifting his hands and dropping them, telling Becca it was all up to her. Becca said to Debbie, "I'll tell you, only not right now. Right now Seth and I have to go to Saratoga Woods. We had to stop here first because that's what happened the day that Derric fell."

"Everything started that damn day, didn't it?" Debbie said.

Becca considered this. She saw it was only partly true. "Most things," she agreed, but then she added, "Not everything, though. That's how I figure it."

WHEN THEY PULLED into the parking lot at Saratoga Woods, there were no cars present and no bicycles locked against the information board. They got out of the car with the dog. Seth said, "Gus, sit," and that was exactly what the Labrador did. He licked his chops, though, and looked toward the woods. He gazed meaningfully at Seth.

"Impressive sit," Becca told Seth.

"Only as long as there're no rabbits or squirrels in sight." Seth bent to the dog and rubbed his head as he clipped on the leash. They headed across the meadow with Gus trotting along beside them.

Becca pointed south where a distant trailhead opened into the towering Douglas firs. "Derric was up that trail, but I didn't get to him from there. I came out that way after I found him, though."

"Yeah. I remember. That's Meadow Loop," Seth said. "You c'n get onto it from Coral Root Link. You want to go that way first?"

"Let's retrace everything, just like it was. Except I don't think we need to let Gus run off."

"Glad of that," Seth declared. "I can't promise he'd come back. He's not *that* well trained."

They headed for the main trail, directly in front of them at the end of a path through the last of the season's rustling meadow grasses. Seth gave the dog more leash so that Gus could sniff the nectar of a thousand other dogs, and they made their way onto the trail into the woods.

It was hushed among the trees, which made Becca think of how many sounds she'd heard on that day when Derric had fallen. There had been whispers coming at her from all directions, as well as scent and the barking. She remembered how everything had seemed to stop suddenly except the barking of the dogs, which went on and on.

Seth said to her as if reading her mind, "What I remember is that Gus heard dogs barking. He took off. I went straight after him up Indian Pipe Trail."

So that was what they did, following the trail on the damp ground with the scent of decomposing vegetation rich in the air. When they came to the first junction, Seth paused and said, "Yeah. I remember I was happy he hadn't gone onto Wintergreen. It was muddy in that direction, and there weren't any paw prints. So I figured he stayed on Indian Pipe until Twin Flowers Trail, and that's what I did, too."

"This is where I got lost," Becca said. "You disappeared and I heard the dogs. I turned left somewhere but I didn't know the forest, so I ended up on a trail that went way up and through some private land. That's where I ran into Diana Kinsale. Gus was with her, and she gave me a leash to use, but he still got away."

"Private land?" Seth repeated. "That sounds like the Coral Root Link. It connects this woods over to Putney Woods. To Metcalf Woods, too. If Gus was with Mrs. Kinsale on that trail, we need to head that way."

Seth led her to the left onto the secondary trail and they began to climb. The ascent was immediate and narrow, carving an edge into a hillside covered with shrubbery and trees. The only sounds came from Gus's snuffling along the sides of the path and from a woodpecker *rat-tat-tatting* against a dead tree trunk.

Some distance along the trail, another veered off and the area looked familiar. Becca saw a flat-topped rock backed by a thick wall of ferns from which spiderwebs stretched like Halloween decorations. She remembered sitting on a stump here, she recalled the sounds of dogs coming closer. She said to Seth, "This is where I met up with Diana Kinsale and the dogs. Then Gus took off on that trail"—she pointed to it—"and I went after him."

Seth pointed to a small sign onto which M.L.T. had been carved. "Meadow Loop Trail," he said. "Let's go."

Becca followed him. It was all coming back to her now, but what came back most strongly was how it felt, not what she saw. She remembered the moment when the scent that she associated with Derric had disappeared, as if cut off peremptorily by a slap in the face. She remembered the feeling of all at once being set adrift in a place that she didn't know and couldn't understand. She remembered the solitude and emptiness of it.

Seth said over his shoulder, "So where'd you see that footprint? Seems to me we need to find that next."

She told him that the footprint had been at the steepest point of the trail, above the spot where Derric had fallen. He nodded and went back to the hike, and in a few minutes of climbing they had come to it. Becca said, "Here, Seth," and she pointed to the tree far down the bluff against which Derric's body had rested. "Gus was down there. It was like he knew Derric was hurt. He was lying right next to him."

"Where was the footprint?"

Becca looked around to see if she could remember the precise spot, but instead of spying where the footprint had been, she saw that there was a secondary trail leading up the hill that comprised the other side of Meadow Loop Trail. This was more of a path, like the myriad paths that people made on their own throughout the woods. Like those, this one wasn't official. It forged a way up to the remains of a large moss-covered trunk of an old-growth hemlock. Leaning against this were the remains of several other fir trees, long ago downed by storm. Together they formed the shape of a small teepee covered in ferns and moss.

"Oh my gosh," she said, "Seth, look at that," and she began to climb up to it, not knowing exactly why she was doing so, only knowing it felt right to her.

Seth said, "Be careful. There's a lot of deadfall. If it slides out from under you and . . . Gus, stay. I don't need you going up there, too."

At the top, Becca crawled into the teepee, and sat cross-legged. She was some thirty feet above the trail, looking down on Seth and on Gus next to him, his tail whisking the ground. She said slowly, "Seth . . . this is . . . It seems very special."

"It's probably a raccoon den, and you're probably sitting in the middle of a pile of raccoon poop. Better hope they're out for the day 'cause they can be nasty. You better come out."

Becca looked around. The hollow was deep and dimly lit from the daylight. There didn't seem to be any poop, and the place didn't smell of animals or anything else except vegetation. But then she spied something tucked into the deepest part of the hollow, and she crawled to inspect it as Seth called up, "What're you *doing*?"

Becca said, "Found something," and she saw that it was a plastic supermarket bag, covering two other plastic supermarket bags, and all of them were tightly fitted around what felt like a box. The box turned out to be an old *Star Wars* lunch box, a little rusty but otherwise usable.

Becca crawled out of the teepee and opened the lunch box. Inside, she found envelopes. There was a stack of them, each with the same word printed on the front of it. The writing started out as simple block printing, became clumsy cursive, and then gained confidence. Becca was somehow not surprised when she read the word written over and over again as she flipped through the collection: *Rejoice.*

———

THEY WERE LETTERS, dozens of them. They began "Dear Rejoice" and no matter the block printing or the cursive, they all ended identically: "Your loving brother, Derric." Becca read this with the dawning understanding that Derric had crept up to this place to hide letters he'd written to a beloved sister.

Dimly, Becca heard her name called again. She said, "It's a *person*, Seth. Rejoice is a person!"

"What the heck . . . ?" Below her, Seth's face was screwed up in confusion. Hastily, Becca put the letters back into the box, wrapped the plastic bags around it, and got to her feet.

She felt dizzy for a moment. Then she understood. She said, "Oh my *God*. He just fell. Seth, he just fell. No one pushed him. You rushed by looking for Gus and he probably stood up quickly, but then . . . He just fell."

"How d'you figure that?"

She held up the package. "These're letters he wrote. He came here to write them or maybe just to hide them but it doesn't matter because he stood up and he slipped and he fell all the way down to—"

"No way," Seth said. "Good try but no way."

"Why not?" She began to descend, but within four steps, she

slid and went down. As if to prove Seth's words, a root broke her fall. She clambered up, went the rest of the way down to the trail, and Seth caught her arm when she got there.

"Rest my case," he said. "Anyway, Derric could walk on a shoe-string across Niagara Falls. He's an athlete, Becca. He's an excellent athlete. No way did he slip. Even if he did, he only would've slipped to here, the main trail. He wouldn't've kept going. He would've hit a root or some salal or something. Nice try, though." He nodded at the box. "What's that?"

"Letters," she said. "Like I said. To someone called Rejoice."

"What the heck kind of name is Rejoice? How d'you even know it's a person?"

"'Cause he told me about her right when I met him," Becca said. "Only I didn't understand what he meant till now."

FORTY-TWO

Even Gus knew something had happened. He was lying flat on the backseat of the VW instead of sticking his head out of the window or leaning it on Seth's shoulder. Becca was sitting with that lunch box clutched in her lap. The only thing she had said since they'd hurried down the rest of Meadow Loop Trail was, "We've got to get to the hospital." She had said it so urgently that, for a second, Seth had thought she was sick. Now as they drove she was just chewing her lip and he wondered if she was thinking that he'd hurt Derric after all.

Out of nowhere, Becca said, "I know you didn't hurt him. Your footprint was there but I bet your footprints were all over the forest that day."

Seth was freaked. It wasn't the first time Becca had said something that clicked right into his thoughts. He said, "That's just what I was thinking about."

"I figured."

"There's Dylan, though."

"He doesn't like Derric," Becca agreed. "He hassled him at lunch one time when I was there. But do you see Dylan going after Derric by himself, Seth? I mean, he seems to be the kind of kid who only does stuff for an audience. And there were no other footprints as fresh as that one I saw. It had to be yours." She opened the box and flipped through the letters.

Seth glanced over and saw how the printing changed to inexpert cursive and then to nice script. He said, "I don't get why he didn't just mail them. Or d'you think maybe Rejoice is just an imaginary friend? I had one when I was a kid. Jeter."

Becca looked at him from under her eyebrows and smiled. "What kind of name is Jeter?"

"The perfect name for an imaginary friend. A non-name. They don't need *real* names. Rejoice could be like that."

"Did you write letters to your imaginary friend?"

"Why would I? He was always there."

"That's just it," Becca said.

Seth considered this. She had a good point. They said nothing more until they arrived in Coupeville and pulled into the parking lot of the hospital.

Then Seth said, "You sure about this? His dad could be in there with him."

"He doesn't really know what I look like," Becca pointed out. "And anyway, it doesn't matter now. This box is what matters. Derric needs to know that someone knows."

"What's that going to do?"

"It'll take too long to explain. Just trust me, okay?" She looked at him earnestly when she said this, and Seth got the distinct feeling that she knew a lot of things that she wasn't revealing. He thought about this for a moment and decided that just as he had unfinished business in his life, she probably had unfinished business in hers and some of it might have to do with Derric Mathieson.

She nodded as if he'd said all this aloud, which made a shiver go down Seth's spine. He said, "Okay, let's go. Stay, Gus," and he cranked the window down halfway so the dog could enjoy the scents of Coupeville.

When they got to Derric's room, the door was open but no one was there visiting. This was the first time Seth had seen the other boy since his fall, and he looked around the room and noticed that there were wilted flowers that could be dumped in the trash. He thought about making himself useful and doing this, but instead he made himself look at Derric. The other boy was hooked up to tubes and peeing devices and whatever. Seth saw how the athlete he'd envied was now completely reliant on other people's willingness to care for him.

Becca went to the bed. She said over her shoulder, "C'n you stay by the door? If someone tries to come in, c'n you ask them to wait?"

Seth nodded. He eased the door closed and asked Becca what she was planning to do. He thought about Sleeping Beauty and the kiss from the Prince and then about Snow White and the kiss from the Prince, and he thought about how being kissed by a prince was something every girl was supposed to be waiting for: someone to save her when the reality was that there was no saving anyone, really. There was only saving yourself.

Becca glanced back at him. Seth saw in her eyes a kind of knowing. He couldn't work out what to make of this, but he suddenly trusted her completely.

He watched Becca put the lunch box on the bedside table and open it. She flipped through the letters and selected one, which she took out of its envelope. She unfolded it, smoothed it out, then put it on Derric's chest, faceup so that she could read the writing. Then she took up a framed picture from the bedside table and held it. With her other hand, she laced her fingers with Derric's flaccid ones. She leaned over the bed so that she could see the letter on his chest. She began to read it to him.

Seth heard only the first part, which was "Dear Rejoice," and after that he caught the occasional phrase like "track team at school this year" and "likes to talk to me about the Peace Corps" and "Goss Lake for the bicycle trials." He listened to this and tried to stay patient, but it wasn't easy. It seemed wildly unlikely that reading a letter was going to do any good, and he was about to say this when Becca reached the phrase "miss you so much, Rejoice," followed by "bring you here," and then the impossible happened.

Derric's foot moved. Then his free hand eased up to his chest. It moved across the letter and settled there so that Becca couldn't read any more of it. Only this didn't matter because she'd reached the end of it, which Seth could tell by the way she'd said "loving brother" and then "Derric." She'd said this last the way you'd say it if you were calling to a person, and that was what she was doing, Seth realized. She was calling to him.

Seth felt his heart seizing up in his chest. He said, "Becca, Becca, he's waking up."

She said, "Yeah," and then she spoke to Derric, saying, "I found the letters in the woods, Derric. I know about her. I understand."

At this, Seth saw Derric's eyes flutter. He saw his head turn with enormous effort so that he could look at Becca. His lips parted and his voice, when he spoke, was cracked by disuse. Just before Seth crashed out of the room in order to get to the nursing station, he heard Derric's words. They were clear in every possible way.

Derric said, "Where'd that stupid dog come from, Becca?"

They'd all been such fools, Seth thought.

———

SETH'S GRANDFATHER ALWAYS liked to use the expression "Can't see the forest for the trees," but Seth knew that for him and for most everyone else the opposite had been true. They'd all been unable to see the tree for the forest. The single tree of truth had been in front of them all along. But no one had seen it because everyone had been confused by their own individual, personal stuff.

Seth had chased Gus all over Saratoga Woods that day. He'd gone up one trail and down another and Becca had been doing the very same thing. Gus, of course, had thought it was a game. The faster Seth ran, the faster Becca ran, the faster Gus ran. How easy it would have been, then, for the Labrador to come racing around a bend in the trail where he'd come upon Derric just down from his hiding place, where he'd leaped upon the boy in a joyful Gus greeting, causing him to lose his footing and go over the bluff. So minutes later Seth had crashed by just running after Gus who was already streaking up ahead. And Seth had noticed nothing at all because in that moment when he'd passed by, there was nothing *to* notice. The fall had occurred, and he wasn't thinking about someone falling anyway. He was only thinking about finding his dog.

No one's fault, Seth thought. Absolutely no one's frigging fault.

At the nurses' station, he said, "He's waking up," and they knew at once what he was talking about. One of them picked up a phone and began to punch in numbers while another got to her feet and headed to Derric's room.

From all of this, Seth knew that the undersheriff would be arriving in short order to see his son. Because she was still a missing person to him, Becca was going to be someone the undersheriff probably would want to talk to. Plus, there was still the matter of that cell phone and how it would look to Dave Mathieson if he made the connection between her, it, and leaving the scene of Derric's accident. So Seth went back to the hospital room and stood in the doorway to get her attention.

The nurse was bustling around the bed saying, "Look who's awake! My, my, we've had a sleep, haven't we," and generally talking to Derric in the way someone talks to a five-year-old. She was writing on a chart and checking the IV bag and chatting away about "Mom and Dad are going to be very happy with *this* turn of events," and completely ignoring Becca who was sitting next to the bed with Derric's hand in hers like a lifeline he was clinging to.

Seth was about to call out to her and tell her that they should split before the undersheriff showed up when she stood and said to him, "Yeah, we should go," and then said to Derric, "I'll be back. I'll keep them safe for now."

Derric didn't seem to want to let go of her hand, though. The nurse didn't like this one bit. She said with false heartiness, "Now, Derric, the doctor's going to want to have a look at you and we can't have your little friend here when that happens, okay? She'll be back, won't you dear?"—this to Becca—and then, "See there? She's nodding. That means yes. You can let go now."

Derric, though, looked only at Becca. She bent over the bed and kissed his forehead. Then her lips met his and they lingered for a moment. His hand touched her cheek. Her hand touched his.

"Enough of that, now," the nurse said in a jolly fashion. "Let's not get him all excited, dear."

"I'll be back," Becca said again to Derric.

He nodded. He turned his head as she moved toward the door. His eyes met Seth's. He nodded again in the weak greeting of someone whose strength has been depleted. Seth said, "Hey, man. Good to see you again," and when Derric murmured, "Care of," Seth knew he was referring to Becca. He said, "Sure. You get better now, okay?" When Derric nodded again, Seth felt a link had been forged between them.

He and Becca ducked out of the room. In Becca's hands was the lunch box of letters. He said, "You don't want to leave those with him?" but Becca shook her head and said, "He wants me to keep them for now."

"They mean something, don't they?" Seth said. "I mean, they have to do with him and you, huh?"

Becca looked at him and then at what she was holding. She said slowly, "I didn't think about that. But I guess you're right."

Seth said, "It was weird, but when he looked over at me . . ."

He didn't know how to complete what he wanted to say, but it turned out he didn't need to because Becca said, "Yeah. I felt it, too."

They went down the corridor. As they headed across the hospital lobby, Undersheriff Mathieson came in the door at a run. Seth thought about hiding. He thought about stuffing Becca next to an artificial plant with large dusty leaves. But this wasn't necessary as it happened. The undersheriff was intent upon getting to his son. As with the forest and the trees, he saw nothing else.

FORTY-THREE

Becca descended from the bus into the cool afternoon air of Coupeville to feel a soft mist blowing up the street off the waters of Penn Cove. She yawned and slung her pack to her shoulders. It was heavy with books and with makeup work for the time she'd missed at school.

She'd been busy making things up to Debbie Grieder as well. She was back to cleaning rooms and helping the kids with their homework, and there was a form of peace among everyone in their little group. Josh, especially, was a joyful boy now that the prospect of seeing his Big Brother Derric again lay in front of him.

Becca and Debbie had talked about trust, but it seemed to Becca that something was not being said between them. *Seth* and *who he is* and *what I thought* constituted the only whispers from which Becca could derive a few clues, though. From these she figured that Debbie knew she'd been wrong about Seth but was having trouble apologizing for this.

At the door to the hospital, Becca fished the AUD box from her backpack and plugged it in. She went to Derric's room but found it empty. He'd been moved to a regular room, she was told. Out of a coma, he didn't need constant care any longer.

Becca felt a surge of happiness. It seemed, then, that Derric was entirely back in body. What remained to be seen was whether he was back in spirit as well.

At his room, she was stopped by yet another nurse, who informed her that the patient was allowed only two visitors at a time and she would have to wait. The nurse was all business, and she made it clear that there were *no* exceptions.

Becca figured there was no point to arguing. She could return to the lobby and wait awhile there because she had enough homework to do to keep her busy till the end of the semester. She was about to do this when the door to Derric's room opened. Rhonda Mathieson and Jenn McDaniels stepped out. It would *have* to be Jenn McDaniels, Becca thought.

A smile broke over Rhonda's face. She cried, "Jenn, look who's here! The very person Derric was just asking us about." Jenn scowled at this, but Rhonda went on, saying to Becca, "I wasn't sure how to get in touch with you."

"No one is." There was an edge to Jenn's voice. "If you don't run into her sneaking around Langley like an FBI agent, you just don't see her."

Becca ignored this. She said to Rhonda, "I'll give Derric my number. He had it before but he might've lost it."

Jenn scowled again.

Rhonda said, "Good. You go in and see him. And when you've finished your visit . . . Jenn and I are heading to the cafeteria for a snack. Join us there if you can, okay?"

Jenn shot Becca a look that said she hoped that Becca's snack would be slugs on toast. Becca told Rhonda she'd try to come to the cafeteria. Her real intention, though, was to hightail it back to Langley as soon as her visit with Derric was over.

She went into his room. Derric's leg was raised in traction as it had been earlier, and seeing him like this with his leg trussed up, Becca was reminded of how bad the break had seemed when she found him in the woods. She wondered what kind of athlete he'd be able to be when this was all over.

"They're saying it's going to be okay," he told her as her gaze met his. "Not this year, though."

"Did you just read my mind?" she asked him.

He laughed. "If I could read chicks' minds, I'd have all the right moves and I'd be dating that chick from the vampire movies. But nah. You were looking at my leg, which is what I spend most of my time doing, so I figured you were wondering the same thing I wondered when I woke up and saw it." Then his face softened noticeably. He patted the mattress next to him. "Glad you came."

Becca knew he meant her to sit on the mattress, but she was suddenly shy. She sat on the chair next to the bed instead. He looked wonderful, she thought. He looked as good as the day she'd met him, all smooth dark skin and dazzling smile. She tried to figure what she should say to him and felt knotted up inside with everything she wanted to tell him but still could not. She saw on his table a pile of schoolbooks, so she forged a path in that direction. She nodded at the books and said, "You and me both," and he said "Yeah, bummer," in a way that told her he knew what she meant. It was odd and yet perfectly natural that they would communicate in this shorthand fashion. It made her want to reach for his hand and hold it, but she was acutely aware that he was no longer a boy in a coma but a boy watching her closely with his great dark eyes and an expression of anticipation on his face.

He said, "I don't remember very much. There was just . . . all of a sudden this dog was there and he was crashing into me. I guess I was off balance or something. I think I scared him and he sure as heck scared me. And then I woke up and Dad was bending over the bed and here I was."

From this, Becca understood that Derric didn't remember anything about regaining consciousness with her at his side. She felt unaccountably sad, while at the same time not knowing what her sadness actually meant. She said quietly, "Derric, I think Rejoice brought you back."

His dark eyes seemed to grow darker. Cautiously, he said, "What?" and she told him about finding the letters, bringing them to the hospital, reading one of them to him. She looked around for a moment and saw the photograph she'd held that day, and she picked it up once again. She said, "Rejoice is one of these little kids, isn't she?"

He said nothing, and Becca looked from the picture to him and saw that his eyes were filled with tears. She whispered, "Oh no. Did she *die*? Is that why you hid the letters?"

He shook his head. No, no, no. Tears began to roll down his cheeks. He turned his head away from her, and she saw how hard his throat was working and from this she knew he was struggling to stop crying, which was only making him cry even more. From this Becca realized that he wanted to leave again, to go to that place he'd been in his coma, so she grabbed his hand. She said,

"*Tell* me what happened to her. I'm your friend. Now and always. Derric, you *have* to tell me." She thought of all the terrible things that happen to people in Africa because of political insurrections, civil war, genocide, famine, and disease. "Please, tell me," she repeated.

He said, "I left her."

"What?"

"I never said she was my sister." The tears continued to roll down his cheeks as he turned back to Becca. "I had the chance to be adopted and I *still* didn't say. So they didn't know."

"The Mathiesons?"

"Everyone," he said. "She was three years old and I was eight and I never said. There were so many kids and the boys and girls lived in separate buildings. My mom came with her church group and she said she wanted me and the only way . . ." His fingers closed into a fist. "So I didn't say anything and I didn't tell her about Rejoice and when she came back with my dad and he and she said 'Do you want to be our son, Derric?' and she didn't say anything about adopting a daughter, I didn't tell them. I was so scared they'd change their minds." He turned his head away in grief.

Becca saw how it had occurred. She saw that this secret was the heaviness and the sorrow she'd always felt in him, and she understood why his soul had persisted in crying out *Rejoice*. She sat on the edge of the bed. She took his hand. She said to him, "It's okay."

"It'll never be okay," he said. "I thought if I wrote to her and she could see how happy I was and if I promised to bring her here when I could . . . Only how could I do any of that when

I couldn't even mail the letters because then they'd know, and even if I mailed them, she couldn't read them . . . ?"

"You need to tell them now," Becca said, "They'll find Rejoice. They'll bring her here."

"I can't tell them. What kind of kid leaves his own sister behind? What kind of kid pretends he *has* no sister? Would you have done that? *No one* would have done that. They'll *hate* me. I hate myself."

Becca was silent because she had no answer. He'd done a terrible thing but he was far from being a terrible person. And yet he'd just come face-to-face with one of those facts that her grandmother had always called "a real gut stabber, hon." In life, there were no do-overs. There was simply what you did and then living through what happened next.

She said, "Derric, you were desperate. There isn't anyone who wouldn't understand that. You were a little kid. You wanted parents who would love you and take care of you and that's who you were and that's what you did. But the person you are now wouldn't do that. You wouldn't even be able to."

"I don't *know* that," he wept.

"I do," she said.

She hugged him then and he clung to her. She caressed his back and she cupped her hand around his head. Then over his shoulder she saw the door to his room swing open.

Jenn McDaniels walked in. But she stopped dead at the sight in front of her: Derric and Becca in each other's arms. Pure hatred chiseled its way across her face. When she saw this, Becca absolutely knew it was a hatred that wasn't about to dissipate anytime soon.

She left, then. There was nothing more to be said in front of Jenn, and Becca could tell from Jenn's expression that she wasn't about to leave her alone with Derric again. So she told him she would be back soon, and she headed in the direction of the lobby.

Once there, though, she saw that Undersheriff Mathieson had just entered with a stack of magazines in his hand. Becca figured she could get by him without a problem because he still didn't know who she was, but just at the moment she was set to do this, she heard Rhonda Mathieson call out from behind her, "Becca! Don't leave without saying good-bye." And then what was worse, she went on to her husband, "Dave, here's your mystery girl. Here's Becca King."

Becca cringed inwardly but she faced the undersheriff. She said, "Mystery girl?" with as casual a smile as she could manage.

Dave Mathieson looked her up and down. He said, unaccountably, "*Chubbette?*"

Becca eased the earphone of the AUD box from her ear. She knew that if there was ever a time to catch whispers, this was it. But all she caught were *nuts to think . . . what's wrong with boys . . .* and she was trying to make something from all this when she realized the undersheriff was speaking to her asking her where the dickens she'd been staying and did she know how much she'd worried her aunt? From this, Becca realized that, despite her every suspicion, Debbie Grieder had not betrayed her, even when she'd felt betrayed herself by Becca's relationship with Seth Darrow.

"Couch surfing," Becca told Dave Mathieson. "Aunt Debbie and I . . . We had sort of a misunderstanding about a guy—"

"Seth Darrow?" the undersheriff asked sharply.

"—but we got it straightened out. I'm back home now."

"Back at the motel?"

"Room four-four-four, where I was before."

"I didn't know Debbie had a niece," Rhonda Mathieson said. "But I guess we're finding out we don't know a lot about other people, even people we think we know better than we know ourselves."

The undersheriff turned a deep crimson at this. He said to Becca, "You never heard I was looking for you? Hayley Cartwright didn't track you down and tell you? The Darrow kid didn't tell you? Jenn McDaniels didn't tell you?"

"I missed a lot of school."

"We need to talk about that, too. What're you doing, going truant from school? *And* running off? You know where this kind of nonsense leads?"

All of this might have put Becca on the defensive except his whispers where flying around fast and furiously. *Motel . . . always knew . . . Tatiana . . . damn stupid . . .*

Becca looked at Dave Mathieson and then at his wife. Whatever was going on at the moment really didn't have anything to do with her, with being truant from school, or with running off, and she got this. So she said, "I was acting dumb for a while. But I'm back in school and I'm making up the work."

"I better not hear otherwise," the undersheriff told her.

"You won't."

"Dave," Rhonda said, "she's been good to Derric. I think we can cut her a *little* slack."

He looked at his wife and then back at Becca. He nodded. He said, "Derric told me some damn fool dog was loose in the woods. He remembers that. He's remembering other things, too. Kids reading to him, music playing, people talking to him. But he says he feels a special bond with you. So . . . thanks for being part of things here, for being there for my boy. For my *son*." His face softened at last and he smiled at her. "I hope you'll keep coming back, Becca."

She said that she would. He extended his hand. She shook it. But he pulled her to him and gave her a rough hug, and from this she felt how much he loved Derric and how little he was able to say about that love. He released her and she said good-bye. She was just about out of the hospital door when Dave Mathieson spoke again, however.

He said, "You ever hear of someone called Laurel Armstrong, Becca?"

Becca swallowed. This was her moment to reestablish the possibility of contact with her mom, but she knew the reality of her situation because it hadn't changed one bit. Laurel tied her to Jeff Corrie and danger. So she shook her head slowly and said, "I don't think so. But I'm new on the island so there's lots of people I don't know yet."

"Debbie tells me you come from San Luis Obispo. How far is that from San Diego?"

Becca thought about this, trying to see San Luis Obispo near the coast of the state, just a few miles inland from Morro Bay. She'd been there once. She'd met the real Becca King before her death, a happy girl struck by acute leukemia, a brave battle fought and then lost forever. She said, "I dunno exactly. Maybe three hundred miles?"

He nodded but he looked at her for a longer time than seemed necessary. So she said, "Why?"

He said, "Laurel Armstrong was connected to the cell phone that made a call from the woods the day Derric was injured. We've traced her back to an address in San Diego but we still can't reach her. So we still don't know for sure who made that call."

Becca said, "Maybe someone who didn't want to get involved?"

He thought about this. "Well, that wouldn't be you, would it?" he said.

FORTY-FOUR

Seth recognized the sound of a pep rally going on when he climbed out of Sammy, telling Gus to stay in the car. From the general direction of the gym came the stamping of feet on bleachers, followed by yelling. He dwelled for a moment upon the thought of how nothing ever really changed about high school.

He sauntered over to the administration building, trying hard to look like a guy who felt confident about being there. He went into the reception area where he sent a prayer of thanks to whatever god had arranged for this *not* to be the time of day when Hayley Cartwright sat at the desk and greeted visitors. But no one else was at that desk, either. So he wandered down the corridor, past the nurse's office, to find himself in front of the registrar's desk.

Ms. Ward knew him. Ms. Ward knew everyone. She looked up over her glasses and said, "Seth. Coming back to school? It's been boring around here without you."

"Nah," he said. "Me and South Whidbey High School? Not a good fit."

"So what can I do for you?"

Here was the difficult part, the revealing-of-self part that

Seth wasn't looking forward to. But he was tired of breaking his promises to himself and to others, so he said, "I wanted to talk to Ms. Primavera about getting a tutor for the GED."

Ms. Ward smiled. "What an excellent idea." She got to her feet and went to the counselor's office, which was behind her own with A–L in block letters above the door. In a moment, she was back, telling him to go on in because Ms. Primavera would be delighted to see him.

He doubted the delighted part, but he ducked behind Ms. Ward's desk. Tatiana Primavera was working on something, and Seth could see she didn't look very well. Her nose was red, and there were two boxes of Kleenex on her desk. Seth said to her, "Oh hey, I c'n come back later. You feeling bad? A cold or something?"

She said, "Allergies," with a faint smile.

Seth thought this was baloney. It was hardly the time of year for allergies. But he also thought, Whatever, chick, and he told her what he needed and wanted. First was a tutor. Second was passing the GED.

She seemed to rouse herself at this. "Good for you. What're your plans?"

He said, "Same as before. Professional guitar. But I want to take care of this thing first."

"Still playing gypsy jazz, though, aren't you?" she asked.

"Course," he said. "With the trio. But I'll probably do something on the side, too, at least for a while. I'm good at carpentry, so I figure I'll work part-time with a contractor."

She looked at him earnestly. "And you're okay with that, Seth? I know that lots of island people have jobs that support the art they do, but I remember how intent you were on the guitar and nothing else."

"Still am," he said. "But I figure I need to be realistic, too. It's time."

"SETH? SETH!"

He knew who it was. He'd been close to a clean getaway from the school, but the pep rally had altered the schedule for the day and now Hayley had seen him. She had also seen Gus, and she was saying, "You've got Gus back? Great," as she crossed the parking lot to the VW.

Seth felt awkward around her because he hadn't seen her since the morning she'd come by the Star Store asking him to help Becca. He still wasn't sure why she'd done that, considering how the last couple of their encounters had gone before that early-morning visit.

She stopped on Gus's side of the car. The window was down, and she let the Labrador slobber on her in his usual enthusiastic greeting. She said hi to Seth and he said hi to her and then there seemed to be nothing else to say at all until Hayley asked him if he'd heard about Derric.

He said, "Yeah. You hear about Gus?"

"You mean about Gus knocking Derric off the path?" And when he nodded, she said, "Yeah." She looked to the edge of the parking lot, where the maple trees were finally shedding the rest of their russet leaves. She said, "I'm sorry for what I thought . . . about you pushing Derric."

He shifted his weight. "S'okay. It's not like you turned me in or anything. And anyway, I'm sorry for what I thought, too."

"About what?"

"You and Derric hooking up."

"He's always been my friend, Seth. We were kissing and I know that hurt your feelings, but that was all we did. Just that one time."

"I get it now."

Both of them hung their heads, examining their feet and the damp ground they stood on. It seemed to Seth that they'd said all they had to say to each other, so he reached for the handle of his door. At the same moment, Hayley said, "That day at the farm when you came over to tell my mom about Lyme disease . . . ?"

He said, "Yeah?"

"That's when I knew you hadn't hurt Derric. See, I've been worried about . . . about *stuff* in my life and none of it has to do with you. You just took the heat for it."

Seth thought about this and said, "Your dad."

She looked at him across the top of the old VW. She swallowed hard. "Seth, I can't be anyone's girlfriend right now. There's too much going on at home. It's just too hard." She brushed her hair off her face in that gesture she had that Seth had always loved seeing, but when she did it now, he felt the pain of it, in a place beneath his heart. She said, "I thought my life was going to be so simple. I'd graduate here, go to U-dub on a scholarship. Then I'd go into the Peace Corps for a few years. Then I'd go to grad school. Only it's not working out that way. And you know . . . it hurts."

"I get that," Seth said.

"So I can't be your girlfriend or anyone else's. I don't even want to be. It's not you. It's me. It's how things are right now."

Seth thought about this: about how things were for all of them. He said, "What about being someone's friend, Hayl?"

"Sure. I can be someone's friend. I can be *your* friend."

"I'm okay with that," he told her. "But c'n I ask you something?" And when she nodded, "What were you doing in the woods that day? Why'd you hide the truck?"

She didn't answer at first, and Seth knew she was trying to decide how much more to tell him. She finally replied with, "I thought Mrs. Kinsale could help make my dad better. We met in the woods to talk about that."

"Why'd you think she could make him better?"

"It was just . . . It was something I thought, something about who she is and how she is. But I was wrong. The things she does for people . . . they don't work that way. She explained that to me."

Seth wondered about all this. He thought Hayley probably meant that Diana Kinsale practiced alternative medicine because there were practitioners of all sorts of things around the island: from eastern medicine to dowsing for lost articles. He'd never taken Mrs. Kinsale for one of these individuals, but he was learning fast that there was a lot he didn't know about people he saw every day.

He said, "I'm sorry, then. I wish she could've helped him."

"So do I. But no one can."

"What's that mean?"

Tears came to her eyes, but she didn't shed them. "You know, Seth. You *know*. It's why I can't be anyone's girlfriend, why I'm not going away to college, why there's no Peace Corps in my future. He's going to die. It'll take a while but he's going to die. We all know it but we don't mention it. It's just the way things are."

"But he only seems a little clumsy," Seth said.

"Clumsy is how it begins." She brushed at her eyes and added quickly, "I've got to go now. I've got to pick up Brooke."

He nodded and she hurried away. As he watched her go, Seth thought about how you never really knew anyone, not even the people you thought you knew. He also thought how you never learned a single thing about them as long as you only stayed in your head trying to understand what was inside theirs.

FORTY-FIVE

Becca locked her bike at the information kiosk on the edge of the meadow. Saratoga Woods rose up the hillside in an army of silent Douglas firs, but Becca knew she wasn't going to be alone in the forest. Diana Kinsale's truck was in the parking lot. She didn't want to be seen on this particular mission, however. So once she had the bike locked, she quickly took the sealed plastic bag and its contents from her backpack.

Across the meadow, she climbed Meadow Loop Trail. The day was cool but bright, and the trail was dappled with sunlight. It hardly seemed the place any longer where Derric had had such a terrible fall.

At the bottom of Derric's little trail, Becca looked right and left and listened hard to make sure she'd be able to get up to the teepee of trees in secrecy. There was still no sound other than the cry of the blue Steller's jays above her, so she picked her way up the steep hillside.

Derric's hideaway was as before: dry and secure. Becca worked her way to the back and wedged the package into the spot where she'd found it. As she did so, she wished that things were different for Derric. She wished he would tell his parents the truth.

But she knew this was *his* truth to tell and not hers. She had her own secrets, and perhaps it was this that they recognized in each other, the thing that felt like a bond between them.

After she had put the package safely into its place, she crawled back out. She waited again, listening for noises that would indicate someone coming along the trail. But Derric had chosen his hiding spot well: The Meadow Loop Trail was rarely used.

Becca didn't see Diana and her dogs until she was unlocking her bike. At that point, Diana emerged from the trees, coming from Wood Nymph Way, which was not across the meadow but rather just to the west of Saratoga Road. It led through the forest in an entirely different direction from the trails from the meadow.

Diana said, "Hello, girl with bike," as the dogs began to circle Becca, bumping into her in their usual pack greeting. "This is becoming something of a tradition. You, the bike, the dogs, me, the truck . . . Are you coming or going?"

"Going," Becca said.

"Would you like a ride back to town?"

Becca said that she would and, as before, Diana lifted the bike into the bed of the pickup. Once everyone was in his proper place, they set off for town.

Diana said, "Debbie tells me you're back at the motel," and when Becca wondered about this, Diana added, "We've had coffee a few times, Debbie and I. Want me to drive you there? To the motel, I mean."

Becca said yes, that would be fine, and Diana added that she needed to make a stop first at the cemetery. She wanted to check on a corkscrew willow that she'd planted to shelter both Charlie's grave and the concrete bench that was part of it. Becca was agreeable to this. She hadn't been to Reese's grave recently. It would be good to clear from it whatever dead leaves had blown there.

When Diana parked the truck, she let the dogs out for a run. Becca walked across the lawn to Reese's grave while Diana strode to Charlie's, where the willow made a pretty sight at one end of the bench.

At Reese's grave, Becca dropped to her knees. The lawn was damp from recent rains, and the fallen leaves were sodden. She began to gather them and when she got to the stone, she noticed something with a rush of surprise and pleasure. Reese's mildewed picture had been replaced with another. It was a school picture of her, grinning happily, and it was protected on the stone with a new cover of Plexiglas, sealed properly. Only one person could have done this, Becca thought. When she looked around, she saw her.

Debbie Grieder had seemed to materialize out of nowhere. She was sitting next to Diana on the bench at Charlie's grave as if they'd intended to meet each other all along. Diana had her arm around Debbie's shoulder. They were speaking.

As Becca watched them, Debbie rose. She turned and came toward Reese's grave. In her hands, she carried a pot of chrysanthemums, brilliantly yellow against the black fleece that she was wearing.

She lowered herself to her knees next to Becca. Together they looked at Reese's grave. *Now . . . hurts . . . making you free I don't believe* came from Debbie. What she said, though, was, "I appreciate how you fixed her grave, Becca."

"It seemed sort of lonely."

"It was good of you to do it. You've done a lot of good things. I couldn't see that at first but I see it now."

"Oh. Gosh." Becca wasn't sure what else to say. She had the feeling that Debbie wanted to tell her something, but she didn't know how to encourage her.

Debbie, though, didn't need encouragement. She said, "Ms. Ward hit her when she was riding her bike on Langley Road. That part of what I told you was true. The part that was a lie was whose fault it was."

Becca was silent. She knew something big was coming. She hardly dared to breathe because she also knew that, somehow, it was important that Debbie finished what she had to say.

"I was dead drunk," Debbie said. "I was coming down the stairs. I fell and hit my head and sliced it open. That's what this scar is." She pointed to the jagged route across her forehead. "There was blood everywhere. Reese wanted to call nine-one-one, but I screamed at her no. The last thing I wanted was for *anyone* to see. But she was afraid because of the blood. So she got on her bike and she set out to find Sean because I was screaming 'No ambulance' and she didn't know what else to do. I guess I said 'Get Sean for God's sake' and because she was a good girl, she wanted to help me. She was on Langley Road and she was in a panic because for all she knew her mother was going to bleed to death before she could find her brother. A deer jumped out and she wasn't prepared. She swerved, right into Ms. Ward's path. And that's how she died."

Becca said, "Oh gosh. I'm so sorry."

Sorry isn't . . . it won't . . . past returning came to her along with the power of Debbie Grieder's sorrow. Debbie said to her,

"You don't ever pay for a crime like that. You live with it, but you never pay." She reached out and touched Reese's name on the gravestone. She said, "I couldn't come here. I couldn't face looking at her picture and knowing I was the person who'd trampled the light of her and had made it go out. People say to me that her death made me finally stop drinking so some good came out of it. What I say is I'd drink myself into the grave if it would only bring my little girl back."

"That makes sense," Becca said. "I think both parts of it make sense."

Debbie rested back on her heels and gazed at Becca. She said, "Outside of my AA meetings, I've never told anyone that story. Everyone probably knows, but no one says anything to me about it. So what kind of almost-fifteen-year-old fairy are you, Becca King, that I'd talk to you about all this?"

"I'm just some kid you decided to help," Becca told her. "Because, I think, that's what you do."

"I suppose," Debbie said. "You want to go back to the motel together?"

Becca nodded. "I'd like that a bunch."

Epilogue

It was three weeks later when Hayley Cartwright stopped Becca on her way to her English class. She said, "Seth's playing jazz tonight with his trio. Over at Prima Bistro. Want to go?" Hayley added with an impish smile, "Derric's going, by the way. I'm picking him up. You in?"

Becca thought about this. Seeing Derric outside of school and outside of his get-togethers with Josh would be great, but she hesitated. Mostly it was a safety issue. She was becoming more comfortable out and about on the island, but always in the back of her mind lingered Laurel's warnings about keeping her head low. Still, Prima Bistro seemed secure enough. It wasn't out in the open. It sat on First Street up above the Star Store, a small restaurant and bar where local musicians played in the evenings. At this time of year, only Langley people went to the place. Tourists were long gone, and they wouldn't be back till Memorial Day.

She said, "I'm in."

"Pick you up at seven-thirty, then."

Becca was ready. She'd found a pair of jeans at the thrift store, along with a top and a hip-length cardigan. She threw on a belt and borrowed a scarf from Debbie. She looked okay, she thought, aside from the glasses and the hair. She eased up on the makeup for the evening. A little compromise wouldn't kill anyone, she figured.

Derric was in the Cartwrights' farm pickup waiting when Becca dashed through the rain to it. He flashed that smile of his and patted the seat. "Put it here," he told her as he scooted over.

"You'll have to share the seat belt," Hayley told them.

"Not a problem," Derric said, and put his arm around Becca to fit them both in.

Becca saw Hayley's small smile. What a matchmaker, she thought. But she didn't mind. She liked the feeling of Derric's arm around her. She liked the feeling of his hip pressed close to hers.

"How's the leg?" she asked him, tapping on the cast.

"Hurts some," he said. "I guess it's getting better."

They took off. It was a very short jaunt into town, and Becca knew she could have walked it. Hayley knew it, too, and so did Derric. But Hayley, it seemed, had plans for them.

She'd reserved a table. It wasn't one close to the spot set aside for the evening's musicians, though. Instead it was tucked into a corner, where the only light came from a single candle. "Wow, pretty romantic," she said. "You two take the far side. I'm sitting here."

Sitting here meant sitting with her back to them and her front facing the musicians. It was logical, considering that Seth and the two other young men of the trio were taking their places to start playing. But it was also obvious, and Becca grew hot with embarrassment.

Derric, however, said, "Cool. Thanks, Hayley," and when he and Becca sat, he moved his chair close to hers and said, "This is great. I haven't been out of the house except to go to school. That chick Courtney—she leads the Bible study group?—she keeps asking me to come to their meetings, but I'm not much for the Bible. This is better."

"Yeah. Me neither," Becca said. "The Bible I mean." Then she didn't know what else to say. She wanted to ask him questions about his letters to Rejoice, about whether he'd told his parents about her. But she had the feeling that the magic of the evening would be spoiled somehow if she asked about his sister, so she said nothing. Those questions could wait.

Seth and the other members of the trio began to play. As she had been the day she'd heard them rehearsing at South Whidbey Commons, Becca was at once engaged by the gypsy jazz. She watched the musicians' fingers moving on the strings with a speed that looked nearly impossible to her. Seth was amazing on guitar, she thought.

She looked at Derric. He was smiling at her. "Pretty cool, huh?" he said. "Next September I'll take you to the festival. There's gypsy jazz all over town. Seth'll probably be performing."

The idea of *next September* warmed Becca throughout. For a moment, even, she forgot about Laurel, about British Columbia and the town of Nelson, where her mom was setting up their home. It was enough to think of *next September* and being with Derric. They'd listen to the music together. They'd sit shoulder to shoulder, hand in hand.

He took hers, as if sharing her thought. He twined his fingers with hers, leaned over, and said, "Thanks."

She looked at him. "What for?"

"Everything." He kissed her.

The softest lips, the sweetest breath, she thought. She wanted the kiss and the evening to go on forever.

"Think Mrs. Grieder'll care if you come over for Thanksgiving dinner?" he asked her, close to her mouth, so close that she wanted him to kiss her again. Which he did when Becca said Mrs. Grieder wouldn't mind at all. And then he added with a smile, "What about Christmas?"

Becca felt light-headed. It was a special moment, and she promised herself she would never forget it.

———

SHE HELD ON to all of it when Seth took her home later. That had been the sensible way to arrange things. Derric and Hayley lived in the same direction, after all. And four people could not fit into Hayley's truck. So Becca and Derric had parted with a long look at each other and a longer smile. Then Becca climbed into Sammy and patted the ever-present Gus, who roused himself from sleep in the VW's backseat. She said to Seth, "You were great."

Seth smiled and asked, "Were you guys even listening? Didn't look that way to me."

Becca felt herself blush. "You can kiss and listen at the same time, you know."

"Whoa," Seth teased, "too much information!"

He put the car into gear. He honked a couple of times at people he knew who were also leaving the bistro, and he pulled out into Second Street for the quick jaunt over to the Cliff Motel.

"You like him, huh?" he said to Becca.

"I like him a lot," Becca said.

"Ready to fight half the chicks at South Whidbey High School for him?"

"I guess I am."

"Even the cheerleaders?"

"Rah rah rah," Becca said.

Seth chuckled. They made the turn into Cascade Street and zipped along the bluff high above the water. Soon enough they were in front of the motel and Seth was preparing to pull into its parking lot.

At that moment, Becca's life crashed shut.

A man was getting out of a car in front of the motel. There was something familiar . . . a set to his shoulders . . . the shape of his head . . . He turned to glance in the direction of Seth's VW. Becca saw him clearly. She cried out.

"Seth! Turn around!"

Seth said, "What the heck . . . ?" and then saw the man himself. "Oh hell," he breathed. "That's *him*? The guy—"

"Yes! Yes! Please, Seth. Go! If he sees me, if he finds me . . . You've got to go!"

Seth didn't need to be told twice. He reversed the car in an instant like a tourist who'd made the wrong turn. He floored it in the opposite direction, back up Sixth Street, heading out of town.

"Take me somewhere," Becca begged. "Take me someplace safe."

Seth gave her a look. He measured her panic and made his decision. "How d'you feel about tree houses?" he asked.

"I feel just fine."

"Done," he said.

AUTHOR'S NOTE

One major liberty had to be taken with Whidbey Island, and those who live here will recognize what it is: Coupeville General Hospital would not be equipped to care for a patient with Derric Mathieson's injuries and he would have been airlifted to Harborview Medical Center across the water. Other than that, at the time of this writing of the novel, everything is as described, although locals will recognize that some of the names have been slightly altered.

I'd like to thank Mike Hawley of the Island County Sheriff's Department for a tour of that facility and of the county jail, as well as for information he provided me about police investigations. Dane Heggenes, Bayley Heggenes, and Trevor Heins were terrific interviewees about their experiences at South Whidbey High School as well as at Bayview School, and erstwhile principal Rob Prosch unlocked actual doors for me at that former facility. I'm extremely grateful to Ralph Hastings for his willingness to become a character in the novel, as well as for allowing me the use of his amazing garden and house as one of the settings. My wonderful personal assistant Charlene Coe researched everything from trees to wildflowers while simultaneously keeping the ship afloat at my home, and my husband Tom McCabe put up with my disappearance into my office to write two novels simultaneously.

In New York, my editor Regina Hayes showed remarkable and endless patience as she guided me into and through the world of young adult fiction, and I'm deeply indebted to her as the learning curve was a steep one for me. As always, I must thank my literary agent Robert Gottlieb for everything he does to support me and to promote my work around the world.

Elizabeth George

WHIDBEY ISLAND, WASHINGTON